Return of the Bad Girl

By Codi Gary

Return of the Bad Girl
Bad Girls Don't Marry Marines
Good Girls Don't Date Rock Stars
Things Good Girls Don't Do
"The Trouble with Sexy" in *Kiss Me:*
An Avon Books Valentine's Day Anthology

Return of the Bad Girl

CODI GARY

AVONIMPULSE
An Imprint of HarperCollinsPublishers

Excerpt from *Bad for Me* copyright © 2015 by Codi Gary.

Excerpt from *An Heiress for All Seasons* copyright © 2014 by Sharie Kohler.

Excerpt from *Intrusion* copyright © 2014 by Charlotte Stein.

Excerpt from *Can't Wait* copyright © 2013 by Jennifer Hopkins. This novella originally appeared in the anthology *All I Want for Christmas Is a Cowboy.*

Excerpt from *The Laws of Seduction* copyright © 2014 by Gwen T. Weerheim-Jones.

Excerpt from *Sinful Rewards 1* copyright © 2014 by Cynthia Sax.

Excerpt from *Sweet Cowboy Christmas* copyright © 2014 by Candis Terry.

EPub Edition DECEMBER 2014 ISBN: 9780062372222

Print Edition ISBN: 9780062372239

AM 10 9 8 7 6 5 4 3 2 1

*This one is for all the readers who
fell in love with Rock Canyon.
Thank you so much! This book would not
have been possible without you.*

Chapter One

> "Ladies, lock up your men! Caroline Willis is
> back in town."
>
> **—Miss Know It All**

CAROLINE WILLIS SNORTED as she read the entry in the *Rock Canyon Press*. She'd seen her name on the cover and paused to pick up a paper before heading into Hall's Market. When she'd turned to page three, there had been a picture of her leaving her sister Valerie's house. Twelve years ago, gossip was spread on Sundays after church, at the local salon, and on any bar stool in town. Now every juicy tidbit was being printed in the local paper by an anonymous big mouth.

Miss Know It All was the town gossip columnist-turned-blogger. No one knew her identity, although there had been much speculation bandied about by Caroline's sisters. Valerie was certain it was Gracie McAllister, while Ellie thought it was Mrs. Andrews, the town's biggest bitch and gossip. Caroline had no idea. And yet, over the last few weeks, whoever it was seemed to have taken a particular interest in her.

Still, it wasn't like Miss Know It All could make her return any worse. Caroline had decided over a month ago that she wanted to come home to be with her sisters. As for her father, well...she had hoped that at least he would be willing to put the past behind them and start over. It wasn't like they'd ever been a picture-perfect family, at least not behind closed doors, but despite all their bad blood, he was still her dad.

Working things out with him probably wouldn't have been so urgent if he hadn't had a heart attack two weeks ago. Valerie had called Caroline to tell her the morning it happened. As Caroline had raced home, she'd imagined her father's relief at seeing her doing so well after twelve years away with no contact.

Man, had she been living in a fucking fantasy land.

If her father's refusal to even see her hadn't proven how she'd over estimated time's ability to heal all wounds, she definitely wasn't prepared to face the citizens of Rock Canyon, Idaho. Lord knew she'd burned more bridges before she was eighteen than most people lit up in their lifetimes. She'd only bumped into a few people since being back, but when she'd tried to be friendly, she'd been met with chilly nods as they hurried away.

Walking into Hall's Market offered a perfect example of how her return was definitely not met with cheers and parades. The first thing she noticed was the stares. Hope Weathers was putting out boxes of cookies in the bakery department and just about dropped one as

Caroline passed. Marci Andrews, Betty Harwood, and Willa Fullerton—Rock Canyon's version of the morality police (they were just like the Fashion Police on *E* but meaner)—were standing in line at checkout stand one, a wall of open disapproval as they whispered back and forth with the blonde clerk, whose scowl was so ugly that Caroline almost paused. She didn't even recognize the girl, but she was sure giving Caroline the business.

Even Danny Cordova, who was stocking an end cap, stopped what he was doing, his eyes bugging out of his head as she gave him a tiny wave. Although maybe he was staring at her for another reason. She smiled at the thought that straight-laced Danny might be checking her out, especially considering how shy he'd been in high school. She'd never seen him even look sideways at a girl and had actually assumed he played for the other team.

Caroline was tempted to stop, spin around, and yell *Boo!*, but then they would say she was crazy. Lord knew she'd called herself the same thing for the last fourteen days. Crazy for coming back, crazy for expecting her father to have grown and softened in his old age. Who knew that when he'd told her to never come back twelve years ago, he'd meant it?

"Oh my God, Caroline Willis? Is that you?"

Caroline stopped in her tracks. Six feet in front of her—and holding a bundle of celery so tightly that Caroline imagined it would snap in half any second—stood her former best friend, Shelby Donovan. She definitely couldn't blame her for being tense, though. They hadn't exactly ended on the best of terms.

What with Caroline having stolen Shelby's boyfriend and all.

On second thought, maybe today *hadn't* been a good day to venture out of her sister's house and brave the world. Judging by Shelby's red-faced, lemon-sucking expression, Caroline had every reason to hide, but she wouldn't back down from Shelby's anger now. She'd embrace it and attempt to make amends. It's what she'd told Valerie she would try to do. Take the high road. Turn the other cheek.

"What brings your skanky ass back here?"

Sparks of temper prickled Caroline's skin. Sucking in a calming breath, she forced a smile. "That is so classy, Shelby. Congratulations, by the way; it looks like your boobs finally came in. Or was that a little surgical gift from Mom and Dad?"

Okay, so maybe the high road was overreaching.

Shelby's cheeks flushed an unhealthy shade of violet, probably because despite the obvious surgical enhancements, she had gained about thirty pounds. Shelby had always moaned and groaned about her lack of curves in high school, voicing her jealousy over Caroline's hourglass frame, but it looked like she had finally gotten her wish. Only where Caroline's body had always been toned, Shelby looked a bit…lumpy.

"Well, Marcus doesn't seem to think there's anything wrong with me," Shelby said, smirking.

Ah, Marcus Boatman. Shelby's dream man was the same guy who hadn't hesitated dumping her like a hot potato the minute he'd thought Caroline was interested.

"I find it interesting that you're still holding a grudge against me, when your supposed boyfriend," Caroline said, making air quotes, "cheated on you. How come you forgave him?"

"Because men are weak. Besides, he has more than made up for his one transgression, where as you violated the rules of friendship and sisterhood."

Caroline had to bite her cheek to keep from laughing. "Okay, first of all, you were never my sister in any way. And you, of all people, know that I was not in a good place. Where were you when I needed you?" Caroline shook her head. "Face it, Shelby. We both failed each other in a big way, and I apologized a long time ago for my part in it, but don't you think it's time to just let it go?"

Obviously not, if the flush of her former friend's face was any indication. "You haven't changed at all!" Shelby said. "You act like you're God's gift—"

"Is there a problem here, ladies?"

Caroline looked over her shoulder to find Mr. Hall glancing between them sternly.

"Yeah, there is. You let this tra—"

"Actually, Mr. Hall, I was just picking up a few things to take over to my dad and bumped into Shelby," Caroline broke in, shooting Shelby a warning look. Obviously, age had not matured the spoiled, entitled little snot, but if she thought Caroline was going to stand there and be bad-mouthed to her face, she was wrong. Caroline could only be pushed so far. "It seems we still have some things to work out, but unfortunately, I am in a hurry."

Shelby huffed and tossed the celery back onto the pile. "We have nothing to work out, and you can be sure I'll be doing my shopping elsewhere from now on."

Caroline wanted to tell her exactly how ridiculous she sounded, but before she could, Shelby stomped around the two of them toward the exit.

When they were alone, Mr. Hall ran a hand through his silver hair, clearly uncomfortable. "How's your dad doing?"

Caroline smiled. She'd always liked the kindly grocer. "As far as I know, he's ornery as ever. We'll see if he lets me through the door."

"Yes, he can be stubborn," Mr. Hall said, his eyes shifting away.

His whole demeanor screamed that he had something to say and was struggling with it. Caroline tried to put him at ease. "It will all work out, I'm sure. I am sorry about the way Shelby spoke to you, and I'm sure she didn't mean what she said about shopping elsewhere."

Although, Mr. Hall, it shouldn't surprise you if she does stop coming here...the spiteful little bitch.

"Yes, well...I understand you're moving back here." He paused a second, as if waiting for her to confirm his statement, so she nodded. "You know I don't listen to gossip, but I can't afford to lose my regular customers. Do you understand what I'm saying?"

So much for thinking at least one person might give her the benefit of the doubt.

"Sure. You're saying if I offend the respectable people of Rock Canyon, you won't let me through the door," she said, no longer smiling and hanging on to her temper by the skin of her teeth. "And that's called discrimination. I thought you were better than that, sir."

Without waiting for him to stop blustering, she walked back toward the front of the store and down to the candy aisle, trying to hold on to her dignity. It shouldn't surprise her that Mr. Hall would warn her off; she was a fly in the ointment for quite a few good citizens, and he had a business to run.

Still, did he have to make her feel like some kind of second-class citizen? It wasn't like her money was worth less. As she stopped in front of the candy display, she realized she'd been squeezing her hands into fists so hard that her nails had dug into her palms. She opened them to find purplish-red crescent moons indented into the flesh and winced.

Since she began running her own businesses years ago, she'd tried different tricks to control her temper. Sometimes they worked and sometimes they didn't, but at least she hadn't popped anyone in the face today. That was progress.

Caroline pulled a gold-and-yellow bag off the shelf, ignoring her sore flesh. Her father loved these disgusting butterscotch candies, and she was hoping a bag of them might ease his hostility. He definitely hadn't been as receptive of her last visit to the hospital a few weeks ago.

At first, she'd laughed off her father's refusal to see her as a sign that he must be feeling better, but when he'd denied her a second time, irritation had settled into the pit of her stomach and simmered. Why couldn't he just set aside some of that stubborn Willis pride and put the past where it belonged?

After three days, she'd barged into his hospital room and faced off with Edward Willis for the first time in twelve years. After a few minutes of telling him exactly what she thought of his rejection, the nurse had shoved her out the door. But not before she'd had the satisfaction of watching her father's face turn purple with rage after she'd said, "You're the one who missed out, Dad. I survived without you. In fact, I thrived in spite of you."

Edward Willis never liked to be wrong, especially when there was proof.

Of course, if he'd known anything about those first two rough years after being kicked out, he probably would have glowed with satisfaction. Within just the first few weeks, Caroline had had less than fifty bucks to her name and had been sleeping in her car outside of Las Vegas, eating a lot of dollar tacos.

And then she'd run out of money.

But when she went around to local businesses, none of them would hire a high school dropout who was living in her car. None except Diamond of the Desert Gentleman's Club.

Caroline had hated stripping more than she could express, but she couldn't deny that it paid well. Within a year, she'd saved enough to move on, and when one of her favorite patrons, a kind, lonely man named Carl Jackson who owned a bar nearby, asked if she'd be interested in a bartending position, she'd agreed—with the stipulation that there'd be no dancing, stripping, or teasing involved.

Caroline ended up working for Carl longer than she'd thought she would. Along with getting her GED and taking college classes online, she found her calling in drawing people to Carl's bar, the Whiskey and Wine Saloon, using fun theme nights. Soon she was managing the bar and eventually, two years and one bachelor's degree in business later, Carl offered to sell it to her. Three days after her twenty-sixth birthday, she was able to sell the bar for a profit and leave Nevada in her rearview mirror.

After that, she'd taken on five more failing bars around the country, leaving every one of them in a better place than when she started and making enough for the next project in the process. But the work was exhausting and after a while, it started being more labor than love.

When her father had his heart attack, she'd already planned to stop flipping. But once she decided to move back to Rock Canyon, it had been Carl who'd suggested she start a consulting business for bars that were struggling. Now, she already had a few consultation jobs lined up in Chicago and New York, but she wanted to get settled before she did any traveling. All in all, she had high hopes for her future and her business. With little thanks to Edward Willis.

So no, Caroline hadn't been putting on a brave face when she'd thrown her success in her father's face. She *had* survived without his help. Without his money. She had worked hard, done whatever it took, and even graduated from college. His lack of approval or forgiveness hadn't broken her, and no way would the opinions of a few idiots tear her down now.

Pulled back to the task at hand, Caroline walked up to the checkout stand and saw that the three biddies were still there, standing at the front of Hall's, watching her.

"Good morning, ladies," Caroline said, oozing sweetness. "So lovely to see you again." Mrs. Andrews sniffed and headed toward the exit with her cart, the other two hurrying after. Innocently, Caroline handed the blonde clerk her candy and debit card. "Was it something I said?"

Chapter Two

"The past will always catch up to you, no matter
how fast you run."

—Miss Know It All

CAROLINE STOOD AT the end of the walkway leading to
her childhood home. The April breeze blew her hair into
her eyes, obstructing her vision as she stared up at the
two-story ranch house. It hadn't changed much besides a
fresh coat of paint, but the perfectly landscaped fortress
still seemed like a strange place instead of the warm, welcoming hearth that coming home was supposed to be.

Reaching up to tie her hair back in a loose ponytail,
she rotated her shoulders and cracked her neck, trying to
ease the tension.

*You can do this. You just have to face him, to show him
that you're here and you aren't going anywhere, no matter
what a bastard he may be.*

Caroline headed up the path and the steps, the hard
candy in one sweaty hand. She shouldn't be this nervous,

especially since she'd already faced his anger in the hospital.

But there, they'd been in a less personal setting, neutral turf. Now, she was stepping into the lion's den, where a thousand memories, both good and bad, would be waiting to add to her already emotional state.

It was funny. She'd spent three years hating him before she left and another two blaming him for everything that went wrong once he was out of her life. Yet he was still her dad. Though the times he'd been there for her were few and far between, those were the memories that stuck out to her. Like the time he'd coached her for the state spelling bee, which she had lost. But for a week there, having his complete attention had been all she cared about.

Yeah, he definitely hadn't been the dad of her dreams, but she was almost thirty-one. She didn't need him to be a dad now. But she would at least like to have some kind of relationship with him. If only so she didn't add any more regrets to her list.

Once she stood on the stoop, she knocked twice and waited, expecting their housekeeper, Teresa, to open the front door.

Only when the door opened, it wasn't Teresa.

Caroline's heart stopped cold before resuming at an unhealthy tempo, beating against her chest painfully. Icy blue eyes stared back at her from a too-handsome face, a cupid's-bow mouth splitting into a leer that knocked the wind out of her.

Kyle Jenner.

Valerie had warned Caroline that he worked for their father now and was basically his right-hand man. It didn't surprise her that Kyle and her father were attached at the hip, considering how far up Senator Jenner's ass her dad's head had been. But she'd never thought Kyle would be in their home, especially since her father was still recovering.

"Well, hello, beautiful."

His tone, arrogant and too familiar, sent her stomach twisting. Bile rose up and burned the back of her throat. She was being strangled by her fear, and there was nothing she could do. Every self-defense and martial arts class she had taken hadn't cured her of the paralyzing fear this one man could create. She'd faced down three-hundred-pound drunks and an angry husband with a two-barrel looking for his wayward wife, yet Kyle's sly smile still made her want to piss her pants.

She resisted the urge to close her eyes in an effort to block out the memories clawing to the surface. Who knew someone so beautiful could be so rotten?

"Cat got your tongue, sweet Caroline?"

"Don't struggle, sweet Caroline."

Fifteen years had passed since that night, and his words, his tone, still made her skin crawl with disgust.

Her father had asked her to attend a dinner party at Senator Jenner's home in Boise, where they were going to spend the night. It wasn't the first time she'd met the senator's son, Kyle, but his attention on her was definitely new. He'd spent the whole night courting her, fetching her drinks and sweets, and dancing with her out on the porch. She'd felt like a princess.

Until she'd been woozy and excused herself to go lie down upstairs. Kyle had offered to help her, but she'd said she would be fine. Before she blacked out, she remembered feeling weightless and dreamy but somehow different from the sensation of being drunk. Besides, she hadn't been drinking alcohol that night.

Later, she woke up in pain. Kyle was on top of her. Inside her. He was *raping* her, and she was too dizzy, too weak, to do much but whimper and cry.

"Please…stop…"

He hadn't stopped, though; he'd laughed. He'd insulted her and mocked her until he finished with her.

"*A virgin is just a whore in training.*"

When she'd woken up the next morning, her memories had blurred together. Her head had pounded painfully, and when she'd tried to sit up, the room still spun. As she started to climb out of the bed, she'd cried out sharply at the shock of soreness between her legs. Caroline had pulled back the blankets and realized her dress was torn, her underwear gone. When she stood up, she winced, trying to fight past the fog and the hurt to remember what had happened, and then she saw it.

Blood on the sheets.

Nausea had rolled up her throat until she was doubled over on the floor, vomiting up everything she'd eaten the night before. A flash of Kyle's laughter intensified the pain in her head, and she'd curled up on her side, sobbing.

When her father had come knocking at her door to let her know they'd be leaving in an hour, she'd been so shaky and confused, she hadn't been able to say more than okay. Once she heard his footsteps retreating, she'd changed out of her destroyed dress and stuffed it into her backpack. She had tried to scrub the vomit out of the carpet with one of the bathroom towels, but it only seemed to make things worse.

Once she'd dressed, she headed for the stairs, but before she could take one step, someone had grabbed her arm and pushed her up against the wall.

"Where are you going in such a hurry?"

Caroline closed her eyes against the evil sneer of Kyle's voice and whispered, "Let me go."

"Not until we have a little talk about what happened last night," he said, pulling her into the hall closet, despite her struggles against his grip.

"What happened last night? You raped me!"

Kyle closed the door behind them with a chuckle, and Caroline backed away from him, her heart hammering as she remembered that laugh, mocking her when she was begging him to stop.

"Now, if you have any thoughts of walking downstairs and telling your father I raped you, I'm going to advise that you reconsider."

Caroline would have laughed if her throat hadn't been closing with apprehension. Being stuck in such close quarters with Kyle had scared the hell out of her, and his dark tone hadn't helped. Had he always been so much taller than her?

"It's the truth—"

Kyle's forearm was suddenly there, pressing into her throat as he shoved her back against the closet wall.

"The truth? The truth is your dad has his head stuck so far up my father's ass, if you say anything, he'll tell you to shut the fuck up," Kyle hissed, increasing the pressure on her throat until she couldn't speak. "I'm going to save him the trouble."

He brought his face close to hers, his disgusting breath hitting her nose. She'd reached up to his arm, digging her nails into the fabric of his shirt to get him away from her neck, but he just cursed at her.

"If you tell anyone about last night, it will be your word against mine," he said, releasing her neck only to grab her hands and pin them above her head against the wall. "But on the off chance that I *am* arrested, you can bet your ass I'll make bail. And when I do, I'll be coming not just for you, but your little sisters too. Val's…what? Thirteen?" His lips ran across her cheek until they reached her ear, and nausea roiled again in her already empty stomach. "It won't take much effort to get them alone, and when I do, well, they won't be as lucky as you."

"What do you mean?"

"I won't bother to drug them."

Caroline shook with fear and anger, picturing Val fighting Kyle, screaming for help. And Ellie…

"You wouldn't hurt Ellie," Caroline said harshly. "She's only six."

"So?"

Disbelief and terror clawed their way through her until she was heaving. Kyle released her as she doubled over, but his hand fisted in her hair before he left. "Remember what I said, sweet Caroline. I mean every single word."

Caroline had looked up into that icy blue gaze and known he wasn't bluffing. His father would probably swing bail, and who's to say he'd be prosecuted anyway? With the Jennerses' connections, Caroline herself could be the one to disappear. Or he could do exactly what he threatened...

Only, what were the chances they would survive the encounter? Kyle would be an idiot to leave behind three witnesses.

In the end, he'd gotten exactly what he wanted; Caroline was scared out of her mind for her sisters and had kept her mouth shut for more than a decade. Even after Kyle had hurt another girl.

Right after Valerie had started at Boise State, she had told Caroline that Kyle had raped her roommate at a party. The girl hadn't pressed charges either, and Val figured Kyle's father had paid off the victim and her family. Caroline had been surprised the girl's parents wouldn't want the man who had hurt their daughter to pay. If it had been her child, she would have gutted him.

Regardless, the thought that Kyle had gone on to victimize more women made her stomach churn, even now.

But because you never told anyone what he did to you, he was free to do it again.

She had been a kid, barely fifteen, and scared shitless when it had happened. The possibility of reliving the whole thing for the world and nobody believing her had kept her silent. That Kyle might get off anyway and come after her family was enough to give her nightmares for years.

Sometimes she'd wished she was Jennifer Connelly in *Labyrinth*, able to say, *"You have no power over me."* But life was never like the movies. The bad guy didn't always lose, the losers didn't always win, and the guy and girl didn't always ride off into the sunset.

And despite all the drunkards and bullies she'd encountered over the years, Kyle's eyes could still render her catatonic. Just as they were now.

"I'm…I'm here to see my dad," she finally managed to choke out.

He leaned against the door jam and tsked. "He's resting, actually. Just fell asleep half an hour ago."

"Then why are you still here?" She was proud; there was hardly a tremor in her voice.

"I'm just answering his phone and helping him. We've become quite close, you know, with Valerie causing him so much trouble and Ellie moving out…well, he's been under a tremendous amount of stress."

The veiled attempt to place the blame on Val and Ellie for Edward's heart attack wasn't lost on Caroline, but she had no witty comeback, no biting retort.

Instead, she said, "Just tell him I stopped by and give him these."

She held out the bag of candy, and Kyle took it, but before she could pull away, his fingers wrapped around her wrist and brought her close enough to whisper, "Wouldn't you like to stay and keep me company, sweet Caroline?"

She jerked away from him and snapped, "Touch me again, and I'll gut you."

As she walked away, he called, "Oh, how I missed that fire. For a second there, I thought you'd lost it."

As she climbed into her car, she caught sight of him kissing two of his fingers and waving them at her. She wished for half a second she'd gone with a lifted 4x4 truck instead of her little Corolla, just so she could climb over the rocky, landscaped yard between them and plow into him. If she took the house down too, so be it. It would be worth it to never see his smug, disgusting face again.

Peeling out, she sped down the road, oblivious to speed limit signs. She wanted to put as much distance between her and the bastard as possible. She had planned to spend at least half an hour or more with her father, but that was shot to hell. It was only ten in the morning, and she wasn't due to pick up the keys to her new apartment until eleven thirty. Maybe Gemma Bowers wouldn't mind if she stopped by early.

Caroline had decided several days earlier—right after the third night in a row of her sister Ellie coming home at three in the morning, giggling and bumping into things—that she needed to find a place of her own. When Val had offered to let Caroline stay at her place, she'd failed to mention that Ellie was already taking the spare room and the only place available was the living room couch. The first week had been fine, with them taking turns at the hospital, but by the time her father was released, it became business as usual at Casa de Val, which essentially meant sexy noises from Val's room and Ellie's midnight stumbling.

So she'd jumped onto Val's computer and found Gemma Bowers's ad on Craigslist for a two-bedroom,

one-bath apartment with private parking. She'd called
Gemma that morning and set up the showing. The
place was perfect, and they'd shaken hands on the spot.
Gemma had agreed to have a one-year lease drawn up to
be signed that morning. Val hadn't been happy about the
news, acting like Caroline was abandoning her again, but
Caroline had been living on her own for too long. Plus,
all of the "what have you been up to since you left home"
talks were grating on her. She was used to having space to
breathe, and that was exactly what Gemma Bowers's two-
bedroom apartment was going to give her. Space and an
excuse to get away from all the probing questions.

And, of course, seeing Kyle had sent her into a twister
of rage and turmoil all its own. Even the shaking in her
hands hadn't subsided.

She needed a place to chill out, to feel safe. A place to
decorate however she wanted and to relax in when she got
home, where she wouldn't have to listen to Val's disturbing sex noises or deal with Ellie tripping in at all hours,
waking her up. Caroline needed all that and a comfortable bed. Valerie definitely hadn't bought her couch for
guests to sleep on, that was for damn sure.

Exiting off of Main Street, Caroline turned down a
narrow alley behind the row of shops. The older stone
and brick buildings of Rock Canyon looked dingier from
the back, but her new parking spot was behind Gemma's
bookstore—Chloe's Book Nook—and right next to the
stairs that led to her new place.

Caroline wasn't worried about the stairs, since everything she owned currently fit in her trunk and on her

backseat. She usually rented furnished apartments to keep from having to sell stuff when she moved on, but once she had everything unloaded here, she planned on making a few shopping trips to Twin Falls to pick up new furniture and décor. She had been saving up for so long, it was about time she splurged.

Caroline saw the parking spot, but as she began to pull in, she almost plowed into the back of a midnight blue motorcycle already parked there.

What the hell?

Glaring at the crotch rocket, she thrust her gear shift into park and turned off her car, not giving a tinker's damn if someone else tried to come through the alley. She couldn't wait to kick this asshole out of her parking spot.

She jumped out and passed the bike slowly, reading the license plate with disgust.

BBYBLUE.

What a sissy name for a street bike. It was probably some jerk who was afraid of his poor baby getting scratched out on the street. But that was no excuse for taking her spot. Trying to cool her already-hot temper, she hummed the lyrics to her favorite Fleetwood Mac song as she came up to the bookstore's back entrance and knocked. First, she would pick up her keys, and then she would call a tow truck to remove the motorcycle.

Gemma Bowers opened the door, her dark hair pulled back from her face, drawing attention to the paleness of her skin. Gemma was curvy in a natural way and soft-looking, with a sweet face. Her hazel eyes were wide behind her glasses, and Caroline could see how she'd won the heart of country rock star Travis Bowers who was, from what Caroline remembered, a total hottie. And although Caroline hadn't known her in high school, when she'd come to see the apartment the other day, Gemma had been very nice.

"Hey, Gemma, I'm sorry to show up so early, but my morning plans fell through. Is it okay if I sign the lease now?" Caroline asked, wondering now at the woman's deer-in-the-headlights look. "By the way, do you know who I can call to get a tow? There's some douche wad in my parking spot."

Gemma opened her mouth as if to speak, but a deep voice out of sight beat her to it.

"It's my parking spot."

Caroline poked her head past Gemma to see who it belonged to. The man behind the voice was a panty-dropper for sure. He was leaning against the counter of the shop's break room, but Caroline had a feeling he was as tall as he was muscly. Wide shoulders and rippling arms were hugged by the light cotton of a tight, army-green T-shirt, and she couldn't miss the bumps and ridges of his pecs and abs—proof that this guy worked out hard, in all the right places.

Caroline tried to say something, but her mouth was too dry, her tongue glued to the roof of her mouth.

She hadn't even gotten to his face yet. How long had it been since a man had tongue-tied her with his body alone? Too long, apparently.

Her gaze finally met his obsidian eyes—complete with ebony lashes framing them thickly, unfairly. His coffee-and-cream skin was smooth except for the hint of scruff around his chin and a two-inch strip of dark hair running down the middle of his head, like a short, tamed Mohawk. She could see the tip of a tattoo on the side of his neck, just above his T-shirt, but it was his smile that finally brought her back to reality.

It was stretched wide—with an edge that told her he knew exactly what he was doing to her, that it happened to him all the time—and his arrogance was like a bucket of ice water. This man was dangerous, cocky…and he had stolen her parking spot. Worse, he'd called it *his* spot, and here she was, basically going into heat. She wasn't this girl, the one who panted after whatever hot guy crooked his finger at her.

Gearing up for battle, she placed a hand on her cocked hip. "As pretty as you may be, I am going to have to call bullshit on that one. Gemma leased the upstairs apartment to me and the parking spot along with it."

Tall, dark, and douchey stood up, forcing her to tilt her chin skyward and curse her lack of heels. She normally wore them everywhere, but since today was moving day, she had worn comfy shoes for running up and down stairs. Which put her about four inches shorter than normal; at five foot three and a quarter, she was on the shrimpy side when dealing with average men. This guy was definitely above average, probably six foot two in his bare feet. What really pissed her off, though, was the way he was leaning over her now, as if he was trying to intimidate her with his bad-boy aura.

Please, I eat assholes like you for breakfast.

He took a few steps closer, that smug smile never slipping. "Well, Travis, Gemma's husband, rented the apartment—and parking spot—to *me* as well. So, looks like we have a bit of an issue here."

That threw Caroline, and she swung her focus to Gemma, who looked like she was ready to wring her hands and cry. "Please, tell me he's kidding."

"I wish he was, but apparently, Mr. Moriarty—Gabe—met with my husband yesterday. I didn't even know about this until last night."

"And you couldn't have given me a heads-up?" Caroline snapped.

"I tried to call your cell phone, but it kept going to voicemail."

Damn it. That's because her sister's monster of a dog had taken a shine to stealing her things. Her socks, her phone, her underwear. By the time she'd realized it was gone this morning, it was dead, and there was no way to coerce information out of a dog.

Crossing her arms over her chest, Caroline glared at the man who was trying to steal her apartment. "So, what happens now?"

"Now you take your sweet little ass out of here and find another place to live," Gabe said. Caroline had the sudden urge to flip him off or kick him in the balls. Maybe both.

"Bite me."

"If you can wait until I get my bed moved in, I'd love to take you up on that." His voice had taken on a dark, husky tone, and she told herself it was so *not* going to work on her—even as goosebumps prickled her flesh.

The thought of those white teeth nipping along her skin made undeniable heat pool between her legs, but she had learned a long time ago that talk was cheap. Despite a short wave of curiosity, there was no way this guy was ever going to get in her pants. Or her apartment.

"Tempting, but I'm not interested."

"That's not what your girls are saying."

Following his gaze down, she saw her nipples were hard and pushing against the sheer bra beneath her T-shirt. Her eyes snapped back up to his, and she sneered, "So, I can add *inappropriate perv* to the long list of nicknames you've already earned in our short acquaintance."

"Just stating the obvious, princess," he drawled.

Before he could open his mouth further, Caroline turned to Gemma. "How are you going to fix this?"

"I—"

"There's nothing to fix. I was here first, and I'm taking the apartment."

Caroline clenched her fists and counted silently to calm herself. Places to rent were hard to come by in Rock Canyon, and she didn't know how much longer she could stand listening to Val and her boyfriend getting it on while she slept on the couch.

Focusing her attention on Gemma again, she asked, "Has he signed the lease yet?"

"No, I—"

"Good. Then you can just hand me the lease you drew up for me, and I'll sign it now," Caroline said, giving Gabe a shrug. "Sorry, but I saw the apartment first."

"Like I said, princess," Gabe said, moving closer until he was nose to nose with her. Unconsciously, her eyes moved to those damn kissable lips. "Get your sweet ass out of here—"

"I'm very sorry about the confusion," Gemma broke in loudly, and when both of them swung their attention her way, Caroline saw her swallow hard. "I think I need to talk to Travis before I make any decisions."

Caroline gritted her teeth and wanted to scream in frustration, but Gabe's dark eyes were watching her again. It was on the tip of her tongue to rip into Gemma about having to ask her husband's permission, but she refrained for the sake of pissing off her potential landlady.

Besides, if she threw a bitch fit, it might make hot shot look like a better choice of tenant, and she couldn't let him win. Especially when he was so damn sure of himself.

Taking in a deep breath, Caroline said, "Fine. I'll call you with another number to reach me in about ten minutes."

With one last hostile glare at Gabe, Caroline stormed out of the shop.

His apartment? Not gonna fucking happen.

Chapter Three

"Attention all the single ladies: Fresh meat has arrived! Oh, and get this, he has a motorcycle. Mmm...I smell a bad boy."

—Miss Know It All

GABE MORIARTY WALKED out of Chloe's Book Nook, yanking on his gloves. He had been *this close* to signing the paperwork to the Bowerses' apartment until that little wildcat had stormed in, making demands. Now he had to wait until Gemma talked it over with Travis and they decided what to do.

Gabe could tell that Gemma had been distraught, and he hadn't wanted to add to her stress by voicing his displeasure, but damn it, he was there first. That uppity witch could go take her attitude somewhere else to live. Speaking of Miss Temper, there was no sign of her. She was probably off to speak to her lawyer or maybe off looking for that tow truck. He snorted. As if anyone was going to touch his bike but him.

It was too bad too, 'cause despite her putting a monkey wrench in his plans, she was fucking hot. With her long dark hair pulled back from her face, her brown eyes had drawn him in, and although he'd tried to play cool, he'd felt his heart beat faster with every sassy word out of her mouth.

You mean that lush mouth? The one that was probably good at a number of things?

Straddling his bike, Gabe shrugged into his jacket before grabbing his helmet off the back and slammed it down onto his head, cursing.

It didn't matter how hot she was, she was the pain-in-the-ass reason he wasn't getting his apartment, and that pissed him the hell off. Gabe had a plan, and he hated when things didn't go smoothly.

He'd driven into town the day before yesterday, planning on surprising Chase Trepasso, an old friend of his, only to find out that Chase was out of town until today. He'd wanted to be settled, already set with a place to live before he dropped in on Chase, just in case the welcome wasn't as warm as he'd hoped. It had been sixteen years since he'd seen his former best friend, and that last time had been a blur of disbelief, confusion, and rage. Now, he was stuck staying at the Rock Canyon Inn, and when he walked into Chase's tattoo shop, there was a chance that Chase would tell him to get the hell out of town.

He wasn't going anywhere, though—even if the Bowerses gave into that prickly princess's temper tantrum.

One of the things he'd been working on—during the five years he'd spent in that tiny Nevada state prison cell—was a list of all the mistakes he'd made to get there.

And the way he'd treated Chase was on it.

It had taken him about a year to stop blaming Chase for his own mistake, mostly because he hadn't been ready to admit what an idiot he'd been. His prison psychologist had helped him come to that conclusion, and actually, it had been his idea to form the list in the first place.

The list had started with the obvious—making sure Honey was taken care of—and from there, it had grown. Gabe had been checking things off for years, but it seemed like for every wrong he made right, another two wrongs popped up. It had started as a way to help him assuage his guilt but had grown into much more.

It quickly became the right thing to do. He'd always known right from wrong, but the lines had blurred for a while there. He'd been trying to walk the line for the last nine years, though, and being in Rock Canyon was just a part of that.

It was a central location for what he was trying to build for himself and for his future. Being rural Idaho, halfway between two sets of mountains, with beautiful areas to explore, it was also perfect for a man trying to get a custom motorcycle shop off the ground. And it was only two hours from one of the best assisted-living facilities in the country.

"I wanna see the mountains, Gabey."

When he'd quit his job in Colorado and uprooted his sister, Honey, and her nurse, Sharla, from the facility where they'd been living for five years, neither had been happy with him. But he'd been tired of Denver and tired of working for someone else. So, when he'd started researching areas with the best facilities, Sun Valley, Idaho, had come up on his radar. It was surrounded by the Sawtooth Mountains and fulfilled Honey's only request.

Backing up his bike, he pulled out and down the alleyway until he hit a side street, making his way back to the main stretch where Chase's tattoo parlor sat. It was too early for Chase to be open, but Gabe couldn't stand the idea of lying around the hotel another day either. Instead, revving up the bike, he headed out of town and took a left toward the highway.

It was a two-hour drive to Sun Valley. Of course, he'd have to take a little detour through the McDonald's drive-through for a large fries and vanilla shake, or Honey would pitch a fit. But in the big scheme of things, it was a little thing to do for his sister; he had a lot to make up for.

Like the fact that he had cost his sister the chance at a normal life.

Gabe passed over Highway 84, and the cold wind bit through the leather of his jacket, causing goosebumps to prickle across his skin. He normally wore a hoodie under his jacket for long rides, but he'd been too pissed off by the events at Gemma's bookshop to bother going back to the hotel to grab one. He had thought everything was settled; hell, he had been damn excited to move into the little two-bedroom apartment. It would be quiet and private, with plenty of space for just him. In Denver, he'd been living in a cramped little studio apartment with his TV, bed, and an old recliner he'd bought at a garage sale years back. Right now, everything was locked up in a storage unit in Twin Falls. He'd had plans to move everything today, but that was shot to shit.

By the time he pulled into the center's parking lot two hours later, his skin was numb, but the cold had helped him think a little more clearly. Maybe Rock Canyon wasn't the right town. This could be a sign that he was on the wrong track and should start looking around at other locations.

Grabbing the shakes and bag of fries he'd picked up, he walked into the building, calculating all the costs he was looking at for setting up shop in Rock Canyon. Since arriving, he'd noticed that places for rent were few and far between, and spaces large enough for his custom-built motorcycle shop were even scarcer still. He'd driven by what looked like an old firehouse on the edge of town with a SPACE FOR RENT sign out front, but when he'd called, the price had been a little steeper than he'd banked on. Especially if he ended up staying at the hotel for an extended length of time. Maybe in another town, he'd have better luck.

Gabe had been saving for his dream shop for nine years, but the money he'd saved was meant to go toward the equipment he needed. He didn't want to have to take out large business loans and have some small-town bank manager delving into his past. His past was his own, and he didn't want it spread across town. Especially when it detailed that he'd spent five years in prison for an accident he'd caused while riding drunk.

An accident involving his sixteen-year-old sister, who had been on the back of his bike at the time.

As he came through the front door, the woman at the check-in desk, Gillian, waved at him happily.

"Hello, Mr. Moriarty!"

"Hey, Gillian," he said, signing the visitor log. "Is she in her room?"

"Yep, just got back from the pool."

"Thanks," Gabe said, heading for the stairs that would take him to the second floor and Honey's room. The nice thing about the facility was that it had all the medical staff of a hospital but with studio and one- and two-bedroom apartments. Residents could eat in the main dining hall or have their meals in their rooms. It allowed the more-independent, functioning occupants the freedom they wanted, along with structured plans for others like Honey.

Slipping the other shake between his arm and his body, he knocked on Honey's door. Sharla Baker, Honey's nurse for the last six years, opened the door, her dark eyes widening.

"Well, bless my soul, Gabriel, we didn't expect you until the weekend."

"Hey, Sharla." Gabe gave her a hug. The facility offered a fantastic nursing staff, but Sharla had an almost maternal bond with Honey, and she knew his sister's moods. There were times when he wondered what they'd do if she retired, but for now, he loved the gentle, compassionate woman for everything she'd done for them—above and beyond what she was paid for. She was family. And although she shared Honey's care with other nurses at night and on her days off, none of them could replace her.

"I had some time today, so I figured I'd come for a visit," he said, walking past her into the room. He caught sight of Honey, sitting by the window, painting. Suddenly all his anger, frustration, and worry drained away as he watched his beautiful sister focus so intently on the canvas. Her hair was cut short, a riot of corkscrew curls that stopped at the back of her neck. She was wearing a simple white dress with light pink flowers that made her caramel skin appear darker.

"Hey, baby girl," he said softly, knowing that startling Honey when she was consumed by an activity could bring on an episode.

She didn't turn around, but Sharla patted his arm before she went to stand next to Honey.

"Honey, your brother is here."

Honey turned slowly, as if coming out of a trance, and Sharla repeated herself. Shifting toward the door, Honey's pretty face broke into a bright, joyful smile.

"Gabey!"

Honey struggled to her feet with her hand on the back of the chair, and Sharla put an arm around her waist to steady her. Gabe set the food down on the round table in Honey's little kitchen just before Honey launched herself against his chest.

Gathering her close, Gabe's stomach twisted as he rocked her back and forth. "How you doing, baby girl?"

"I painted the mountains! Come and see—oof!"

She had tried to pull away excitedly and would have fallen if he hadn't kept a hold of her.

"Easy. I'm not going anywhere."

Honey's lower lip started to quiver and her eyes filled up with tears as she rubbed her hip. Gabe hadn't meant to hurt her feelings, but she easily forgot her limitations, and the last thing he wanted was to see her hurt again. Because of him, she'd already had her leg pieced back together, using screws and pins that had left one leg shorter than the other. Walking too much was painful, and fast movements could sometimes throw her off balance.

"Hey, come on now, where is this picture? You know I want to see it. Maybe I'll hang it up in my new place."

Honey's face immediately split into an excited smile, the sheen in her eyes disappearing. It was one of the side effects of her brain injury that he would never get used to—how rapidly her moods could shift. One minute she'd be laughing and teasing him, and the next she'd be screaming and throwing things. It had scared the shit out of him the first time he's seen it, and even now it unnerved him.

With his arm still around her waist, she led him over to her easel. Despite her issues with impulse control, Honey hadn't lost any of her artistic talent. She had captured the snowcapped mountains and the cloudy spring sky. It might not have been as cleanly detailed as her work before the accident, but it was still beautiful.

It had actually been Honey's love of art that had brought her and Chase together when they were teenagers. They had been too afraid to tell Gabe that they were seeing each other, worried about how he would react to his best friend dating his baby sister.

It turned out that they had been right to be concerned. Gabe had taken it hard and had overreacted. He could blame the alcohol he'd consumed, but it wasn't just that. When he'd caught them, he'd been fighting his own issues, which had only fueled the violent pummeling he'd given Chase before ordering Honey onto the back of his bike. Looking back, Gabe had a feeling that even if he'd caught them kissing when he was stone-cold sober, he'd have probably flown off the handle anyway.

Only he might not have overcorrected on that curve and sent his bike careening off the road. He definitely wouldn't have spent five years in prison, and his sister would have had a real future.

"Gabe?"

He realized that Honey had been repeating his name. "Sorry, I was just so caught up in your painting. You did good."

Honey beamed at him. Her dark eyes and long lashes reminded him of when she was six, and she'd wanted a piece of his Halloween candy because she'd already demolished hers. He'd given in, unable to resist her puppy-dog eyes or the way she'd thrown her arms around him, squeezed him tight, and whispered, "You're the best brother ever."

If only that were still true. He'd been trying every day to make it up to her. He'd gotten out of prison and spent the last nine years fighting for her, doing everything he could to make her life better. This place was definitely better than the state hospital his mother had left her in.

He still wanted to rip his mother apart for putting Honey in that place, despite the fact that she'd been dead for almost seven years now. While he was awaiting trial, his mother had sued the hospital for missing a brain bleed on Honey's scans. She'd been awarded millions—plenty of money to give Honey the best care—but instead, his compulsive gambler of a mother had locked Honey up in a place where he wouldn't put his worst enemy. By the time he'd gotten out of prison, his mother had blown through nearly everything.

When his mother was shot outside of a gaming hall in one of the rougher areas of the city, Gabe couldn't muster too much sadness for her. In the end, she'd been a selfish bitch. He could forgive her for a lot, but the way she'd turned her back on Honey had been enough for him. He'd claimed her body, used the money in her account to pay for cremation, and then sold everything she owned to pay for Honey's care.

If that made him a hard son-of-a-bitch, then so be it. But he'd needed to be that way. To survive prison. To be able to protect Honey. Hell, just to deal with life and the uphill battle he was fighting, he had to learn to harden up.

"Do I get to see your place?"

Honey's question jarred him, and he hesitated. If it were up to him, Honey would live with him, but Sharla and Honey's former doctor had convinced him that Honey needed structure to avoid the confusion that might lead to violent outbursts. Too much stimuli and change could upset her, and after witnessing Honey's episodes firsthand, he had agreed with them.

"Soon. Hey, I brought you something," Gabe said, helping her sit down at the little table. Her face lit up when she saw the bag and drink cup.

She dove into the bag and pulled out the fries, shoving several into her mouth with a groan. "I love French fries."

"I know," he said, watching her take off the lid of her shake and dip her fries into the ice cream, just like when they were kids.

"So, tell us about your new apartment," Sharla said, sitting down at the table.

"The other shake and fries are for you," Gabe said as he sat down next to Honey.

"That was sweet of you, but I'm trying to watch my figure," she said, her eyes twinkling. "These days, I can't eat just anything like you young people can." It didn't stop her from sneaking a few fries, though, before repeating, "So, your new place…"

"I haven't even moved in yet. It turns out that while the husband had agreed to rent it to me, the wife had promised it to a woman, and when we both showed up to sign the lease, they decided to talk about it first."

Gabe was talking more to Sharla than Honey, who was too busy eating to pay attention.

"That's terrible," Sharla said.

"Yeah, and I get the feeling the other potential tenant will make some major waves if the decision goes my way. She just seems like the real uptight, self-involved diva type, you know?"

"They should go with the first person to claim it."

"I agree," Gabe replied, appreciating Sharla's loyalty. "But I also don't want to start sh—" He caught himself at Sharla's warning look. "*Stuff* in a new place and cause problems. I'm trying to turn over a new leaf."

"Psh, just because you're trying not to make waves doesn't mean you let other people push you under the water."

He laughed, shaking his head. "I'm not. But whether they pick me or not, it's out of my hands."

"You should share," Honey said, her words garbled by a mix of fries and milkshake.

Gabe stared at his sister, fighting a smile. "You think I should share my apartment with a strange woman?"

"Is she strange?" Honey asked.

No, she's not strange. She's hot and sexy and trouble on two legs.

"I just mean that I don't know her."

"If you lived with her, then you would get to know her, wouldn't you?"

That gave him pause. It *was* a two-bedroom apartment. If he shared the rent, it would help with the unforeseen expenses he hadn't counted on. Women liked things neat and tidy, didn't they? They could split the housework, and he'd hardly be there anyway, what with getting the shop off the ground.

All in all, it wasn't a half bad suggestion.

He leaned over and kissed the top of her head. "Thanks, baby girl."

"Wanna watch a movie?" she asked, jumping up from the table so fast, she almost took out his chin.

"Sure." Following his sister to the day bed, he sat against the headboard and wasn't surprised that she picked *Homeward Bound*. It was a favorite of hers.

As she climbed up next to him, she leaned her head on his shoulder. "You're the best brother ever."

His chest tightened. *Not yet, but I'm working on it.*

GABE RODE BACK into Rock Canyon at just after six in the evening and took the main stretch so he could stop by Chase's tattoo shop. He parked his bike around the corner on Oak Avenue and realized, as he took his gloves off, that his palms were sweating, and he couldn't seem to slow his heart rate.

It was no surprise that he was nervous. The last time he'd seen Chase, he'd been screaming at him from a hospital bed the morning after the accident, blaming him for everything and telling him to get out. Chase had even visited him once while he was in prison, but he'd refused to see him.

Gabe had tried to find him when he got out, to make amends, but no one knew where he'd ended up. It wasn't until Gabe had taken a trip to Reno and stopped in at a little diner off the highway where Chase's mom had worked that he'd been able to track him down. Chase's stepdad had told him that Chase had moved to a small town in Idaho and was living a really good life there, writing comic books while running his tattoo shop. Gabe had been curious about Rock Canyon and why Chase would have chosen to settle there instead of LA or New York. Chase had always talked about moving somewhere big and booming, where artists were "appreciated," whatever that meant.

Despite their rocky past, Gabe had kept up with Chase's comic book career. He'd even bought a ticket to a comic book convention in Denver, once he'd learned that Chase would be signing books there. But in the end, he hadn't made it past the parking lot.

Chase was the only person who had been there the night of the accident and who had stuck around for the aftermath. He'd seen Gabe at his worst, and for Gabe, that was the reason facing Chase was so terrifying. Honey could remember bits and pieces sometimes, but for the most part, she was blissfully ignorant and had forgiven Gabe easily.

It wouldn't be that simple with Chase.

Gabe stepped inside the brightly lit parlor. Chase was standing with his back to him, hanging up some artwork on the wall.

"Hang on; I'll be right with you," Chase said.

"No problem."

Chase straightened the picture, turned, and paused for a moment, staring at Gabe.

The silence and tension became stifling, overwhelming Gabe. He shoved his clammy hands in his pockets to dry them. "Bet I'm the last person you expected to see here."

"Not the last but close," Chase said dryly.

"Yeah," Gabe said, searching for something else to add but coming up empty.

Neither of them said anything else, and Gabe could feel his throat start to tighten with anxiety.

This was a mistake.

"So, what brings you to town?" Chase asked finally. "From what I remember, you said if you ever saw my face again, I was a dead man." He stood in the same spot, hardly moving.

Better to just rip off the Band-Aid. "And yet, you still tried to see me."

"What can I say?" Chase said, a wry smile twisting his mouth. "I'm a risk taker. Plus, I figured they'd have you in restraints."

"It's not like I was Hannibal Lecter," Gabe said, looking around the shop. "It looks like you've done well for yourself."

"I'm doing all right."

Chase seemed to be waiting for something, and Gabe shuffled his feet, unable to meet his gaze. "Look, man, I'm sorry I refused your visit. I appreciate it now, but at the time, I was still pretty raw and wrong. I couldn't face you, for a lot of reasons." Chase said nothing, so Gabe added, "I was all messed up. It took me several years to get my head wrapped around everything I'd done, and I just need you to know...I was a major dick. Nothing that happened was your fault."

"Dating my best friend's sister probably wasn't the smartest move," Chase said.

"If I could do it over, I can't say I would have been happy about it, but I definitely wouldn't have attacked you. Or ridden my bike wasted."

"Still riding those testicle ticklers?"

Gabe choked on a laugh, easing some of the tension in his shoulders. "My bike could take whatever hog you have stashed away." Chase's smile was small, but it was there. Maybe there was hope for forgiveness after all. "I'm actually thinking about moving here. I've been saving for years to open my own custom bike shop."

Chase was silent, seeming to mull over what to say next. "Why here?"

The question was reasonable enough, but for Gabe, the reasons behind his decision were emotional, and emotions would make him even more vulnerable in an already awkward situation. Just when it seemed like they were starting to relax around each other.

"The facility where Honey's staying is in Sun Valley, and this place is only two hours from her. It's centrally located between many outdoor recreation areas, which would be perfect for selling my bikes," Gabe said, fidgeting as he added, "Besides, your stepdad said you'd be here, and I needed to try to make amends."

"Aw, you came all this way for me," Chase said, jokingly clasping his hands to his chest. "Be still my heart."

"Shut up, man," Gabe said.

Chase laughed but the tone wasn't mocking. Waving his hand toward one of the chairs, he said, "Well, you're here. Have a seat. Where you living, anyway?"

"That's currently up in the air," Gabe said, adding, "I'm working on it."

"Well, let me know when you get settled, and you can come over for dinner. Meet my wife."

The word *wife* was so foreign—especially coming out of Chase's mouth—that Gabe was still having trouble believing it. "Yeah, I heard you settled down. Congratulations or condolences?"

"Congratulations, man," Chase said, his face taking on an almost dreamy quality. "Katie is amazing. You'll love her."

"Great," Gabe said, surprised at the changes in Chase. Granted, it had been sixteen years, but still....Chase had been the guy who thought serious relationships were just short of castrating yourself. Just another reason Gabe had been sure Chase would hurt Honey. But now he was a healthy, contributing member of society, with a wife, a home, and a successful business.

Everything you once imagined for yourself.

"So what all do you need to work out with your new place?"

Gabe's thoughts shifted to the dark-haired beauty currently making his fresh start more difficult. "I have to deal with a pest problem before I move in."

Chapter Four

> "In my opinion, men and women cannot live
> together without at least some friction."
>
> **—Miss Know It All**

CAROLINE WAS LYING on the couch at eight o'clock, trying to go back to sleep. Between Val and Justin coming back here instead of going to his house, and Ellie sneaking in at four in the morning, only to trip over Gus, the bulldog, Caroline hadn't slept more than a few hours. The last time she'd woken up, it had been to Ellie's releasing a string of curses—and a mumbled apology after she'd asked if Ellie was okay. Then, just as Caroline was about to drift back to sleep, Justin had come out of the bedroom with Val on his heels. After a ten-minute smooch fest by the door, Justin had left, and Val had made her way back to her bedroom.

There'd been no more sleeping after those disturbing noises, so Caroline had spent the last few hours debating how she was going to get into that apartment. She had a feeling Mr. Bad Ass wasn't going to give it up without a fight.

If she was her father's daughter, she'd do a little digging into her competitor's past. A guy like that probably had a few skeletons, some undesirable qualities—besides the fact that he was a snarky, chauvinistic jerkoff. Telling her to find someplace else. Calling her "princess."

Once upon a time, maybe, but she hadn't been pampered or sheltered since before her mother died. But that was a long time ago. That girl wouldn't have made it in the world on her own. Caroline had needed to adapt, change, and grow with every situation.

But if she wasn't going to resort to dirty tactics or legal recourse now, what other options did she have?

A loud knock at the front door startled her, and she jumped, nearly rolling off the couch. Dressed in a pair of boxers and a T-shirt, she got up and walked to the entryway. Her hand was on the knob before another knock shook the wood.

Opening the door, her mouth fell open when she found Gabe the Badass standing on her porch, looking sheepish.

And hot. Can't forget hot.

"I take it you're surprised to see me," Gabe said, a smirk turning the corners of his mouth up in a knee-weakening way that didn't affect her at all.

Not one little bit.

"What do you want?"

"You dropped out of charm school, didn't you?" Gabe asked.

"When it comes to you, this is about as charming as I get," she said, resisting the urge to smooth out her messy ponytail. She didn't even want to think about what her breath smelled like.

Why do you care? It's not like you're going to be kissing him. Maybe you can scare him away with your dragon breath.

"Fair enough," he said, and she hated that he looked so damn good in a pair of faded jeans, a cotton shirt, and a leather jacket. If it weren't for the piercings, he could have been in the cast of *Grease*. "I know we got off to a rough start—"

"You mean when you tried to steal my apartment and throw me out?"

Satisfaction raced through her as his jaw clenched. So she irritated him. Too bad. He irritated her, too.

"I meant that the confusion over the apartment caused us both to leave empty-handed," he said.

"So what? You've come to convince me why I should just let you have it?"

"Actually, I was going to suggest we share it," Gabe said, the smirk back in full force as he added, "if you think you can handle it."

Caroline blinked at him. "Please tell me you're joking."

"Nope."

"Why would I want to live with you? I can't even stand to breathe the same air as you."

He shrugged. "You seem like the type to get all sue-crazy over something like this, so I figured I'd be the bigger man and lay out a compromise. It's up to you, though."

"I am not sue-crazy," she muttered.

"Whatever you say, princess."

"*See?* We can't live together. It would be a war zone," she said.

"I'm hardly going to be there, so it's not like we'd have to interact," he said, holding out his fingers as he ticked them off. "Since I'll be busy, it will basically be a crash pad for me, and it would only be temporary. Once another place opens up, one of us could move out. Plus, it would be cheaper to split the rent."

She eyed him up and down as a voice in her head screamed that it was a crazy, stupid idea. That tattoo just above his collar continued to taunt her, and she thought she caught a flash of silver in his tongue that matched the bar going through his eyebrow. Not that she cared—she had her fair share of tats—but she knew danger when it flashed her a charming smile.

Besides, trading two noisy sisters for one potential serial killer didn't seem like the brightest idea.

"I can't live with a strange man who I know nothing about. You could be some kind of Dexter, and I'll come home to you dissolving bodies in the bathtub."

"That's up to you," he said, shoving his hands into his pockets. "But you don't have to worry about me. I'm as harmless as a kitten."

With that, he walked inside, brushing against her—on purpose, no doubt—and she ignored the tingles the close contact caused, protesting, "Hey, I didn't invite you inside."

"And I don't usually conduct business on people's porches."

Caroline slammed the door and followed him into the kitchen. He was standing in front of an open cupboard, perusing the contents. Caroline noticed that Gus, the monster dog, was sitting at his feet, panting at him, with his massive jaws spread into a wide grin.

Evil is attracted to evil, apparently.

"You know, illegal trespassing and breaking and entering are serious crimes. So is looting and burglary."

With a long, amused look, he grabbed a package of Hostess cupcakes, and he had the nerve to laugh. The bastard. "I didn't break anything, and like I said, we're talking business." He ripped the package open with his teeth and took out one of the cakes, opening his mouth wide.

"If my sister catches you eating her cupcakes, you're a dead man," Caroline said, eyeing the sugary treats longingly. She'd sworn off sugar last month after she'd stress-eaten herself ten pounds heavier. Just imagining the sweet, orange frosting caused her mouth to water.

"Want one?" he asked, holding out the package to her, tempting her. "We could be criminals together."

When she didn't reach for it right away, he set it on the counter and concentrated on demolishing the rest of the one in his hand, licking his fingers with quick flicks of his tongue.

Yep, that tongue was definitely pierced.

As he sucked the frosting off his hands, her nipples tightened, imagining the sweetness of the frosting mixed with the warm, salty taste of his skin. In her mind, she was the one licking and sucking on each long digit as her hands slid up under his T-shirt, over those abs, until she found out if his nipples were also pierced.

Stop it! Do not think about him like that. He is an ass!

"So, what do you think?"

His question caught her off guard. "What?"

"Wanna be my roommate?"

"No," she said, going to the fridge for a protein shake.

"Suit yourself," he said.

"Goddamn it!" Caroline heard Val scream from her room. "Eleanor!" A door slammed, another opened, and the screaming continued. "Did you take the new Jimmy Choos I just ordered?" A muffled reply that Caroline couldn't make out followed, and then, "I said you were not to look at them, let alone borrow them. I haven't even worn them yet!"

Caroline could feel the headache coming on as her sisters continued to squabble, her forehead becoming the center of the pounding pain.

"Those your sisters?"

She glanced his way and said sarcastically, "Yeah, how'd you guess?"

"Gemma said you lived with your sisters when I called for your address last night," he said.

So that's how he'd found out where she lived.

The screaming had intensified in the other room; Ellie apparently finally was awake enough to yell back at Val. Suddenly, even a homicidal roommate didn't seem like the worst thing in the world.

"Okay, let's just say I was interested in a temporary living arrangement," she said, rubbing her temples and forehead with her fingers. "We would have to establish some ground rules."

"It's simple," he said, leaning back against the counter. "You stay out of my business; I'll stay out of yours. We split the rent and utilities fifty-fifty—"

"What about Internet or a house phone?"

"I've got my cell phone, so I don't need a house phone, but I'll split the Internet with you. And cable."

"I don't need cable. I stream off the Internet," Caroline said. With how often she moved, it was easier than getting new service every six months.

"Whatever floats your boat, princess," he said, and her hackles rose.

"And stop calling me princess," she said.

Before he could answer, Caroline saw a flash of dark hair out of the corner of her eye and turned in time to see her sister Ellie slam the front door. Seconds later, Val appeared, opened the door, and yelled after her, "If you ever get into my closet again, I'll rip your hair out!"

She shut the door with a loud bang and turned toward them. Her angry expression melted into surprise before her face flushed a deep red. Was she embarrassed that someone else had witnessed one of their family fights?

Or maybe it was that it had been witnessed while she was in her underwear and a tank top.

Caroline shook her head. "Valerie, this is Gabe. Gabe, this is my sister."

"Pleasure," Gabe said. Caroline saw his mouth twitch, as if he were fighting a grin.

"Nice to meet you. Excuse me," Val said, running from the room.

Caroline sucked down her protein shake and tossed the bottle in the garbage. "So about this living arrangement...I'm in."

"HERE YOU GO," Gemma Bowers said with a relieved smile, handing Gabe the keys. "I'm really glad you were able to work something out. I am sorry this happened, and I'm so embarrassed—"

"Think nothing of it, Mrs. Bowers," Gabe said, all charm. He thought he heard a gagging noise coming from Caroline, who was standing by the door. Gabe grinned. He wasn't surprised she'd said yes to his proposal, not really. Over the years, he had learned a thing or two about strong, independent women, and the foremost lesson was that it was hard for them to back down from a challenge.

And sure enough, this tiny brunette with attitude was no different.

Plus, the last thing he'd wanted was to cause a problem between Travis Bowers and his wife. Especially because Travis had gone out on a limb for him after he'd come clean about his time in prison. He'd shared enough of the details to prove he wasn't a rapist or a murderer, but he hadn't bared his soul. Luckily, Travis had said it would stay between them. He'd been surprisingly cool about everything.

"Everyone deserves a second chance."

For Gabe, it was a little hard to believe that a perfect stranger was willing to give him a clean slate, especially since so many of his friends from his past had written him off.

It wasn't all their fault. He'd been angry, filled with self-loathing, and jealous as hell of their futures, especially Chase's. Chase had been getting out of town to go to Berkeley on a scholarship. That had been eating Gabe alive for months before he'd caught Chase and Honey together.

Jealousy was an ugly thing.

"Can I get the second set? I want to start unloading," Caroline said, right next to his shoulder now. Gemma handed over the keys, which Little Miss Attitude snatched up in a hurry. Damn, she was a brat. He watched her storm out the door, her jeans hugging her ass like they were made just for her.

Gabe had to admit, if he was up for a detour on his road to redemption, the sharp-tongued woman would be the perfect pit stop. Today, she looked fresh-faced and sweet, except for that angry gleam in her eyes that said she definitely wasn't ready to make nice with Gemma.

Or him, for that matter.

Even if she had been ready and willing for a little action, he wasn't looking for anything more than someone to satisfy his needs, and he wasn't about to become fuck buddies with a woman he'd be sharing a bathroom with. That scenario was just too domestic for his tastes.

Even if she did have an amazing body.

He followed her out the door and caught a sweet, flow-ery scent that told his body that finding a friend-with-benefits might need to happen sooner than later. Living with a woman like her, twenty-four/seven, was not going to end well. He had too much work ahead of him—on his new life, his shop, and repairing his friendship with Chase—to be tempted into trouble.

Gabe joined her at the top of the stairs as she slipped the key in the lock.

"God, do you have to breathe down my neck like that?"

He resisted the urge to bend over and blow in her ear, just to piss her off.

"Are you ever pleasant, or does the 'I'm better than you and I know it' act work for some guys?" he asked, following her into the apartment as she pushed the door open.

"So far, I haven't had any complaints," she said, sar-casm oozing from every word.

"Probably 'cause they're pussies that are scared to death you'll cook and eat them," he said, ignoring her gasp behind him as he headed for the room on the left.

"You're taking the bigger room?" she called out after him, outrage evident in her tone.

Turning at the door, he said, "You can wrestle me for it if you want, princess."

"Ugh, why did I think this would be better than my sister's?" she groaned, turning her back on him. He admired her backside again before she came back toward him with a determined, angry glint in her eye. "Let's get a few things straight: this is not going to be anything but a living arrangement. Two strangers, sharing one dwelling, and nothing more. So, stay out of my room and away from me. And stop calling me princess."

God, she thinks she's tough shit. Her challenge sparked something inside him, and he crossed the hallway without thinking. She backed up against the other closed bedroom door at his approach. Warm satisfaction curled through his body as he boxed her in, hovering over her with one arm against the wall. She was so tiny compared to him, but her glare was defiant as she raised that pointed little chin and met his gaze.

Dipping his head a bit lower, he whispered darkly, "What should I call you then? Angel? Baby?"

He swore he saw her shiver, even as she snapped back, "My name is Caroline."

It would have been so easy to lean over and see if those berry-pink lips tasted as good as they looked, but instead, he pushed off the wall and away from her. "I'm not one of those choir boys you can push around or manipulate. Unless you want to test my patience, I suggest you stop trying to control me, Caroline."

Shoving him out of her way, she headed back toward the front door. "I'm going to unpack my car, and then I'm going to the store."

Just to annoy her, he called, "Great plan. I think I'll join you. We should probably take your car, though, since I've just got my bike."

"Screw you. You can starve."

And on that friendly note, Caroline slammed the door behind her, leaving Gabe amused and turned on, despite the warning voice in his head.

Focus on what you're doing here, and forget about her.

As if that were possible, when her scent still lingered throughout the room.

Chapter Five

> "Everyone has baggage. Whether or not you can leave your baggage at the door of a new relationship is up to you."
>
> —**Miss Know It All**

CAROLINE HAD GOTTEN in and out of the grocery store without bumping into any "old friends." Not that she was scared of her past. She'd made plenty of mistakes, but she was an adult now. She could take the fallout with maturity and just hope that the people she wronged would follow suit.

And if that didn't work, she'd just turn the other cheek. How bad could it be?

Shelby's reaction to their run-in yesterday was a mild version of what she'd been expecting. Still, Shelby had barely begun dating Marcus Boatman when Caroline had drunkenly seduced him at a party. Considering the guys who had come before and after, there were probably a few more former girlfriends who would rather sock her than look at her.

She didn't dare stop for gas at the Shell station, afraid of what Mr. Nelson would do if he saw her again. After she'd made off with a six-pack of beer stuffed into her jeans, jacket, and shirt, he'd hung her picture in the window as a reminder that she wasn't allowed near his store. She had managed to get away only because he had been chasing one of her companions who'd boosted a bottle of whiskey out the other door. Her father had swooped in to smooth things over when Mr. Nelson had called the cops.

Good old Dad, always there when the family name was on the line.

Back at the apartment, Caroline was glad to find Gabe gone. *Gabe.* She snorted. Most likely short for Gabriel, which made her think of the show *Supernatural.* The archangel on the show had been short and funny.

Her new roommate was the polar opposite.

As she put her groceries away, she thought of the way he had stepped up to her, his body so close she'd felt the heat radiating off him like the sun. If it hadn't been for his expression, she might have been nervous, but he hadn't been trying to scare her. He had wanted to prove something.

Caroline knew exactly what she was dealing with. He thought he was charming and was used to having women fawn all over him and probably doing anything and everything he wanted. But she wasn't one of them, and he was going to learn pretty damn quick that she played the game better than most women.

At least, that's what the second stall in the Rock Canyon High School boy's bathroom had said years ago.

Looking around the empty apartment, she doubted Gabe the Babe Slayer had brought any decent furniture with him. Guys like him thought lawn chairs and a TV made a living space.

It was still early, not quite noon, so she decided to make the forty-five-minute trip up to Twin Falls. A few hours later, although it had taken a good chunk out of her savings, she left with a promise of next-day delivery on everything, including her brand-new bed.

When Caroline pulled into the alleyway, she saw that Gabe's bike was parked in the spot again.

You're going to have to explain to him that the spot is yours, and he can park that stupid tricycle somewhere else.

She swung back onto Main Street and parked in front of Gemma's shop. Caroline got out of her car and walked past the front window of Chloe's Book Nook, catching the friendly wave from Gemma. Caroline waved back. Although she was still perturbed at the pretty bookstore owner, she didn't want the drama to continue. She had enough of that from outside sources.

As she headed back down the alley, she saw the back of her sister's dark head sitting on the third step of the staircase leading to her new place.

That morning, Caroline had knocked on Val's bathroom door to let her know that she'd decided to take the apartment, not bothering to mention that Gabe would be sharing it. Luckily, she'd caught Val midshampoo, so they hadn't had a chance to have a long conversation. Her sister had already protested her moving out.

"Just give me a day or so, and I'll send Ellie packing back to Dad's. You don't have to go."

Caroline hadn't had the heart to tell her it wasn't just that she needed space from Ellie, Gus, or the dreaded lumpy couch.

As she stopped at the bottom of the staircase, she saw that Val had her missing cell phone in her hands. "I see you finally got my phone back from that demon you call a dog."

"Hello to you too," Val said, brushing her short bangs off her forehead. Although Caroline wasn't a fan of short hair, she had to admit the new cut looked good with her sister's delicate features and big brown eyes—their mother's eyes. Caroline had been blessed with the same eyes, but with her rounder face, they didn't stand out as much.

She held out her hand for the phone and noticed the bite marks in the rubber case. Luckily, the canine's massive jaws hadn't cracked the screen. "Sorry, but that dog is evil."

"No, he just likes you. A lot," Val said, grinning. "So, are you going to show me your new place or what?"

"Sure, but there's not much in there. I've got furniture scheduled to be delivered tomorrow." Caroline climbed past her sister as she stood up.

"That's fine. I thought I'd drop the phone off when I found it, but if you don't want me to see your place..."

"Oh, will you knock it off?" Caroline said as she put the key in the door. "I was just sharing pertinent information. Stop acting like a brat."

"I'm not a brat," Val snapped behind her, and Caroline's insides warmed with happiness. It hadn't taken them long to fall back into their old roles, and it made Caroline glad that Val didn't really hold a grudge against her for leaving. One less person hating her guts was a plus in Caroline's life.

Unlocking the door and stepping inside, she held her arm out. "Mi casa es su casa."

Val stepped past her and looked around the empty rooms. "I can't believe you don't have any furniture."

Caroline shrugged as she shut the door. "It made it easier to drop everything at a moment's notice and move on."

"Hmmm…so, who was that guy this morning?"

Well, that took a lot longer than expected. If Caroline had walked into the kitchen in her skivvies and encountered a strange man, she would have asked then and there instead of running away to put clothes on.

"My new roommate. Remember how I showed up to get my keys and found out that some wires got crossed? Travis rented it to Gabe, the guy from this morning—"

"Wait, the douche with the crotch rocket is the same gorgeous man who was leaning against my sink, looking like sex on a fucking stick?"

Caroline rolled her eyes. "Yes, but—"

"Is that who's in your shower?" Val asked.

Caroline had been so tuned in to her sister's reaction that she hadn't even heard the shower running. "Must be."

"Well, I can't wait to officially meet him. What changed, by the way? Yesterday you were ranting and raving, and now you're sharing a bathroom. So, what's he really like?"

Arrogant. Bossy. Hot.

"He's just a guy. I haven't even really talked to him, besides the initial argument about who this place belongs to and what our living situation is going to be like."

"I'm surprised you didn't run him out of here with an icy glare."

"I tried. Seems I might be losing my touch."

"There's never been a man you couldn't charm or chase off if you put your right mind to it," Val said, chuckling.

Except for Daddy...

That last fight with her father before she'd left, when she'd fought so hard to go to San Diego for a fresh start, had been a total surprise to her. She'd never thought her father would deny her the college of her choice.

"I'm not paying for you to go to a known party school two states away so you can squander my money and flunk out. Boise State is a perfectly acceptable school."

It hadn't been about the parties or the beach. She'd wanted to get away from her past and never come back. She couldn't go to Boise State, not when Kyle was there. She couldn't take the chance that she'd bump into him and have to deal with his knowing sneer. She tried everything, from begging to bartering, before finally delivering an ultimatum.

"If you don't let me go, I'll walk out that door and do it on my own. I will figure it out."

She'd been bluffing, of course, hoping he'd change his mind to keep her in his life, but she'd overestimated her father's fondness for her.

"This is my house, and you will follow the rules or you will get out. And there are no second chances, Caroline. If you leave, you'll stay gone."

So she'd gone. A scared seventeen-year-old whose bravado had backed her into a corner. She'd called Val to beg her for some money and a bag of clothes, just so she wouldn't have to face their father again. Val had made her promise to call, but the calls home became fewer and farther between, partly because she had one of those pay-as-you-go phones for a while, and most of the time, she couldn't pay.

The other reason was because every time she heard her sister's voice or listened to her complaints, Caroline wanted to beg her father to take her back. Especially on the nights when she'd gone to bed hungry. But at the time, she'd been too stubborn to give up and admit that he might have been right, that she couldn't make it on her own.

Like father, like daughter.

"I think the water turned off," Val hissed, drawing Caroline out of the past and into an entirely new and dangerous train of thought.

Thinking about Gabe in the shower, water trailing down that brown skin, caused her nipples to tighten. Damn, she wished she would stop imagining what the jerk looked like without his clothes on.

Suddenly, the bathroom door opened and out stepped Gabe, a blue towel wrapped around his hips. Caroline's heart stopped along with her breathing for half a second and then kicked back into high gear. His chest looked even better out of a T-shirt, and the tattoos intermingling along the muscles of his arms drew her gaze all the way up to those wide shoulders. Some of the designs were hard to make out, just swirls of color and black, but the one on his neck looked tribal. She scanned down over the top of his towel and a tiny, evil part of her wished it would fall open so she could see the rest of him.

"Sorry. Didn't realize you were here."

His deep voice jerked her eyes back up to meet his amused gaze. Damn it, she didn't want to be flustered by him or his abs.

"Hey, I'm Caroline's sister, Valerie. You might remember me as the screeching, half-naked lunatic from this morning," Val said, her brown eyes twinkling. "You're Gabe?"

Caroline heard the tone of her sister's inquiry, as if she had told Val so much about him, and she gave Val a dark look.

Val ignored her and slid her gaze up and down. "You weren't at all what I was expecting."

Gabe grinned as he took the hand Val held out, and Caroline got a closer look at his tattoos. The one that drew her attention first was the barbed wire wrapped around his bicep, a cliché that still looked massively sexy on him.

Stop thinking about how sexy he is!

But the barbed wire continued down, wrapping around his whole arm like a rope until it stopped at his wrist, and she saw the red drop on the back of his wrist. As if the tattoo had pierced his skin. Within the loops of the tattoo were smaller colored images, but she didn't have a chance to study them further before he pulled his arm back.

"Really? You weren't expecting a man in a towel?" Gabe asked Val, glancing at Caroline with his eyebrow raised. "Then what were you expecting?"

"Definitely not you," Val said.

"She is just messing with you," Caroline snapped when Gabe's gaze drifted back to Val. "I just said you were my new roommate." She didn't like the way his face softened as he checked out her beautiful, petite sister. Like he was wondering what she'd be like in bed.

Why do you care?

Because Val has no business flirting when she has a serious boyfriend.

Right.

Even the voice in her head was condescending. Awesome.

"It's true; she did just say you were her roommate. I was the one who brought up your hotness," Val said, smirking.

Could you plead justifiable homicide if you strangled her?

"Well, thanks," Gabe said, that small, arrogant smile in place, the one he'd given Caroline the first time they'd met and was getting on her last nerve.

"She's got a boyfriend," Caroline said abruptly, and her cheeks warmed with a blush when the two of them turned to look at her, one amused, one exasperated.

"Thanks, Caroline, for making a friendly introduction awkward as hell," Val snapped.

"First of all, *you* were flirting," Caroline said, ignoring Val's attempt to protest. "I'm just letting *him* know, in case he had any ideas."

"I was just being polite," he said.

Polite, my ass.

"Her boyfriend is also a former marine," Caroline added, wishing her brain could override her mouth. The arrogant ass probably thought she was jealous or something.

Which she wasn't. At all.

"Both of my sisters are off limits, regardless."

Gabe ran his free hand over his strip of hair, as the other held onto the top of his towel. "Got it. You'll have to introduce me to the other one so I'll know who to stay away from." Nodding at Val, he said, "It was nice meeting you."

"Likewise," Val said as he turned and went into his bedroom.

When they were alone, Val laughed. "You are in so much trouble."

"No, I'm not," Caroline argued.

"Are you kidding me? He is H-A-W-T."

"I'm going to tell Justin."

"No, you won't, and besides, I'm just making an observation. I love Justin, and I know he's it for me."

Caroline's chest tightened. She was so happy that her sister had found love after everything their father had done to keep Val and Justin apart. Val deserved it.

Just then, she thought of something. "That reminds me, I was hoping I could stay at your house one more night. My bed comes tomorrow, and as uncomfortable as your couch is, it's better than the floor. Unless you're going to be with your man, in which case I am stealing your bed."

Val looked sheepish. "I'm sure he wouldn't mind if I came over tonight."

"Good, then can we get out of here? I want to avoid run-ins with my unwanted roommate as much as possible."

"Sure you do."

Caroline wasn't amused.

Chapter Six

> "If one person says it, it's a rumor. If two people
> say it, it's gospel."
>
> —Miss Know It All

"YOU'RE LIVING WITH *Caroline Willis*?"

Gabe's beer stopped inches from his mouth when he caught the look on Katie Trepasso's face. It was as if he'd just told her he'd decided to go on a homicidal rampage.

"Yeah. Something I should know?"

Katie's big blue eyes swallowed up her face as she cleared her throat and got up from the patio table. "Nope. I'm just surprised. She just got back and everything. I figured she'd be staying with her sister."

And before he could ask her anything else, she hightailed it into the house. Giving Chase a questioning look, Gabe waited for an explanation.

"Don't ask me. I've lived here over a year and never heard of her."

Gabe let it go and looked out over the flat farmland behind Chase's white house, searching for something to say. Things had been tense between the two of them since he'd arrived for dinner half an hour ago. He knew he had a lot to make up for, but he hated that it was so hard. So awkward.

The elephant in the room loomed over them both, but neither wanted to talk about it. Katie came back outside then, carrying a platter of chips and salsa and another beer for Chase. Setting down the platter, she handed him the bottle over his shoulder. "Here ya go."

"Aw, thank you, beer wench," Chase said, looking up at her with a wide grin.

She reached over his shoulder to slap his chest, and he grabbed her hand, pulling her forward. When her head was almost on his chest, Chase turned his head to kiss her.

Gabe looked away. He'd never been comfortable with public displays and such. Of course, the last woman he'd ever been with long enough to get like that had been Cherise, but that hadn't lasted much longer than it had taken him to get back on his feet after being released. Cherise had been one of those women who liked to take care of people, to fix them. When she'd realized he didn't want or need her help, she'd lost interest in him. It was nothing to break his heart over.

Not that he had been looking for the white picket fence, the sweet wife, or the handful of kids since he got out. Things that everyday Joes—and now, even Chase—had just weren't in the cards for him after what he'd done.

He'd lost any chance he had at having a normal life the minute he'd driven his bike that night.

"So, Gabe, Chase said you want to open a custom motorcycle shop?"

"I said *bike*," Chase said, pulling Katie down onto his lap, despite her yelp of protest.

"But you hate that word," Katie argued.

"When you talk about *my* baby, yes, but we're talking about his."

Gabe laughed while Katie rolled her eyes.

"I was actually hoping your husband might want to stop in a few days a week and help out with some of the artwork. He designed the emblem on the first bike I built from scratch."

"How old were you?" Katie asked, leaning across Chase to snag a chip.

Gabe didn't miss the shadow that passed over Chase's face. "Seventeen."

Seventeen. They'd been seniors and best friends, getting into trouble and partying together.

Only…the last few months of high school had tested their tight bond. All Gabe had been able to think about was how Chase was getting out, but he was going to be stuck there, working for the local mechanic, with nothing but a small-town future ahead of him. Something he could only dream about now, but at the time, he'd envied Chase so much that his jealousy had started to consume him.

And then he'd caught Chase kissing his baby sister, and he'd lost it. How could Chase make the moves on Honey when he was just going to take off and leave her? Like he was leaving Gabe.

He'd been a fucking idiot.

The scene still played through his head like it was yesterday, even though sixteen years had passed.

"Come on, man, I'm sorry," Chase had said, stepping back from Honey, his hands in the air. Gabe had been too drunk to care that Chase was his best friend; he'd just been kissing his sister. His sister, who was only a sophomore. She was smart, talented, and deserved more than a guy who was just going to take advantage and then leave her behind when he took off.

The bastard had to pay.

"Fuck your sorry," Gabe had roared, charging Chase and knocking him to the ground.

Sitting on his chest, Gabe had thrown punch after punch until his sister had jumped on his back, screaming in his ear, "Stop, Gabe! I like him!"

He'd climbed off Chase and grabbed Honey's arm, dragging her to his motorcycle. Chase had yelled at him, tried to stop him from driving, but he hadn't listened.

It was no wonder Chase was reluctant to accept his apology, even now. The day after the accident, Gabe had woken up in the hospital, handcuffed to the bed. Chase had been sitting in the corner.

"What happened? Where am I?"

Chase had stood up grimly. "You're in the hospital. You wrecked your bike last night and broke your arm."

Dread had pumped through him as he'd tried to remember, to shake the clouds from his brain. His bike, Honey flying through the air...

"Where's Honey?"

Chase's expression had darkened. "She was stable and talking when they brought her in, but then she started seizing. They missed a bleed on her scans, and her brain swelled. They took her back up to surgery and put in a shunt to drain it, but they aren't sure if she'll wake up. And if she does…"

"If she does, *what*?" Gabe had shouted.

"She probably won't be the same girl."

Gabe had gone berserk, throwing whatever he could reach until nurses had come in and sedated him. He'd cursed Chase, blaming him, and Chase had left.

Only none of it had been Chase's fault. It was his.

Maybe moving here had been a mistake. It seemed like any time he was around Chase, memories flooded up and crashed over him.

Trying to change the subject, Gabe asked, "So, Katie, why did you freak out when you heard I was rooming with Caroline?"

Katie blushed. "It's nothing, really—"

"You might as well give up," Chase said. "My wife doesn't like to gossip."

"It's not gossiping; it's sharing intel," Gabe said, relieved when Chase grinned. If he could just break down this wall between them, he could start mending the rift. And then, maybe, they could be real friends again.

Katie opened her mouth, probably to shoot him down, but then Chase said, "Don't you think he should know what kind of character he's living with?"

Her cheeks flushed, and she slid off of Chase's lap into her own chair. "Caroline and I went to school together and would have graduated the same year, but she took off and left town. Nobody really knows why, except that she had a falling out with her father just before."

Gabe didn't get why that alone would make Katie look like she was going to shit her pants.

"There's got to be more to it than that."

Sighing, she continued. "She just had kind of a wild reputation in high school."

"Ooooooh, a reputation," Chase teased, and Katie smacked at him.

"What kind of reputation?" Gabe asked.

"With parties and"—Katie paused, looking very uncomfortable—"guys."

Gabe sat back in his chair with a smile. "So?"

"Nothing. I just remember rumors flying a lot where she was concerned and was surprised when you said you were living together," Katie said, adding, "I just kind of got the impression you were trying to fly under the radar."

Ah, so Chase has told her about your past.

Why wouldn't Chase tell his wife who was coming to dinner? She deserved to know, and the fact that she'd been warm and welcoming made him like her even more. Chase was right about his wife. She was special.

"I am trying to keep a low profile, but I also miscalculated my expenses, and she was there, willing to pay half the rent. I just couldn't pass it up."

"I understand," Katie said.

"So, was she as notorious as her little sister is now?" Chase asked, popping a chip into his mouth.

"Valerie?" Gabe said.

"You met Valerie?" Katie asked.

"Yeah, she came by the apartment earlier."

"No, not Valerie. Ellie, the youngest. She's…what?" Chase paused, turning to his wife. "Twenty-one?"

"Yes."

"So, what's this girl done? Screw the football team?" Gabe joked.

"Probably, but her latest stunt—"

"It's not nice to gossip, Chase Trepasso," Katie teased, her blue eyes sparkling.

"I'm just sharing intel."

Gabe waited for Chase to continue and finally prodded, "Come on, man. Don't leave me hanging."

"She was screwing the Thompson brothers, and when one caught her with the other, they started fighting. They plowed through a wall and almost took down the whole barn. I heard from one of my clients that Mr. Thompson was going to sue Ellie's dad for damages."

"I didn't hear that. Who told you?" Katie asked.

Chase pretended he was buttoning his lips. "I cannot reveal my sources."

While Katie tried to get the truth from Chase, Gabe couldn't stop his mind from mulling over what kind of dirty deeds his uptight roomie might have committed in high school. Had she been wild like her sister? He'd known from their first meeting that she wasn't a straight-laced goody-goody, but she was so uptight, he had a hard time imagining her cutting loose and wreaking havoc.

Whatever it is, it's in the past. Don't dig at hers, and she won't dig at yours.

"What did you think about her, Gabe?" Katie's question broke into his thoughts.

"Sorry, what?"

"What was your impression of Caroline?"

That she would look great on her back, lying across your bed.

"Just that she's stubborn, angry, and probably going to be a giant pain in the ass."

They both laughed, and Katie patted his hand. "Don't let her get to you. Remember, it's only a temporary arrangement."

Gabe appreciated the encouragement, but it was hard not to react to Caroline, especially when she got all bossy. Man, was she hot with her eyes flashing and that long dark hair falling around her shoulders. She was definitely the type of woman men chased after.

But not me.

Chapter Seven

> "The Spice Girls once sang, 'Friendship never ends.' Apparently, they'd never fallen for the same guy. Or seen the movie *Heathers*."
>
> **—Miss Know It All**

CAROLINE WAS CURLED up on her new couch the next day, running her hand over the soft leathery fabric. She'd spent one last night at her sister's house, only to be woken at two in the morning by Ellie and a few of her friends' raucous laughter. It had gone on so late that Caroline hadn't fallen back asleep until six o'clock and almost missed her alarm to let the movers in. When she'd arrived at the apartment, Gabe was gone, but the truck had arrived right on time.

Looking around the blank walls, she thought about checking out the thrift stores and maybe even an art studio. It would be nice to bring in some artwork to match the colors in the coffee table and the rest of the furniture. She'd already picked up sheets for her new bed and some other things at Target, and after unpacking her meager belongings into her new dresser drawers, she was eager to get out and do something.

What she should be doing was promoting the consulting business she was trying to get off the ground. She'd already been getting plenty of interest online—especially from several bars in Chicago and New York—but she also wanted to work locally, which meant hitting up the local bars and pitching her abilities.

After a brief shower, she threw on a tunic sweater and a pair of comfy jeans with her tennis shoes. It was April in Idaho, and the weather was unpredictable; by the looks of the dark clouds rolling in, she assumed rain was coming their way. She grabbed her business-card holder, figuring she'd stop off at Hank's Bar—since it was right on the Main Street—before she shopped for décor.

She stopped by Chloe's Book Nook first, pasting a pleasant smile on her face. She definitely wasn't over the mistake Gemma and her husband had made, but she was in such a good mood, she was willing to overlook it. The bell over the door dinged as she entered, and Gemma stopped talking to another woman to glance her way, blinking behind a pair of black-framed glasses.

"Hey, Caroline. How are you?"

"Fine. Just stopping in to see what you've got," Caroline said, smiling at the other woman. "Hey, I'm Caroline Willis."

The woman brushed dishwater blonde hair out of her face, the wild ringlets a hair dresser's nightmare. She took Caroline's hand and said softly, "I'm Callie Jacobsen. I host the morning show down at the local radio station. Kat Country."

Suddenly, the woman was a hell of a lot more interesting, and Caroline beamed. "Awesome. I am starting a consulting company targeting bars, honky-tonks, and nightclubs. Maybe I could come in and talk a little bit about my experience and what I do. Do you mind if I give you my card?" Before Callie could open her mouth to say anything, Caroline added, "And I could probably swing a sit-down interview with Jax Dillon."

"Jax Dillon? He's—"

Caroline had the DJ's attention now. "Yeah, Jax is predicted to become bigger than Tim McGraw and not just for his hard-partying ways and crowd-pleasing hits. I met Jax six years ago. He played in the bar I was renovating before he got picked up by Big Machine. Jax is a great guy, down-to-earth. We became friends, both of us from small towns, and he is the nicest guy you'll ever meet," Caroline said with a secret smile. "We keep in touch."

The two women exchanged a look, Callie probably assuming Caroline had slept with Jax, but the truth was, despite the smooth-talkin' Texan's attempts to charm his way into her pants, she'd said no. As much as she'd liked Jax, she just hadn't felt that zing she usually did when the chemistry was rocking.

Like what I feel with the bad boy sharing my living space?

She wanted to slap the stupid voice in her head for even suggesting that. Thinking a man is hot and feeling a zing were two different things.

"If you can swing it, you've got yourself a deal, but I would have given you air time regardless."

Callie's words sank in, and Caroline blushed, something she rarely did. The words were spoken so softly, they were almost a reprimand, as if Callie was trying to say that Caroline didn't need to bribe anyone or use her feminine wiles to get what she wanted.

But she was wrong. Everyone wanted something.

"I appreciate that," Caroline said, handing over the card she'd fished out of her purse.

Gemma piped up. "Oh, you should head over to Buck's tonight. Travis is doing a show, and it'll be packed. You can network and give Eric Henderson your pitch."

Caroline smiled. Eric worked for her family when he was a teenager, doing yard work and such. She didn't think she'd have any problem convincing him that he needed her services.

Still grateful for the tip, Caroline warmed a little more toward Gemma. "Thanks."

"Also, Hank's is a few doors down and pretty quiet this time of day. You should stop off there too," Callie suggested.

"I'll do that. Thanks for the help, ladies. I'm also looking for a cute place to get some inexpensive paintings and knick-knacks."

Gemma's face lit up. "Oh, I love Canyon Classics down the street. They have some great stuff, but if it's not what you're looking for, you could take the ten-minute trip to Buhl. There are several little shops I love there."

Caroline wasn't sure if she wanted to drive anywhere, but she thanked them just the same. As she walked out the door, she almost plowed right into a couple.

"I'm so sorry, I didn't see—" She stopped talking once she recognized the icy blue eyes glaring at her with blatant dislike.

Ah, shit. This is gonna be bad.

Shelby's face was twisted up into a scowl so dark, Caroline was tempted to warn her that it might freeze that way.

"Didn't anyone tell you that bitches aren't allowed off leash?" Shelby said, gripping the arm of her companion tightly. Caroline wondered if Shelby was imagining her neck as she squeezed. Probably.

Caroline followed the arm up to a pair of wide shoulders, and the irony almost made her laugh. Marcus Boatman, the whole stupid, meat-headed reason for their falling-out, was staring down at her with an expression Caroline didn't like at all. It was a mix of astonishment and lust.

Do not engage. Do Not Engage. DO NOT ENGAGE.

"First I'm a skank, and now I'm a bitch?" Caroline said. "Really, Shelby, if you're going to toss around insults, you should at least stick to ones you can't be lumped into."

"What the hell do you mean?"

"Let's see. Since you've sunk into immature name-calling…what's that old saying? I'm rubber, you're glue, whatever you say bounces off me and sticks to you?"

Shelby's lips thinned as Marcus stepped in. "Come on, Shelby, can't you just let it go?"

"Let it go?" Shelby squealed, dropping his arm like he was diseased. "The only reason she ever slept with you was because I wanted you, and she wanted to hurt me. How can you just let that go?"

Marcus turned away from Shelby, his face beet-red as he asked, "So, how long have you been in town?"

"Three weeks," she said. "I've been lying low."

"That shouldn't be much of a challenge, considering how low you can get," Shelby said with a sneer. Shelby's innuendo was not lost on Caroline, and despite her personal vow to rise above and make amends, she just couldn't do it.

"Still pouting, Shell? Didn't anyone tell you that sulking is one of the least attractive qualities in a woman?" Caroline said.

Shelby stepped forward, as if she was going to hit her. Considering that the last time Shelby had started a fight with her, Caroline had kicked her ass, she had to give her former bestie props for being scrappy.

Or stupid.

"I didn't come back to cause trouble or fight," Caroline said calmly, though she knew her stance belied her soothing words. If the bitch threw a single fist, she was going to drop her to the pavement. Hard.

Yes, what Caroline had done to Shelby had sucked, and she regretted the petty mistake, but the fact that Shelby hadn't gotten over it by now spoke volumes about her own issues.

Poor Shelby. Still chasing after the perfect guy and the perfect life.

The two of them had met in pre-K and, while they had both gotten good grades and stayed out of trouble over the years, Caroline had been the extrovert, and by the time she'd started her freshman year, she'd begun turning heads. Shelby had been pretty but shy, tagging along behind Caroline to parties and such but always hanging back.

It wasn't Shelby's fault that she had been sheltered. She'd grown up as an only child, with perfect parents who had spoiled her and promised her she would have everything her heart desired if she just worked hard. She had been raised to be a little self-centered, but Caroline had loved her anyway.

Until Kyle had taken everything from her—including her virginity—and she had needed her best friend. Deeply depressed, she had called Shelby to confide in her.

The minute she picked up, Shelby went on and on about something amazing Marcus had done, how hot he was, and if he would only notice her. For almost an hour, Caroline couldn't get a word in, until finally she'd exploded, "I was raped!"

Shelby went dead quiet on the other end of the phone for a moment. "What?"

Taking a deep breath, Caroline repeated, "I was raped. By Kyle Jenner."

"The senator's son?" Shelby said.

"Yes."

"Tell me what happened," Shelby said, and as Caroline told her everything she could remember, Shelby's silence was deafening.

When she finally finished, Caroline asked, "What should I do? I was going to tell my dad, but he stayed behind to talk to the senator and isn't home yet."

"You can't tell your dad," Shelby said quickly, surprising Caroline.

"Why not?"

"Because…I mean, what are you going to say? You were flirting with Kyle before it happened, right?" Shelby said.

"Yeah, but…but that doesn't give him the right to…and he must have slipped me something, because I don't remember most of it—"

"So, how do you know you didn't say yes?" Shelby asked.

Caroline lost it. "Because I wouldn't have!"

"But if you press charges, everyone is going to know what happened," Shelby said, fueling Caroline's hurt when she added, "I just don't think I could do that. It would be so embarrassing."

"I didn't do anything wrong," Caroline said, nearly sobbing.

"Okay, but what if he didn't realize he was doing anything wrong, and then you accuse him—"

"Shelby, he laughed at me! He threatened me and my sisters! Does that sound like an innocent man to you?" Caroline's throat began to close, raw emotions choking her as a vortex swirled inside. Uncertainty, guilt, anger, helplessness, embarrassment…she had been fighting them all day, and now, she could add another one to the list.

Shame.

"I thought you would be on my side," Caroline said softly.

"I am. I just want you to be sure that you know what you're doing before you potentially ruin your reputation."

Caroline scoffed. "Why, Shelby? Because Little Miss Perfect can't hang out with a girl who cries rape?" The silence on the line made Caroline's hand shake with rage, and she screamed, "Fuck you, Shelby! You are a selfish, arrogant snob who can't pull her head out of Marcus Boatman's ass long enough to realize that he's not interested."

After that night, Caroline started avoiding Shelby, who had become one of those perky, giggling simpletons they'd once made fun of together. She avoided everyone, in fact. But the more Caroline isolated herself, the more she resented Shelby's perfect life with her two healthy, caring parents. It even seemed like Marcus had started to notice Shelby more.

One day before Christmas break of their sophomore year, Caroline had seen Marcus lean over and give Shelby a sweet kiss after walking her to class. The whole scene was so sweet, so innocent. Two people sharing something good and pure and right.

Witnessing that, something had snapped inside Caroline. Everything she'd been told about love and guys and the best years of her life had been bullshit. She had no one to turn to, and she was utterly alone.

Until New Year's Eve. Caroline had gone to a party that one of the football players was having. She'd started drinking shots of whatever was handy and when she was totally shit-faced, she'd bumped into Marcus, who had offered to get her some water, to take care of her. But it hadn't taken much to flirt Marcus Boatman out of his tighty-whities and into one of the empty bedrooms.

It had been mean and spiteful.

Caroline hadn't been drunk enough to ignore the fact that there would be serious consequences to her actions, but at the time, she hadn't cared. All she'd wanted was to hurt Shelby the way she was hurting. Shelby had everything, and Caroline had nothing.

The next morning, when she woke up next to Marcus, the self-loathing sank in. She hadn't even liked him, but she had screwed him to get at Shelby. To try to make herself feel better by hurting someone else.

After that, her reputation preceded her. She flirted with whomever she wanted and didn't give a fuck what anyone thought. Looking back, she could hardly remember all the "fun" she'd had, but maybe that was for the best. She'd traded self-loathing, frustration, and anger for a void of emotionless hook-ups and numb oblivion.

That was a long time ago. Move forward.

"I need to get going. I'm looking at stuff for my new apartment."

"Oh, where are you living?" Marcus asked, ignoring Shelby's glare.

"Up there," she said, pointing above Chloe's Book Nook.

Marcus's clear blue eyes looked into hers earnestly. "Maybe we can get together and *catch up*."

"We'll see," Caroline said, avoiding Shelby's murderous gaze. "Nice seeing you."

She passed Marcus and could hear Shelby behind her, hissing angrily. "Why would you say that?"

As she headed down the street to Hank's Bar, she wondered for the hundredth time if she had made a massive mistake in coming back here. There were so many people she had hurt and betrayed in one way or another. She had taken her pain and anger out on everyone else and made a lot of enemies.

You are a different person now. Leave the past in the past.

That had been her plan, but the whole turn-the-othercheek thing might be too much for her. Edward Willis hadn't raised his daughters to back down from a fight.

Chapter Eight

> "I've been told, 'To assume is to make an ass out
> of you and me,' to which I reply, 'I don't have to
> assume. I know you're an ass.'"
>
> **—Miss Know It All**

GABE WASN'T SURPRISED that Caroline was parked in the
lone parking spot when he got home; he'd been counting
on it. It gave him the perfect opening to discuss a few
roommate conditions.

However, when he walked into the apartment and
found it fully furnished and decorated, he stopped dead in
his tracks. The living room had a gray sectional against one
wall, separating the carpeted area from the tile of the dining room. Across from it was a cherry wood entertainment
center, with his flat screen smack in the middle of it. He had
brought his belongings over from his storage unit yesterday,
but now, there was no sign that he even lived here. The walls
held several gray paintings with splashes of red and yellow.
Finally, a modern silver clock was hung above the end table.

The dining room was complete with a dark wood table and six chairs surrounding it. A gray table runner with black and red birds printed on it ran up the middle, the look finished by a black ceramic bowl filled with red apples. From there, the decorations spread into the kitchen.

The words "woman's touch" flashed through his mind, and he clenched his fists. This was supposed to be *their* apartment, at least for now, and it looked like Martha Stewart had waved her magic wand and sprinkled the place with décor dust. There wasn't one item, besides his TV, that said a man lived here.

Gabe marched down the hall, fully intent on giving Caroline hell for not consulting him, until he heard the shower going.

Don't do it.

Against his better judgment, he pushed the bathroom door open, his fury boiling over at the flower-covered shower curtain and the shaggy pink rug in front of the tub.

"What the hell is this shit?"

His angry shout got the result he was looking for. Caroline grabbed the curtain and pulled it back just enough so that she could look at him with outrage.

"Get out of here, asshole!"

"I'm not going anywhere until you explain where you get off putting your shit everywhere without asking."

"You are fucking insane! This *is* my apartment, was my apartment *first*, and it's not like you had anything but a TV, your bed, and a funky old chair."

"That doesn't mean you can come in here and frou-frou up the place without talking to me first."

"Like I said, it was my apartment first, and since this is only temporary, you won't have to go out and buy anything until you find somewhere else to live."

He should have tried counting to ten or taking a walk, but the way she stood there, hiding behind the curtain, with only her smug little face visible…well, he lost his temper.

"You. Out," Gabe said, pointing his finger at her.

He heard her loud sigh as she ducked back behind the curtain and shut the water off. Tough shit if she was annoyed. They were going to have it out—now. He wasn't going to be her whipping boy, taking whatever she dished out. If she wanted to stay, she was going to have to learn to share.

The pink towel that had been hanging over the shower bar disappeared, and Gabe couldn't stop his brain from imagining all the lush curves she was probably drying with it.

Little droplets of water clinging to her nipples…

What was it about this infuriating woman that reduced him to a twelve-year-old at the pool?

If certain parts of his body realized what a pain in the ass she was, he wouldn't be having issues with the hard-on currently pressing against the front of his jeans.

When the curtain pushed back again, it revealed Caroline wrapped in the pink towel, her legs smooth and tan as she stepped out of the tub. Her dark hair hung around her shoulders, drops of water falling from the ends as she stood on the rug.

The pink, frilly chick rug.

Before he could say anything, she stepped up to him and pushed against his chest with one hand. "You cannot kick me out, and if you don't hightail it out of this bathroom, I'll show you how fast I can castrate a man with just some dental floss and a Bic razor."

"Don't threaten me, princess," Gabe said, catching her hand against his chest.

"Oh, it's not a threat. Believe me," she said, her voice hushed and raw. "Barge in on me uninvited, and you'll be peeing out of a straw."

He had to give her credit. He was at least twice her height and weight, but she stood toe-to-toe with him without even a tremble.

"Maybe you should lock the door next time."

"I tried, but the lock is busted. I thought you'd hear the shower and show some respect."

Damn, she was trying to school him. And the worst of it was, he could picture her all respectable with a suit and glasses, that dark mass of hair in a tight bun as she slapped a ruler against her hand...

When had he started having bad-teacher fantasies?

Still, despite her point, he had his own to make. "And you should have asked before turning the place into a fucking tearoom. This place is so female-centric, I feel like I'm living in a sorority. If I bring a woman back here, she's going to think I'm married."

Caroline tossed her hair back with a snort. "Like any woman with taste would marry you."

Well, that hurt a bit. "You can think anything you want, princess, but I've never had a problem with women.

But the minute they see this place, they'll head for the door."

"Oh, you never know. Some women are into married men."

The implication brought his anger back up to simmering. He had made a lot of bad decisions, but he would never get involved with a woman who would chase a married man. "Well, I'm not into those women."

She seemed to be considering him seriously for the first time, with her head tilted to the side and her gaze thoughtful. Sighing finally, she asked, "What do you suggest then? A video-game chair and naked women posters all over the walls, held up by thumbtacks?"

The suggestion was exactly what most of his friends had had in their apartments when he'd gotten out of prison, but he wasn't a horny twenty-three-year-old anymore.

Okay, he wasn't twenty-three, but apparently he was still horny as hell. His gaze drifted down to the top of the towel, which gave him a tiny glimpse of the valley between her breasts. She was so damn sexy, and he had been an idiot to think he could resist her when she was going to be right here, under his nose. Within reach.

Unable to resist, he reached up and brushed a strand of wet hair off her shoulder, trailing his fingers over the coolness of her skin. "I'm way classier than that. The posters would be framed."

CAROLINE WOULD HAVE jerked back if his gesture hadn't been so fast. Before she could do much more than catch her breath, his hand was gone.

No, she wasn't going to smile at his joke. He wasn't charming or funny. He was rude and condescending and—

"You're right. I should have asked your opinion, since we both have to live here."

Wait… What? Did you just apologize to him?

His dark, pierced eyebrow lifted, as if he couldn't believe it either. "Somehow, I didn't expect that from you."

"You don't know me, so quit acting like you do," she snapped.

He crossed his arms and had the audacity to look casual. "I don't have to know you personally. I can read people pretty well."

"Oh, really?" she asked, mimicking his stance. "Please, tell me exactly what you think you know."

He moved closer, and her heart quickened as she smelled his cologne; light and male, it didn't overwhelm like some. Her nipples hardened against the roughness of the towel, and she hated that he could do this without touching her. He was wrong for her. Trouble. She could read people too, and this guy probably had *bad news* tattooed on his ass.

"I'd say you have issues with authority and men in general. You like to be in control, and you do not like to be told when you're wrong. You have never been in a relationship that lasted longer than a few months, and not one of those guys ever knew you, not really," he said, his tone dropping to a harsh whisper. "How close am I, princess?"

Too close for comfort; that was for damn sure. She squeezed past him, her body brushing against his as she scoffed, "Whatever."

But before she made it to the door, he reached out and took her arm gently. "Are you saying I'm wrong?"

His hand was hot against her chilled skin, and she imagined the rest of him was just as heated. The image of them pressed together, his hands leaving trails of fire across her skin, reminded her it had been a while since she'd pulled out her battery-operated buddy for a little alone time. She was going to have to schedule that in some time soon.

For now, she needed to get away from Gabe's dark, penetrating eyes before she forgot herself and took him for a test drive...an idea that spelled all kinds of bad.

"I'm saying that you probably shouldn't start offering psychic readings," she said, pulling her arm out of his grip and stalking to her room.

As she closed the door, she heard him laugh, and it made her stomach flip over. The last thing she wanted or needed was to feel anything for the man she was sharing a two-bedroom apartment with. Which meant avoiding situations that put them in close proximity and nearly buck naked.

First thing Monday morning, she needed to fix the lock on the bathroom door.

Grabbing underwear and a bra from her new oak dresser, she shimmied into them swiftly before wrapping her hair up in the towel. Her phone started blaring the Britney Spears song "Boys," and she picked it up off her bed. Ellie's smiling face flashed across the screen.

Sliding her thumb across the talk icon, she said, "All right, what kind of trouble did you get in now?"

"You know, I resent that, especially when I'm calling to help you," Ellie said, sounding insulted. "Why do you and Val always assume the worst of me?"

Caroline grinned. Val and she were closer, that was for sure, but Ellie was wild and funny, easy to be around. Val almost tried to mother them both, even though Caroline was older.

"Well, you know us Willis girls," Caroline said, grabbing a simple black dress from her closet. "Even when we're trying to be good, we seem to find trouble."

"Don't I know it! Did you see Miss Know It All's blog this morning? She said if I was a super-villain, I'd be the Enthraller, because I can control the male population with a flip of my hair. I swear, that woman either hates me or loves me, but I'm not quite sure which yet."

"I didn't see it but sounds about right."

"Very funny, but it's not important. Two things. I was calling to see if you wanted to go to Buck's with me tonight. I want to go to Travis Bowers's performance, but all my friends are busy, and Val is going with Justin and his friends."

"Aw, nothing like being last choice," Caroline teased, not taking it personally. Ellie and she had been getting to know each other again as adults, but they still had their awkward moments.

"Come on, don't give me shit. Just say you'll go. I can't go to Buck's alone or guys will think I'm available."

"And you aren't?" Caroline asked. She hadn't realized her little sister had a boyfriend.

"No."

"Okay, are you going to tell me about him?"

"Nothing to tell yet," Ellie said casually. "We're hanging out…testing the waters."

Oh well. If Ellie wasn't ready to share, then Caroline wasn't going to push her. "Fine, I'll go with you."

"Awesome. Can we take separate cars, though? I might have to cut out early."

Even though she wouldn't push, it didn't stop her curiosity from almost getting the best of her. "Fine. I'll meet you there around six thirty. I want to do a little networking before it gets crazy."

"Great!"

"And the other thing?" Caroline prodded.

"Oh, right, I need you to handle the birthday cake for Val's birthday. Justin and I are planning a barbecue, but if I make the cake, she's gonna know what's up."

Caroline groaned. "Seriously? Can't I just order one from Hall's?"

"No, this is tradition! We always have homemade cakes for our birthdays!" Ellie said, adding with a giggle, "Remember that cake Val and I made for your sixteenth birthday? We tried to make it in the shape of a car."

"But it came out looking more like a shapeless blob. Yes, I remember," Caroline said, her heart squeezing. It was one of the last birthdays she'd celebrated at home.

"See, and you loved it. Val's favorite is rainbow chip, in case you forgot. I'll see you tonight!"

Her sister hung up the phone before Caroline could protest again. The fact that Ellie hadn't wanted to share her boyfriend's name bothered Caroline. Most women wanted to be seen with their significant others, not hide them away.

Unless there's something wrong with him—like being married.

Which was exactly why she avoided getting involved in other people's business. Dealing with other people's baggage was too much for her emotionally. Her own baggage could fill up an airplane's cargo hold.

Besides, she had been so caught up in her work and becoming successful, it hadn't left a lot of time for relationships, except perhaps of the wham-bam, thank-you-man variety.

She heard the shower start up next to her room. Gabe was in there, lathering up all that hard muscle and delectable mocha-colored skin. It would be so easy to walk in on him and offer a little "roommate perk."

You wanted a fresh start, to prove you aren't the same girl making bad decisions. That means a successful business, playing nice with the rest of the townsfolk, and dating a respectable man, not the convenient bad boy you could never get serious with.

Quickly, she headed for the closet to grab her shoes. She needed to get the hell out of there before she did something she'd regret.

Chapter Nine

"For some reason, Buck's Shot Bar is a breeding ground for drama and stupidity. Oh, wait—maybe because it's a bar and there's alcohol. Oh, and the Coulter brothers. Not a night goes by that they aren't there, getting into whatever trouble they can. And yet, charges never seem to stick…Could they have a GET OUT OF DRUNK-TANK FREE card? Police corruption in Rock Canyon…Hmmm, suddenly I feel like Veronica Mars."

—**Miss Know It All**

"WAIT, YOU'RE DITCHING me?" Ellie said loudly.

Caroline rolled her eyes. "No, I'm just going to talk to Eric about doing some consulting for Buck's. I'll be right back."

"But the whole point of us going together was so guys wouldn't think I was here trolling!"

"Ellie, I'll be back before any guys notice you're alone," Caroline said, although her sister's sheer top with the hot pink bra and tight jeans didn't really give off the "not interested" vibe.

As if reading her thoughts, Ellie crossed her arms over her stomach. "Fine, but hurry up."

Caroline pushed her way to the back of the bar where she'd seen Eric Henderson, pulling down the light fabric of her simple black dress. Her dress was conservative enough to be business casual but had an understated sexiness that hugged her curves and said, *"Howdy, boys. I'm available."*

She was surveying the crowd, checking out a few men over by the pool tables, when she saw Gabe leaning over to make a shot, his muscular arms taut as he sent his stick into the ball, spinning it across the green to sink in a corner pocket. He stood up with a pleased look, and she noticed a blonde jumping up and down next to him, squealing.

Irritation shot through her as the blonde jumped on Gabe, throwing her arms around his wide shoulders. Gabe wrapped one arm around her waist and pulled her close, whispering something in her ear. The woman laughed, and Caroline finally got a good look at her.

Kirsten Winters. Why was she even surprised? Gabe was hot, and the one thing Kirsten was drawn to was a good-looking man. Caroline would never call another woman easy—having heard the word connected with her name way too often—but she would say that Kirsten had enjoyed plenty of guys in high school.

So why do you care if she enjoys Gabe?

She didn't. Caroline was only irritated that Gabe seemed to be everywhere. In the apartment, here at Buck's…It was too small of a town not to realize she was going to see way too much of him and his gorgeous black eyes.

Suddenly, she crashed into a hard body and opened her mouth to apologize, but Marcus Boatman spoke first. "We have to stop meeting like this."

Yes, they certainly did. The last thing she wanted was to give Marcus any sort of encouragement, especially since he was obviously dating Shelby. She could deal with the animosity from her past deeds, but no way in hell was she going to hook up with Marcus again. He hadn't exactly been mind-blowing in high school, and somehow she doubted he'd improved with age.

"Hey, Marcus, sorry. I'm on my way back to talk to Eric—"

"What for?" Marcus interrupted.

She caught the narrow-eyed look he was giving her. It was none of his damn business, and she was just about to tell him so when she was pushed from behind. Stumbling forward on her heels, she would have gone down hard if Marcus hadn't caught her.

"Get your hands off her, Marcus!" Shelby squawked over the blaring of the opening band.

Caroline couldn't believe she was getting this twice in one day *and* that the bitch had the audacity to push her. Twisting around to face her assailant, she resisted the urge to shove her back. She was here on business, after all, and it wouldn't do to get thrown out of a bar she wanted to work with. "You really should look into some anger management courses."

Shelby's face turned purple, and she snapped, "Stay the fuck away from my man."

Okay, this was too Jerry Springer for her. A small crowd was already taking notice of them. "Shelby, I'm not interested in Marcus. I bumped into him; that's it."

She'd tried to speak slowly and calmly, but that seemed to just irritate Shelby more. Caroline realized too late that the woman had already consumed a few too many drinks. Before she could get out of the line of fire, Shelby launched herself at Caroline, and all she could do was brace herself for the first blow.

A blow that never came.

Instead, Shelby screeched with outrage, and Caroline opened her eyes to find Gabe standing next to Shelby, his hand clasping her arm in a tight grip.

"Maybe you should get her out of here before she does something stupid."

Gabe's suggestion was directed at Marcus, who almost looked like he was going to argue, but in the end, he took Shelby's arm from Gabe, saying, "Come on."

Shelby hurled insults at Gabe and tried to pull away from Marcus, who finally dumped the drunken wildcat over his shoulder and pushed through the crowd. As the crowd that had gathered dispersed, Caroline was left facing Gabe, hating the fact that he had saved her from a disastrous situation.

"Thanks, but I could have handled it."

"I figured, but now you don't have to."

His cool answer pissed her off. Did he think he'd done her some huge favor? That she wouldn't have to deal with Marcus and Shelby again?

"Do you always jump into tense situations? Is that what gets you off? Saving the poor, defenseless, wronged woman?" Caroline said, sneering. "Don't worry about me, hero. I deserve everything they throw at me and more. If you don't believe me, just ask around. I'm sure someone would *love* to give you all the sordid details."

"Regardless of what you've done in the past, she was out of line. I could tell you were trying to take the high road, and I know what that's like. You try not to fight back, 'cause you figure they'll back off if you don't play their game, but that's not always true."

His observation hit home for Caroline, and a small part of her wanted to ask him about his story, about what he was trying to atone for, but that might give the impression that she cared.

Which she didn't. At all.

"Well, again, thanks. At least now I can do what I came to do," she said, catching sight of Eric behind the bar.

"Yeah, what's that?"

"I've come to see a man about a bar," Caroline said, smiling at her own joke.

"Well, I'll let you get to it," Gabe said, leaning over to whisper close to her ear. "I'll see you at home, princess."

Caroline fought the shiver that the heat of his breath caused across her neck and down her back. As he went back to playing pool with Kirsten, she told herself that the irritation churning in her abdomen was because of Shelby's causing a scene and had nothing to do with the way the stacked blonde slid her hand possessively over Gabe's bicep.

Turning her back on them, she walked straight up to Eric and said, "Well, hey there, handsome."

Eric looked over his shoulder from filling the beer fridge, his forehead furrowed for a minute before he recognized her with a whoop. "T-R-O-U-B-L-E!"

Caroline laughed as the big man came around the bar and wrapped her in a bear hug that lifted her up off the ground. It was good to know that not everyone in Rock Canyon thought she was scum. Being called *trouble* was the friendliest thing she'd heard since arriving back in town.

When Eric set her down, he gave her a smacking kiss on the mouth that startled her, considering he had never done anything like it before. Eric had worked on their yard every summer for years, and after her mom died, she had followed him around and helped out when she could. She'd always nursed a bit of a crush on Eric, but he'd never treated her like anything other than a kid sister. As she'd gotten older, he used to tease her about all the trouble she got into, but it was always playful.

When he caught her surprised look, he leaned over and said loud enough to be heard over the music, "We're being watched."

Caroline pulled away, her eyebrow raised as he gave a subtle nod to the left. Caroline glanced toward the end of the bar and saw a pretty blonde with shoulder-length hair glaring at them. Gemma and Callie, who were next to the woman, waved at Caroline.

Waving back, Caroline tried to place the blonde. "Are you using me to make her jealous or to make her leave you alone?"

Eric's smile was wide and sheepish. "Jealous."

Caroline put her hand on his chest and batted her lashes. "And what do I get out of this little scenario?"

He covered her hand with his and squeezed. "Step into my office, and we'll discuss business."

Caroline let Eric lead her toward the storeroom and close the door. Leaning against the shelves, she asked, "So, who is she?"

"Gracie McAllister. I think she was a year or two behind you."

"Cradle robber," Caroline teased.

"It doesn't matter. She won't give me the time of day."

"Really? 'Cause she was glaring at me so hard, I'm surprised she didn't burn a hole through my skull."

"Yeah, it's complicated," he said, crossing his arms. "So, I hear you've got a business proposition for me."

"Who told you?" Caroline asked.

"One of the bartenders at Hank's said you stopped by."

"I did."

"Well, let's hear your pitch. Lord knows Hank's is already kicking my ass on karaoke night."

GABE KEPT GLANCING toward where Caroline had disappeared, wondering how long she'd been dating the big bartender. When the guy had kissed her, Gabe had barely resisted the urge to snap his pool cue in half.

Is this what gets you off?

Her words had slammed him in the gut and brought to mind all kinds of images that would definitely do it for him. Most of them featured that little black dress on the floor of his bedroom and her sprawled across his bed. He'd start at the top of her head and work his way down, pausing at all the interesting spots until he reached the juncture between her legs. He'd pull her legs over his shoulders and dip his head down to kiss her p—

"It's your shot, Gabe," Kirsten said sweetly, tossing her thick blonde curls over her shoulder and reminding him that he had no business lusting after Caroline.

Kirsten, on the other hand, was *exactly* the type of woman he should be lusting after—casual, sexy, and knew exactly what the score was. She was looking for a good time, just like he was.

He was leaning over the table, lining up his shot, when Caroline came out of the storeroom, her hair tousled. She threw her head back and laughed at something the big guy said.

"Are you going to take your shot or what, man?" one of the cowboys he was playing with asked impatiently. Gabe pulled back, aimed…

And blew his shot to hell.

"Shit," he said, ignoring the laughter from the other man.

Gabe scowled at the two men. He'd been fine playing with Kirsten, taking it slow and just having fun, but when the cowboys had approached him with two hundred on the winner, he couldn't resist. He assumed the two of them were related; not only did they have the same coloring, but even their high-pitched hyena laughs were almost identical.

"Better luck next time," the shorter one said, snickering as he lined up his own shot.

Gabe wasn't happy about missing the shot, but he was too distracted by watching Caroline maneuver through the crowd to dwell on it. He couldn't miss the way men checked her out and a few even tried to engage her in conversation. The smile she gave them was polite, but she kept moving on.

Was she here alone? Despite the fact that she'd grown up here and that Rock Canyon was a small, tight-knit community, he couldn't believe she'd be stupid enough to go to a bar alone. Someone could spike her drink or attack her as she walked to her car.

It was none of his business what she did or what stupid mistakes she made. That's what he kept telling himself as his irritation rose.

"I'm out," Gabe said suddenly, dropping his money onto the table.

One of the men stepped into his path. "Let's finish the game."

Gabe looked into the smaller man's scowling face and said, "You got my money, cowboy. We're square."

Turning away, he heard the other man mutter something that sounded a lot like "pussy."

Gabe swung back around before he could rein in his temper. "What was that?"

"Come on, Walt, he's right," the other man said, wrapping his arm around Walt's shoulders. "We're square. Let's get another round and see if we can't talk to a couple of pretty girls."

Walt followed his brother to the bar, giving Gabe a wide berth. Gabe watched them until a soft hand stroked his arm.

"Don't mind Wayne and Walt," Kirsten said, bending over the table to rerack the balls. "If they aren't starting something, I think they'll wither up and die."

Before he could say anything, Travis Bowers took the stage, and the whole bar exploded into whistles, cheers, and applause. When the crowd calmed down, and Travis started his first song, Gabe spotted Caroline talking to another dark-haired woman, who kept checking her phone.

Wonder if that's the other sister she warned you away from.

Remembering the way Caroline's face had flushed when Valerie had called her out on her rudeness still left him smiling. He hadn't thought much of anything frazzled her, but apparently being called out on her misbehavior could.

"So, do you want to get out of here?" Kirsten asked.

Gabe looked down at the woman with the open invitation and was surprised that he didn't find her nearly as appealing as he had earlier. Maybe it was that she was too available and suddenly, he wasn't interested in the easy conquest.

What's the matter with you? This is exactly what you came out looking for. Someone to have fun with, ease a little tension.

But that was before a vixen in a black dress had walked in and wrecked his night.

Okay, so she hadn't really done anything on purpose. She hadn't even seen him before he'd stepped up and grabbed that drunk woman's arm, but he had noticed her the minute she walked in. While every other woman around wore hip-hugger jeans and flashy tops, she looked classy as hell.

And sexy. He couldn't forget sexy.

It seemed like no matter how many times he told himself he wanted nothing to do with Caroline, he sought her out.

"I was actually going to stick around and grab another drink," he said, realizing that Kirsten was standing there waiting for his answer.

She shrugged. "Maybe another time." Pulling a pen out of her purse, she scrawled her number down on a bar napkin and handed it to him. "Call me."

Gabe put the number in his pocket as she got lost in the crowd. He was a little surprised she hadn't tried harder to get him home. She'd seemed like the aggressive type.

His gaze strayed again to Caroline as she talked to her sister. At least she wasn't there alone. Both women were drinking brightly colored cocktails, and he wondered if he should offer to drive them home. She'd probably tell him to fuck off, but at least then his conscience would be clear. If he checked in on her and she didn't take his help, it was on her.

Gabe took a few steps toward them but paused when another man with sandy hair stopped to talk to Caroline.

You should still go by and just offer to walk her out. It would be the gentlemanly thing to do.

Then he caught the expression on Caroline's face: pure joy and excitement as she reached up to hug the blond man. Obviously, the guy was someone she was happy to see.

That was good. Someone she knew well and would look out for her. It took the responsibility off Gabe's shoulders, and his momentary concern could be chalked up to just wanting to be a good roommate.

And the fact that you're attracted to her and don't want anyone else to have her.

That was crazy. He knew the score. No decent woman wanted an ex-con, especially one with as much baggage as Gabe. Even with Caroline's past reputation, he knew quality when he saw it. Besides, he had Honey and his dream shop. There just wasn't room for anything else.

Pushing the opposite way through the crowd, he went in search of Kirsten, to see if her offer was still on the table.

Chapter Ten

> "I've been told you reap what you sow...Ominous sounding, isn't it?"
>
> —Miss Know It All

"WILL YOU STOP checking your phone every five minutes?" Caroline snapped. Since she'd returned from talking to Eric, Ellie had looked at her phone at least a dozen times, even when she'd tried to introduce Ellie to Gregg Phillips and his wife, Ryan. Gregg and Caroline had been boyfriend and girlfriend in eighth grade, and he'd been her first kiss. They'd drifted apart during their freshman year of high school, but Gregg was a good guy. She was glad he was happy now.

"What? I told you I have plans tonight, and I don't want to miss his call," Ellie said.

Caroline itched to question her about this mystery man and why he couldn't just come out and meet them, but it wasn't her place. Ellie was a grown woman who could see whomever she wanted. Even if her sister's secretive behavior was making Caroline's dirt-bag radar go haywire. The only guys who liked secret relationships were already attached. Whether they were married or just dating another woman, it never boded well. Caroline had been the other woman before, mostly unknowingly, and the aftermath was always bad.

"Ellie, it's past nine. I think if he was going to call, he'd have done it by now," Caroline said as gently as she could over the music. "Besides, if he calls you after midnight, he's just looking for a little play, and you deserve better than that."

"Please don't give me the spiel about how I need to 'respect' myself, and men will respect me for it. I get enough of that crap from Val and the biddies of the Morality Squad."

Caroline finished her drink and set it on the bar behind her. Putting her hands up as if surrendering, she said, "Hey now, I have no right throwing stones or advice at anyone. And I'm the last one to lecture you on moral code. I just wanted to caution you, as your older sister who has made plenty of mistakes involving men, that the good guys—the ones you want to marry and have kids with—don't usually make booty calls."

"Who says I want to get married?" Ellie said flippantly. "I haven't seen one instance where marriage did anyone any good in the long-term. I mean, every week it seems like Miss Know It All is writing about some other couple breaking up or having an affair. I'm just wondering, what is the damn point?"

"Okay, hey, I don't want to fight," Caroline said.

"I'm not fighting; I'm expressing a valid opinion," Ellie said.

Caroline understood now why Val constantly wanted to strangle Ellie. She just couldn't take advice with grace. Couldn't accept the fact that someone older and with more life experience might know what she was talking about. Val had been griping for weeks that Ellie continued to make the same mistakes over and over and never seemed to learn her lesson. But someday she'd learn the hard way what rash decisions and bad choices could get you: a whole lot of heartache.

Bad decisions, like moving in with a guy you hardly know?

Caroline was still trying to wrap her head around *that* decision. Okay, yeah, things had been uncomfortable at Val's, and she hadn't been sleeping well, but she could have toughed it out. She'd slept in her car for months at a time; she could have handled a lumpy couch. But in a moment of weakness and frustration, she had said yes to living with a man she didn't know. Who was even now chatting up a woman, probably to bring her back to the apartment they shared. Just the thought that she might have traded her sister's sex noises for Gabe's made her want to hit someone.

"Well, Ellie, ain't you just as pretty as a picture," Wayne Coulter said as he sidled up to her.

"Fuck off, Wayne," Ellie said, checking her phone again.

"Now, that's not very nice," his brother, Walt, said, his gaze traveling slowly over Caroline.

Caroline remembered the Coulter brothers, although they were even older than she was and had continued to hang out at high school parties after they graduated. Even at her worst, she'd avoided them like the plague, trusting the instincts that told her they were bad news.

"Finally," Ellie said, putting the phone to her ear and heading toward the door.

Was she going to take the call and leave, or would she be back? Caroline wasn't sure, but having the Coulter brothers' full attention was enough to tell her it was time to go, either way.

"Gentlemen," Caroline said, starting to walk past them, only to be stopped by Wayne's hand wrapped around her bicep.

"What's your hurry?"

Caroline tried to shake off his arm, but he didn't let go. "You have about two seconds to get your hands off me before I scream for Eric."

Wayne dropped her arm. "Now, come on, I was just trying to be friendly."

"Maybe you should try not being an asshole. I hear that works sometimes."

Wayne's face flushed. "You bitches think the sun rises and sets on your ass. Acting like a man oughta lick the mud from your boots before he even speaks to ya."

"Not every man. Just you."

"You're gonna regret talking to me like that. You just wait."

"Wayne, are you bothering this lady?" a friendly voice said at her elbow. "'Cause if I remember correctly,

Eric told you if he caught you bothering any more of his patrons, you were going to have to find another place to drink." Caroline turned to look up at her would-be savior, unable to place him.

"Fuck you, Stevens," Wayne said before turning away from them and heading toward the door, with Walt close behind.

Caroline shook her head. "I can't understand how women aren't falling all over themselves to get with them."

"Maybe because they have taste?" the man said, his brown eyes shining as he grinned down at her. "Not sure if you remember me, but I'm Mike Stevens. We had English junior year with Mrs. Selk."

Caroline remembered a skinny kid with Coke-bottle glasses and long hair who'd sat behind her named Mike, but this guy looked nothing like him. He was clean-cut, from the almost shaved head to the collared shirt and khakis.

"Mike. Right. You look good," she said.

"You too."

And he did look good. Taller than her with lean muscle and a nice smile. No tattoos or piercings in sight.

"So, what do you do for a living?" she asked.

"I own a computer repair shop on Oak Avenue."

Self-employed and tech-savvy. A nice, stable guy.

"What about you?" he asked.

"I'm starting a consulting business. I've spent the last eleven years managing and flipping bars, but I wanted to come home. Instead of trying to buy and flip another bar here, I figured I could travel for work but still be home to spend time with my sisters."

"Yeah, I saw Ellie hanging around."

"Yeah, well, she sort of bailed without telling me. Hot date."

"If you want, you can join me and a few of my friends," he said.

Caroline wasn't in the mood to socialize with a bunch of strangers, no matter how nice Mike seemed.

"Thanks, but I think I'm going to just take off," she said, holding out her business card to him. "But maybe another time? My cell is on there, if you want to get dinner some time."

Mike took the card and slipped it into his wallet. "I'll give you a call, then."

"Oh, and thanks for helping me out with the Coulter brothers."

"No problem. Any time."

Caroline headed toward the exit and bumped into Ellie as she was coming back in. It didn't take a genius to see Ellie had been crying.

"Hey, you okay?"

"I'm fine," Ellie said, wiping at her cheeks. "I was just coming in to tell you I'm taking off."

"Me, too," Caroline said. "We can walk out together."

Ellie didn't argue, but she was quiet the whole way out to her car.

"Are you okay to drive?" Caroline asked.

"Sure. I only had one drink," Ellie said, slipping her key into the door. "Plus, it's not like I have to go far."

Before she could think, Caroline said, "I just want to say that if this guy doesn't treat you right, he doesn't deserve you."

"That's sweet," Ellie said, the darkness shrouding half her face. "Cliché but sweet."

Caroline didn't have a response to that as Ellie climbed into the car and started it up.

Caroline had begun weaving back through the cars to where she had parked when she heard a drunken giggle.

"Dance with me."

Nearby, a very drunk Kirsten was dancing up against a guy. With sparse lighting in the lot, it was hard to make out the guy's features.

"Give me your keys," a deep voice said. A voice Caroline was very familiar with.

Gabe.

She heard a jingle. "You want them? You gotta find them."

Rolling her eyes, she passed them and continued on to where she'd parked. At least Kirsten wouldn't be driving.

Then, in the dim light, Caroline noticed something on her window. Pulling out her phone, she flipped on the flashlight app and saw that someone had written all over her car with what looked like shaving cream.

Bitch. Whore. Leave.

"Charming," she muttered, wondering if she should call the Rock Canyon Police Department to report vandalism. Unlocking her car, she grabbed some napkins from the glove department and started wiping at her window.

Caroline heard footsteps behind her but didn't look.

"Hey, isn't that her?"

"Yeah, I'm surprised she even had the nerve to come back to town. I heard her dad kicked her out because she refused to go to rehab for her coke addiction."

"Seriously?"

Giving the windshield one more swipe, she turned around to catch two women she didn't recognize passing her. "Actually, it was sex addiction. If you're going to spread gossip, at least be accurate." They hurried away, and she called, "Have a nice night."

Great. Miss Know It All will probably have that rumor by tomorrow.

Caroline climbed into her car and flipped on the headlights. Her wipers and cleaning fluid helped a little, but she was going to have to take her car through a wash before the shaving cream sat too long. The smell of smoke and bar funk filled her car. With the place packed so full, it had been impossible *not* to get funkified.

Ugh, she wanted a shower.

As she pulled out of her parking spot, her headlights illuminated Gabe and Kirsten, locked in an embrace. For some reason, seeing them together, so close they could be making out, made her grip the steering wheel harder. She didn't like Kirsten's draping herself all over him like that, and why was he letting her, anyway?

For someone who doesn't care about him, you sure are getting pissy.

Caroline suddenly realized she'd been sitting there too long with the glare of her headlights on them. And Gabe was looking right at her.

Shit. Pulling forward, she drove past without looking at them. She hoped he couldn't see who was driving, but he'd probably recognize the car. Damn it; she didn't want him thinking that she was spying on him, because she wasn't. She didn't care who or what he did, as long as it wasn't illegal and didn't affect her.

Which is why you were basically Fatal Attraction *stalking him, right?*

Fuck, the voice in her head needed to shut the hell up. Okay, so she was attracted to him. So what? She was attracted to lots of jackasses, and not one of them had turned out okay. This was her chance to turn over a new leaf and not follow her same old patterns. No dirt bags, assholes, or criminals. Item number two put Gabe smack in the middle of the undesirable list.

It took about fifteen minutes to go through the car wash at Mr. Nelson's Chevron station. Once she was finished, she headed down Main Street to Oak Avenue, pulling down the alleyway slowly, just in case she hadn't beat Gabe home. The spot was empty.

After she parked, she climbed out of the car and took a deep breath as she tried not to run for the stairs. No matter how many times she told herself that Rock Canyon was a safe place, the fact was, her rapist worked with her father just a little way down the street. And she'd accidentally forgotten her Mace and Taser tonight. But she wasn't worried about Kyle making trouble, especially since he had no reason to. She'd kept his secret.

Still, the quiet of the alley was making her nervous. She glanced over her shoulder nervously before rushing into the apartment the minute her key turned the lock. The door slammed harder than she'd intended, her heart pounding against her breastbone as she twisted the dead bolt into place.

She was jumpy as hell and had no idea why. Just nerves, she supposed, but she'd lived in way rougher places than this. Maybe it was because she still hadn't shaken the run-in with Kyle, and tonight, Wayne Coulter's cold blue eyes and tight grip on her arm had brought on a rush of unease. Not that the two men looked alike, but the expression in Wayne's eyes had reminded her of Kyle's: untouchable, able to get away with anything.

And why not? He had. Aside from Shelby, who obviously hadn't cared, she'd never told anyone what Kyle had done. She'd simply shoved that bag of bloody sheets under a loose floorboard in the back of her closet and kept quiet. It was her fault that he'd been allowed to move on and become successful.

There had been so many chances for her to come clean, but every time she found an opening, Kyle's words would creep back in. If she tried to press charges, would he hurt her sisters? Kyle was sick, but as long as she didn't give him a reason, he would stay away from Ellie and Val.

But now with Kyle being nearby, Caroline's old fears had returned. Though she wasn't as worried with Justin staying at the house most nights, what about Ellie? Any time she left the house, she was vulnerable.

It wasn't the first time Caroline had worried about her sisters' safety since Kyle's threat.

A few weeks after he raped her, Caroline still hadn't been able to sleep without the nightmares. Every night, she'd dreamed of Kyle's attacking her, only in her dreams, she felt and remembered everything. But one day, just as she was at her wit's end and had been ready to tell her father, she'd shown up at her sisters' school to walk them home…and they hadn't been there. She'd been frantic, racing to the house to see if they were there, but they weren't. She'd called Val's phone, but there was no response. Just as she was about to call the police, Val and Ellie had come through the door with ice cream cones…and a smiling Kyle behind them.

Caroline hadn't been able to breathe. When she'd told Kyle he needed to leave because her dad wasn't home, he'd just smirked at her.

"I'll see you around, then."

The minute Kyle was out of the house, she'd dead bolted the door and started yelling at Val and Ellie that they were not to go anywhere alone with Kyle. Despite their confusion, she'd dragged a promise out of them and went upstairs to her room. Once inside, she'd closed the door and slid to the floor against it, sobbing.

Now, Caroline headed into her room, and when she went to open her dresser drawer, she realized her hands were shaking at the memory.

Get a grip. Kyle has no interest in you anymore, and you—and your family—are perfectly safe.

Gathering up her night clothes, she went down to the bathroom to shower. She was just getting ready to turn on the water when she heard the front door open.

Hearing Kirsten's high-pitched giggle, followed by Gabe's low voice, helped Caroline relax. She felt better having him there, which was mind-boggling, because she had left her sister's to get away from all of the noise.

Letting the heat rush over her body, she scrubbed herself until the water ran lukewarm. After drying off and pulling on her pjs, she stepped out of the bathroom and saw Kirsten dancing unsteadily in the dining room.

Kirsten stopped dancing when she noticed her. "What are you doing here?"

"I live here," Caroline snapped, hardly glancing at the confused blonde when she caught sight of Gabe by the coffeepot, holding two cups in his hand. Their eyes locked, but she couldn't get a bead on what he was thinking or feeling.

Doesn't he feel guilty for bringing home a girl who is obviously too drunk to make good choices?

But Kirsten was a grown woman who had made the decision to get stupid drunk. And Gabe was making her coffee. It wasn't like he'd spiked her drink.

Like Kyle did to you?

Caroline hated that Kyle was so fresh in her mind. "I'm going to bed. Try to keep it down."

Gabe had the audacity to shrug. "I make no promises."

Stomping down the hallway, she resisted the urge to slam her door.

Why are you mad? He's not doing anything wrong.

She didn't answer her inner voice.

Caroline realized she'd forgotten to brush her teeth and walked out of her bedroom again. Gabe and Kirsten were no longer in the kitchen. Another giggle came from behind Gabe's closed door. She brushed her teeth quickly and went to bed, finally slamming the door again before she could stop herself.

She's too drunk, and he should know better.

The thought came unbidden and caused her to catch her breath, trying to bite down the panic.

This happened sometimes. She'd catch the harsh scent of a cologne, reminding her of the one Kyle had worn that night. Or she'd taste that same cherry flavor that reminded her of the drinks Kyle had spiked.

Or she'd see a girl who was out of control from drinking too much.

Closing her eyes didn't help, but she did it anyway and clenched her fists until her nails dug painfully into her palms. That night was still a blur, with patches of memory missing throughout, and *that* was almost more terrifying. Remembering the disorientation as she came in and out of consciousness. The heavy feeling of him on top of her, inside her. The pain so sharp it had made her sick. She remembered vomiting over the side of the bed and his laughter. He always seemed to be laughing at her.

He was still laughing at her.

Taking slow, even breaths, Caroline grabbed her iPad from her dresser and her Wi-Fi plug. Nothing could chase the past away, but sometimes an episode of *The Big Bang Theory* could push the memories back down.

Caroline set the iPad up on her nightstand and rolled onto her side, concentrating on the characters on the screen instead of the demons in her past.

Chapter Eleven

"I've been told if you want to find a good man, look at the way he treats his mother. I disagree. You want to find a good man? Watch the way he treats his dog."

—Miss Know It All

CAROLINE WOKE UP to the sound of the front door slamming. Rubbing her hands over her face, she glanced at the clock next to the bed and groaned at the red 6:07 A.M. mocking her.

Climbing out of bed, she went to the bathroom and brushed her teeth. After washing her face and twisting her hair up in a clip, she came out of the bathroom and smacked into Gabe.

He grabbed her, steadying her, and she caught herself staring up at him. The lids were heavy over his obsidian eyes, as if he were only half-awake. His face sported some scruff that made him look a little less perfect but no less handsome. His warm, firm grasp on her arms felt good, and the close proximity made it hard to resist stepping into him and snuggling against that hard chest. Would he wrap his arms around her, or would he pull away?

"You okay?" he asked, his voice gravelly with sleep.

Are you okay? No. You're fantasizing about a man you despise, who takes advantage of drunk women. Stop it.

It still took her another moment to pull away. "Yeah, just sleepwalking. I'm guessing that was your sleepover guest who slammed out of here."

"Yeah, she was running late for something."

"Nothing like the walk of shame on a Thursday morning."

"I wouldn't know," Gabe said, running his hand up and over the top of his head. His muscles flexed and bunched as he moved, and she silently told her body to stop swaying toward him. He wasn't hot, and she needed to stay away from him.

"You've never left a girl's apartment after a one-night stand?" Caroline asked, taking another step back.

"Not that I can remember," he said, moving around her into the bathroom. Spreading toothpaste on his toothbrush, he added, "And I don't usually have overnight guests either."

"Aw, so Kirsten is special? How romantic," Caroline said sarcastically. Without giving him a chance to respond, she walked out into the living room. She was angry again, wondering what had happened to Kirsten after Gabe had taken her back to his room. Had she woken up this morning with a fuzzy recollection? Had she realized what had happened and regretted it?

Needing something to do, anything to occupy her, she grabbed a few of the empty boxes left over from unpacking and headed for the front door.

"Actually, I'm just not as big of a dick as you seem to think I am," Gabe called after her.

Caroline dropped the boxes to open the door and turned to snap at him. "Well, you certainly aren't a good guy, or you wouldn't have slept with a woman who could barely walk a straight line."

His handsome face twisted into a glare. Had she struck a nerve?

"I wouldn't be casting stones, princess. I heard all about your sins the minute I hit town."

Furiously, she threw the boxes down the stairs outside and reached back for the knob. "I guess you know what I'm capable of, then."

Slamming the door, she cursed all the way down the steps, her breath fogging in front of her as it hit the cold air. She saw frost coating the metal handrail and realized she was wearing only a thin long-sleeved shirt, pajama bottoms, and house slippers. She was too pissed off to go back and put on a sweatshirt, though. Picking up the boxes at the bottom of the stairs, she walked down the alley toward the Dumpster.

Gabe didn't know her or what she had been through. He had no right to judge her.

You mean, the way you judge him?

Grumbling, she opened the Dumpster and had just dropped the first box inside when she heard a faint cry coming from within. She froze and heard it again. Heart pounding, her first thought was that it sounded like a baby. Someone had thrown a baby away.

No, that's not right. Babies don't mewl like that. It has to be an animal, right?

Caroline wasn't much of an animal person, but the thought of someone taking something helpless and throwing it out like garbage infuriated her.

Looking around for something to stand on, she saw a stack of pallets behind the Local Bean Coffee Shop. It took her a few minutes to drag them over, but once they were stacked five high, she stood on top and looked over the Dumpster's edge. It was pretty full, and reaching out, she moved the box she'd just thrown on top of the pile. At that moment, she saw a black plastic garbage bag move.

What if it's a rat?

"What if it's not?" she said aloud and climbed inside, crawling across the top until she reached the moving bag. Gripping it with both hands, she ripped it open wide and looked inside.

A lump formed in her throat as she stared at the tiny fuzzy bodies. A litter of kittens. She picked up one with fur the color of butter, but its body was cold.

"What the hell are you doing?"

Caroline looked up to find Gabe standing in front of the Dumpster, his expression blank.

"Someone just threw them away," she said, her voice sounding hollow as she picked up the next kitten. And then the next.

But she'd heard a cry.

One of them must be alive.

To her surprise, Gabe took a few steps closer. "Here, hand them to me," he said, holding his hand over the side.

She didn't argue. Handing him the yellow kitten, she saw him grimace before he set it down outside the Dumpster. He held out his hand again and one by one, she handed him the cool, lifeless bodies. When she reached the last two, a fluffy gray tabby and a short-haired, cream-colored kitten, she noticed that they were warmer than the others but still motionless. And then the cream one moved and meowed.

"Oh!" she cried, a wet laugh escaping. She hadn't even realized she was crying. "This one's moving."

"What about the other one?" Gabe asked.

Her smile disappeared. "It's warm still, but not moving."

"Here," he said, and she placed the kitten in his out-stretched hand. To her surprise, he started rubbing the kitten gently.

"What are you doing?"

"I worked at an animal shelter once and saw the vet do this to a puppy that had stopped breathing."

"Did it work?" she asked, hope constricting her chest as she held the squirming cream kitten close.

"No," he said, before placing his mouth over the kitten's tiny mouth and nose and breathing into its body. He pulled back and began rubbing it vigorously all over, turning it over and over in his hands.

"I've got him," Gabe said, his handsome face shining as the kitten cried weakly and squirmed in his hands.

Caroline watched him cradle the small cat, amazed by his gentleness. "You saved him."

Gabe glanced up from the kitten, and their gazes locked. Electricity crackled around them, and suddenly, she had the urge to crawl across the garbage and kiss those full lips. Just to thank him.

"Hey, what are you doing in there?"

The connection was broken by a woman's voice, and Caroline turned to see Gracie McAllister, the jealous woman from last night, racing toward them from the back of the Local Bean.

Caroline cleared her throat. "Someone dumped a litter of kittens into the trash."

"Oh my God! Bastards!" Gracie looked at both of them and then down toward the ground in obvious horror. Caroline wondered if Gabe had just set the other kittens on the ground and that was what Gracie was seeing. "Here, I'll take him while you climb out," Gracie said, finally, holding her hands up to Caroline.

For some reason, Caroline was reluctant to release the kitten. He had called out to her, after all, but in the end, she wanted to get out of the Dumpster. Handing Gracie the little kitten, she crawled out with the help of Gabe's other hand under her elbow. As soon as her feet were back on the ground, she took the creamy furball back from Gracie, her heart melting a little as he nuzzled her neck.

"The veterinarian is down the street, but she's probably not in yet," Gracie said as she pulled out her cell phone. "Luckily, I have her cell number. I'll let her know you're coming down."

"Thanks, Gracie," Caroline said.

Gracie shook her head and hugged her before Caroline could react. "You are my new hero, Caroline Willis. There are not many women who would climb into a Dumpster—for any reason."

Caroline had never been called a hero in her life and had no idea what to say as Gracie released her to make the call. With Gracie just a few steps away, Caroline didn't want to say anything to Gabe that Gracie might hear, but damn it, the man had gone from being a total asshole to the type of guy who gave mouth-to-mouth to a kitten.

It was unacceptable.

That action alone said he had some redeeming qualities, and she didn't want to think about him like that. From their first meeting, she'd put him down as self-centered and bad-tempered, but he'd followed her outside for some reason. To explain about Kirsten maybe? Had she jumped to the wrong conclusion? Maybe she'd been too drunk to drive, and he'd just taken care of her.

Was she reading too much into his actions? She'd tried too many times to see the good in people that just wasn't there and learned the hard way that men would screw you and disappoint you every time. It made forming attachments almost impossible, waiting for the other shoe to drop.

"Okay, she's on her way to the office and will meet you there," Gracie said, stepping close enough to stroke the top of the cream-colored kitten's head. When she spoke again, she was talking to the kitten in a high-pitched baby voice. "I'm sorry people are assholes, but you're going to be in good hands."

Caroline glanced over at Gabe, whose expression warred between amused and *how fast can I get out of here*. Caroline understood what he was feeling as Gracie took her hand and squeezed it. "You come in for coffee anytime you want. It's on the house."

Before she could argue, someone opened the back door to the coffee shop and yelled Gracie's name. As she hurried away, Caroline and Gabe stood alone.

Clearing her throat, Caroline said, "You're the one who should be getting free coffee. I didn't do anything but get a little dirty."

"I didn't do anything. Hell, I didn't even think that shit would work," he said sharply.

"Still, it did, so really—"

"Look, princess, I like animals and all that, but don't go thinking I'm a hero because I got lucky. I'm no fucking hero."

Caroline was taken aback at first, but then her temper flared to life. "Of course you're not. But for a minute there, I thought you might at least be a human being."

He didn't say anything right away, and it burned her that she'd actually felt warm fuzzies toward him. He held the kitten in one hand and a box in the other. Since the other kittens weren't on the ground, she assumed they were in the box, and she held out her hand.

"Why don't you give me your kitten and the box. I can make it down the street on my own."

"Not without dropping a kitten. They're squirmy," Gabe said, confusing her further. She'd given him the perfect out, and he wasn't taking it.

Throwing up her free hand, she snapped, "Fine. Whatever. Let's go."

But as she started down the alley, her little kitten began to nuzzle and knead her neck, its tiny body vibrating with a clicking purr, effectively melting Caroline's heart and diffusing her anger.

He's not worth your anger or your energy.

Which killed her, because for just a moment, she'd thought he might be.

GABE, WHY THE fuck do you have to be such an asshole?

Gabe couldn't answer the question.

It was true he'd seen the vet use mouth-to-mouth on the puppy at the shelter, but the rubbing trick he'd remembered from watching *101 Dalmatians*, Honey's favorite movie.

Now, all he could think about was the time Honey had brought home a very pregnant stray dog when they were kids. Their mother had bitched that they didn't need another mouth to feed, but she'd let them keep the dog anyway. When the mutt gave birth, one of the puppies hadn't been moving. Honey started crying and praying, but he'd grabbed a towel from the bathroom and started rubbing.

Gabe had told Caroline that it hadn't worked because he didn't want to get her hopes up, but it had worked. The little puppy had started moving and squirming, and Honey had thrown her arms around him.

"You're my hero, Gabe."

Hearing the same words from Caroline had sent panic bubbling up his throat. He wasn't a good guy or a hero.

If she started thinking he was anything but an arrogant dickhead, he would only disappoint her. Even at his best, there was too much bad surrounding him to combat the good. It haunted him constantly; if Honey hadn't sustained brain damage, would she remember the accident? Would she blame him? Hate him? He could only imagine, and the scenes that played out in his mind were never ones of forgiveness.

Which was why allowing Caroline to get close to him would be a mistake. Despite the rocky start between them, he liked Caroline's spunk. But he didn't want to feel anything for her, especially when it would only lead to hurt later on. What could he offer any woman but a broken man with a checkered past?

But when he'd come down the stairs and found her in the Dumpster, she'd looked so sad and vulnerable, he'd wanted to help her. Protect her.

And now, the best way to do that was to keep her from getting too close.

"I think this is probably her," Caroline said, breaking into his thoughts when they arrived at the vet's office just as a large truck pulled up in front. "I can take the kitten if you want to go."

"I'm good." He rubbed his thumb across the fuzzy little baby's back and almost smiled when it arched and mewled.

"You must be Gabe and Caroline," said the young black-haired woman who jumped out of the lifted diesel truck. "I'm Zoe Carver."

Zoe was tall and leggy, and as she passed them to open the office, Gabe noticed she walked with a small limp. She pushed open the door and turned to him with a sad smile on her face. "I'll take the box, if you'd like."

Gabe handed her the box of dead kittens and let Caroline go ahead of him as they followed Zoe through the lobby and into a small exam room. As Zoe clucked and tsked over the box, Gabe glanced toward Caroline and saw she was fighting to control her expression. It surprised him; he hadn't pegged her for the type to cry over anything. Ever.

"Most likely, they died from hypothermia or suffocation. Gracie said you found them in a Dumpster?" Zoe asked. She didn't give them the opportunity to answer before she continued. "Some people just suck." Zoe came around the exam table and held her hands open. "Why don't you hand over your little darling, and I'll examine him or her."

Gabe released the kitten to her and balked when she said, "You two should get medals for heroism."

"I didn't do anything," he said quickly. "It was all her. I just held the box." He avoided Caroline's gaze but could feel it boring into him. The intense stare finally pulled his gaze up to meet hers, and he saw the confusion. The disappointment.

If she knew the truth, she'd understand.

The air around him became hot and stifling as he imagined telling Caroline everything he had done. The disgust and resentment it would cause.

People who found out about his DUI assumed he was an alcoholic, that he just couldn't help himself. But he hadn't been drunk or high since that night. He could have a beer or drink, but never more than one if he was out. Still, people didn't want to hear that. They just assumed the worst and wrote him off.

Which was probably why he'd never gone back to his hometown, except to bury his mother. The Welcome Wagon definitely hadn't been waiting for him.

No, he wasn't brave or a hero. Caroline was the brave one, coming back here and facing her past.

All he could do was try to make up for his.

When Zoe tried to hand the kitten back to him, he backed away, glancing toward the door, toward escape. "If you've got this under control, I've got things to do."

He hadn't meant to sound so sharp, but he was still surprised when Caroline said, "Then go."

"See you at home, princess."

As he left the room, he heard Zoe ask, "Are you together?"

"No, just roommates. Thankfully," Caroline replied.

He gritted his teeth, irritation flashing through him.

What do you expect? Instead of trying to keep a casual, comfortable living arrangement with the woman, you barge in on her showers, fight with her at every turn, and can't stop thinking about what she looks like naked.

After exiting the vet's office, Gabe jogged back to the apartment, hoping to blow of some steam, but it just left him more keyed up. A cold shower didn't help either, and by the time he climbed down the stairs to his bike, he wished for a pair of gloves and a sparring partner to unleash his demons on.

After he found the perfect spot for his shop, he was going to have to look for a boxing gym or something close to it. Living with Caroline wasn't going to be easy, especially when he kept pissing her off at every turn.

In fact, this morning she'd seemed downright hostile about finding Kirsten in their apartment, but what was he supposed to do? He'd brought Kirsten back to have some fun, but when he'd had to help her up the stairs, he'd realized exactly how drunk she was. He'd tried making them coffee in the hopes of sobering her up, but she'd lain down on the living room floor after Caroline went to bed and wouldn't get up. So, he'd done the right thing and picked her up, carrying her back to his bedroom. He wasn't going to kick a woman out in the middle of the night, especially one who could barely stand, so he'd put her to bed and spent the rest of the night trying to sleep on top of the covers while the tiny blonde had snored like a trucker.

He would have probably headed back to bed after seeing her out this morning if he hadn't bumped into Caroline. But after she stormed out, he'd followed her, intending to apologize and explain, only to find her crying in a Dumpster. The sight had left him nearly breathless. It had been the first time in his life he'd ever wanted to pull a woman other than his sister into his arms and comfort her. He had wanted to see her smile, her beautiful eyes twinkling…

Pulling the bike to a stop in front of the Realtor's office, Gabe cursed the crazy turn his mind had taken. Since when did he get poetic about women?

Maybe he'd try to find a shop with an apartment above or in the back. It was obvious he had made a mistake, trying to be a good guy. It just wasn't in his nature. He liked things his way, and he didn't want to answer to any woman. Especially not a sharp-tongued beauty who only seemed to add to the regrets he carried.

Chapter Twelve

"As Cher once sang, 'It's in his kiss.' The first kiss can tell you whether there's a spark or the relationship's doomed. Either way, the first kiss is my favorite."

—**Miss Know It All**

CAROLINE TOOK A deep breath as she knocked on her father's door and waited for Teresa to answer. She looked up and down the street, but there was no sign of Kyle's car this time, thank God.

It had been four days since her encounter with him, and she still hadn't gotten up the nerve to swing by and see her father. Finally, she'd called this morning and asked Teresa if her father was expecting company today. Teresa had said no, and Caroline had begged her not to say anything to her dad; she'd wanted to surprise him. Though it would probably seem more like an ambush to him.

Still, if she was going to help bygones be bygones, she needed to get her dad alone. Even alone, he was a bastard, but with an audience, he was completely unreasonable. It shouldn't be this hard to put this one disagreement in the past, especially when she'd done so well for herself, but she still expected him to drag it out, if only for the theatrics.

Her father, the drama king. Must be where his youngest daughter got it from.

In fact, Val had called Caroline in the middle of the night, asking if Ellie was with her. While they were on the phone, Ellie had come home, and Val had hung up, yelling, blowing out Caroline's eardrum.

Whatever was going on with Ellie was going to come to a boiling point, and Caroline had a feeling it was going to be bad. But as she'd told Val, Ellie was an adult. She had to make her own mistakes and learn from them.

She heard a slight mewl and looked down at the animal carrier she'd bought in Twin Falls after leaving the vet's. She'd picked up this little carrier—a black tote with breathable mesh sides—along with bottles, formula, and some fleece material for the kittens to cuddle into, figuring it would be easy to wash.

Zoe had offered to find them a foster home, and Caroline had almost agreed...until her little cream-colored buddy had curled up against her neck and fallen asleep. She couldn't give up him—or his brother—after that. Zoe had given her instructions, and they were lengthy. At first, the little babies would want to eat almost every one to two hours, but eventually, she would be able to get them onto some kind of feeding schedule. Until then, it was best to treat them like newborns. True to what Zoe had said, the little vermin had already devoured three bottles of formula today.

Teresa pulled the door open, her dark eyes widening before she shrieked. "Ah, niña, you are home." The short round woman grabbed Caroline's arm and pulled her inside, squeezing her so tightly that Caroline could hardly breathe. Wrapping her arms around Teresa's shoulders in return, she realized Teresa was crying.

"Don't cry, Resa, I'm okay," Caroline murmured, awed by the woman's emotions. Teresa had been with them since Caroline was five, and she had always felt more like an aunt than their housekeeper. After her mother's death, she had even snuck out to Teresa's home to cry on the older woman's lap while she'd stroked her hair.

But now, to her shock, Teresa pulled away and smacked her arm. "You. Not a word in twelve years. If it wasn't for Valerie, I'd have thought you were dead in a ditch!"

Caroline bit her lip to keep from laughing. Teresa's accent always thickened when she was angry. She could still remember Teresa shouting at them when they'd eaten half the cake Teresa had made their parents as an anniversary gift. She'd chased them out of the kitchen, slipping into rapid Spanish, and made them scrub the kitchen and take another bath before their parents returned.

"I called you."

"Only after I told Valerie that I would hunt you down!" Teresa reached out and cupped Caroline's cheek, shaking her head. "You have grown more beautiful than when you left us."

Covering the older woman's hand with her own, Caroline took a breath and blinked. She didn't want to cry before she saw the old man. "Thank you."

Teresa pulled away first, wiping at her eyes and huffing, "Well, you stayed away far too long. I'm sure your father will be happy to see you."

Ha. Not if his reaction at the hospital was any indication.

Caroline followed Teresa to her father's bedroom and waited behind her as she knocked on the door. "Mr. Willis, there is someone here to see you."

"If it's Kyle with the new figures, tell him—"

Caroline stepped around Teresa and pushed the door open. "Hi, Daddy."

Edward Willis looked up from a pile of papers on his lap, and although he appeared stronger than he had in the hospital, seeing her once-imposing father sitting in bed in the middle of the afternoon was still hard to get used to.

He had aged twenty years, in Caroline's opinion. His once-dark, silver-flecked hair was nearly white. His reading glassed perched on his nose, and the hard eyes gazing out at her were surrounded by more wrinkles than she remembered. Even his skin looked weathered, although he was still a handsome man. He was like Clint Eastwood; immortal even as he aged, his presence was still strong.

Caroline tried to remember the few times in her childhood when he'd been caring or affectionate—hell, even just proud of her—but they were hard to come by. She felt like those memories belonged to someone else. This wasn't her home, and this wasn't the man who'd raised her. They were just strangers who shared the same blood.

Things could have been so different if he had just tried. Opened up and listened to them.

Acted like a father, you mean?

But the past was the past, and she couldn't change it. She could only try to move forward.

No matter how terrifying it was.

"I thought I made myself quite clear that you were no longer welcome here."

Caroline heard Teresa suck in a breath behind her, but she refused to be rattled. "I thought maybe we could bury the hatchet—preferably not in each other's backs."

Edward watched her, his face flushed as he reached for something from his nightstand.

"How much?"

"How much what?" Caroline asked, knowing full well he was talking about money but wanting him to say it aloud.

"How much money do you need?" Edward asked, enunciating each word with a sneer.

Caroline wanted to wipe that condescending look off his face. Pulling out her scratched cell phone, she opened her bank account app and walked around the bed until she could hold out the screen to him.

"As you can see, Daddy, I'm doing okay for myself. I am here strictly on a personal level."

Edward looked positively ill as he stared at her online bank statement.

Don't smile. You are an adult who made good and do not need to rub it in his face like a child. Don't smile.

She grinned. "Aren't you proud?"

God, why do you have to revert to an angry, snotty teenager?

"If you don't want money, then there is nothing for you here," he snarled.

"So, let me get this straight," she said, slipping her phone back into her pocket. "You don't want me around, but if I did need money, you would be okay with that?"

"Anything to keep an embarrassment like you away from me," he said.

Her eyes stung as if he'd slapped her, but she choked back her tears on a harsh laugh. "You are such a dick."

Teresa gasped behind her, as Edward shouted, "Get out of my house, you little whore!"

During her time as a bartender and owner, Caroline had learned to master her temper, to speak calmly and rationally when dealing with unreasonable and sometimes drunk people.

But all it took was being back in her father's presence to cause her temper to burn out of control.

"I am not a whore."

"Please, do you think I haven't heard about your escapades? I chose to ignore them as long as you continued to excel in your studies and didn't cause undue embarrassment, but I knew everything you did."

"Really," Caroline said, her voice shaking. "So you know about how Kyle Jenner drugged and raped me at his family's house party when I was fifteen? About how he threatened to hurt Ellie and Val if I said anything?" Sucking in air, a heavy weight lifted as she spoke, "Tell me, Daddy, if you know everything about me, then how could you hire the one man who destroyed my chance at a normal life?"

Unsurprisingly, her father's face flushed purple with temper, and he shouted, "You're lying! Kyle is a strong, upstanding—"

"Upstanding? You mean wealthy and connected!" Caroline hollered back, her vision blurring despite her attempt to blink back angry tears. "I know Val told you about her friend in college. Kyle's other victim. You know that Kyle's father would do anything to protect his reputation and his son. If you think Senator Jenner is blind to his son's faults, look again. I guarantee that you'll find a few skeletons in his closet." Dashing at her eyes, she added, "Why would I lie about this now? It's been fifteen years since that night, so why would I bring it up now if it never happened?"

Caroline didn't give him a chance to answer before she continued. "The only reason I've kept quiet was because he said he'd hurt Val and Ellie exactly how he hurt me, only he wouldn't drug them. *That* is the man you hired and treat better than your own children. You let a monster into this house."

As he spoke, the blood drained from his face. "If you think I would have allowed anyone to hurt you or your sisters this way, you are gravely mistaken. I would have handled things. I would have..." He seemed to be collecting himself. "I would have protected you."

He believed her. It was almost unbelievable, considering the several hundred scenarios of this moment that she'd played in her mind over the years; in only a few had he actually believed her. She didn't know what to do with this. For years she'd held onto this secret, assuming that her father wouldn't believe her unless Kyle followed through with his threat—a risk she was never willing to take.

In fact, he was looking at her with more emotion than she'd ever seen from him, even at her mother's funeral. Anger was there but so was regret. Did he regret not knowing? That she'd never told him?

Suddenly, it was too much. Without waiting for him to say more, to voice his thoughts, Caroline spun around and pushed past Teresa, muttering an apology as she rushed out of the house. She heard mewls of protest as the kittens bumped against her hip, and she slowed down, brushing her hair out of her already bleary vision. She couldn't see well enough to get her key in the lock, and cursing, she kicked the side of her car.

"Caroline? Are you okay?"

Caroline turned to find that the DJ, Callie Jacobsen, had pulled up alongside her. Callie was watching her with concern from the window of her SUV, her golden riot of curls pulled back from her face. Caroline opened her mouth to answer but stopped when a monster dog in the back of Callie's car jumped into the passenger seat.

"Killer! Ratchet, dang it! Get down!"

If Caroline hadn't been on the verge of breaking down, she might have laughed. "Killer Ratchet? What kind of name is that?"

Callie grinned sheepishly. "His real name is Ratchet, but everyone in town thinks it's Killer. It's started off as a joke, but you'd be surprised at how many people back away from a dog named Killer, as opposed to Ratchet."

A surprised smile came over Caroline. "Is that to weed out the undesirables?"

"Something like that," Callie said, scratching the giant dog behind his ears. "I'm not much of a people person."

"Funny. Me either," Caroline said.

"So, did you need some help? I thought maybe your car door was stuck or something."

"No, it's fine. I'm just shaken up."

"Well, okay then, if you're sure."

Callie's SUV started to pull forward just as Caroline called out, "Hey, Callie?"

"Yeah?"

"In case you hadn't noticed, I'm kind of a social pariah around here, but right now, I could really use some company. Do you maybe want to come over and hang out?"

Callie hesitated, and Caroline almost opened her mouth to let her off the hook, but then Callie nodded. "Sure, that would be great. I'll follow you. Is it okay if Ratchet comes?"

A mewling reminded her that the kittens were hungry, and she said, "As long as he doesn't try to eat cats or me, we're good."

"I THINK IT'S a great space, man, and for the size, it's the best deal."

Gabe nodded, considering Chase's opinion. He had to admit that he was happiest with the old firehouse too, especially since the rent had just been reduced. It was located at the end of Main Street, far from most other businesses, except for the tire shop next door, but that might work in his favor anyway. It was always a good business tactic to create partnerships with the places around you, especially if you wanted to pave a larger parking lot, so to speak.

As they made their way back to Chase's Blazer, Gabe said, "Yeah, you're right. Hey, thanks for looking at it with me." He had been surprised that Chase had agreed to go with him.

"No problem," Chase said, heading around to the driver's side. "I'm actually a little jealous."

"How's that?" Gabe asked.

"Well, I think, considering price per square foot, you got a better deal than me."

Gabe laughed as he climbed inside, leaning back in the seat. "Sorry about that."

As he started the car, Chase said, "Eh, it's okay. I get better foot traffic in the main stretch of town anyway."

Silence stretched in the car once the radio came on, and Gabe buckled in.

"How's Honey doing?"

Chase's question had been a long time coming, but it still knocked the breath out of him. Gabe swallowed down the knot of guilt and unease that had gathered in his throat and said, "She's doing good. She's started painting again, mostly landscapes. She's got a great view from her room."

"That's great."

The tension in the car thickened. Gabe was glad that Chase had finally brought up Honey, but now it felt like they'd lost what little ground they'd managed to cover over the last few days.

Desperate to get back to that place, Gabe asked, "So what's Katie up to?"

"Katie's working. That's the only thing that sucks about our schedules; she works from ten until six, and I head in to open around five in the evening and don't get home until she's already asleep."

"But you guys seem happy, so it can't be that bad," Gabe offered, catching his friend's sly grin.

"You know, I never pictured this as my life, living in a small town. Hell, even marriage was way off the menu. But when it's right, you just can't help it."

Gabe was glad that Chase was happy, if a little whipped. Then again, had his own life gone differently, he might have gone down the same road. With his past, though, he couldn't imagine a woman like Katie giving him a second glance.

But Katie's blue eyes and sweet smile aren't who you'd want anyway. You prefer dark beauties with smart-ass mouths and killer curves.

He almost snorted out loud. Caroline was definitely not a good girl. She was fire and steel and sex in a pair of painted-on jeans and—

"What the hell are you thinking so hard about?" Chase asked, breaking into Gabe's lust-filled thoughts. Damn, what was it about her that could turn him into a daydreaming fool?

"Sorry. I was trying to picture myself in your shoes, and I just can't."

"You're only thirty-four, dude," Chase said. "You still have time."

Gabe didn't say anything. What was the point?

As if reading his mind, Chase said, "I used to think that I didn't deserve Katie and almost lost her because of it. The only person who can really make you feel less-than-worthy is you."

"And where'd you pick up that bit of wisdom?" Gabe said, sarcasm dripping from every word. "Not many women jump with joy when they find out I'm an ex-con who builds motorcycles for a living."

"First of all, you build crotch rockets," Chase said, ignoring the bird Gabe flipped him. "And second of all, you made a mistake, but you did your time. You paid for your mistake—"

"Yeah, I paid five years, while Honey continues to pay for my stupidity," Gabe said.

Chase said nothing for a moment; then, finally, "You did something when you weren't thinking straight. You were a hot-tempered idiot, but you're making up for it by taking care of your sister. You fought for her and have made sure she gets the best treatment, while putting your life on hold." Chase took a breath before adding, "At some point, you got to forgive yourself. Otherwise, you're just going to end up bitter and alone, flogging yourself every night for the past."

Gabe coughed, trying to cover the emotion choking him up. Chase almost sounded like he forgave him. "I don't need to flog myself. I can find someone to do that for me."

"Like Kirsten Winters?" Chase asked as he parked in front of Chloe's Book Nook.

"How the hell do you know about her?" Gabe asked.

"It's a small town. People talk. I'm just glad it's you and not me, because the last thing I need are the biddies of this town in my business again."

Gabe shook his head. "I will never get used to people knowing my business before I've figured it out for myself."

"Eh, I've learned to take it as a compliment. It means they think you're interesting."

"Well, hey, I am that," Gabe said, holding his hand out to Chase. "Thanks again, man."

Chase shook it. "I really believe that you've changed for the better, Gabe. You don't have to worry about us, as long as you just keep doing what you're doing."

Gabe's eyes were stinging, and he tried to shake off the emotions raging inside. No one had ever forgiven him for that night. Not the people he grew up with or his mother, who had probably died hating him for making her life harder.

But Chase—whom he'd beaten, blamed, and cut all ties with—was forgiving him. Telling him that he knew Gabe was trying and that they were good to start over.

Rubbing his hands over his face to wipe away any moisture, he said, "Thanks, man."

Chase slapped him on the back. "What can I say? I've matured."

Gabe choked out a laugh. "I appreciate that."

"It had to happen sometime, right?"

"Amen."

Gabe climbed out and, with a wave at Chase, headed around the back of the building. Jogging up the stairs to his apartment, he was almost to the top before he heard deep, booming barks and realized they were coming from inside.

The door swung open and although he registered Caroline standing in the doorway, holding a tiny ball of fur in her hand, that wasn't the main focus of his *oh, shit* reaction. No, his eyes were trained on what could only be described as Beast from *The Sandlot*, stepping so close he could feel the dog's hot breath right in his crotch.

Please don't bite my nuts off.

Just as he was starting to sweat, another woman, with frizzy blonde hair, stepped up and called softly, "Killer."

The dog whipped around and went back inside, just as Gabe sagged against the railing, and Caroline laughed.

"That's not funny. I thought that dog was gonna bite my junk."

"Yes, because *that's* exactly what he wants."

"Look, I don't like dogs, especially not giant ones that come charging outside—"

"Caroline, I'm gonna take off. If you wanna meet us later, we usually get to Hank's around seven thirty," the blonde said as she stepped past them, the giant dog sniffing at him as they went down the stairs.

"Hey, thanks for keeping me company, Callie."

"Any time. And thanks for getting that interview set up."

But before he could ask what kind of interview, Caroline was already back inside. He followed behind her, closing the door with a loud click before turning to find her sitting on the couch with a baby bottle in one hand and a squirming, slurping kitten in the other.

"So who was that woman, and why was her giant fucking dog in our apartment?" he asked, hoping the "our" would irritate her. And by the narrowing of her eyes and the clenching of her jaw, he figured he'd hit a bull's-eye.

"I don't bother you about your guests," she said.

"My guests don't bring Cujo with them."

"Killer is an extremely well-behaved dog and goes with Callie everywhere. He's like a service animal."

"Service animals serve handicapped people. She didn't look like there was anything wrong with her."

"There isn't," she snapped.

"Then why does she need a service animal?" he asked, coming around the couch to face her. Caroline was beautiful in pajamas, looking tousled and sleepy, but in a black tank top that showed a generous amount of cleavage and blue jeans hugging her thighs, she was hotter than the blazes of hell. It was all he could do not to push her back on those plush pillows and take that full frowning mouth with his.

But seeing how she currently had her hands occupied, and he was pretty sure she'd bite him if he tried, he refrained.

"For post-traumatic stress. And before you ask what happened, I don't know, and I wouldn't talk to you about it if I did, 'cause it's none of your fucking business—or mine."

Gabe watched her extract the bottle from the sleepy kitten's mouth and place him back into a cardboard box by the couch. Getting up, she tried to move around Gabe, but he stopped her with a hand on her arm. A hand she immediately tried to shake off.

"Let go," she snarled.

Tightening his grip, he said, "You might not like me, princess, but we are living together, so what you do and who you bring into this apartment *is* my business."

"Oh yeah? So I have to explain who my guests are, but you can take advantage of drunk girls in your room, and I can't say anything?"

"First of all," he said, rage clipping his words, "I didn't take advantage of anyone. I would never hurt a woman, and I definitely wouldn't take advantage of her. But I'm also not going to leave some girl too drunk to take care of herself at a bar or her apartment and take the chance of her choking on her own vomit or something worse. So I let her stay here." And just because he resented her accusations, he added, "And the reason why she slammed out of here all pissed off? When she woke up, hung over, and tried to start something with me...sexually, I told her no thanks."

He could tell she was struggling with whether to believe him or not, and it made him wonder how many men had hurt her. How many had taken advantage of her in some way to make her think the worst of him?

"I am not perfect, but I can promise you, I would never hurt a woman—physically or otherwise," he said, loosening his grip on her arm. "But not everyone is like that, which is why it's important to be careful who you bring home."

"You never answered me, though," she said. "Why is it any of your business?"

"Because if you bring the wrong guy home and he starts hurting you, I'm the one who is going to handle him."

She burst out laughing, shocking the hell out of him. "You think you're going to have to rescue me?" Caroline stepped into him, as if trying to back him up against the wall, but he stood his ground. Their bodies were almost touching as she looked up at him and whispered teasingly, "I thought you weren't a hero, Gabriel."

Gabe knew she was baiting him, and it worked. White-hot desire prickled his skin as he leaned into her body. Her smell wrapped around him like a blanket, lemony sweetness making his mouth water. "I'm not. I'm a bad man who has done things that would make sweet little girls like you quake in their boots."

"I'm not wearing boots."

"I'm saying, if you know what's good for you, you'll back up out of my face."

"Let's get one thing straight. You don't—"

He'd given her a chance, but as he'd said before, he wasn't a nice man. Wrapping his arm around her waist, he pulled her flush up against his body, and before she could finish her startled "What the—" his head dipped down as he claimed her mouth in a hard kiss.

Caroline's whole body stiffened, and he felt her tiny fist shove at him, but he held fast, sweeping his tongue out to trail across her lips. Suddenly, he felt her hand splay out against his chest and her body soften, her mouth opening and her breath mingling with his.

Gentling his hold on her, he slipped his tongue inside, the warmth of her mouth drawing him in further. She was everything he had imagined, soft breasts pressing into him as his hands trailed down to rest against the small of her back, just above her ass. He itched to cup her and bring her closer, but he didn't want to spook her. Deepening the kiss, he ran his hands up her back, a thrill shooting through him when her own hands slipped up to his shoulders. He caught her low moan in his mouth and lost all worry that she didn't want him. Despite his resolve to stay away from Caroline, he couldn't stop, not when the reality of having her in his arms was so much better than the fantasy.

To his surprise, Caroline broke the kiss, her hands gripping his shoulders hard. "Stop. What are you doing?"

Her voice was husky, and her eyes were still half closed, but the question was like a bucket of ice water. What was he doing? What were they doing? She had kissed him back and thoroughly enjoyed it too.

Gabe took two steps back to give his raging cock some room. Just the brief press of her curves had given him a full-on erection, and he cursed himself for being weak, but she just kept challenging him, pushing him. He thought he'd outgrown his rash behavior years ago, but apparently, a leopard just couldn't change his spots.

The taste of her lingered on his lips, and just he was about to lick them, she came fully out of her stupor.

And slapped him—hard enough to knock his head back.

"Don't you ever touch me again," she said.

Rubbing his cheek and jaw, he tried to ease the sting. "You kissed me back."

"And that makes it okay, how?"

She fled the living room before he could respond, her bedroom door slamming behind her.

Okay, so he might have deserved the slap for kissing her, knowing she probably wouldn't appreciate it, but she had been daring him. Otherwise, she wouldn't have stepped into him like that, teasing him with that soft voice and those lips he couldn't stop thinking about.

Man, did she have a hard hand. Walking over to the mirror on the dining room wall, Gabe studied the bright-red imprint of her hand and rubbed at it. Most women didn't knock a guy's jaw off for stealing a kiss, especially when they had seemed into it.

This was fucking nuts. He'd lived with this woman less than a week, and all they did was fight. Granted, he'd wanted to keep her at bay, but he never wanted to make her feel threatened.

You were the one who told her you were a bad guy. How can she trust you if you're telling her one thing and doing another?

The fact was, if they were going to survive their temporary situation, Gabe owed Caroline more than one apology. Whatever her issues, he had made the wrong move, and he needed to make it right.

The story of his life.

Chapter Thirteen

"The only stalking that should be done in Idaho is during hunting season."

—Miss Know It All

CAROLINE STIRRED HER Jack and Coke and tried to shake off her shitty day. At least one good thing had come from it; she had made a friend.

Callie sat quietly next to her, smiling and nodding at whatever Mike Stevens was saying. Callie and she had talked for hours earlier, and when she'd asked Caroline to come out with them, Caroline had been hesitant. But after Gabe had kissed her, she'd been emotional and crazed and needed to get the hell out of there. When Callie had texted her, saying they were going to dinner too, she had said yes. She'd been worried about sneaking out without bumping into Gabe, but thankfully, he was gone when she'd come out of her room.

She wanted to put Gabe and his unwelcome kiss from her mind.

Which was hard to do when his stupid face kept popping into her head, bringing a tingling sensation to her lips, which reminded her of how he had crossed a line and how, for a split second, she'd wanted to let him. To let him take control and make her feel something, *anything* besides anger, pain, and being generally unwanted.

But then she remembered they could barely stand each other and that she was no longer sixteen, trying to fill a void inside her. She'd had every intention of picking and choosing her partners carefully, weighing the benefits, taking in the risks...

And Gabe was just too big a gamble.

Forget the fact that she knew very little about him, except that he was a wash of contradictions. Their first meeting, he'd been arrogant and a major dick, but when he'd offered to share the apartment, he'd been almost charming. He hated accepting praise when he was kind and lashed out at her when she started to see the good in him. She just couldn't get a handle on who he was, and it scared her.

But when he'd kissed her, it had felt like she was floating for half a second and then, *boom*, her skin was burning like molten lava, hot and fast. Every stroke of his tongue had left her weak, tingly, and craving more of him. She had been ready to surrender completely until the voice in her head had started ranting.

You aren't in control. He is.

The slap had been a reaction after the fact, but Gabe hadn't been wrong. She *had* kissed him back, *had* moaned and enjoyed him. She'd given him every indication that she liked what he was doing.

What was wrong with her? She might be attracted to Gabe, but he wasn't *the* guy. He wasn't what she needed. He was like every other loser she had hooked up with over the years: selfish, only in it for a good time. That was her past. She was almost thirty-one years old, and she needed to break the cycle. No more Mr. Right Now. She needed a mature, stable guy. Someone who would show the town of Rock Canyon that she had finally grown up.

"So, Caroline, Callie said you flip bars for a living?"

The question came from Travis Bowers, Gemma's country rock-star husband, who was sitting across from her at the round table, nursing a beer. Travis was definitely the type of man her mother would have called a "tall glass of water," with his curly brown hair and five o'clock shadow making him look like a rugged roughneck, looking for trouble.

"I did, but I've switched my focus to consulting. I want to set down roots somewhere instead of picking up and moving every couple of months to a new town, new city."

"I understand completely," Travis said, picking up Gemma's hand and bringing it to his lips for a kiss.

Caroline almost rolled her eyes but caught herself. It wasn't their fault that she wasn't the type of woman to attract the hand-holding, eyes-for-her-only type of man. She never had been.

She attracted weaklings who liked a woman to tell them what to do and usually had no imagination in the bedroom; the charmers who wanted to see if they could land her and then tell all their buddies about their exploits; and the assholes who liked strong women only as long as they could break them.

Every one of them was definitely on her new DO NOT DO list.

"I heard Eric and Hank are fighting over your services," Mike said, reaching over to steal some of Gracie's nachos while she was onstage singing the Judds' "Mama He's Crazy."

It was karaoke night at Hank's, and Caroline had wanted to stake out the little bar in action. She could see why this night was taking away business from Buck's. The karaoke alone was a great draw, but Hank's had a "1-2-3" promotion, too: one-dollar longnecks, two-dollar nachos, and three-dollar margaritas.

"I said I'd give them an assessment and upon retainer, I'd draw up a recommended business plan. First come, first served," Caroline said, sitting back in her chair. "I've got to say, though, Hank's doesn't seem to be hurting on karaoke night."

"The only problem Hank's has is when Hank starts drinking," Gemma said, making a face.

Caroline sat forward. "He drinks in his own bar?"

"More like gets shit-faced in it," Mike said. "I feel bad for the guy because he's on his own, but he can get downright unpleasant."

"Then he's a waste of my time," Caroline said with a sigh.

"How do you mean?" Travis asked.

"Well, for starters, if he gets drunk in his own bar, he runs the risk of his employees and customers not only taking advantage of him but getting out of control. This drink," Caroline said, holding up her Jack and Coke, "is too strong, which tells me the bartender's not measuring shots correctly—wasting alcohol and eating into profits."

They stared at her until, as a group, they each took a sip of their drinks, except Travis, who had the only longneck. A few of them nodded their heads in agreement.

Caroline checked the time on her phone again, and Mike asked, "You got somewhere to be?"

Before she could answer, Gracie finished her song, and their table broke into thunderous applause and obnoxious whoops of encouragement. Gracie sashayed back to the table, demonstrating a courtly bow as she said, "Thank you. Thank you."

She sat down next to Caroline and wrapped her thin arms around her shoulders before giving Caroline a smacking kiss on the cheek. "And how are you enjoying Hank's?" Her smile was slightly silly, and Caroline guessed she had started the party early, especially when she moved on before Caroline could answer. "Did you know that this woman is an honest-to-God hero? She freaking crawled into a Dumpster to save a gaggle of kittens—"

"I don't think kittens come in gaggles," Mike said, earning a scowl from Gracie.

"Whatever. The point is that she is *amazeballs*, and if anyone messes with her"—Gracie thumped her chest and almost fell off her chair—"they are messing with me."

"Lucky you," Gemma said from across the table.

Caroline wasn't sure how she felt about Gracie's admiration but decided it was better than Gracie's hating her guts.

"So are you one of those crazy animal lovers, then?" Travis asked, yelping when Gemma pinched him. "What? I didn't say anything about you."

"Actually, I like animals but have never had any desire to own one. I moved around too much. But now, the reason I keep checking the clock on my phone is because the kittens have to eat every two hours."

"Wait, you aren't an animal lover, but you're keeping kittens that you found in the trash?" Mike asked. "How many are there?"

"Two, and I'm not keeping them. I'm just fostering them until they can be put up for adoption," Caroline said, trying to picture handing over her babies to someone else. In just the few days she'd had them, they had already started to gain weight, and the minute she picked them up, they started that clicking purr she'd come to love. Last night, as she'd watched *The Big Bang Theory*, she'd let them cuddle against her chest. It was hard not to love the little squirts.

"Uh-huh, and how does your roommate feel about that?" Travis asked, a smirk on his face. "When I showed him the apartment, he didn't exactly seem like the warm and fuzzy type."

Travis's opinion irked her. It was true that Gabe wasn't Mr. Sunshine and Roses, but he had saved the gray kitten. He had his moments of actually being a human being.

Too bad they were few and far between.

"Actually, he helped me save them."

"It's true. I was there," Gracie said.

"How?" Callie asked.

"He stimulated the little grey one's heartbeat by rubbing him and even breathed into his nose and mouth."

"Huh. I guess people do have layers," Mike said, mimicking Shrek.

How had the conversation turned toward the very man she was trying to forget?

Standing up, she gave everyone an apologetic smile. "I'm sorry I have to go, I had a lot of fun, but I'd better go feed them."

"Do you need me to walk you home?" Mike asked with a flirtatious smile.

This is the type of guy you should be thinking about, not infuriating Neanderthals who don't know how to treat a woman.

"That's okay. I'm right up the street," Caroline said. She patted Callie's shoulder. "I'll call you tomorrow."

"Okay," Callie said.

Grabbing her coat and purse, Caroline headed for the door. The cold wind hit her face as she walked outside, and she struggled to get her coat on as she made her way back toward her apartment. The streetlamps were lit up nicely, though, and despite the two drinks she'd had, she was nowhere near being drunk.

As she rounded the alley corner, she thought maybe she'd open that bottle of merlot in the cupboard and have a glass before bed. She just hoped luck was on her side and Gabe was asleep or out. She wasn't quite ready to face him yet.

Suddenly, strong hands grabbed her from behind and slammed her into the brick building next to her. Her cheek hit the wall and pain exploded in her skull.

"What did you tell him, you stupid bitch?" A dark voice hissed in her ear, and hot breath dampened her skin. Through the painful haze, she realized it was Kyle. Fear ripped through her as he pressed his body into hers, flattening her between him and the hard, cold surface.

"What—"

"And don't even think about fucking lying to me," he growled low.

"Ky...Kyle...I—"

"Whatever you said to him, you'd better fix it. I'm not going to have the life I've built ruined by some slut who wants to clear her conscience," Kyle said, gripping her hair in his fist until she cried out in pain.

"What the fuck is going on out there?" Gabe's voice called from above. Caroline heard the heavy fall of his feet on the metal stairs and tried to cry out a warning, but her throat had closed and all that came out was a whimper.

"Remember what I said," Kyle warned before he let her go. She heard the clip of running, the sound becoming fainter in the distance.

Tears seeped from the corner of her eyes, and she tried to breathe, to calm her quaking body, but she was scared. And angry, so angry. Her conscience? She hadn't done anything wrong. Did he actually think she felt guilty about what he'd done to her?

Don't you? You are constantly telling yourself that you should have known, should have seen through his charm? Isn't that a guilty conscience?

Suddenly, hard hands grabbed her arms, and she turned, swinging, prepared for Kyle coming back, but Gabe caught her fists instead. "Shhh, it's okay. You're okay."

Unable to hold herself up any longer, she collapsed against him, hating the weakness. She could take care of herself—had been doing so since she was a kid—but she couldn't seem to fight this one fear: the fear of being Kyle's victim again.

Without asking, Gabe gathered her up in his arms, holding her tightly against his chest as he strode toward the apartment. She tried to remember that he was a jerk, a man whom she shouldn't trust at all, but his hard body and comforting arms helped her shaking subside. He made her feel safe, and if he hadn't been upstairs, hadn't been listening...

"Thank you," she whispered against his shoulder as he climbed the stairs.

He didn't respond, just adjusted her in his arms to open the front door. The living room light hit her eyes and stung for half a second. "Yowza, that's bright."

Still he said nothing. Gently, he deposited her on the couch, and before she could miss his warmth, he had dimmed the lights.

Stretching her mouth open, she winced when a lightning bolt of pain shot through her, and she touched the spot where her face had collided with the building. "Well, that's gonna bruise."

"Who was he?" Gabe asked, his voice almost too low to hear.

"He works for my father," she said.

"Your *father* hired someone to rough you up?" he fairly shouted.

"No, no. This was something…else," she said, unwilling to get more personal than that. Despite his timely intervention and rescue, he was still just her roommate. If she hadn't even told her own sisters about what Kyle had done, there was no way she was going to share her feelings with a man she hardly knew.

Silence stretched in the small room, and she looked away from his intense, searching eyes to check on the kittens, sleeping peacefully in the box. "I'm surprised they've slept this long. I figured they'd be up and crying by now."

"They were, which is why I was out here in the first place. The little bastards were pitching a fit, and I fed them so they'd shut up. Then I heard something outside and decided to see what in the hell was going on down there." He reached out to brush her hair back, and his fingertips grazed her forehead, leaving a trail of tingles in their wake. "I'm still trying to figure that out."

"Why do you care?"

"I told you. Your crazy became my crazy the second I let you move in."

"You mean when you stole my apartment." A small smiled stretched his full lips and before she could stop herself, she said, "You should do that more often."

"What?"

Boldly, she placed two fingers on his bottom lip. "Smile."

"I smile," he said.

"Not that sarcastic grin you use or the one you think is charming," she said, dropping her hand from his mouth. "I mean a real smile."

He paused. "I guess I don't have a lot to smile over."

The conversation was fast becoming personal and intimate, two things that made Caroline squirm.

"I appreciate the help, really, and I'm sorry that I sort of fell apart on you, but this really isn't your problem. There's no roommate code, nothing in our little arrangement that says you have to step in and take on my issues."

"When your issues follow you home and assault you in the alley below our apartment, it becomes my business."

She bent over and picked up the kittens' box. "It's going to be better for both of us if you stay out of it, okay? Besides, aren't you the guy who said you're not a hero?"

Chapter Fourteen

> "What's the point of living in a small town if you
> can't get up in someone else's business every once
> in a while?"
>
> —Miss Know It All

GABE WALKED OUT of Honey's assisted-living facility,
carrying the painting she had made for his new place in
his hands. He'd grabbed a protective bike bag to trans-
port it home, once Sharla had given him the heads up.
Honey had been in a good spot today, almost like her old
self, asking him about his motorcycle and what girls he
was interested in.

It was a good day when she remembered nothing of
the accident and still looked at him with hero worship in
her eyes.

He usually called before heading up for a visit, but he
had needed to get out of the house this weekend. Since
he'd started asking questions of Caroline about the man

who'd assaulted her last week, she had been avoiding him like the plague.

And he'd made it easy for her. Not because he didn't want to see her, but because of the emotions her attack had stirred in him. He'd wanted to wrap her up and keep her close, to never let her out of his sight.

Too bad he hadn't gotten a good look at the fucker. Whoever he was, Caroline was clearly scared of him. Holding her in his arms, he could still remember the way she'd trembled. Caroline was a strong woman, and to see her so vulnerable made him want to tear someone apart.

By the time he parked on the street two hours later, it was close to five thirty. He had planned to stop by Chase's tattoo shop to go over the logo design for Moriarty's Custom Bikes, but feeling grimy, he climbed off the bike and pulled out the painting. He would hang it and then get cleaned up.

Gabe walked through the alleyway and took the stairs two at a time. The draw of a hot shower was so exciting, he pushed open the door too quickly and hit the wall behind with the knob.

"Crap, what are you doing?" Caroline yelled as she came around the corner. "I do not want to pay a massive bill at the end of this lease because you come through the door like the Incredible Hulk."

Gabe didn't say a word; he simply stared at her as he set the painting down gently against the wall. She looked good all the time—she had been a knockout in that black dress at Buck's—but tonight...

Tonight, she was like a damn siren in a pair of fuck-me heels.

Her long dark hair was swept back and to the side, her brown eyes surrounded by smudgy black eye shadow. Her lush lips looked wet, and it gave him all kinds of ideas of how they'd feel, kissing their way along his body and around a certain part of his anatomy that was suddenly standing at full attention. The dress she had on was royal purple with a light shimmer to it, the heart-shaped neckline creating a deep *V* of cleavage that made his hands eager to squeeze and test the weight of her breasts. And then there were her shapely legs, sliding down into leopard-print heels. Leave-them-on-while-you-screw-me heels.

He wanted to throw her over his shoulder and carry her back to his room, where he'd strip her out of everything *but* those shoes.

Suddenly, it occurred to him she wasn't dressing for *his* benefit, and his jaw clenched. It was hard to deny the sudden urge to pound whoever she'd had in mind when she'd dolled herself up, and he knew it was unreasonable. He had no right to be jealous; she was a free agent who could go out with whomever.

He didn't have to like it, though.

"Where the hell are you going, dressed like that?"

Well, if her pissed-off look meant anything, *that* had been the wrong thing to say. "I have a part in a Bond movie."

"It's forty degrees outside," he said, trying to gentle his tone and be the voice of reason.

"So?" she said, eyeballing him like he'd lost his damn mind. "I've got a jacket."

"Your tits are going to pop out of that dress if you bend over."

"Gabe," she said as she pulled her jacket off the back of the couch, "when you can manage to put your dishes in the dishwasher without leaving food on them, I might take your advice. No, wait, why would I ever take your advice on fashion? You're idea of style is a T-shirt and jeans."

He ignored her passive-aggressive criticism. Damn, he liked the way she said his name. He'd like it even better in another, more sultry tone, but he'd take what he could get.

Wait…When had he started wanting anything from Caroline?

She was heading right for him, probably so she could escape out the front door, but he was having none of that. Stepping into her path, Gabe asked again, "Well, you have to admit, your girls are popping up and saying howdy in the friendliest way I've seen yet."

"Well, they aren't saying howdy to you," she said, moving to his right.

Grinning, he side-stepped with her. "Then who are they saying howdy to?"

Caroline let out an exasperated breath. "Are you trying to irritate me?"

"I didn't know I had to try. I thought you just woke up, and the annoyance was there."

"Oh, no, some mornings I wake up thinking, *I must've imagined it. He can't be that bad.* And then I see you, and it all comes flooding back like a drunken night of idiocy." When she tapped his chest with a long, glittery purple nail, he resisted the urge to grab it and nibble the tip. "Only it's not *my* idiocy I'm remembering."

When she tried to out maneuver him again, he caught her around the waist and said, "Speaking of idiots, who's your hot date?"

"How do you know I'm going on a date?"

" 'Cause a woman doesn't dress like that unless she's trolling for a man or going out with one," Gabe said.

"You don't know him," she said, struggling against him.

"What kind of man asks a woman like you out and doesn't even bother to come to the door?"

"He's coming to the door. I just didn't want the first thing he sees to be you," she snapped.

"Why? I'll be nice to him," Gabe said.

"Would you let go? He's going to be here any minute, and you're wrinkling my dress!"

Suddenly, there was a knock on the door, and Caroline pushed him away. Gabe leaned back against the couch and waited as she opened the door.

"Hey, Mike," she said to the guy on the porch.

"Wow, you look amazing," the unknown guy said.

Gabe's good humor fled. Heat curled in his stomach, easing out into his limbs until he wanted to punch someone, most of all the faceless guy in his doorway.

That churning in your gut feels a lot like jealousy.

Stepping up alongside Caroline, Gabe leaned his arm on the doorframe and gave the man on the porch his best "don't fuck with me" glare. "Hey, Mike. I'm Gabe."

The guy was average height with brown eyes and short dark hair, and instead of being intimidated, he stuck his hand out with a smile. "I've heard a lot about you."

"You have?" Gabe asked suspiciously, looking down at Caroline.

"Don't look at me. I avoid talking about you."

"Actually, Travis told me about you, that you make custom motorcycles. I was thinking I'd come by your shop and see what you can come up with for me."

The guy was lethal; Gabe would give him that. He'd charmed and disarmed him in five seconds flat. Taking Mike's still-outstretched hand, he said, "I'm by appointment only until I get all the equipment moved in, but you can usually get me on my cell."

The two of them exchanged numbers, and as he slipped his phone back into his pocket, Gabe caught Caroline's irritable expression.

"What?"

"Do you think my date and I can leave now?" she asked.

"Sure, take him. Get him out of here," Gabe said, but as they started down the stairs, he saw Mike's hand move to the small of her back.

Gabe knew what she felt like, right there at the curve of her back, and he didn't want any other man's hands on her, even if that man seemed like an okay guy. Then Gabe realized he was halfway down the stairs, ready to remove Mike's arm from the socket if he didn't stop touching her, and froze.

Caroline turned a few steps down and looked up at him. She must have heard his footsteps or felt the vibration. "Was there something else, Gabe?"

Damn, there was his name again, but this time it had been spoken softly. Their eyes met, and he wanted to close the distance and claim her.

"I just wanted to know if you need me to feed the vermin."

The small smile she gave him unnerved him and made him feel like a kid, trying to please his teacher by asking for extra credit. "Only if they cry. I just fed them half an hour ago."

"All right, then," he said, searching for something else to say. As they started climbing down again, he called out, "Hey, Mike?"

"Yeah?" Mike said from the bottom, holding his hand out for Caroline. When she slipped hers into his, Gabe almost growled.

"Treat her with respect," he said.

"Of course, I—"

"If you don't, I'll chain you to the back of my bike and drag you behind me until your own mother wouldn't recognize you."

Mike's jaw dropped, and Caroline scowled. "I have a father," she said. "I don't need you—"

"Have a good time, princess," he said, cutting off her rant.

She flipped him the bird behind Mike's back before they walked out of sight, and he chuckled until he realized he was hanging out at home on a Saturday night. Alone. There was no way he could sit around the apartment all night, waiting for Caroline to come home.

After his shower, he'd hang up the painting and head out somewhere. Maybe he'd check out Twin Falls nightlife. But as he stepped back inside, he heard a distinct scratching noise coming from Caroline's room. Inside, he found the little gray tabby, Googlie, hanging over the side of his box. Caroline had named him Googlie for his big, googly eyes, and Gabe had to admit that the name fit.

"What are you doing, buddy?"

The kitten meowed in response, and Gabe padded over to pick up the fluff ball. Peeking over the edge of the box, he saw that Possum, the little cream-colored kitten, was looking up at him, as if gauging the distance needed to jump.

"I guess your mom doesn't know what she's talking about, huh?" Scooping up the second kitten, he held them both against his chest, their little purrs vibrating his hands. Stroking their fur with his thumbs, he carried them into the bathroom with him, let the kittens down on the floor, and turned on the shower.

Googlie started to meow loudly, and he bent over to pick up the fuzz butt. "Listen, dude, I'm going to let you chill in here with me while I shower, and if you're cool, I'll let you watch some Dwayne Johnson with me. Sound good?"

Gabe felt the kittens purr and shook his head. He'd officially lost his mind if he was talking to a couple of cats.

"Am I putting you to sleep over there?"

Caroline jerked as Mike's words penetrated her wandering thoughts. "I'm so sorry. I think the wine might be getting to me. What were you saying?"

Mike chuckled. "It's all right. I don't really find motherboards all that interesting anyway."

Was that really what he was talking about on a first date? Geez, no wonder you were thinking of something else.

Or someone, to be exact.

"So, tell me more about you. You're the one who has moved around and worked in exciting places. You must have stories," Mike said.

Stories? Oh yeah, she had stories, but not the first-date kind. She really didn't think a guy like Mike wanted to hear about the first year she spent away from home, how she'd ended up stripping at some dive in Nevada just to get her car fixed. Or about the time she'd been arrested for stealing a waitress's tip off the table because she had spent her last ten dollars on gas.

"Okay, well, I actually got started working in bars when I was nineteen. I'd been on my own for a little over a year, and I took a job working as a waitress in this little sports bar. The owner, who was a wonderful man, liked my spunk, and by the time I was twenty-one, I was head bartender. I kept advancing until he came to me one day and said, 'Look, I want to retire, and I think you've got a gift for this business. I know you've got a little something saved up. Do you want to make a deal?'" Caroline took a sip from her wineglass and smiled, "And that's how I got my first bar."

The waitress came over to clear their plates, and Caroline heard the faint sound of "Let's Hear It for the Boy" coming from her purse. She reached inside to grab it. When she glanced at the screen, it was a text from Val.

OMG, I have no idea why, but apparently, Dad is investigating Kyle.

Caroline's heart started pounding as she remembered Kyle's grip in her hair. *"You fix it…"*

"Shit," she said aloud, immediately covering her mouth when she realized Mike and their waitress had heard her. "I'm sorry."

"Is everything okay?" Mike asked as his handsome face knit with concern.

He really is such a sweet guy. It's too bad there's just no spark.

"Yeah, my sister was just giving me an update on some family drama. No big deal."

"Are you sure? If you need me to drop you somewhere…"

"No, I'm good. She'll fill me in later."

But Caroline's fingers itched to call or at least text Val to find out what she knew. She didn't know whether to be relieved or terrified that her father was looking into Kyle's past. Kyle could still retaliate. Things could go bad fast.

When Mike paid the check and offered to take her home so she could call her sister, she felt a little guilty that she was more excited than disappointed. But as nice as he was, his touch just didn't heat her up like Gabe's did.

Yes, she'd been avoiding Gabe for a week, trying to puzzle through the roller coaster of emotions she was riding. On one hand, she knew what Gabe had told her, that he was no good and she couldn't count on him. Yet when she'd needed him, he'd been there.

But every time you start to feel like there's something more to him, he shuts down.

Besides, she didn't want to add serious complications to their living arrangement. God forbid they hook up and things turn awkward as shit.

Why does it always have to be sex with you anyway? Why can't you just enjoy the fact that you don't want to bash his face in every five seconds?

Which was true. Even his little stint into obnoxiousness this evening made her laugh more than want to kick him in his jewels. It was nice to finally not walk on eggshells around him, and he'd even taken care of the kittens a few times. All in all, the roommate thing wasn't turning out as horrendous as she'd thought.

Well, except the dishes thing…and a few times, she'd found some of his dirty clothes suspiciously mixed in with hers. She'd taken the clothes and left them outside his door. Taped to his door, she'd left a note that read, NOT YOUR MAID OR YOUR MOTHER. DO YOUR OWN LAUNDRY.

Of course, the next day he'd retaliated with his own note on the bathroom mirror. HEY CHEWBACCA, HOW ABOUT CLEANING THE DRAIN EVERY ONCE IN A WHILE? YOU'RE SHEDDING LIKE A SAINT BERNARD.

A week ago, she probably would have gotten mad, but since the night of Kyle's attack, something had shifted between them. He was so moody, but when she'd needed him, he'd been there, and she couldn't ignore the little voice that kept whispering in her head, *Maybe he's different.*

Mike pulled over and parked in front of her building, and she realized she hadn't said a word to him the whole drive back. She'd been too busy thinking about Gabe.

"Thank you for tonight. It was lovely," she said once he'd come around and opened her door.

"You're welcome," he said. "I'll walk you to your door."

She wasn't going to say no, and when they reached the top of the stairs, he leaned over and gave her a chaste kiss on the cheek.

"Good night, Caroline."

"Night," she said, and as he climbed back down the stairs, she realized that he hadn't offered to call her or to try again another time.

Maybe he sensed your lack of interest? Or maybe he realized he was actually not *that into you.*

Unlocking the apartment door, she decided she was relieved. At least she wouldn't have to let him down easy now. She stepped inside and closed the door, clicking the lock into place. As she tiptoed behind the couch, she noticed Gabe stretched out, asleep, while *The Scorpion King* played low on the TV. In the dim light, she could see Googlie and Possum's fuzzy bodies curled into Gabe's neck.

If she was one of those girls who melted and sighed at adorable sights, she'd be goo.

His face seemed darker, cast in the shadows and light from the TV, and more innocent in sleep. Well, except for the piercing and black ink on the side of his neck, but still, he was gorgeous to look at.

Leaning over the couch, she touched his chest softly. "Gabe."

He startled awake, making her jump, he moved so fast. The kittens didn't seem too bothered by it, but Gabe's dark eyes were wide as he looked around the room before finally focusing on her.

"Damn it; you scared me."

"I'm sorry," she whispered. "I tried to be gentle, but I was afraid if I left you there, you'd end up with a kink in your neck."

Gabe nodded before stretching his arms behind his head. "Appreciate it."

Caroline's gaze hooked on those sinewy muscles coiling under his darkened skin, and suddenly she wanted to get away from him as fast as she could. "Okay, well, I'll take the kittens for now, and you can go to sleep or finish your movie."

"I'll probably just turn in," he said, handing the protesting kittens off to her as he stood up. "So, Mike didn't want to come in for another drink?"

"Some men are gentleman," she said, cuddling the fuzzy bodies against her.

Gabe stared at her hard, and when he spoke, his dark, husky words shot pure desire though her body.

"Princess, if I had come to pick you up and seen you in that dress, we wouldn't even have made it to the restaurant."

Chapter Fifteen

"Has anyone noticed that the upcoming weather calls for two days of severe thunderstorms and right smack in the middle of that, a night of clear skies and a full moon? Crazy weather + a full moon = gossip-palooza. So what will this wild weather bring us this time? Stay tuned."

—Miss Know It All

"How the hell did Ellie find this out? I thought she was living with you," Caroline asked Valerie as the two of them sat in her apartment on Sunday morning. Caroline had wanted to get the scoop on their father—and to keep from being alone with Gabe.

After his parting comment, he had gone into his room, all dramatic and confusing, and it had just pissed her off. Two-plus weeks of living together, and he was still a mystery of freaking epic proportions.

"She's trying to find an apartment, maybe a roommate. But she went back to Dad's house to pack up some of her stuff and heard Dad talking on the phone about dredging up any past criminal behavior that the Jenners might have buried on Kyle. Either way, it looks like Dad may finally be shedding some light on Kyle's bastardly deeds."

And she doesn't even know about what he did to you.

"So, will your hot-and-spicy roommate be gracing us with his presence?" Val asked abruptly.

"What? No, I mean…I don't know," Caroline said, jarred from her deep thoughts.

"Well, I doubt he's at church. He doesn't seem like the seeking-redemption type."

"Honestly, I don't know what "*type*" he is," Caroline said grouchily.

Val's face lit up. "I'm sensing a tone. What did he do now? Tell me everything."

"Nothing, he's just…" How could she explain that, with a single sentence, Gabe could send her into a lust-filled state for which there was only one cure, and she was all too aware that he was just down the hall, able to take care of it?

"We wouldn't even have made it to the restaurant."

Why did he have to say things like that? For hours afterward, she had tossed and turned, imagining all the things they would have done, ready to scream in frustration. If things had gone better with Mike, Gabe wouldn't have been able to creep into her mind and make her think all kinds of naughty thoughts.

No, instead, the seed had been planted and firmly had taken root. Weeks of fantasizing and daydreaming about Gabe's body, his kiss, and his touch had been tormenting her, and now that she had tasted a sample, well…

Now, Caroline wanted Gabe in a bad, down-and-dirty, not-coming-up-for-air-for-days kinda way.

"Just what?" Val said. "Come on, stop holding out on me. I know there is something going on with Mr. Tall, Dark, and Pierced. He has this almost dangerous edge about him—"

"He's not dangerous, okay?" Caroline hadn't meant to snap, but she didn't like her sister describing Gabe that way. He wasn't dangerous, no matter how many times he'd told her he was bad news.

Val looked like Caroline had just kicked her dog. "Okay, I was only teasing."

"No, I'm sorry. He's just…weird."

Val's lips twitched like she was fighting a smile, and Caroline was happy her sister's good mood was restored.

"Weird is not the word I would use to describe him, but to each her own," Val said.

It wasn't Caroline's first choice either, but she really wasn't prepared to share her innermost thoughts and feelings on Gabe, especially when she wasn't even sure what her feelings were, beyond wanting to jump his bones.

"Where did you get that painting?" Val asked, looking at something over Caroline's shoulder.

"What paint—" Caroline paused as she studied the landscape canvas, taking in the beauty of the strokes. The mountains were a steely gray with white caps, sparsely covered by green trees. Clouds almost seemed to float over the light blue sky, and the green valley appeared lush and wild at the base of the mountain.

Caroline stood up and walked over to the painting. In the corner were the initials HM.

Who was HM?

"Well?" Val prodded.

"It's not mine," Caroline said, admiring the close-up details. "It's Gabe's."

"Huh, I wonder if he could get me one. It's gorgeous."

Yeah," Caroline said. *Curiouser and curiouser.*

"So, do you want to come over to Justin's for dinner tonight?"

"Hmmm." It was on the tip of Caroline's tongue to say no thanks, but Val added, "You have hardly been around Justin, and I want you to like him. Come on. Everett is a fantastic cook and—"

"Who's Everett?" Caroline walked back over to the couch and sat down, absently wondering whether or not Gabe would tell her who H. M. was if she asked.

"Justin's older brother."

"Justin's older brother, me, and you? Are you trying to set me up or something?" Caroline asked, amused.

Val actually laughed. "You and Everett? God, no. Justin's dad will be there and Ellie too."

Unease settled in the pit of Caroline's stomach. "Why are you laughing? Is thinking that my practically engaged sister might try to play matchmaker for me really so wild an idea?"

"No, it's just…Sorry, but…Everett is this super-nice guy, but he's kind of…emotionally damaged, and you're…"

"I'm what?" Caroline asked, glaring at her sister. "I'm not nice?"

"No, you're secure in yourself and who you are. You're strong and you're successful, and I just think he needs someone a little more…nurturing."

Caroline had been taking care of kittens for over a week—getting up with them, feeding them, making them poo, for God's sake—but she wasn't nurturing?

"Right," Caroline said, smoothing her hair out of her eyes as she stood. "I'm an ice queen. I forgot."

"Caroline, that's not what I—"

"You know, I've been back in this town for a little over a month, and I've gotten nothing but grief from my father, random freaks, and crazy women. Even the fucking checkout girl at Hall's Market has been giving me 'tude every time I go in there! The only people who are willing to give me a snowball's chance, I can count on one hand!"

"Maybe because they've never been screwed by you before," Val said sharply.

"You think I screwed you?" Caroline said, incredulous.

"Yes. I think you fucking bailed because Dad wasn't going to let you do whatever the fuck you wanted, and you left Ellie and me behind to pick up the damn pieces."

Caroline knew Val had been upset with her for leaving Rock Canyon at first, but she'd never given any indication she'd felt betrayed. But regardless, Val's assumptions beat at the flames of Caroline's temper, causing it to flare. "You don't know *anything* about what happened back then, so why don't you shut the fuck up, Valerie?"

"The only reason I don't know things is because you don't talk to me! Since you've been back, it's been all surface stuff and casual conversations. Every time I get too personal, you shut me out."

"Or maybe I'm trying to protect you."

"I am a grown-ass woman who has managed to survive this long without you shielding me from the bogeyman. Is this about Dad and his shady dealings?"

Shady dealings? She knew their dad hadn't always walked the straight and narrow when he wanted something, but...

"What are you talking about?"

Val seemed surprised that Caroline didn't know. "Ellie found a file with all of this evidence against Dad that could potentially put him in prison. I used it to...well, to get him to leave Justin and his family alone. He was threatening to have their farm taken away, and I used the folder as 'incentive' for him to back off."

Caroline believed her. It figured that their father wouldn't stop at intimidation, especially if it came to one of his daughters doing something he didn't approve of. He'd tried to do the same thing to her when she'd left home, but she'd had nothing left to lose.

"So where's the evidence now?" Val asked.

"Ellie has it."

The tense moment wasn't lost on Caroline. Part of her wanted to drop all the defenses and tell Val the hard stuff, but she was afraid Val would pity her. Or worse, challenge Kyle to a duel. Val was finally settled and happy; she didn't need to be dragged down by Caroline's problems. She'd been through enough on her own.

Wanting to reassure her sister, Caroline reached out to Val and pulled her in for a hug. At first, Val held away stiffly but slowly relaxed in her arms.

"I know you think I'm shutting you out, and I'm sorry. Just give me time, okay?"

Val nodded against her shoulder before pulling away. "I know you had it rough after Dad made you leave. I just missed you and want to be close again, like we were when we were kids."

That seems like a lifetime ago.

"We will be."

"Okay," Val said, gathering up her purse. "Well, I have to get home. I'm going to try to impress Justin and his family by making a cake."

"What kind of cake?" Caroline asked.

"The kind that comes from a box and takes about an hour to bake."

Caroline saw her sister out and closed the door with a thud. Leaning back against the cool wood, she ran her hands over her face and hair. Her head was pounding, and she knew it was part emotional exhaustion, part stress. It seemed like the more time she spent with Val, the more Caroline wanted to tell her everything, if only to unburden herself. But how fair would that be? Val would be ready to drag Kyle into the police station and press charges, but so many things could go wrong. Kyle was dangerous—Caroline knew that better than anyone—and if she tried to bring him down and failed...

He would hurt the people you love to get to you.

Suddenly, the apartment walls seemed to be closing in on her. She wanted to get out of there but had nowhere to go, really. She was antsy and irritated, with no outlet.

Heading into the kitchen to grab a bottle of water from the fridge, she noticed a drawing hanging from it: two wheels and a set of handlebars surrounded by flames.

Moriarty's Custom Motorcycles
121 Main St.
Rock Canyon, Idaho

It seemed like fate kept giving her little pushes in Gabe's direction. The question was, did she want to test her resolve?

GABE WAS SWEATING like a fiend in the closed shell of the firehouse. Moving around the work benches he'd bought on craigslist and the office furniture in the back was getting to him, and he'd already taken off his shirt, which hadn't helped as much as he'd hoped.

He wanted to be able to open the shop before his second rent check was due, and that meant working fast and hard. He'd have asked Chase for help, but his friend went to church with his wife, while Gabe hadn't gone to church since... well, ever.

Grabbing a bottle of water from the cooler, he took a few gulps and then poured the rest over his head and shoulders, rubbing the cold liquid across his skin. It felt amazing but did little to alleviate the heat.

Of course, it wasn't just the stuffiness of the room that was getting to him. It also was sharing a small space with a woman he couldn't get off his mind.

"Wow, now that's something you'd see in a chick flick for sure."

Gabe turned quickly and found Caroline standing in the doorway of his shop, as if his thoughts had brought her to him by force of will alone.

"What are you doing here?" he asked, sounding harsher than he meant.

"I saw the flier design on the fridge, and I was bored," she said, either oblivious of or ignoring his obvious irritation. He guessed it was the latter.

"So you just thought you would sneak up on me when I'm trying to work?"

"I thought maybe you could use some help moving things and setting up," she said, her long ponytail flipping back as she shrugged. "But if you don't need me, I'll go do something else." She spun around, her shapely legs walking away from him in dark jeans and knee-high boots. They did nothing to decrease his desire for her.

Eating up the floor between them, he reached out to touch her arm.

"What?" she said without turning around. "I know your first instinct is to be a complete asshole to everyone, but I am not in the mood to take your shit today."

She turned to face him and for what felt much longer than a few moments, their gazes fused until he could have sworn sparks erupted.

Really? When did you turn into a fucking poet?

He could tell himself that what he felt for Caroline was just physical—his appreciation for a beautiful woman—but he'd be lying his ass off. He was protective of Caroline, wanting her safe and sound. Just being in such close quarters amped up those feelings—feelings he didn't want or need.

Especially since she doesn't even know who you really are.

"I know. I know I can be a dick—"

"You said it, not me," she said.

"But I would appreciate the help." She seemed to be waiting for something else, and he added, gritting his teeth, "Please."

"Fine," she said, heading over to one of the work stools. "Where do you want this?"

Chapter Sixteen

"Where have all the real men gone?"

—Miss Know It All

TWO HOURS LATER, Gabe had to hand it to her; for a short girl, Caroline was damn strong. She hadn't balked at the weight of some of the steel benches or whined about being hot. She'd grunted, laughed, and groaned along with him as they'd lifted the last bench into place.

"I think I'm done for the day," he said.

Her voice was breathless as she wiped her hand across her forehead. "I should probably get home to take care of the kittens anyway."

He grabbed a water from the cooler and handed it to her. As he watched her hold the cold bottle to her neck, his eyes were drawn to the swell of her breasts, shiny with sweat.

"I appreciate the help," he said.

"No problem. I needed to work off some tension anyway," she said, finally opening the bottle of water to take a long pull.

"Why are you tense?" he asked, his mind suddenly taking a dark turn. "Did something else happen with that guy who attacked you?"

"What? Oh, no, it's just family stuff. My sister actually," she said, setting her bottle down and walking around him. "By the way, who is HM?"

"What?" he said, surprised by her straightforward question.

"The painting you hung in the living room. It's signed by an HM, and I was curious how you know him…or her."

He took several gulps from another bottle of water and tossed the empty plastic in the trash. "HM stands for Honey Moriarty. My sister."

"I didn't know you had a sister," she said.

"You never asked."

"No, I guess I didn't. I guess I didn't feel it was appropriate, considering that you've said several times—if I stay out of your business, you'll stay out of mine," she said, taking a long draw of her water before continuing. "Although so far, you haven't really done your part, have you?"

"What do you mean?"

"Well, no matter how many times I say I don't need your help, you always seem to be there. It's pretty heroic, actually. Besides, you aren't really the sharing type anyway."

He knew she had chosen "heroic" because it would needle him, but really, he was amused. Over the last week, he'd found that the walls between them were slowly being chipped away, at least on his side.

Though it was still killing him that she wouldn't tell him about the man who'd attacked her or why.

"That's interesting, because every time I ask you about your past or about the guy who assaulted you, you change the subject. Care to bare your soul and divulge all your secrets?"

Caroline sighed loudly. "Point taken."

He waited for her to continue, but instead she said, "So show me some of these designs of yours."

Apparently, sharing time was over. "You like motorcycles?"

"Sure. Had one for a while in Arizona. It was awesome."

Just one more thing that made her amazing.

"What kind did you have?" he asked.

"I had a 2010 Ducati Streetfighter."

He whistled. "What happened to it?"

"I sold it when I moved to Detroit. Too cold most of the year to have one," she said, walking into what would be his office.

He grabbed some of his designs from his portfolio and came up alongside her. The sweet smell of her lotion or perfume mixed with her own scent had him leaning closer as he opened the large folder. "These are the first plans I drew up for my bike, so you can see how it changed," he said.

"Why do you call your motorcycle Baby Blue?"

He shrugged. "My sister is a big George Strait fan."

"Not you?"

"No."

"Where is she?"

"Who?"

"Your sister."

He didn't plan to go there with her, but when he opened his mouth, the words that came out were honest. "She's in a private-care facility in Sun Valley."

"Oh my God, why?"

He clenched his jaw, ashamed. Gabe didn't want to answer and considered blowing her off, but what good would it do? All she had to do was Google his name, and all his dirty little secrets would be laid out for her to see.

What happened to keeping the past under wraps? To a fresh start?

Gabe realized that if he'd learned one thing about Caroline, it was that she knew how it felt to have people judge you based on your past. And if he couldn't tell her about his, then how could he expect her to be honest with him about her problems? It all came down to trust. And though it had been a long time since he'd given his to anyone, for some reason, he felt like this woman could handle it.

"She was in an accident and suffered a brain injury. She has good days and bad, but she needs constant care."

Caroline said nothing, but to his surprise, she pressed her warm hand against his shoulder, branding him with her touch. "I'm so sorry."

Her pity, the last thing he needed from her, had him jerking his shoulder out from under her palm. "Don't be. It's my fault she's in there."

By the surprised intake of breath, he figured she wasn't prepared for that. Turning, he showed her his other arm.

"I got this scar from the same accident. And along with the scar, I got a five-year sentence in the Nevada State Prison System for driving under the influence and being involved in an accident that caused significant bodily harm."

He caught the guarded look on her face, and it pissed him off. "I told you. I'm not a good guy. I'm a selfish fuck who drove drunk because I caught my baby sister kissing my best friend. I shoved her on the back of my bike without making sure her helmet was fastened and on the way home, I overcorrected and skidded across the pavement. I don't remember much—except waking up in the hospital, handcuffed to the bed, and being told my sister would never be the same. I should have gotten longer in prison, but with good behavior, they let me out early. I've been trying like hell to make it up to her, but I'll never be able to. I am a damaged fucking individual, princess."

Turning away from her, he slapped the portfolio closed and took a deep, shaky breath. "I wasn't going to tell you any of that. I just figured you would find out somehow anyway, so why not get it out of the way? I feel like you keep looking for something more to me, but what you know about me is it. There's no deep down, no mistaking my true character. I am bad news."

He waited, listening for the tap of her retreating feet or the slam of the door, but only silence met his ears and then the soft sound of shoes on the cement floor—only they got closer to him instead of farther away.

Fingers trailed feather-light touches over his lower back. "This scar on your back? Is that from the accident?"

Her caress made his skin tingle as he shook his head. "I was knocked down by one of my mother's boyfriends and landed on a glass table."

"What about here?" Her hand had moved to his right shoulder.

"It was a tattoo I had removed. In prison, you're safer if you belong, so—"

"I understand," she said, cutting him off.

Had she heard the pain in his voice, or did she really understand? He turned around before she could point out any more scars. "What are you doing?"

She looked him in the eye and touched the side of his neck, where his tattoo began and spread all the way down, past his shoulder and over his chest. "You say you're damaged. That you're bad news and won't ever change."

"Yeah?"

To his surprise, she dropped her hand to his and brought it up to her collarbone, where his finger felt a rough, puckered line.

"This is a knife wound—just a scratch, really—that I got from a man who used to come see me dance at the strip club. He was constantly asking me out, and I always let him down easy. But one night, after I'd had a shitty day, I told him I would never go out with an old, ugly fuck like him. He was waiting by my car when I got off work."

His rage blazed at this phantom from her past. "What happened?"

"I pulled a move I'd learned from one of the bouncers. Even though he still cut me, I was able to pick up a handful of gravel and throw it in his face. I made it to the front door of the club, and he took off. They arrested him on assault charges, and it turned out he had an outstanding warrant. I never saw him again."

Caroline pulled him closer, lifting her arm for him to see a jagged scar along her forearm. "This was from a broken beer bottle I got sliced with when a woman came into my bar in San Antonio, looking for her husband. She didn't take it well when she found out he had a girlfriend on the side, and when I stepped in to stop her from attacking him, she sliced me."

He couldn't stop his hand from sliding up over her soft skin until it rested on the back of her neck, his fingers pressing into her flesh until she tilted her chin up to meet his gaze.

"What's your point with all the show-and-tell, Caroline?"

She reached out and smoothed his chest with her hand. "I don't care how damaged you are, because I am just as broken, maybe more so."

Her words tore at him, twisting him up inside as his other hand cupped the back of her head. "You don't want to go here with me, princess. I'm only going to break your heart."

The laugh that passed those beautiful lips was bitter and sad. "Trust me, my heart was shattered long before I ever met you."

Gabe wanted her, wanted to believe that he could find comfort in her body without the complications that would inevitably come, but he'd seen her heart firsthand. She had one. It might be wrapped up in a mile-thick layer of cowhide, but a part of Caroline Willis was still open to new emotions. New love.

And he wasn't.

But he wanted to kiss her anyway.

He dropped his head until his lips hovered above hers, and he watched as they parted, the closer he came. Her hot breath teased his mouth, and he couldn't stop while she was warm and willing. He might not get another chance to taste her, and while a better man would have walked away, he wasn't that guy.

So he took her mouth with his, sweeping his tongue inside, savoring the sweet and salty taste of her. His fingers slid up into her ponytail, and he knew he was being rough, that he should slow down, but the way her hands gripped his shoulders told him she didn't mind. He took her soft moan into his mouth and, slipping one hand out of her hair and down her body, he did what he'd been dreaming of for weeks. Gripping one of her lush ass cheeks, he lifted her onto his desk and stepped between her legs.

Damn, but his cock did love pressing against her.

Her legs hooked around him, bringing him closer as he dragged up her tank top. Gripping the fabric in his hands, he broke the kiss, leaning his forehead against hers, his breath coming fast and hard.

"You have exactly three seconds to get out of here before I do everything I've been thinking about since the first day I saw you. You decide. Now."

Her hands slid into the back pockets of his jeans and, gripping his ass, brought him back into her body, giving him her answer.

Using both hands, he pulled her tank up and over, tossing it across the room as he took in her lush breasts, curving above the cups of her bra. Covering them with his hands, he squeezed them, molding them into his palms until the gasps and moans escaping her were too much.

"You are so fucking sexy," he said, bending down to tease the lobe of her ear, drawing it into his mouth with his teeth and loving that she countered his teases with the scrape of her nails on his skin.

"Oh, yeah?" Her voice was hushed and breathy.

He reached between them and cupped her through her jeans. "Hell yes."

Her head fell back, and he took advantage, kissing below her chin and delivering open mouth nips and sucks until he reached the top of her breasts. He'd been dreaming of her like this, and as badly as he wanted to savor the taste of her skin, he found himself feeling frenzied. What if she changed her mind? She had to know that he'd let her go in an instant if she asked.

God, please, don't let her ask that. It might just kill him.

Reaching behind her back, Gabe released her bra, and after slipping it down her arms, he cupped one breast in each of his hands before dipping down to take one of her nipples into his mouth. Her hand cupped the back of his head as he closed his lips around her and sucked hard, gently grazing the peak with his teeth until she was writhing under his ministrations. Her soft cries were music to his ears and encouraged him to experiment. He wanted to please her, to make her feel safe and cherished.

Cherished? You need to stop thinking like that, man. This is sex—raw and hot, heat-of-the-moment play, and the minute it's over, she's gonna walk away.

Which is exactly what he'd been looking for, right? He'd wanted sex with no strings, just pure physical release. So why did the thought of meaningless sex with Caroline make him almost hesitate going further?

"Oh, Gabe," she whispered softly.

It was exactly how he'd imagined she'd say it.

Gabe pulled away from her breast and moved his other hand down her body until he had the button of her jeans flicked open. The zipper was tricky one-handed, but when it finally opened, he pushed his hand down the front of her jeans. His fingers slipped inside her panties, pressing between her folds until he found the hard button of her clit. When her hips jerked up, he leaned over and placed his mouth against the shell of her ear.

"The ride's not over yet, princess."

Chapter Seventeen

"Sex is supposed to be messy, chaotic…and fun.
Otherwise, what's the point?"

—Miss Know It All

"Ohhh!" Caroline cried as Gabe swiftly lay her flat on the desk.

Before she could move, he was removing her boots, tossing them to the side so fast, it caused laughter to bubble up her throat.

"Are we in a hurry?"

Her teasing was met with such heat, she sucked in her breath. Sure, she'd thought of sex with Gabe, imagined all the mechanics, but the raw wanting in his eyes made her weak. His gaze was possessive, and as his hands started inching her jeans down over her hips, every touch felt like a brand against her skin. His lips touched every inch of flesh he revealed, and she wasn't sure anymore whether she was arching away from or toward his mouth.

She had always liked to be in control, had never just let a man do what he wanted, but after their turbulent first meeting and the last few weeks of back-and-forth, somewhere along the way, she had begun to trust Gabe. She trusted him to know what she would like and that he wouldn't hurt her.

At least not physically, she amended, as her jeans hit mid-thigh, and his mouth hovered over her hips. There was no way she'd trust Gabe with more than her body. Even if he wasn't the bastard she'd originally thought, she still couldn't picture a future with him.

She felt the hot, wet press of his mouth through the black cotton of her panties, and the hard nub of his tongue piercing made her squeal with delight, the sensation dragging her out of her head for just a moment. He stopped tonguing her long enough to take her jeans all the way off, pulling her panties down her legs until she was completely exposed. It wasn't the first time she'd been bared to a man in the daylight, but as the fabric of her underwear scraped softly down her skin, she felt nervous and jittery. Maybe because his hands were so gentle, suddenly in no hurry to rid her of this last scrap of clothing.

And then her panties circled her ankle before, with one final pull, they silently fell to the floor.

Gabe sat down in his office chair, gliding forward until he was right in front of her. Then he spread her legs and hooked them over his shoulders. As she looked down the line of her body to meet his dark gaze, she felt too exposed, the whole situation too intimate. Most of the men she'd been with hadn't been all that interested in foreplay, and she'd never had a man in the position to see...well, everything. She started to tell him to stop, but he spoke first.

"Hang on."

Without further ado, his big hands cupped her ass and brought her to his mouth. The wet heat sent her body lifting off the desk as the first sweep of his tongue set her aflame. Pushing his tongue inside her, Gabe flicked that metal bar against her clit in hard, swift strokes that had her nails digging into the wood to the point of pain.

God, sex had never been this intense or hot. Maybe it was the tongue ring or the way he took charge—never asking, just doing what he wanted—that had her dripping wet and throbbing. Then that familiar pulsing began, and whether it was his skill or the fact that her last orgasm had been over two months ago, she was suddenly lost moments later, shaking from the inside out—and it was a-fucking-mazing.

When she finally started to come down, all she could think was that she wanted to do it again and again and again.

The sound of metal on metal drew her gaze back to Gabe, who had already unbuckled his belt and was standing there with his jeans spread open, revealing the tops of his boxer briefs and the hard bumps of his abs above them. She stared at his six-pack, and a silly smile spread across her lips.

"You know, when you came out of the shower that first time in a towel, I thought your abs were hypnotizing."

He stopped his movements, and she saw a square condom wrapper in his hand. "What?"

"Yeah, I pretty much think you could get away with walking around town nude, and no one would mind."

"Have you lost your damn mind?" he asked before ripping the package open with his teeth.

"Just stating the facts. You…are…fucking…ho—"

Before she finished, he was kissing her, his hands cradling her face as his tongue slipped into her mouth, sweeping along her teeth. He tasted musky, and she realized it was her essence.

When he pulled away, he was sucking in air as he said, "For the last two weeks, I have done nothing but think about you. About how good you smell and the way you would feel if I could just get you into my arms. The thought of being this close to you has haunted me, and I have a feeling I'm never going to be able to get the reality of you out of my head."

What did he mean? Was this not just a one-time thing? No, if his behavior hadn't shown her how much he despised intimacy, he had told her as much.

Caroline reached up to pull his mouth back down to hers, wanting to cut off anything else he might say. Gabe let her take the lead for a few minutes, but when he pulled away from her to push his jeans down, she saw his cock stretching out the fabric of his boxer briefs and sucked in her breath. He was just so beautiful, so perfectly put together. She ran her hand over his flat stomach to the top of his boxers and slid her hand inside, gripping his velvety breadth, and pumped him with her hand. Caroline rubbed her thumb over the tip of him, and his cock jerked in her hand.

He grabbed her wrist and lifted her hand from his shorts. "Not that I don't like the way you're touching me, but I want you too bad to wait."

Most guys would have sat back and let her continue, hoping it would turn into her going down on them. The fact that Gabe wanted her so bad he couldn't wait to be inside her was new and tantalizing.

And it turned her on so bad, she was ready to leap off the table and tackle him.

It was a fantastic feeling, and as he shoved his boxers down his legs, she licked her lips, watching him roll the length of latex over himself.

Without another word, he stepped between her legs and grabbed her ass with both hands. As he lifted her up, she wrapped her legs around his hard waist and rubbed against the stiff erection pressing at her entrance. She felt the brick wall at her back as he adjusted himself and slipped inside, inch by inch, slowly tormenting her until her eyes rolled back, and she whimpered with impatience. She didn't want slow and sweet. She wanted fast, crazy, buildings-falling-down-around-them sex, and to get her point across, she gripped his shoulders and rolled her hips sharply. He looked up at her, their eyes locking across the inches, and she saw need in those dark depths...but also uncertainty.

Gabe? Uncertain?

She must be losing her mind.

Suddenly, he thrust up, hard and deep, seating himself all the way inside her, and the motion left them pressed tightly against the wall. They were so close, eyes and mouths close enough to touch, yet he didn't kiss her or say anything. Still, their breath mingled with each movement, and he never looked away.

Caroline had had sex, had been fucked—but she'd never had a guy watch her so intently. It was like he was searching for an answer in her expression while he took her. But it didn't matter what the question was; she wasn't prepared for this.

When he slipped out again and pumped her several times with quick strokes, she closed her eyes, breaking the eye contact to hang on as each zing of pleasure shot through her body. She tried to concentrate on the way her body felt and to push those dark, searching eyes from her mind.

Her moans gained pitch with each pass, and she buried her lips into his shoulder as her muscles clenched, and her second orgasm of the day brought about wave after wave of relief. Spent and relaxed, she held on as he shouted her name, a warm smile spreading across her lips when she felt his cock flex inside her as he came. His chest heaved against her, and while she waited for him to collect himself, she drew lazy patterns over his back.

Besides, she was quite out of breath herself.

He pulled away enough to look down at her. "If you want to go again, you might have to give me a minute."

A breathless giggle escaped her as she admitted, "When you said sex with you was a ride, you weren't just whistlin' Dixie."

"Whistlin' Dixie? Who are you, Granny Clampett?"

"My mom used to say it. She was originally from Mississippi and moved here when she was thirteen."

His harsh laugh caused her stomach to flip-flop all over. She'd never heard him laugh, and damn, it was sexy. But Gabe's laugh also sounded hoarse, like he didn't use it very often. She'd always loved to make people laugh, especially as a kid.

Involuntarily, she smoothed her fingertips across his lips, lingering on the edges and then trailing up to the crinkles at the edge of his eyes.

"You searching for more scars?"

"No," she said, removing her hand. For just a minute, she had forgotten this was a fluke—a one-time thing—and had been trying to memorize the moment. As if she wanted more.

Unwrapping her legs from his waist, she felt him slide from her body and shivered as her muscles clenched again. Still, Gabe didn't release her right away, holding her at her waist until she dropped her arms from his shoulders.

She could definitely go another round, but she didn't plan on making a habit of jumping Gabe whenever she had an itch her vibrator wouldn't satisfy. He was a self-proclaimed bad guy, and although she wasn't perfect, she did want to find someone she could have a future with. A mature adult with his life together.

Besides, if she was ever going to breach her father's defenses, there was no way she was going to do it with a tattooed ex-con by her side. If her father pitched a fit at Val's squeaky clean former marine Justin Silverton, he'd have another heart attack if she introduced him to Gabe.

Damn, have you always been a snob, and it's just been lying dormant? You aren't exactly the type of girl nice guys bring home to Mama…

"I should get dressed and get back home. The kittens are probably hungry, and I—"

"You don't have to explain," Gabe said as he walked to where his briefs and jeans lay. "I get what this was."

"You do?"

"Yeah," he said, his back to her. She saw him drop the condom into the wastebasket before he stepped into his boxer briefs, pulling them up and over those hard, drool-worthy calves and thighs until his sculpted ass disappeared beneath the navy cotton.

She bit her lip to shut her mouth. If she didn't stop staring at him, drool was going to start dribbling down her chin.

He turned around to face her as he shook out his jeans and pulled them back on. "You were horny as hell, and I was available. I understand, and believe me, I didn't mind."

Okay, so maybe she'd been thinking almost the exact same thing, but that didn't mean he could just assume that she was using him to get her rocks off.

Why not? That's what it was. Why can't he call a spade a spade?

Because despite her best efforts not to let it get to her, when he'd looked into her eyes, part of her had felt like he could see into her soul.

"Is that what it was for you?"

He had the damn nerve to shrug. Bastard.

"Huh." She moved over to where he'd tossed her jeans and took several long, calming breaths.

"I say something wrong? Was this supposed to be something more?"

"No, of course you're right," she said, pulling her jeans on without her underwear. "I helped you move your shit around just so you would fuck me. I had this whole thing planned. I'm like some kind of moving prostitute. I help you move, and you—"

He pulled her to him so fast, her mouth snapped shut.

"I think I liked you better when your mouth was making those little moans against my neck."

She jerked away from him. "You're a pig."

"Wanna get dirty?"

"Hell no," she said, gathering up her shirt and undergarments and heading toward the front of the building to get dressed. "In fact, the next time I'm feeling horny, I'll be sure to go elsewhere to get my jollies off."

Her shoulders stiffened when Gabe called, "I'll see you at home, princess."

"Asshole," she muttered as she slammed the office door.

Why are you pissed at him? He gave you an incredible orgasm—twice, in fact—and you act like he insulted you.

As she climbed into her car, it struck her; she'd been deluding herself when she thought maybe he'd felt something more. The whole time she'd been worried he might be thinking this would lead to a more permanent situation, maybe even a relationship, but the minute it was over, he was all business.

So were you.

Had she wanted him to want more from her than just sex? She'd been telling herself for weeks that he was not the guy she wanted to make a fresh start, yet she was drawn to him and not just because he was her type. She'd seen subtle signs that maybe he wasn't all that he seemed. That this was the strongest attraction she'd had for a man in years, and now that she'd given in, she couldn't shake the desire for more.

Lord, was she a hot mess. How the hell was she going to survive living with him, knowing exactly what he could do to a woman?

Chapter Eighteen

"Communication is the key to any healthy relationship...which explains why the silent treatment is a woman's favorite form of torture."

—Miss Know It All

CAROLINE DROVE HOME to feed the kittens, but once she was done, she didn't really feel like sticking around and hashing things out with Gabe. She'd calmed down enough to realize she had blown up at him over nothing, let her own issues fuel her crazy, and now not only had she slept with him, but she'd been *that* girl, the one who wigs out after sex and scares the hell out of a guy.

Looking for something to take the edge off, she grabbed a beer from the fridge and chugged down half of it without taking a breath. Water would've probably been better, but despite her reasonable deduction that the awkwardness after sex had been her fault, stealing Gabe's last beer gave her perverse pleasure.

He was going to be pissed, and she didn't even care. Actually, she was sort of looking forward to it.

Jumping in the shower, she cleaned herself up and decided to head over to Justin's family farm for dinner after all. She needed advice, and the only person she felt comfortable enough asking was Val.

Thirty minutes later, she was kicking up dust with her tires down the long dirt road leading to the Silverton farm. Green fields went on for miles, the only trees being closer to the white ranch house, tall green pines to block the wind. As she pulled up next to Val's truck, nervousness settled in the pit of her stomach. What had she been thinking to drive all the way out here without calling? What if Val told her to take off?

Val would never bail on you. Ever.

But still, Justin's family was here. How was she going to get Val alone without drawing attention to herself? She might as well wait and call her a little later.

Hand on the gear shift, she was just about to throw her car into reverse when the front door opened, and Val stepped out onto the porch. A few seconds later, Ellie followed, and before she could escape, both of her sisters were standing next to her driver's side door, staring in at her.

"I thought you couldn't make it," Val said.

"I changed my mind," Caroline said, opening the door. "If the invitation is still open."

"Of course it's open," Ellie said, pulling the car door open wider. "We were just getting ready to eat."

As Caroline stepped out, a dark smudge on Ellie's cheek caught her eye, despite the layer of cover-up she'd tried to apply. Reaching out her hand, she touched Ellie's face. "What happened?"

"I got into a fight with one of my girlfriends at Buck's," Ellie said. It was entirely plausible, but Caroline didn't buy it. Not with the way Ellie's eyes shifted away. Her baby sister might be a hell of an actress, but she couldn't fool Caroline.

"Don't get me started," Val said, shaking her head. "I'm just thankful she didn't get arrested, or I might have had to bail her out."

Caroline didn't miss Ellie's pleading eyes and decided to back her sister's play. For now.

"Val, I just wanted to say I'm sorry for the way I acted earlier. I've just been a little on edge lately."

"You don't have to apologize. I know I handled my invitation badly. You've got a lot going on, and I didn't mean to lash out at you."

"No, look, I haven't been exactly available to you, and I know my taking off twelve years ago was sudden, but there are things you don't know. Things that are hard for me to talk about. But that last argument with Dad...He asked me to do something I just couldn't do, and when I refused, he told me to get out and never come back."

"He said you refused to go to college at Boise State," Val said, her voice laced with confusion.

It was time. With Kyle's attack weighing on her mind, she had been considering telling her sisters, especially now that their father knew.

Before she changed her mind, Caroline drew in a deep breath and her courage. "I couldn't go to Boise State because the guy who raped me went there."

Both of her sisters gasped, but Val was the one who reacted first. She pulled Caroline into her arms roughly, squeezing her so hard she almost couldn't breathe.

"Oh my God, Caroline, why didn't you tell me?"

Tears pricked Caroline's eyes, and she swallowed hard. "I didn't tell anyone."

"But why?" Ellie asked, joining in on the hug.

"Partly, to protect you guys," Caroline said, second-guessing herself. If she told Val everything, her sister might lose her shit and confront Kyle. "The other half was because I was afraid no one would believe me."

"Of course we'd believe you! Who wouldn't believe you?" Ellie said, pulling away to look Caroline right in the eye.

At least, that's where she assumed Ellie was looking, but her vision was too blurry to know for sure. Val pulled away too, but she was giving off waves of rage that told Caroline her prediction wasn't far off the mark.

"I want to know who it was," Val said. "I'm going to kill him. Eviscerate him. Stake him to the ground in Justin's cornfield and run him over with the harvester."

Caroline was already shaking her head, despite the insane urge to laugh at her five-foot, hundred-pound sister taking Kyle out. "I can't tell you."

"What?" Ellie and Val both cried, but only Val added, "Why the hell not?"

"Because what good would it do? It's in the past, and if I was going to do something, I should have done it right after it happened, but I was so afraid—" She caught herself before she finished saying that she was afraid Kyle would hurt them and said instead, "You two just need to be careful, okay? Make sure you aren't going off alone, especially at night."

Val opened her mouth to say something else, but Justin popped his head out at that moment, flashing an apologetic smile. "Sorry to interrupt, but dinner's on the table," Justin said, raising his hand to wave. "Hey, Caroline, glad you could make it."

"Thanks, Justin."

"We'll be in," Val said, waiting until he'd shut the door again before hissing, "This is not over. I will have that bastard's name."

"Down, girl," Caroline said, reaching out for Val's hand. "I appreciate you wanting to avenge my honor, but I don't need you to go all vigilante justice, okay? I just need you to be careful and take care of yourself." Caroline held up her hand, stopping Val's protest. "Let's just enjoy dinner with your future in-laws."

Val started sputtering that they weren't engaged and the normal, safe conversation warmed Caroline, who was trying hard to get her emotions in check. For years, she'd imagined what it would feel like to unburden herself on someone else, and even though she hadn't shared everything, it was still relieving to have this one secret off her chest.

And to know that her sisters had been supportive. Between Ellie's compassion and Val's protective nature, Caroline felt cherished and loved; she had forgotten how good it felt to be accepted.

Val headed for the porch first, while Ellie and Caroline trailed behind. Caroline touched Ellie's arm and pointed to her eye.

"This better not happen again," Caroline whispered.

"I told you, it—"

"What are you two talking about without me?" Val asked, holding the door open for them.

"Nothing," Ellie said, quickly.

"I was just giving her a little advice about what to do in a fight," Caroline said, catching Ellie's eye meaningfully. "The first rule is, don't get hit."

Ellie pushed past Val to get inside.

"What the hell is her problem?" Val asked, rubbing her chest where Ellie had bumped her.

"She's a Willis; we've never been very good at taking advice."

GABE HAD BEEN stewing for hours at the apartment, waiting for Caroline to get home. Despite all the warning signs that getting involved with her would lead to disaster, he hadn't been able to stop once they'd started, and sure enough, it had ended with him pissing her off.

That hadn't been his intention, of course. He'd been nervous as hell, as hard as it was to believe, and when he got nervous, he said stupid shit. He just hadn't wanted her to read too much into his reaction to their sexcapade—which had been fucking mind-blowing. He'd been reduced to a sixteen-year-old kid, shocked as hell that the hottest girl he knew wanted to "do it," and he'd embarrassed himself. For a minute there, when their gazes had met as he slid into her, he'd thought there was a connection. Something more than sex, more than just lust. As if their souls had recognized one another.

Something was wrong with him, that was for damn sure. Flowery thoughts and obsessing over a woman just wasn't his style.

Still, he'd wanted to give her time to calm down, so hopefully they could have a reasonable conversation. He hadn't been prepared to walk into a disaster zone.

The formula bottles for the kittens had been left on the counter without even being rinsed out. Clothes were littered across the bathroom floor, and her towel was thrown across the back of the couch.

So, she was in a hurry. You aren't exactly Mr. Clean when you're rushed.

Heading over to the fridge, he'd opened it and reached in, wanting to sit down with a cold beer while he tried to find something to watch.

Only there was no beer.

There had been one can last night when he'd gone to bed, and he hadn't been home at all today. Which meant Caroline had come in here and taken his last beer, just to be spiteful.

Maybe she planned to pick up more on her way home.

It was almost nine, though, so he wasn't holding his breath.

A knock at the door interrupted his dark thoughts. Who the hell would come calling at nine o'clock on a Sunday? He pulled open the door and found a pale blond guy standing on the porch. The guy seemed surprised to see him.

"I'm looking for Caroline."

"She's not here," Gabe said gruffly, eyeing the blue suit the guy was sporting. It looked expensive, but then again, the last suit he'd worn had been a rental, so what did he know?

"Will you just let her know that Kyle came by?"

There was something about the guy Gabe didn't like, and it wasn't just that he looked slicker than snot.

"Sure, Skip, when she gets home, that's the first thing I'll do."

Ole Kyle didn't like that. "It's important."

"I'm sure it is, but I gotta ask, if you need to see her so bad, why don't you just give her a call?"

That made Kyle angry, if the deep red of his skin was any indication. "I lost her number."

"Well, that sounds like a personal problem, Kyle," Gabe said and started to shut the door.

"Kyle?" Caroline's voice sounded from the bottom of the stairs.

Gabe opened the door again as Kyle turned toward her.

"Caroline. I was hoping we could talk."

Caroline paled for a half second before Kyle started down the stairs, and every muscle in Gabe's body tensed. *This is the guy.*

Gabe came out the door with a vengeance and grabbed Kyle by the back of the jacket. There was no way he was letting the fucker take one more step toward Caroline.

"What the fuck do you think you're doing?" Kyle shouted as he tried to shake Gabe's grip. Gabe let Kyle's jacket go long enough to allow Kyle to turn around and face him. "I'll sue—"

Gabe's fist connected with Kyle's pretty face, and he stumbled back against the railing.

"*Gabe!*" Caroline screamed, starting up the stairs. "Don't!"

But he wasn't going to stop, not until he scared the piss out of the little prick.

"This is the guy, right?" Gabe said, collecting the front of Kyle's shirt in his hand, ignoring the blood from Kyle's split lip as it dripped onto his hand.

"I didn't tell you that," she said.

"You didn't have to," Gabe said, pushing and shoving Kyle down the metal steps. The fact that she hadn't denied it told him all he needed to know. "Get out of the way, Caroline."

Though Gabe might have sounded calm, he was anything but. He reached the ground with Kyle and knocked him backward with a hard upper cut. He wanted to see this piece of shit quake in his fancy suit, for him to beg Gabe to stop.

Caroline tried to get between them. "Gabe, you can't do this. He's a lawyer, and you have a record! Think about it!"

Gabe's arms shook with the need to twist Kyle's neck until it snapped, but her words broke through the fog of rage. He couldn't go back to prison, not with Honey depending on him. And what would happen to Caroline if he was locked up? If he wasn't here, would Kyle hurt her?

With one last punch to Kyle's middle, dropping him to the ground, Gabe stood over him menacingly.

"You stay away from her, do you hear me? Do not come to this house again, or I'll make sure you disappear."

Kyle groaned and rolled onto his side, coughing. He looked up at them with hatred and rasped, "I'll be pressing charges."

"No, you won't," Gabe said, rubbing his sore knuckles. "People might start asking questions about what you were doing here, and I doubt Caroline will back you up when the police want an explanation."

Without waiting for Kyle to say more, Gabe turned to Caroline and put his hand on the small of her back. "Come on."

She let him gently propel her up the stairs, and when they got through the door, he shut and dead bolted it behind them. Caroline stood by the back of the couch, her shoulders shaking. As Gabe drew closer to her, all his earlier irritation melted away, and he just wanted to comfort her.

Wrapping his arms around her from behind, he pulled her back against him. His palms rubbed her bare skin, and he rocked her. He wanted to ask her again why Kyle was harassing her, but by the quake of her body, he didn't think she'd be up for talking yet.

It killed him that this strong, beautiful woman didn't feel like she had anyone she could turn to. Nobody to keep her safe.

But it wasn't true. And he wished he was the kind of guy to tell her that. That he could be open about what he was feeling, but he wasn't very good with words. He was the thug, the tough guy who used violence to get his point across.

Apparently, he hadn't changed as much as he'd thought. He'd lost his head over a threat to his woman, and he'd dealt with it the only way he knew how.

You just called her your woman.

Deep down, it was how he felt. Like she belonged to him. Like she needed him.

And he wanted her to need him.

"It's okay. You're safe. You're all right," he said, holding her a little tighter.

"I told you not to get involved," she whimpered, her hands gripping his forearm as she tried to turn around. He loosened his hold enough to let her, and when she faced him, he was surprised by her dark scowl.

"That guy assaulted you," Gabe said.

"And I'm still standing. Believe me, he's done worse. But the things he could do to you…Gabe, do you really want to go back to prison?"

"That punk is a fucking pussy," Gabe said, dropping his arms from around her waist. "He's not going to do shit to me."

"You don't know what he's capable of, especially when someone humiliates him," Caroline said, taking his hand and bringing his bruised knuckles to her mouth.

He caught his breath at the gentle brush of her lips, his heart hammering. Trying to play it cool, he used his other hand to tilt her chin up, and he studied her face.

"You trying to say you care about me, Caroline?" She tried to look away, but he wouldn't let her. "Answer me."

"I think you're an idiot who's going to get hurt if he keeps getting involved in my problems," she snapped.

"Hey," he said, releasing her as she struggled. "I'm a big boy. I can handle it."

"I don't need you to fight my battles for me," she said, pushing him all the way back. "I was handling my own shit just fine before you came along, so don't think you're going to come in here on a white horse and save me. Is that your plan? To make me indebted to you?"

Gabe tightened his fists, his muscles aching with rage. "Forgive me, princess. I promise, it's the last time I get involved in your drama."

"Good. That's all I want!"

Without saying anything else, he grabbed his jacket and slammed out the door. Fuck her. If she didn't know the difference between someone stepping up because he cared and someone trying to get something from her, then she was more damaged than he was.

Taking off down the street on foot, he headed toward Chase's tattoo parlor with his mind racing. What the hell was going on with her? Something had happened to her, and that bastard Kyle was involved in it. Was he blackmailing her? Did she owe him money or something? It seemed unlikely, but what else could it be?

Maybe he was a lawyer. Had he helped her cover up a crime or just gotten her charges dropped? Had the charges been buried in exchange for…what?

Maybe you've just been watching too many procedural cop dramas.

As he opened up the door to Jagged Rock Tattoo Parlor, he saw Chase inside, sitting down with Eric, the bartender.

"Hey, man, sorry to interrupt."

"Naw, we were just shooting the shit," Chase said. "Eric, have you met Gabe? We grew up together."

"Not officially," Eric said, holding out his hand. "You're the guy living with Caroline Willis, right?"

Gabe didn't correct him that they weren't *living* together, still remembering the too-familiar way Eric had kissed Caroline. "Yeah."

"She's a good kid," Eric said, squeezing Gabe's hand hard enough to be painful.

"She's not a kid," Gabe said, returning the grip.

The silence stretched as the two men sized each other up, and it was Chase who finally broke the tension. "Whoa, are you two about to throw down or kiss?"

Both of them swung around to face Chase, yelling, "What the fuck are you talking about?"

Chase laughed. "You both looked intense. I was just trying to lighten the mood."

Eric was the first to speak. "I'm just looking out for her."

"Well, good luck with that, because she doesn't need that from anyone, according to her," Gabe said bitterly.

Eric seemed to be fighting a smile. "Yeah, why do you think she got the nickname Trouble?"

The tension eased out of Gabe's shoulders. "So, you two never…"

"Hell no. Like I said, sweet kid, but have you met her daddy?" Eric shook his head as he let out a whistle. "Let's just say, even if I *had* been interested, working for her daddy dissuaded me from any future plans."

Gabe walked over to one of the tattoo chairs and sat. "Tell me about him."

GABE RETURNED TO the apartment two hours later and, thanks to his new bartender friend, knew a lot more about Caroline's father than when he'd walked in. Eric had had a lot to say about the former Rock Canyon mayor, Edward Willis, and the way he treated his three daughters—and none of it was good. After hearing about what a control freak her father was—when he wasn't tearing the girls down for every infraction, that is—he could understand why Caroline had a hard time accepting help. It seemed like everything her father had given them had come with a stipulation.

Flopping down on the couch, he turned on the TV, but before he'd even made it through the beginning credits of *Turner and Hooch*, he was asleep.

Suddenly, he sat bolt upright. At first, he wasn't sure what had woken him, but then he heard Caroline screaming. Jumping up from the couch, his heart hammered in his ears as he burst through her door. He flipped on the light, ready to grab her attacker, but there was no one there—just Caroline thrashing on the bed, still asleep.

Relief swept through him. He'd thought there was someone attacking her, but she was just having a nightmare.

He took her by the shoulders, gently shaking her. "Caroline…"

She thrashed harder, whimpering, "Stop…please."

"Caroline, it's me. It's Gabe," he said. "Come on, baby, stop. Wake up. It's just a dream."

She came to slowly, blinking up at him and then throwing her hands over her eyes to block the light. "Gabe?"

"Yeah, you okay?" he asked.

"Can you turn off the light?"

"Sure," he said, getting up to flip the switch before coming back to her side. Taking her hand, he added, "Seemed like some dream."

"Yeah," she whispered. "It was."

Neither one of them said anything for a minute or two, and Gabe released her hand, figuring she'd fallen back asleep. But when he started to rise from the bed, she grabbed his hand.

"Stay with me...please?"

He sat back down and said, "Are you sure?"

"Not for...I don't want that," she said softly. "I just don't want to be alone."

Climbing in with her, he lay down on his back and smiled as she snuggled into him, her cheek pressing against his chest. As he stroked her back, he waited for her to say more, and when she didn't, he said, "I know you say you don't need anybody, and I believe you. You are one tough woman, and I respect that. But I'm here if you change your mind. Okay?"

Seconds ticked by before she answered him.

"Thanks, Gabe."

Gabe brushed her hair back with one hand as he pulled her closer with the other. After several minutes of quiet, Caroline's breathing evened out, and her body relaxed. Once he was sure she was asleep, Gabe slipped out of her bed and headed for his own, a volcano of thoughts erupting inside: Caroline's anger at him for having Kirsten stay over, how she'd accused him of taking advantage of her, Caroline's reaction after his kiss. The nightmare...

Gabe didn't want to even think it, but it made a lot of sense. Especially her fear of that bastard, Kyle. But if Caroline had been raped by him—when had it happened? And why hadn't she reported it?

She'd said the man who'd assaulted her in the alley had worked for her father. Is that why she hadn't told? Because she'd thought her dad wouldn't believe her? But then why was Kyle stalking her now? Had she finally threatened to expose him after all this time?

So many unanswered questions, but one thought outweighed all the worries. Despite her protests, Caroline *did* need someone. And Gabe was determined to show her that someone was him.

Chapter Nineteen

"Anyone who says he or she has never experienced the walk of shame was just never caught sneaking out."

—**Miss Know It All**

GABE WAS STILL kicking his own ass on Friday as he closed up the shop. He had received the last of the tools he needed and would be ready to open in a couple of weeks, as long as he had customers. So far, things were looking pretty slow for custom bikes in Rock Canyon.

But it wasn't the lack of orders that was eating at him—it was Caroline.

Slamming his helmet into the front door of the shop, he cursed. There were too many unanswered questions, and he wasn't even sure he had a right to ask them. Since Sunday, Caroline had been pleasant with him, but that was as far as it went. They hadn't talked about the sex or the fight with Kyle, and it had put Gabe in a fucked-up mood all week.

Chase had given him hell on Wednesday for being a dick, telling him he needed to get laid, and he'd just about thrown his friend across the room, he'd been so on edge.

Damn it, it was bad enough that he couldn't get the feel and taste of her out of his head, but the knowledge that she slept down the hall had him in a constant state of arousal. The smell of the bathroom after her shower, the sound of her sweet-talking the kittens, and fuck, even the brief glance she'd given him when she came home last night had kept him up, imagining those dark eyes lit with pleasure as he rose above her, riding her body.

God, he needed a drink and something to get his mind off of her.

He headed over to where his bike was parked, and after securing his helmet, he took off toward Buck's, hoping to engage someone in a not-so-friendly game of pool. It took him less than ten minutes to travel across town, but when he pulled into the parking lot, there wasn't a spot left, the place was so packed. Pulling up alongside the wood building, he took off his helmet and called out to a couple of women walking past.

"Hey, why is the place so busy?"

"Ladies night!" the girls squealed together, giggling as they walked inside.

"Ah, hell," he said, swinging off his bike.

At the door, he looked inside at the wall of people, mostly women, dancing and laughing. Men were stationed around the perimeter, watching.

"You heading in, man?"

Gabe hadn't even noticed the tall burly kid hanging by the door.

"Should I?"

The "kid" grinned, and Gabe realized he was probably in his late twenties, just with one of those youthful faces.

"That's up to you, but I've seen some fine-looking women pass by."

"Shit, that's all I need," Gabe muttered as he stepped inside. The last thing on his mind was adding another woman to his plate, especially when not one of the chicks he'd met since moving here held a candle to Caroline.

There was a DJ playing Katy Perry on the stage, and the tables had been pushed to the edge to make more room on the dance floor. As Gabe walked toward the bar, he caught sight of Caroline behind it and stopped, surprised to see her there. He hadn't known what her plans were for tonight, but he hadn't expected her here. Yet there she was, whispering back and forth with the big bartender, Eric, who Chase had introduced him to last week. Remembering the kiss between the two, Gabe clenched his fists involuntarily. It was too bad; if it hadn't been for Eric's interest in Caroline, Gabe might have liked the guy.

Pushing his way up to the bar, he called out, "Hey, can I get a beer?"

Caroline looked his way and had the fucking nerve to give him a polite smile, like he was the fucking postman. Like there was nothing between them.

Like he'd never seen her naked and writhing.

Eric glanced his way, a wide grin spreading across his face. "Hey, Moriarty. Nice of you to drop in for our first official ladies night."

Eric popped the top on a bottle and handed it to him. With his eyes on Caroline, who was looking toward the stage, Gabe said, "Wouldn't miss it."

Eric, as if picking up on the tension, squeezed Caroline's shoulder as he took off toward the back. "Okay, well, I'm gonna get some more bottles from the stockroom. Great job, Trouble."

Gabe flexed his fist and resisted the urge to plant it in Eric's face. The guy was a little too free with his hands, even if he swore he had no designs on Caroline.

Alone together for the first time in almost a week—except for the hundreds of bodies surrounding them—Gabe said, "Seems like you two are awfully friendly."

"He's an old friend of the family."

"Of course he is. That's why he has a pet name for you and everything," he said, sarcasm dripping heavily from his tone.

She leaned over the bar until they were only a few inches apart, and his eyes drifted down to appreciate the low-cut neckline of her shirt.

"Are you jealous?" she asked, quietly enough that he was the only one who heard.

"No, just making an observation."

"Right," she said and started to pull back, but he grabbed her arm in a flash, keeping her close. Her large eyes widened, and those lush lips parted invitingly.

He ran his thumb across the bare skin of her arm, pleased with the goosebumps that rose in response, and she sucked in a breath sharply. He tried fighting a cocky grin but failed; as much as she tried to deny it, she was just as affected by him as he was by her.

"I think we need to talk, to clear the air," he said.

Seeming to have recovered, she said, "I'm good."

"Apologies don't come easy to me."

"You call that an apology?"

"Can I finish?" he asked, exasperated.

"By all means," she said, waving her hand in front of her like a queen.

Satisfied that she would keep quiet for a minute, he released her arm. "I'm sorry about the way I acted after we... well, had sex. Intimacy is not my strong suit."

She looked away from him, brushing her hair off her forehead as she nodded. "Yeah, it's not exactly mine either."

"Does that mean we have something in common?" he asked playfully.

"Oh, the horror."

He shook his head, choking on a laugh. Man, he liked this woman. She was smart and fiery, funny and so damn sexy in her simple navy dress that he had a hard time not coming over the bar and kissing her senseless.

"Yeah, well, I was hoping we could call a truce. Living together is hard enough without feeling like we have to avoid each other. I know you want me to stay out of your business, and I've tried, but it's stupid to walk around pretending we hardly know each other," he said, adding wickedly. "Especially since that couldn't be further from the truth. Parts of you I know…intimately."

"And just when I thought you had an ounce of maturity," she said, trying to step back, but he reached out to touch her hand.

"I'm sorry; it's a habit. I'll try to act like a grown-ass man, if you'll stop pretending I'm some strange acquaintance that you have to run from whenever you see me."

A moment passed before she reached back into the fridge and pulled out a beer. "We could try that," she said, popping the top and tapping it against his. "To behaving like adults."

She tipped the beer back, and her dark hair fell over her shoulder, exposing the clean column of her throat. Gabe's mind flashed back to kissing her soft skin.

"Yeah, yay for maturity."

"What was that?" she asked.

"Nothing."

CAROLINE TRIED TO ignore Gabe's gaze on her while she danced with Gemma, Gracie, and Callie, but just knowing he was watching had her on high alert. She kept swaying her hips slowly, dipping and turning. Lifting her hair up in a move she'd used hundreds of times to get a guy's attention, she glanced back at him to see if it worked.

Score one for Caroline. He was watching her, all right, and the expression on his face was heavy with need.

So much for being mature. You're teasing the hell out of the man.

She couldn't seem to help it. She was fascinated by him—and not just by his body or the things he'd done to her on Sunday. He was a conundrum, made up of a soft side he hardly ever showed and the snarky asshole that most of the world saw. Sure, most guys didn't like to show emotion or weaknesses to others, but Gabe had built the freaking Wall of China around himself—and she really wanted to chip away at it, brick by brick.

Despite her insistence that he stay out of her business, there had been a small part of her that loved watching him beat the shit out of Kyle. Hell, who was she kidding? She'd wanted to jump in there with him and get a few kicks in herself, but she knew the score. Kyle wouldn't hesitate to lash out at Gabe, especially if he thought Gabe meant something to her. After all, she had been the one to rock his perfect boat by coming back to Rock Canyon.

Why wouldn't he try to take away the man she was living with? Someone she cared about?

Of course, Kyle didn't know the truth, that Gabe and she were just roommates.

But is that really the truth? You know there's more to it now.

It didn't matter that she'd been trying to convince herself all week that she didn't care. The thought of Kyle hurting him made her physically ill. In the end, she realized she'd do whatever it took to make sure Kyle didn't go after Gabe. Even if it meant staying away from him.

The other part of her, the weak part, had been tempted too many times this week to confide in Gabe about Kyle and why he was targeting her. To lean on him and his strength, but she'd told him she didn't need him. That she could handle her life on her own, and she could.

But sometimes, she really didn't want to.

And for some crazy reason, she felt like Gabe could be trusted.

He had scars—just like her, that was for damn sure—but it was the sensitivity he kept under wraps that really softened her toward him. Like when she'd come home from her sister's house yesterday and found him on the floor, playing with Googlie and Possum, rubbing their stomachs and growling, "You think you're so tough?" It had been so damn adorable, and she'd hated that he'd stopped when he noticed her.

It had been on the tip of her tongue to tell him everything then, to sink to the floor and let him hold her as she confessed all. But then the insecurities had surfaced. Would he think less of her? He saw her as strong now, but if she admitted how vulnerable she really was, would he see her as a victim?

Or would he lose his cool and go after Kyle? He'd end up back in prison, and she'd end up exactly where she'd always been. Alone.

"Who are you making cow eyes at?" Gracie asked as she shimmied, pulling Caroline back to the present.

"Me?" Caroline said innocently. "No one."

"I call bullshit!" Gemma said, giggling. Caroline had learned that Gemma was kind of a lightweight and tended to giggle when she got tipsy.

"Let's see," Gracie said, tapping a nail on her ruby red lips. "If I had to take a stab at it, I'd say it's…the hot roommate?"

"Or Eric," Callie said, a wicked grin on her face. Caroline was pretty much in love with her new friend, who had a sharp tongue and quick wit beneath her quiet exterior.

Gracie shot Callie a glare.

Caroline smothered a laugh. "It's not Eric. Believe me, he's all yours."

Gracie blushed. "I don't want him."

"Which is why any time another woman even glances at him, you look like you're about to Hulk out," Gemma said, earning her own glare.

Before Gracie could open fire on her bestie, Wayne Coulter sidled up next to them.

"Good evening, ladies."

They all made disgusted faces, and Gracie snapped, "What do you want, Wayne?"

"I was seeing if I could buy you ladies a round, and maybe my brother and I could join you," Wayne said, ignoring Gracie's tone and making no attempt to hide his eyeing Gemma and Caroline's chests.

"No one wants to have a drink with you," Gracie said. "You're an asshole, and you smell like moldy cheese."

Gemma smothered a giggle, while Caroline watched Wayne's expression twist into an ugly mask of rage. "You think you're so hot, that you're too fucking good for us?"

"Please, a sheep is too good for you," Gracie said, and Caroline inched closer to her, waiting for Wayne to either make a move or take off.

Wayne took a step toward Gracie, fist clenched. "Bitch, someone shoulda taught you when to shut up."

Caroline pushed the petite blonde behind her and, closing her eyes, waited for the pain. It wasn't the first time she'd been hit, but when the blow never came, she opened her eyes, her mouth dropping open in surprise.

Wayne was flat on his back, and Callie was standing over him, her legs bent in a fighting stance. She heard a scuffle to her right and turned in time to see Gabe put a struggling Walt on the ground, placing his knee over Walt's throat as he shouted, "Simmer down!"

"What in the Sam Hill?" Eric yelled over the music as the crowd parted.

Caroline was sure Eric was going to kick them out, but his gaze sought Gracie, a scowl screwing up his handsome face. Then suddenly, his anger shifted to the Coulters, and he said, "This is the last time, Wayne. You and your brother get the fuck out of my bar."

"This crazy bitch assaulted *me*, and you're kicking *us* out?" Wayne shouted as he climbed to his feet. Caroline reached out and pulled Callie back, wrapping her arm around the woman's shoulders. She could feel Callie's trembles and rubbed her hand over her arm.

"It's okay," Caroline whispered so only she could hear.

"I'm sure you gave her a reason," Eric said coldly. "I've warned you again and again—you start shit in here, you find another place to patronize. Gabe, I think you can get off him."

Gabe stood up and stepped back toward Caroline and the rest of the women. The way Walt was rubbing his neck, she figured Gabe hadn't been gentle, and it gave her a little thrill that he was on their side.

"Come on, Eric, we were just offering to buy them a round of drinks, and Gracie insulted us," Walt protested.

"I don't care what she did. Every week I've got to deal with some shit you start in my bar, and I'm fucking tired of it. Now get out, or I'm calling the cops."

The two men stared Eric down before they started walking. As they passed by, Wayne shot Gracie and Callie a killer glare.

"See you around, sweethearts," Wayne said, sneering.

"Move!" Eric's bark propelled them a little faster.

Caroline still had ahold of Callie, and when Eric turned his attention back to them, Callie's quaking intensified.

"Okay, Eric, tone it down a notch," Caroline said, squeezing Callie to her side. "When we told them we weren't interested, Wayne acted like he was going to hit Gracie, and—"

"Wait…Did he touch you?" Eric asked Gracie. His whole demeanor, from the clenched fists to the snarl, said he was ready to pound someone.

Oh yeah, there's nothing going on between those two. Nope.

"No, Caroline and Callie had my back. He raised his hand up like he was going to, but Callie took him down faster than any of us could blink," Gracie said, waving Caroline off so she could take Callie's shoulders. "You have to teach me how to do that."

"Are you okay?"

Gabe's question startled Caroline. He was standing right next to her, but she had been so distracted by

Callie's distress that she hadn't sensed him. Looking up into his concerned face now, she had the strange desire to throw herself into his arms and let him comfort her.

"I'm okay, although I think the fun's kinda been sucked out of the evening," Caroline said.

"Why don't I take you home?" he suggested.

Her heart rate went from zero to sixty in two seconds flat.

"Actually, I drove Callie, so I have to take her home first."

"I can get a ride with Gemma and Gracie," Callie offered, and Caroline turned to look at her, relieved that she'd stopped shaking.

"Are you sure?" Caroline asked, noting the small smile Callie gave Gabe.

"Yeah, you should let him drive you."

"I still have my car," Caroline said, getting the feeling that Callie was setting her up.

"Then I'll just see you there," Gabe said, brushing against her as he passed. She turned to watch him slip through the crowd and licked her lips as those wide shoulders disappeared outside.

"He wants you bad," Callie said, beside her.

Caroline gave her a sheepish look. "Yeah, well, the feeling is kind of mutual."

"I knew it," Gracie said, coming up behind them. "Let's bail, before Eric starts yelling at me again. I don't know why he always starts shit with me. I'm a fucking ball of sunshine."

"I think the best way to get Eric into a good mood is for Gracie to—"

"Gemma!"

Gemma giggled and headed for the door as the three of them followed behind.

BACK IN THE apartment, Gabe was on the couch, waiting for Caroline to walk through the door. When he'd seen Wayne Coulter raise his arm and Caroline step in front of Gracie, his whole body had shut down for a split second before adrenaline rushed through him, propelling him out of his seat.

By the time he'd reached them, the blonde girl—Callie—had knocked Wayne off his feet with a sweeper kick, and Walt was about to jump in. He'd caught Walt around the neck and slammed him to the floor. All he'd wanted was to keep the son of a bitch as far away from Caroline as he could.

Just then, the lock turned in the door, and Gabe got off the couch, facing Caroline as she came in.

"Hi," she said.

"Hey."

She shut the door, turning the lock with a click and walked along the length of the couch. "So, you took down Walt pretty fast."

"Yeah?"

"Because you were watching me?"

"Uh-huh."

Before he could blink, she grabbed the hem of her dress and pulled it up and over her head. "Do I still have your attention?"

He came around the couch in three strides, catching the back of her head in his hands. Dropping his mouth to hers, he took those soft lips in a hard, hungry kiss, pulling back just enough to whisper, "Undivided."

Her hushed laugh was cut short as he claimed her mouth again, backing her toward the hallway. With every step, another article of clothing dropped to the floor, like a trail of bread crumbs, but when Gabe hit the wall with his elbow, he broke away to curse.

"Watch where you're going, slick," she said, pushing him against the wall and cupping his cock through his boxer briefs.

Sucking in air through his teeth, Gabe wrapped his arm around her waist and brought her flush against his body. All night he'd been watching her body move, and it had been impossible not to remember how it had felt to be connected to her, moving inside her body. Before the fight had ensued, he'd been tempted to get up and dance with her, if only to stop the teasing looks she'd been throwing his way.

With her hand trapped between them, teasing his length, he trailed his hand over her hip and beneath the scrap of lace covering her. She liked to be in control, to drive him to distraction, but she needed to learn that when it came to sex, he was the boss.

When his finger found her, he rubbed between her lips and circled her clit, enjoying her little gasp.

"Speaking of slick…"

"God," she said hoarsely, reaching up to grab the back of his neck, trying to pull him down for a kiss. "You always have to have the last word."

He dipped his mouth to hers, nipping and sucking on her lips as he stroked her. Her breathing hitched, and one of her legs came up, trying to hook around his hip. Her little groan of frustration was damn hot; he loved the way she didn't hold back what she wanted or needed from him.

If she wanted to be closer, he could help her with that.

Gabe grabbed her thighs and lifted her easily, carrying her the last few steps to his bedroom. As they came through the open door, he noticed Googlie and Possum sleeping on the bed.

"Shit, we have company."

She looked over her shoulder at the sleeping kittens. "We could go to my room."

He did an about-face, mumbling about "damn cats," and headed back down the hallway to her room. As he reached her cracked door, he forgot everything else but the feeling of her mouth on his neck, sucking hard before dragging her teeth across the wet spot.

"You're gonna kill me," he said.

"Don't worry; you'll like it," she teased, running her nails across his back hard enough to bring a growl of pleasure from him.

Once inside the room, Gabe dropped her to her feet. "Turn around."

She did as he asked, and he slid his hand up her back, unclasping her bra. The smooth skin of her back drew him to kiss his way up her spine. As he slid the straps off her shoulders and down her arms, he flung the lacy lingerie across the room before clasping her breasts in his hands. Squeezing her and massaging them, he pulled her back against him, nuzzling her neck as he rubbed his cock against her ass.

Slowly, she reached back and wound her arms around his neck as he tweaked her nipples, pulling and pinching them into hard nubs that left her arching and gasping. He wanted her, to be inside her and make her scream; there was no question. But more than that, he didn't want her to ever forget what was between them.

Because no matter how hard he'd tried to convince himself that she deserved better, he couldn't leave her alone now. She was his.

"Bend over the bed."

She didn't argue as he slid the lacy thong down her legs. She stepped out of it, one delicate foot at a time, while he ran his palm over her plump rear in awe.

"Spread your legs, princess," he said, the nickname rolling off his tongue sweetly. There was no mocking this time; he meant it. He wanted to worship at her feet and treat her like she was nothing less than royalty.

"Shit, I need a condom," he muttered, as his fingers slipped inside her, her hot, tight channel squeezing him.

"Mmm, nightstand drawer," she said breathlessly.

He grinned and kissed his way down her back as his hand worked her. "I love that you're prepared."

"Well, I'd love it if you would—oh!"

His wet fingers had moved up to her clit, pressing into the tight little nub with fast, circular motions, playing with her flesh until she was quivering, and he felt her muscles spasm.

"Oh, God, I'm…I'm gonna…"

She screamed his name as she came, and he kept her riding the wave until her body relaxed under him. Swiftly reaching into the drawer, he pulled out a condom.

Once he was sheathed, he gripped her hips and angled himself. Thrusting hard, he watched her hands grip the comforter in the dim light as he pulled out, heard her breathy moan as he went back in high and came out low. Then he stopped thinking about anything but the softness of her skin beneath his calloused hands and the way her channel squeezed him as he moved within her, and he realized he didn't want to stop, didn't want her to come up from this and tell him it was another fling, just a release or that it meant nothing. He'd never wanted a woman this way, and damn it, he wanted her to crave him. To want only him.

Gabe took her hair gently in one hand and tugged lightly. Taking her from behind had just happened, but as she lifted up off the bed, the angle changed, sending him deeper.

Shaking and fighting his desire to move inside her, he pressed his mouth against her ear. "Do you like this?"

"Yes…"

"Say you want me."

"I do. God, don't stop…"

"My name. Tell me you want me."

He noticed her body stiffen for a split second, but it was so brief, he wondered if he'd imagined it. He took her earlobe between his teeth, and she moaned. "Caroline. I want to hear you say my name."

She turned her face to the side so she could look back at him. Their gazes held in the twilight, and then she turned, breaking the connection of their bodies to wrap her arms around his neck. When she pushed at the back of his neck, he let her bring his mouth down to meet hers. The kiss was wet, messy, and damn, he loved it.

Against his mouth, she whispered, "I want you, Gabriel."

CAROLINE PROTESTED AS Gabe pulled away from her. "Don't go—"

His dark eyes were so intense that her stomach twisted up. "I want to watch your face as you come."

Hotter words had never been spoken and despite his demanding, say-my-name bedroom manner, she had to admit it turned her on. Usually, she wore the pants in the bedroom—taking the lead and offering suggestions—but damn, Gabe didn't need any help getting her off.

As he laid her back on the bed, she arched up, waiting for him to cover her with that big, hard body, but he hovered above her on his hands. When she opened her eyes, she saw him watching her with a half-smile on his lips.

"What?"

He lifted one hand to smooth it over her cheek but didn't answer. The moment was almost tender, and she swallowed back the panic.

This was Gabe. Gabe, her savior. The man who played on the floor with four-week-old kittens and thrashed men who abused women. He was a good man, despite his protests. The look on his face wasn't what she'd expected from the large, dark man, but she just kept telling herself there was nothing to be afraid of.

She was safe with him.

She placed her hands on his shoulders as he came down on his elbows and kissed her, stealing her breath and the last of her reservations. Gabe's lips were like magic, sending tingles through her with every brush, and her arms wrapped around his neck, wanting to keep him there.

He pulled back, and she lifted her hips to take him inside once more, an active participant as they moved together. Each time he thrust, the pressure built, and she held on tightly, chanting his name as pleasure erupted inside her. A few minutes later, he stiffened above her.

When he came down on his elbows again, his lips buried themselves in the side of her neck and hair, his breath warming her as he tried to catch it.

This was the moment she hated; usually, she wanted the man to just get up and go, so she could clean up and go to bed. Her first instinct was to tell him, "Time to go," but the light kisses just under her ear were nice, relaxing her already liquid body as her eyes started to flutter shut. She didn't even realize he had moved off her until he was bringing the covers up over her, and she reached out sleepily for his hand.

"Stay."

The brush of his mouth on her shoulder was the last thing she felt as she fell into a deep, dreamless sleep.

Chapter Twenty

"There are some people who can forgive and
forget...and then there's the rest of us."

—Miss Know It All

"Son of a bitch!"

Gabe woke up to the sound of Caroline's cursing in
the kitchen and the smell of burning food. Groggily, he
pushed himself up onto his arms and yelped as tiny claws
dug into his back.

He'd slept the whole night in her bed.

A warmth of satisfaction spread through him as he
remembered the aftermath of their lovemaking,

"Stay."

Just like the night of her bad dream, he hadn't been
able to resist her request. He'd lain back down after he'd
cleaned up and wrapped his arms around her waist. It
wasn't that he'd never slept with a woman before, but last
night with Caroline had felt different.

Because you've never felt this way about a woman before?

He didn't want to examine that possibility; it was too soon. Just being with her and sharing that level of intimacy had allowed him to experience another emotion he'd thought lost to him.

Hope.

Hope for a future with a woman who made him feel good about who he was. Who knew about his past and accepted him, not because she wanted to fix him, but because she saw something more.

Turning slowly, he felt the kittens slide farther beneath him, and he sat up, twisting to look at the two furballs blinking up at him grumpily.

"Little shits, what's your problem? You clawed the hell out of my back."

Googlie was the first one to stretch and pad toward him, rubbing against his arm. Gabe had never been much of a cat person, but damn if these ones hadn't gotten him, hook, line, and sinker.

Kind of like their mama.

"Damn, damn, double damn!" Caroline shouted beyond the closed door.

Grabbing his boxer briefs, he pulled them into place and walked into the kitchen. Caroline was standing in her robe with her back to him, in front of the stove, her long hair on top of her head in a messy bun. He came up behind her and looked down at a charred, smoking rectangle on the counter.

"If you were making me breakfast, I guess it's the thought that counts."

She jumped and turned so that their bodies were mere inches apart.

Gabe loved that she seemed nervous.

"It's Valerie's birthday, and I'm in charge of the cake. But it seems like my culinary skills come only in the form of microwavable dinners and boiled pasta."

"Why don't you pick one up at Hall's?" he asked.

She threw her hands up. "Exactly, right? But no, Ellie said it had to be this rainbow chip crap, and Val's party is tonight, and—"

"And it only takes about an hour to bake, two to cool, and fifteen minutes to ice it," he said and then shrugged at her shocked expression. "What? My mom worked a lot, and when she wasn't working, she was gambling."

"What about you and your sister?" Caroline asked, her dark eyes shining with sympathy, but he didn't want her to feel sorry for him. He understood why she would, but there was nothing that pity could change about his past. So he'd had a shitty parent—a lot of people did. Those were just the cards he'd been dealt.

Still, he could remember his public defender planning his defense and telling him that it wasn't his fault. A lot of kids who got into drugs and alcohol were raised by abusive, single parents. If his arm hadn't been broken in the accident, he probably would have decked the guy for assuming shit. It didn't matter that his mother had been abusive as hell and just plain mean.

It had been on him to protect Honey, and he'd failed her, time and again.

"Honey and I were usually on our own unless Mom had enough for a sitter, which wasn't often. We were usually the last on her priority list, so I learned to cook dinners and make birthday cakes for my sister and me. We never really had parties, but at least we had cake."

She took his hand and squeezed it. "I'm sorry."

Again, with the sympathy; he tried to be gentle, but his reply probably came off sharper than he meant. "Don't be; we had fun." Then, remembering, he added, "We used to make each other homemade gifts, but this one Christmas, Honey wanted this doll at the mall. I had almost saved up enough for it, but my mom found my coffee can and took everything I had. So Christmas Eve, I went into the store and tried to sneak it out in my backpack."

He didn't know why he was telling her this story; as a kid, it had been terrifying. He'd almost made it out the door and onto the street when the sales clerk had grabbed him.

Would Caroline consider his early shoplifting a prelude to his ending up in prison? He didn't think of it that way, but he could see why she would. He just thought back on that memory as a time when he'd tried to give Honey everything she deserved. After all, it wasn't her fault she'd been born to a loser of a mother. And as for him, well, he wasn't a gem either. Honey had deserved better than both of them.

Damn it. His eyes were starting to sting, and he coughed to hide the emotion this story roused in him.

He felt her squeeze his hand and step closer, her warmth comforting him. "You don't have to tell me."

"Ah, it's fine. I just had a tickle in my throat."

"Okay," she said, releasing his hand to wrap her arms around his waist. "Go on, then."

Gabe could tell Caroline wasn't buying his throat clearing but appreciated that she didn't tease him about it. Lord knew this was the only time he'd ever told this story to anyone besides Chase, and if she teased him, well, he wouldn't be able to take it.

Isn't that why you're telling her, though? Because deep down, you know you can trust her with your past and your baggage?

It was true. Despite their rough start, Caroline was the most understanding woman he'd ever met, and he knew she wouldn't judge him for his mistakes.

Realizing she was poking his back for him to continue, he said, "Anyway, that was the first time I got arrested. I felt like shit, especially when my mom showed up and started screaming at me about having to quit during her winning streak. Then I got pissed, and told her if she hadn't stolen all the money I'd earned, I wouldn't have had to steal. I called her a thief in front of the whole police department, and she slapped me."

"Oh my God, that's awful," Caroline said, pulling far enough away to look up at him, her expression appalled. "They didn't let you go home with her, did they?"

"One of the officers stepped in and threatened to arrest her. She started crying and apologizing, giving him a sob story about raising the two of us all alone and that it would never happen again. She was just emotional. The officer was an older guy who bought her shit and started talking about how he had three teenagers. His advice to her was to let him drive her home, since she was obviously distraught."

"I can't believe no one did anything!" Caroline said furiously. "They should have taken her into custody, and—"

"It was a small town during the holidays," Gabe broke in, rubbing her back to calm her down, although he was secretly pleased that she was angry on his behalf. Made him think that maybe she cared a little.

"I'm sorry, but I think it's ridiculous that no one protected you from her," Caroline said, adding weight to his suspicion. Though really, it wasn't just that he wanted her to care but that he wanted to believe there could be something between them. If sharing a painful part of his childhood could show her he was trying, it was worth opening up old wounds.

Especially when she looked so adorably ferocious, ready to go back in time and challenge his mom.

Without thinking, he leaned over and kissed her, softly. Just a brush of lips before he said, "Maybe if there had been someone like you there, it might have gone differently, but there weren't a lot of choices for us. They might have been able to put me with one of the families at church temporarily, but then I wouldn't have been home with Honey. Honestly, I thank God he didn't do that. I don't think Honey and I would have been any better off in the system, and I doubt if, once she lost us, my mother would have fought very hard to get us back."

"But she's your mother," Caroline protested. "How could she not fight for her children? I couldn't do that."

He shrugged. "It turned out okay, actually. The next day, an officer and some woman showed up at our door. It turned out that one of the guys at the station had called child protective services after my mom slapped me. While my mom and the woman talked in the other room, the officer pulled out two packages and a stocking for each of us, filled with candy and toys. When my sister opened her gift, it was the doll she'd wanted."

"Oh! What a wonderful man. Did child protective services ever come back?"

"No," Gabe said, thinking back on what happened next with sadness. "We were in good health, without a mark on us, and the house was clean, though mostly because Honey and I did all the housework. I guess she determined it was a one-time deal, and there were other children at higher risk than us."

"Well, that was still nice of the officer to do that," Caroline said, squeezing him around the waist.

Gabe tried for irony, but his tone sounded bitter, even to his ears. "Yeah, except my mother took the toys and threw them in the Dumpster right after they left. Something about punishing us for causing her trouble and being greedy or some shit." It was hard not to think of that Christmas and want to smash his fist into something.

Caroline's face flushed. "What a bitch!"

Gabe let loose with surprised laughter and hugged her. "Thanks."

"I'm sorry, but—"

"You don't have to apologize to me. I fully agree with you," he said, rubbing her back. "We didn't have it as bad as some, but after Honey's accident, I wasn't there to protect her."

"Protect her from what? Your mother?" Caroline said with disbelief. "What did she do to her?"

He sighed and leaned back against the counter, bringing her with him and cradling her against his body. "After the accident, my mother sued the hospital for malpractice when they missed a brain bleed on Honey's scans. She was awarded millions, and she was supposed to use it for Honey's medical expenses."

"But she didn't." It wasn't a question, and he gave her a sad smile.

"No, she didn't. She stuck Honey in a state hospital and blew through the money like crazy. By the time I got out and found out what was going on, maybe a couple hundred thousand were left."

"Oh my God."

It was exactly what he'd thought when he'd found out what his mother had done, but had he been surprised? Not really. His mother was who she was, and it had never done him any good to expect more from her than the very least she could give.

"Yeah, never trust a gambler with a large sum of money," Gabe said, trying—but failing—to make light of one of the most difficult points of his life. "I hired an attorney who was willing to work for a percentage and sued my mother for power of attorney for my sister's care and her settlement. We were in the middle of court proceedings when some junkie shot her for her purse in Reno."

"Shut up," Caroline said, searching his face. "Are you kidding?"

"Nope," he said, thinking back to that morning when the police had shown up at his apartment to give him the news. For the longest time, he'd actually been ashamed that his first reaction at their news had been relief. Relief that his mom couldn't gamble away any more of Honey's money and that he might have a chance to recoup some of the money his mother had lost. Of course, he'd never share that with Caroline. Some things were just better kept to oneself.

"And she'd never changed her will from the time she had coffee cans buried in our backyard, so everything went to Honey and me. Right after the funeral, I sold everything she owned and put the money in an account for Honey's care that gains interest. Paid off the legal fees and found her a new facility in Colorado. We lived there for eight years, but it was too expensive for me to start up a new business, and that's what I wanted to do."

"So, that's why you moved here? But why *here*, of all places?" she asked, playing with the fingers on his hand.

The soft touches were innocent enough, but coming from her, his thoughts started to stray to other places her fingers could skim. "Well, 'cause I didn't want to live in a place that got a lot of snow ever again, so Sun Valley was out, and because my best friend from high school lived here."

"Who is that?"

"Chase Trepasso. He owns the tattoo shop down the street," he said, reaching up to trail his thumb across the skin of her neck.

He saw her lips twitch like she was fighting a smile. "Of course your best friend is a tattoo artist."

Reaching out to cup the back of her neck, he growled, "What's that supposed to mean? What are you trying to say, woman?"

"Nothing," she said, giggling.

"Are you trying to say that us bad-boy types stick together, huh?" he said, poking her ribs with his other hand until she was screaming.

"No! I'm sorry! Stop!"

Gabe brought her closer as her laughter subsided. "If I'm going to help you make this cake, I better go with you to the store. Since you lack my mad culinary skills, I can't rely on you to get everything I need."

Caroline tried to hit him playfully, but he caught her hand. Dipping her, he kissed her hard and fast until she was clinging to him. When he had her right where he wanted her, he lifted her back to her feet and smacked her ass.

"Come on, sous chef! Time's a-wasting."

DESPITE GABE'S CAVEMAN-LIKE teasing, Caroline was glad he'd offered to come with her. It had only taken a few minutes to get to the store, and when they walked inside, Gabe ripped off the bottom of the list they'd made and handed it to her.

"You go grab this, while I get everything else."

She glanced down at the scrap of paper. *Birthday card*.

"Very funny," she said, smacking his arm before she grabbed a cart.

"Give me that cart, and go pick out the card. You can meet me in the cake aisle when you're done," he said, leaning down like he was going to kiss her. Just before their lips touched, he turned his face away and propelled the cart forward, placing both feet up on the lower bar.

"Jerk," she called after him, ignoring the stares from several shoppers as she headed toward the card aisle. Caroline saw the clerk at checkout stand one and was tempted to stick her tongue out at her. Every time she came in, the clerk pretended not to see Caroline standing in line unless other people started lining up behind her. She vaguely remembered the woman from high school but had no idea what she'd done to her.

Stopping in front of the wall of cards, she started picking them up one at a time, reading the front and inside. After several duds, she found one with an old woman and a funny innuendo about gravity on the inside and picked up the envelope that went with it.

When she spun around, she ran smack into Marcus Boatman.

"Yikes, sorry, I didn't know anyone was there."

"It's okay, beautiful," Marcus said, shoving his hands into his jean pockets. "What are you up to?"

Caroline didn't like him calling her that but let it go for now. "Just getting some stuff together for my sister's birthday."

"Yeah? Ellie or Valerie?"

"Valerie."

"That's cool," he said, cracking his knuckles, something he used to do to intimidate people or when he was nervous. "So, I guess you can't go out to dinner or anything later, huh?"

Seriously? He is not asking you out!

"Um, considering your girlfriend assaulted me for bumping into you, I really don't think a date is a good idea," she said, grabbing a hundred-dollar gift card to iTunes too.

"Oh, Shelby and I aren't seeing each other anymore. What she did at Buck's was out of line, and I'm really sorry about the whole thing."

Great. "That's nice of you to say, Marcus, but I'm really not interested."

He seemed surprised. "Are you seeing someone?"

"Yes, I mean, maybe," she said, still unsure what to call her thing with Gabe. "Besides, you and I just aren't compatible."

"How do you know that?" he asked, stepping into her path when she tried to leave. "You've never given me a chance."

Frustrated, she snapped, "Marcus, I'm just not interested, okay?"

He was angry—she could tell by the clench of his jaw—but what was she supposed to say? She'd tried to be nice, and he hadn't taken no for an answer.

"You know what? I always thought the women of this town were just being bitches about you, but I think I was wrong," he said, sneering at her. "You really are a teasing slut who likes attention."

"What the fuck are you talking about? Are you high? I have never given you any encouragement. If anything, I've avoided you since I got back to town. But somehow, I just keep bumping into you. Please, explain to me how I've led *you* on and teased you?"

His mouth opened but no sound came out. People were gathering at the end of the aisle, but she ignored them as she continued. "Get this through your thick skull. I. Don't. Want. You. Never have. The only reason I ever hooked up with you in high school was because I was drunk, and I wanted to get back at Shelby. Since then, I haven't thought about you once."

Gabe appeared behind the crowd, his face a mask of concern. Smiling at him, she gave a little wave. The crowd turned around to look at him, but he ignored them, his gaze shifting between her and Marcus.

You've got this.

Staring into Marcus's beet-red face, Caroline spoke softer. "You can call me a slut if it will make you feel better about yourself, but I never teased you. That was something you created in your own mind. If I was you, I'd crawl back to Shelby on my hands and knees and beg her forgiveness. I don't even like her, but there aren't very many women who will put up with a stupid man like you."

Marcus rushed past her, but she didn't even turn around. She just walked up to the edge of the crowd and said, "Excuse me."

The group parted, and even Mr. Hall stood back silently as she made her way to Gabe. She could feel the hard stares of the people around her, but she wasn't going to turn the other cheek. Not anymore. She wasn't going to just sit back and take their abuse. If they wanted to talk to her about the past and move on, that was one thing. But she wasn't the same girl, and she wasn't going to keep asking for their forgiveness.

"You okay?" Gabe asked, taking the card from her hands. He held his arm out to her, and she snuggled into his side.

"Yep, I'm good," she said and took the cart.

"I have to say, I'm usually the one who people want to start shit with," Gabe said.

"Welcome to my life," Caroline whispered. "Did you get everything?"

"I did. What do you say we get the fuck out of here and bake that cake?"

A few horrified gasps let Caroline know that even though most of their audience had wandered away, there was still an eavesdropper or two who didn't appreciate the F-bomb. She saw that the rude clerk and Mrs. Andrews were standing in front of the nearest checkout stand.

Pushing the cart toward them, Caroline smiled. "We're ready."

"Well, I'm going on break," the clerk said, flipping off her light.

"Becky, turn that light back on and check out Ms. Willis," Mr. Hall said from behind them.

Becky…Becky…

Images of a punk-rock girl screaming at her in high school flashed through Caroline's brain. She couldn't remember what she'd done to piss off Becky, but obviously, it had been worth holding a grudge.

Mrs. Andrews walked behind the checkout stand and addressed the blonde bag girl. "Jenny, don't forget to bring home milk."

"Sure, Mom."

Mrs. Andrews lowered her voice but not before Caroline heard, "And do *not* talk to them."

Becky snickered, and Caroline looked right at her. "Do I know you or something?"

Becky's mouth dropped open, as if shocked. "You don't remember me?" she cried.

"Should I?"

"You hooked up with my boyfriend, Charlie!"

Caroline turned to Gabe and said, "I don't remember a Charlie."

"That's too bad," Gabe said. "Charlie sounds like a swell guy."

Caroline smothered a laugh as she dug for her wallet. She found a couple of twenties and handed them to Becky, who counted her change in short, jerky motions. When she slammed the drawer shut and slapped the change down on the counter, Caroline shook her head.

"I don't remember hooking up with your boyfriend, but if I did, I'm sorry. I was kind of a mess."

Becky's lip quivered like she was going to cry, the only sign that she'd heard Caroline.

"You're Valerie's sister, right? Caroline?" the blonde bag girl asked as Caroline and Gabe picked up their groceries.

"You couldn't tell by the villagers with the pitch-forks?" Caroline asked.

Jenny laughed, and held out her hand. "I'm Jenny Andrews. Val used to be friends with my older sister."

Caroline remembered her older sister, but their mother was even harder to forget. It was tough to find a more judgmental, self-righteous bitch than Mrs. Marci Andrews.

"Oh, yeah, I remember," Caroline said.

"Is it true you've been all over the world?"

"Well, I've lived lots of places, but I've never been any-where overseas except London," Caroline said, giving Gabe a one-minute sign with her finger before he contin-ued toward the door.

"Oh, wow, what was it like?" Jenny asked, taking their empty cart back toward the front.

"Why don't I give you my number, and you can call me about it sometime?" Caroline said, searching her purse for a pen. "I normally wouldn't mind hanging out, but it's Val's birthday, and I have to bake a cake."

"Oh, I'm so sorry. My mom always says I talk too much and that ladies should be of few words."

"Do *not* listen to your mother," Caroline said firmly. "You are unique and fun. Don't change for anyone. In case you haven't figured it out yet, adults don't know everything."

Jenny giggled. "No, they sure don't."

Chapter Twenty-One

> "A man who can cook is worth his weight in gold.
> Or at least in chocolate."
>
> **—Miss Know It All**

THEY MADE IT home from the grocery store, and Gabe sent her off to feed the kittens while he got situated. When she returned fifteen minutes later, Gabe was standing by the sink, washing his hands, and she saw that he had not only cleaned up her mess but the kitchen as well.

"Have I mentioned how much I hate doing dishes?" she asked as she kissed his back. "So thank you."

Before he could answer, she grabbed a doughnut out of the box they'd picked up and jumped onto the counter.

"What do you think you're doing?" he asked.

She paused midbite and chewed slowly before answering. "I'm savoring this delicious chocolate doughnut while I watch you make my sister's cake?"

Taking an apple fritter from the box, he bit into it and shook his head. "No. This is not rocket science, and you are going to learn how to make a box cake if it takes us a hundred tries."

Grumbling, she finished her breakfast and jumped down to wash her hands. The minute they were dry, a mixing bowl and a carton of eggs were shoved in her hands.

"Hup two, let's get this cake made."

Despite her protests that she'd just ruin it, Gabe's gruff instructions and teasing did make the process fun. While she was beating the eggs, oil, and water into the powder with the mixer, he came up behind her. Before she knew what he was about, he'd wrapped his arms around her and covered her hands with his.

"First of all, you're spraying batter all over the walls because the speed is too high," he said, adjusting the mixer, "and if you do this kind of circular motion, it helps."

With his hands covering hers, he helped her guide the mixer in a circle, going around the base of the bowl and back into the middle. She realized that as their arms were moving, so were their bodies, and with every circle, he was rubbing against her.

Caroline didn't even bother hiding her grin as she felt his hard-on through the back of her yoga pants. "Ah, that really does help."

"See? You got this," he said, his lips grazing her neck. He released her hands and splayed his across her stomach.

When he grasped her right breast, kneading the flesh through her T-shirt, she bit back a moan and forgot to keep the mixer in the batter.

"Whoa," he said, laughing. "Maybe you can't multitask."

She noticed the spots of batter on the counter and the front of her shirt, and groaned. "Does it at least look smooth?"

"Mmm hmmm," he said as his other hand slipped inside her yoga pants.

For a moment, Caroline wondered what he would think about her lack of panties. Then she grabbed his wrist and yanked his hand out. "You are supposed to be helping."

"I am helping."

"No, you're playing with me," she said, unlocking the beaters from the base and turning in his arms with a beater in each hand. "Wanna lick the batter?"

"Depends," he said, running a finger along the metal and spreading the batter across her exposed chest.

"You are such a"—Gabe bent down and dragged his tongue across her skin, the bar of his tongue ring sliding smoothly along the top of her breasts, causing her nipples to tighten and her stomach to bottom out—"perv."

"I'm making baking interesting," he said, pulling her scoop neck T-shirt down, along with the cup of her bra, and dribbling batter over her nipple.

"You know, consuming raw eggs can cause salmonella poisoning," she said, even as her eyes closed at his first flick on her hard peak. When his whole mouth closed over her areola and sucked, she dropped both beaters on the counter and held onto the back of his head. Releasing her breast and pulling her bra and shirt back in place, he came back up, grinning.

"I like to live dangerously."

GABE RINSED OFF the beaters and put the mixer back in the cupboard as Caroline bent over to slide the cake in the oven.

"I hope this one cooks right."

"I told you; you just had the rack too high," he said, drying his hands. He was just about to take her for that shower he had been fantasizing about, when Googlie and Possum came running into the kitchen, meowing loudly.

"I think someone is hungry again," Caroline said, pulling formula, canned food, and bottles from the cupboard.

"I think they're a couple of cock-blocking fuzz butts," Gabe grumbled.

When Caroline laughed, his chest tightened and his stomach turned in knots. In the last twenty-four hours, he had teased and played and laughed more than he had since he was a kid. Since before the accident.

And it was all because of this woman.

Since you met Caroline, you've been spouting internal poetry. Remember, she said this wasn't anything more than convenient.

But as she passed by him to feed the kittens, she kissed his cheek. And actually patted the front of his jeans. "Be patient, big boy. I'll get to you in a minute."

He knew she was teasing him, but damn, he hoped she wasn't kidding.

Caroline bent over but before he could fully admire the view, she stood back up with two frantic kittens. "Here, take one."

He grabbed Possum and one of the bottles, wincing as the sharp claw dug at his hand. "Chill out, buddy, it's coming."

Gabe followed Caroline over to the couch and sat next to her. She let Googlie knead her chest as he sucked down his bottle.

"When do these things stop nursing?" Gabe asked as he rubbed Possum's tiny ears.

"Zoe said that the mother usually weans them at six to eight weeks. I'm supposed to start them on gruel this week."

"I think they need another bath," Gabe said, wrinkling his nose.

"I'll give them one before I leave," Caroline said.

"What time is your party?"

"Five," she said. Then, almost as an afterthought, she asked, "Would you wanna come with me?"

He almost dropped the bottle, he was so surprised. "Family functions aren't exactly my strong suit."

"Understood. I just thought that since you helped me with the cake, you might want to reap some of the benefits."

"Wouldn't your family be upset if you brought me at the last minute?"

"No, there's going to be a bunch of people there," she said, pulling the empty bottle out of Googlie's mouth.

Gabe watched her stand up, thinking about what the invitation meant. No woman had ever invited him home to meet her family.

Realizing that Possum was sucking nothing but air, he pulled the bottle away. "Sorry, bud, I was thinking."

After taking the kitten into Caroline's room and setting him in the litter box, he stood there for a minute. He'd decided last night that Caroline was what he wanted. Was this her way of showing him she'd changed her mind about this being "convenient" for her?

When he was done washing his hands in the bathroom, he walked out into the kitchen and found Caroline washing bottles in the sink.

Slipping his arms around her waist, he asked, "So, is this party casual, or do I have to wear a tie?"

"It's casual," she said, drying her hands before placing them over his.

"Hmm, so I should wear my T-shirt that says, 'I am the party'?"

"Please tell me you're joking," she said, turning in his arms.

"Fine. I'll pull out my shirt that looks like a tux."

"Okay, maybe I've changed my mind," she said, frowning up at him. "I rescind your party invite."

"Shit, I'm just trying to class the place up," he said.

"Right," Caroline said, wrapping her arms around his waist. "So, does that mean you'll go with me?"

"Yeah, I guess. It's like you said; I helped make the cake," he said, leaning down to kiss her softly. "I should enjoy all the benefits."

"Hmm, so what do I have to bake to get you to take me to the airport on Thursday?" she asked against his lips.

"You can't bake."

"Okay, what can you *teach* me to bake, so you'll drive me to the airport?"

"I don't know. That sounds like a lot of work, with very little re—"

Her mouth dipped to take his nipple, T-shirt and all, into her mouth, stopping whatever he was going to say. Her hand slipped down and between them, cupping him through his pants, and he groaned, "Yeah, sure, I can drive you."

"Good," she said, pulling away and wrinkling her nose. "Now, how about you just go shower, so I don't show up with Stinky McGee?"

"You gonna join me?" he asked, stepping away to pull his T-shirt over his head.

"I already showered," she said.

Sniffing her playfully, he said, "I think you missed a spot."

When she smacked out at him, he grabbed her arm, dipped his shoulder to hoist her up, and carried her like a sack of potatoes. She laughed as she screamed, "Gabe, no! It takes forever to dry my hair!"

"I never said anything about your hair. I said you missed a spot. I'm sure there are other places besides your head that need washing."

CAROLINE LED GABE up the walkway to the front door of Valerie's house. Val had bought the little house on a few acres last year, when she'd moved from Boise, and although other houses were close enough to see, there was still space between them for privacy.

"Lots of cars," Caroline said when they reached the top of the porch.

"Yeah, looks like the party is in full swing," Gabe said, holding the cake in his hands.

Caroline rang the doorbell before she said, "I apologize in advance."

"For what?" he asked.

The door swung open, and Valerie squealed. "Gabe, I'm so glad you could make it."

"That," Caroline said as Valerie came out and gave her a hug.

"Come on in, you guys," Val said, leading them into the house. "We've got the fire pit going out back, and Justin's at the barbeque, although I saw his hot dogs, so I'd go with a hamburger."

"Who is this?" Ellie said from the couch.

"Umm..." Caroline said, unsure how to introduce him.

"I'm Gabe."

"Oh, *you're* Gabe," Ellie said, getting up from the couch and walking over to them slowly.

Caroline noticed her sister's wrist was wrapped with a nude nylon bandage and anger burned through her. "What happened to your wrist?"

"Oh, I just sprained it trying to change my tire."

"Yeah? Well, that sucks," Caroline said, blown away that her super-confident and sexy sister would let someone abuse her.

Why not? You did the same thing, letting Kyle get away with what he did.

"If anyone wants a dog, I believe they're ready," a male voice called from the back of the house.

Gabe touched her arm and said, "I'm going to grab some food. How many hot dogs do you want?"

"One, thanks," Caroline said, waiting until Gabe had walked away before she grabbed Ellie's good wrist. "Come with me."

Ellie started to protest, but Caroline ignored her until they reached Val's room. She pulled her sister inside and shut and locked the door.

Turning to face Ellie, she said, "This has to stop."

"I told you—"

"And I'm telling *you*, I know what it looks like when my sister is getting knocked around," Caroline said, thinking of a bartender she'd employed. The woman's husband was a mean son of a bitch and had beaten her so badly, he'd put her in the hospital.

"You need to tell someone what he's doing to you, Ellie."

Ellie laughed, though there was no humor in it. "Who are you to tell me what I need to do?"

Ellie sounded so hostile that Caroline hesitated, and for a minute, she wasn't sure what to say.

"I just don't like seeing you hurt, that's all."

"You don't know anything, so why don't you just mind your own fucking business?" Ellie snapped, heading for the door.

Caroline blocked her way. "I know you deserve better than black eyes and bruised wrists. You deserve a man who wouldn't hurt you for the world."

"Oh, 'cause it's so easy for you to give me advice. 'Cause you've never made any mistakes or messed up, right?"

"Of course I have, which is why—"

"Why, what? You think you can give me advice 'cause you've been there?" Ellie countered. "You don't know anything about what I'm going through, so don't start butting in on my business and telling me what I should do, Caroline." Ellie pulled Caroline out of the way and left the room. Several seconds later, the front door slammed.

Way to ruin the party, Caroline.

Everything Ellie said was true. Caroline didn't have any right casting stones.

"Hey, what's going on?" Val asked, peeking her head in.

"Nothing," Caroline said, clearing her throat. "I suggested that maybe Ellie needed to see a doctor about all this clumsiness, and I guess I overstepped."

"She has been crazy accident prone," Val said, coming fully into the room and shutting the door. "I invited Daddy."

"What did he say?" Caroline asked, surprised.

"He couldn't come to the phone, but I gave all the details to Teresa," Val said sadly. "I was just hoping he might make an effort, you know?"

"I know, honey," Caroline said, wrapping her arms around her sister. Caroline could've told Val that they'd spent too many years as kids, waiting for their dad to make an effort, but considering how well her most recent sisterly advice had gone over, she stayed quiet.

"Speaking of Daddy, have you heard anything else on why he's digging stuff up on Kyle?" Caroline asked casually.

"Nothing new, but I imagine Senator Jenner is very thorough at hiding things. Why are you asking?"

"I'm just curious. Dad's adored Kyle since we were kids."

"That's because they're both assholes, and like follows like."

"Dad is nothing like Kyle," Caroline snapped.

"Trust me; they are both cruel, unfeeling bastards. You don't know—"

"I do know," Caroline said, avoiding Val's gaze.

Val paused, studying Caroline's face, and then she turned white. "Son of a bitch!"

Val headed for the bedroom door, and Caroline knew exactly what she was doing. "No!" Caroline landed on top of Val, pinning her against the door.

"Get off me! I'm going to kill that motherfucker and roast his dick on my barbeque!"

Someone started pounding on the other side of the door, and Caroline stumbled back as it was pushed open.

"Is everything okay?" Justin asked. Gabe stood just over his shoulder.

Val pushed past them, with Caroline hot on her heels.

"Val?" Justin called.

"Caroline?" Gabe echoed.

Val was halfway down the walkway outside when Caroline caught her arm and swung her around. "Will you just *stop*?"

"Are you fucking kidding me? I can't believe you didn't kill him after it happened," Valerie cried, sucking in air. "When did it happen? Did you tell Dad?"

Caroline saw Justin and Gabe in the doorway and pleaded, "Can we not do this here?"

"Answer me!"

Caroline grabbed her arm hard and snapped, "You listen to me. This is my business, and you will not embarrass me."

"Why would you be ashamed of anything?" Val asked. "You didn't do anything."

"There are reasons why I didn't tell you or anyone else about this."

"But did you tell Daddy? Is that why he really made you leave?" Val asked insistently.

"No. I only told him recently."

"Oh my God," Val said softly. "*You're* the reason he's digging shit up on Kyle."

Caroline took a deep, shaky breath. "Please, Val, just stay out of it, okay? I don't want you involved."

"But—"

Caroline shook her head. "I promise I will tell you everything, every reason why I never said anything, but now is not the time."

Val said nothing for several long minutes, and then: "When I told you what he did to my roommate, why didn't you tell me then?"

Tears stung Caroline's eyes. "I was afraid you'd blame me for what happened to her. Because I never told." Caroline looked away from her sister, ashamed by her admission, but when Val wrapped her arms around her, she froze.

"I don't blame you." Val's softly spoken words made Caroline sag against her, sobbing. "Shh, it will be all right."

"I can take her," Gabe said, next to them, but Caroline looked away from him. She didn't want him to see her like this.

Val squeezed her again and shook her head. "She's my sister."

"I know," Gabe said, before adding, "I promise I'll take care of her."

Val released Caroline, and Gabe scooped her up in his arms, carrying her toward the car.

Caroline looked up in time to see Justin come down the walk and hold out his arms to Val. She went into his embrace, wrapping her arm around his waist and looking up at him with so much love. Caroline was happy for her, glad she had come out of their dysfunctional childhood whole and made the best of it. Hell, Val had made the best of it and then done better. She was happy.

Happiness had been elusive to Caroline for most of her life.

When they reached the car, Caroline whispered, "Did you hear?"

Gabe let her slide down his body as he took her keys from her.

"Did you hear?" she asked, louder, angrier.

"I had already guessed," Gabe said, opening her door. *What?*

"But…how?" She felt his rough palm brush her hair back, but Caroline couldn't look him in the eye.

"It was just a feeling I had. I didn't want to ask you about it, in case I was wrong."

"And now? Do you want to ask me something?" she said, climbing into the front seat.

Still outside the car, he squatted down next to her and took her chin in his hands, forcing her to finally meet his gaze.

"Whether you tell me or not is up to you," he said, stroking her cheek. "It won't change the way I think of you."

Raw emotion choked her. "How...how do you see me?"

He leaned forward, brushing her lips with his. "I see a woman who was hurt and lashed out at others because of it." She bit her lip as he continued. "And then that woman overcame her pain, grew from all that anger, and turned her life around. And I see a woman who, because of everything she's been through, can look at the people around her and find the good that she thought was lost a long time ago."

With a sob, she wrapped her arms around his shoulders and kissed him, cradling the back of his head.

He returned the kiss for a minute or two before he pulled away and squeezed her hand. "To be continued."

Chapter Twenty-Two

> "Being loved is not the greatest gift. The greatest
> gift someone can give is acceptance."
>
> —Miss Know It All

CAROLINE HAD NOT been blissfully happy in her entire life—except for brief times during her childhood—but lying in bed now with Gabe was pretty damn close.

They'd come home from her sister's and fallen into bed, taking their time with each other until they'd been too sated to move. Now, in the afterglow, Caroline's mind drifted to all the things she hadn't shared with Gabe. It didn't seem fair that he had told her about his mother and sister, about his accident, and yet she had shared nothing about herself.

Had she closed herself off from true intimacy? Was she cutting Gabe short because she really didn't think they were right for each other or because vulnerability scared the shit out of her?

Clearing her throat, she took a chance. "My dad didn't really have much time for me or either of my sisters when we were growing up. Not until Mom died just after my fifteenth birthday."

Gabe's hand stroked over her back. "I'm sorry."

"It's okay, it was just..." Caroline swallowed hard, trying to ease the emotional ball welling up in her throat. "Sudden. I mean, one minute we were chasing each other around the backyard and the next, she was on the ground."

The memory still played out in her mind, clear as day, and she could remember the panic that engulfed her as she yelled for help. Kneeling down next to her mother's body, she had grabbed her shoulders to shake her, pleading with her. "Ellie was screaming, and Val was...She just stood there like a statue. I had to call nine-one-one and take care of my sisters until they got our dad. It's funny," Caroline said, sniffling, "the police officer who notified my dad only told him there had been an accident, so he didn't leave the office right away; he didn't think it was an emergency."

Gabe's arms tightened around her, and he murmured into her hair, and she couldn't deny how much she craved that. The understanding and the comfort. Snuggling into his chest, she continued. "The doctors said she'd had a heart murmur, but that it wasn't life-threatening." Laughing bitterly, she whispered, "I guess they were wrong about that, huh?"

"They make mistakes; they're human," Gabe said, rubbing her back. "Believe me, I cursed doctors for the longest time after what happened to Honey, but it didn't do me any good to blame other people."

"Instead, you continue to blame yourself," Caroline said, looking up from his chest to meet his gaze. Gabe's eyes shifted away, and she lifted her hand to touch his cheek. "Stop it."

He heaved a huge sigh and said, "We're not talking about me right now."

The gentle reminder made her wonder if he thought she was trying to avoid talking about Kyle.

He's probably right, but once you tell him, you can't take it back.

"It's…hard to talk about. Before a few weeks ago, I'd only ever told one person, and that didn't go quite how I expected," Caroline said, sliding her hand back down until it lay on his chest. "I just don't want you to look at me differently."

Gabe shook his head and rolled to his side, kissing her gently. "Crazy girl, I think you are one hell of a woman to have overcome the cards you got dealt. A lot of people would have made worse mistakes to deal with their pain."

Gabe's words warmed her, and she kissed him again, just a short press of her lips, but it meant so much for him to try to put her at ease. "Thank you."

He pulled her close again and kissed her hair. "What happened after your mom died?"

You can do this. You've come this far.

"Well, I was a wreck for months, and then my father started asking me to attend political functions with him."

"Political?" Gabe asked.

She tilted her head back and said, "My father was the mayor of Rock Canyon before he started aiming for higher offices in the state."

"Look at that. You really are a princess," he said teasingly. She slapped his abs, and he groaned.

"Be nice."

"I'm always nice," he said, threading his fingers through hers. "But actually, I already knew that about you."

"You did?" she asked, surprised. "How?"

"Hanging with Chase and Eric. I asked why Eric called you Trouble," Gabe said.

"Oh, really? You didn't beat it out of him?" Caroline said, feeling like her emotions were all over the place. One minute she was crying and the next she was smiling.

"I didn't have to." Gabe traced his thumb across her palm. "But I did warn him if he kissed you again, I was going to beat the shit out of him."

Caroline choked. "You did not tell Eric Henderson you were going to beat the shit out of him."

"No, but just so you know, if he does kiss you, he's dead meat."

"Okay, first of all, you don't own me or my lips, buster," she said, pushing away from his chest, "and second, dead meat? Really?"

Gabe tried to kiss her but only got cheek when she turned her head. His warm breath grazed her ear as he whispered, "Hey, I know I don't own you, but that doesn't mean I want you kissing anyone but me."

Caroline's heart skipped and then beat out a hearty tempo. "So, we're kissing exclusively?"

"Well, if Jessica Alba shows up…"

Caroline squeezed his hand hard, and he kissed her cheek. "Yeah, we're exclusive."

Silence stretched between them, and her mind raced at the implications. Was he freaking out, putting everything out there and admitting they weren't going to be seeing anyone but each other?

She could admit; it was freaking *her* out. But just a smidge, really.

"We keep getting off topic," Gabe said.

"What? Oh…" On top of the intimacy associated with exclusivity, he wanted to hear about the most painful parts of her past.

This is what people do in relationships. They share things.

But things were getting heavy, fast. And now she wasn't sure…

"Look, there's no pressure. You don't have to tell me."

"No," Caroline said abruptly. "Sorry, I'm just…I'm ready, okay? Just give me a minute."

Gabe lay there quietly while Caroline collected herself and finally continued.

"There was this senator my dad was good friends with, and we spent a lot of time with his family. He had a son a year or so older than me, and when he started paying attention to me, I didn't mind. I was flattered," she said softly, ashamed that she had been so taken in by Kyle's deadly charm. "So about six months after my mom's death, I go to this dinner party with my dad. They were usually pretty boring, and I never liked most of the girls who attended, but Kyle took me to a private game room."

Closing her eyes, she held Gabe's hand tighter as she spoke. "I wasn't supposed to leave the party, but it felt good to be a little bad, you know? I was excited, because out of everyone, he'd picked me to hang out with. He brought down this cherry-flavored punch that was a little syrupy, but I didn't want to complain. Honestly, though, whenever I smell or taste that artificial cherry flavoring now, I get sick."

Gabe didn't say anything; the only move he made was to kiss the top of her head, which was good. Any more interruptions, and she might've lost her nerve.

"After a while, though, I just started feeling out of it, and when I tried to get to my room, Kyle took me the rest of the way," she said, choking on the words as she finished. "I kept drifting in and out of it, but I remember him on top of me, laughing when I begged him to stop."

"I should have killed the son of a bitch," Gabe growled.

"As much as I would have loved to see that, it wouldn't have helped, and you would have gone to prison."

"Still, the fucker needs to pay," he said, and the quiet that followed was lengthy. Caroline had a feeling he was wondering why she'd never done something about Kyle.

"You want to know why I never told anyone." Gabe said nothing, and it was answer enough. Sighing, she sat up with her back to him, pulling her knees into her chest. "Fear, mostly. I was scared as hell of what Kyle might do to me or my sisters. He threatened to…" God, even saying the words out loud were terrifying. "The night after it happened, he threatened to do the same thing to my sisters. That if I pressed charges, he'd get out on bail, and they wouldn't be as lucky as me, because he'd make sure they were awake for everything."

"How old were your sisters?" Gabe asked, his voice guttural.

"Val was thirteen," Caroline said, wiping at her watery eyes. "Ellie was only six, though."

"Jesus, Caroline, the man is sick as fuck," Gabe said, and she felt the bed shift as he sat up.

"Yeah, I know, but it wasn't just Kyle's threats that kept me quiet. I was selfishly afraid that no one would believe me, that my father wouldn't believe me. I mean, I told my best friend and she didn't seem to believe me."

"Listen, no matter what anyone said to you, what that bastard did was not your fault," Gabe said, his hand on her shoulder. "You have to believe that."

"You don't think I told myself that, over and over? I just felt like I couldn't take the chance. I couldn't let Kyle take everything from me," she said, laying her cheek on her kneecap. "But it turns out I did that to myself anyway by letting my emotions eat at me."

She felt Gabe move before his lips pressed against her bare shoulder. "We all do it. I did it to my best friend, Chase. He had this full-ride academic scholarship to Berkeley, and I was so jealous, I couldn't even see straight. He was going to get out of town, and I was staying behind. I'd tried not to let it affect me, but when I caught him kissing my sister, suddenly it wasn't just me he was deserting," he said, wrapping his arms around her. "We all do stupid shit as kids—hell, even as adults. The key is whether or not you can forgive yourself and move on."

Turning to face him, she asked, "Have you forgiven yourself yet?"

Gabe's expression clouded, and she almost took it back, until he said, "I'm working on it."

Caroline snuggled into him and whispered, "I don't know how to move on from this."

"I think you already took the first step by talking about it," he said, trailing kisses across her skin. "The rest will just take time."

"Is that what helped you? Time?" she asked, enjoying his ministrations.

"That," he said, dipping his head to kiss along her jaw, "and I realized there was something I wanted, but because of self-loathing, I didn't feel like I deserved it."

"Your shop," she said as her hands smoothed up his arms and over his shoulders.

"No," he whispered just below her ear. "You."

Caroline jerked in surprise at his words, unsure how to take them.

"Relax. I just mean that I've never risked getting close to a woman because I didn't think I deserved to be happy," he said, his hand skimming down her arm. "But with you, I think maybe my karma is starting to turn for the better."

Laughing nervously, she said, "I don't think anyone has ever considered me a karmic gift before."

"Just think of what you'd be called if you could actually cook," he said, kissing her before she could respond.

But it was a futile effort. The minute he broke the kiss, she muttered, "You're gonna pay for that."

As he pulled her down, he said, "Bring it on."

THE NEXT MORNING, Gabe was up early and at the firehouse, fighting a brick wall.

Despite Caroline's help moving the tables around, he'd gotten in the rest of his equipment and now needed to set that up before he officially opened for business. Not to mention all the cleaning he had to do. The place had been sitting so long, there were bionic cobwebs in every window and dust bunnies the size of wolverines. He hadn't realized exactly how big the place was until he'd started getting rid of the junk that had been left behind. Plus, there were several posters of bikes he'd designed that weren't going to hang themselves, and he'd had a feeling brick walls were gonna be a bitch to mess with.

He'd been right.

Why had he left the comfort of Caroline's arms for this?

"Gabe?" Chase's voice called from the front of the fire-house.

"Yeah, hold on," Gabe said, gritting his teeth as he tried to get the stick-and-hang hooks to work on the brick. "Damn it."

"Um, hey, man, I brought some help."

Gabe looked up and saw Chase standing in the door-way with a group of guys behind him. Justin Silverton, Travis Bowers, Eric Henderson, Mike Stevens, and a couple others Gabe had seen but didn't know stood holding on to a couple of ice chests, grinning.

Gabe climbed down awkwardly and said, "Hey, thanks for coming guys, but—"

"You're feeling so overwhelmed with gratitude, you don't know what to say?" Eric asked.

"No, I was just going to say that you don't have to help me out with this," Gabe said.

"We know that, but Chase said you were giving a discount to anyone who helped you set up shop," Mike said, grinning.

Gabe glared at Chase, who shook his head. "He came up with that on his own. *I* said it was a party, and they had to bring their own beer."

"Look, I left my baby-crazy wife to come help you out, but if you aren't going to use me, then I got somewhere to be," Travis said.

"Dude, you're oversharing again," Mike said, grimacing.

"I don't mind hearing more about Bowers's wife. She's hot—"

"Finish that sentence, and I'll use this saw on you," Travis said to one of the younger guys, nodding toward the steel blade in the corner.

Gabe looked around at the group of guys he hardly knew and was at a loss.

Chase came up alongside him and patted his shoulder. "Just give us something to do, Gabe. We're here for you."

As Gabe started handing out assignments, he was surprised by how fast the time flew. It had been a while since he'd worked with a bunch of guys, but that had been in a mechanics shop, where he was just another grunt. Here, he was the boss, and the rush of pride he felt when they finished the setup was overwhelming.

"Thank you, guys," Gabe said, holding out his hand to each of them. "You fucking rock."

"Nice," Mike said, rubbing his hands together. "Now about my discount…"

What the hell, right? They had sweated their asses off for him.

"Discounts all around, gentleman," Gabe said, grabbing an order pad and tossing Chase his sketch book. "Moriarty's Custom Bikes is open for business."

CAROLINE WALKED INTO Hank's Bar and shook her head at the waste. If Hank had been serious about increasing business and actually running a business, she wouldn't feel like she was about to step on someone else's dream. But she couldn't put in her time and effort when the owner was just going to run the place into the ground anyway.

Waiting, as the bartender ran to grab Hank, Caroline studied a few of the pictures behind the bar. In one, a young woman leaned back against the counter, laughing. Caroline wondered if maybe she was Hank's daughter.

"Sorry to keep you waiting, Caroline," Hank said, coming from the back. He held his hand out to her, and she took it, catching the scent of whiskey as they shook.

Ole Hank likes to hit the sauce early.

"Hey, Hank. I would love to help you out, but I got to be honest, I just don't think I can," she said.

"What? Did Henderson offer you money not to take me on as a client?" Hank asked.

"No, sir, this is my decision, based on my own observations," she said, waiting for the explosion.

"What in the Sam Hill do you mean, *your* observations?"

Preparing herself to deal with the stages of denial, she said bluntly, "Hank, I'm not going put in the time and effort it would take to improve this place if you're just going to let your employees waste your booze."

"Waste my...What do you mean?"

"You need upgrades, Hank. Upgrades that will control your bartenders' habits to overpour," she said, picking up one of his bottles. "But even that won't help you if you don't stop drinking in your own bar."

"I don't—"

"Please do not insult me by lying. I can smell it on you now."

Hank blustered for a moment before explaining. "I like to have a wee nip in the morning. It wakes me up."

"Yeah, and I bet you have nips here and there throughout the day until you're three sheets to the wind by close," she said, shaking her head. "Look, I just came by to tell you that I appreciated the offer. You have a great bar with lots of potential, but it's just not for me."

"But if I don't start turning a profit, I'm going to lose everything."

Caroline paused at the door and gave him one last piece of free advice.

"I suggest you hire a manager. Someone tough and business-savvy who will control the employees—and you. Good luck, Hank."

Chapter Twenty-Three

> "It's true that absence can make the heart grow
> fonder...but why tempt fate?"
>
> —Miss Know It All

WEDNESDAY WAS A bad day for Caroline, and by the time she walked through the apartment door, she was ready to crack a few skulls.

It had started out awesome.

Gabe had brought her French toast covered with powdered sugar in bed, and although Gabe used most of the sugar as an excuse to lick her all over, it had been delicious. But then, after Gabe left, she'd jumped into the shower only to find he'd used all the hot water. By the time she was done, her teeth were chattering too hard for her to curse.

From there, the downhill slope of badness had been almost comical.

A dead battery and the hour-long wait for AAA had made her late for a business consultation in Twin Falls. The bar owner had been understanding until they'd started talking about her commission. Then he'd thanked her for the advice and shown her the door.

She'd made it back to the apartment only to find Googlie lying listlessly on the kitchen floor. Frantically, Caroline had run down to the veterinary hospital. As Zoe had examined him, she kept making these clucking and hmmm-ing noises that had grated on Caroline until she couldn't keep quiet any longer.

"What does that mean? Is he going to be okay?" Caroline had asked, rubbing his little ears nervously.

"Well, if it's okay with you, I'd like to keep him for a few days. I'll run some tests and give him some fluids, since he seems a little dehydrated," Zoe said. Almost as an afterthought, she reached out to hold Caroline's hand. "We'll take good care of him."

Caroline couldn't help but notice that Zoe hadn't told her he would be fine. Guess she didn't want to give her false hope.

And so, by the time she got home, she was emotionally drained and just wanted to crawl into a dark cave and never come out. She was crying into a box of Lucky Charms when someone knocked on the door.

Getting up from the couch, she pulled the door open, and her jaw dropped.

Her father scowled at her. "Are you going to invite me in or not? I am still recovering from a heart attack, you know, and these stairs were hell."

Jumping forward, she took his arm and helped him inside. He was breathing hard, and once she had him settled, she asked, "Do you want something to drink?"

"Just water, please," he said, leaning his cane against his leg.

Caroline stood up to get him a glass, and when she came back, some of his color had returned.

"Thank you," he said, taking the glass from her.

After several quiet minutes, she finally prodded him. "I'm surprised to see you, Dad."

"I wanted to speak with you about what you told me, but I needed time to process everything," he said, setting his water glass aside.

Again, he was silent, and she shifted in her chair. "And gather information?" she suggested. At his surprised look, she said, "Ellie told Val, and Val told me you were investigating Kyle."

"I'm going to have to talk to Ellie," he said, clearing his throat before continuing, "I needed to have more information on Kyle's…extracurricular activities before I could decide where to go from here. I just needed you to know that I would never allow anyone to hurt my daughters this way, no matter who his father was."

Caroline raised her eyebrow. "But it's okay for you to write your daughters off and pretend that they don't exist?"

His lips thinned with displeasure. "I haven't always been a pinnacle of patience."

"Ha, that's an understatement," Caroline said, recovering from her initial shock. When she'd run out of his house after she told him about Kyle, and he hadn't contacted her, she figured he'd taken Kyle's side after all, that he'd found something in Kyle's background that made him believe Kyle was innocent.

Her father gave her a long-suffering look. "After your mother died, I didn't know what to do with any of you, but at least you seemed to realize the importance of a good education. If I'd known what that—" He cut himself off, and Caroline wondered if he'd been about to call Kyle a nasty name.

Edward Willis almost cursing *and* admitting he was wrong in one day?

"If I'd known what Kyle had done, I would have pressed charges," he said, adding, "No matter who his father is, he had no right to hurt and humiliate you."

Caroline couldn't seem to stop blinking in surprise. She was on the verge of asking if he was on painkillers. It was one thing for Edward Willis to be a blustering hard-ass but for him to be almost…well, comforting? Talk about a personality adjustment; the man had had a damn transplant!

"Dad, I don't want to be rude, but…are you high?"

Her father's face snapped into a scowl. "Excuse me?"

"Okay, you have never, *ever* in your life admitted that you might have been rash or made a mistake," Caroline said, laughing a little. This was a scenario she never thought would come about, but the fact that her father was actually acting like a father as well…weird. "And I'm sorry, but the complete one-eighty of the personality is kind of freaking me out."

"I pushed you girls, I know, but I wanted you to be the best. To do the best thing for—"

"For the Willis name," Caroline finished for him. "We know. We've had the Willis name and everything it means beaten into our heads since we were born, but honestly, do you think it helped any of us? I mean, I left home before I graduated; Val married the man you wanted her to, yet she was miserable; and Ellie is so screwed up, I don't know what to do about her. So explain to me how having a distinguished name and money has turned any of us into a sane, functioning adults?"

"You seemed to have turned out just fine," he said.

White-hot anger shot through Caroline. "Oh no. You can take credit for my stubbornness and my will to succeed, but what I did after I left your house...that's on me and a few friends I made along the way. Everything I have, I worked my ass off for, and yeah, at times I did some things I wasn't proud of, but the Willis name had nothing to do with my success."

"Fair enough," her father said, far too reasonably, further confusing Caroline.

"Is this some kind of near-death experience thing?"

"Really, Caroline, I am trying to control my temper, but your obnoxious attempts to bait me are grating," her father snapped.

The crack in his bizarre Stepford-ness made her smile. "That's better."

Huffing, he said, "All I wanted to make clear was that if you would like to press charges against him now, I will do whatever I can to help."

It was still hard for her to believe her father was here for her, but she needed to give him the benefit of the doubt if she wanted a real truce between them. Besides, she couldn't deny his support warmed her and gave her hope that maybe old, stubborn dogs could learn new tricks. "Thank you, Daddy," Caroline said, adding, "I take it the investigation is going well?"

"Yes," her father said, his tone clipped.

A small part of Caroline pitied her dad. He had put his faith in a man who had violated that trust. It had to sting.

Then again...

"We don't need to talk about the investigation right now," he said, taking another drink of his water. "I want to talk about this man you're living with."

Oh, no, we are not going there. Struggling for another subject, Caroline decided to push his buttons a little. Since he was in a good mood and all, she might as well try to get him to bridge the gap between him and her sisters.

"Or we could talk about this newfound humbleness and how it's going to lead you to Val's doorstep to apologize for being a judgmental ass."

"I will not. If your sister wants to throw her life away on a lowlife farmer who will never—"

"That lowlife farmer is a veteran who loves your daughter. You should be proud that she chose a good man, even if his pedigree isn't what you were hoping for."

Her father spluttered angrily. "Caroline—"

"No, you need to accept the fact that your daughters are grown and are starting their lives. We are not asking for your permission; the only thing we want is your blessing. Your acceptance of who we are. You don't have to like our spouses, our professions, or what we chose to do with our future; those are our choices, not yours,"

Caroline said, emotion clogging her throat. "You're right. You weren't much of a dad to us growing up, but you can take this opportunity to change that now." Reaching out, she took his softly wrinkled hand and said, "All I've ever wanted was for you to love me."

"Oh, you're my daughter. Of course I—"

"No!" Caroline shouted, dropping his hand and standing over him. "Don't you dare say you love me like it's so obvious, how could I stupidly miss it? When you love someone, you show that person every day. There isn't a day that goes by that I don't remember Mom hugging or kissing me, but with you…I don't have any of those good memories. I remember the times you told me to try harder, to do better, to be the best."

Her father didn't speak for several minutes. Finally he said, "That's how I showed you…I tried to make you three into productive members of society."

"That's not love, Dad," Caroline said, sniffling. "If you had truly loved us, seeing how miserable we were would have broken your heart."

After several moments, Edward stood up.

"Fair enough," he said. Then he reached into his jacket and pulled out a manila envelope. He held it out to Caroline, but when she didn't take it, he set it on the couch. "This is for you."

As hobbled to the door, she stared at the envelope with warring emotions. "What is it?"

"Open it and see," he called from the doorway. "And Caroline?"

"What?" she said.

"I just don't want to see you make any more mistakes," he said, opening the door. "You've come so far and surpassed my expectations. You know, I gave you six months before you'd come home, begging to be taken back."

"I guess I proved you wrong, huh?" Caroline said, watching the man she'd once thought larger than life lean on his cane.

"Yes, I suppose you did," he said, starting to close the door.

"Hey, Dad," she called.

"Yes?"

"Go see Valerie," Caroline said, picking up the envelope. "Out of the three of us, she's the only one who loved you enough to try to follow the plans you laid out for her. She should get points for that."

Her father didn't answer as he shut the door, and Caroline sat down heavily on the couch, the manila envelope in her lap.

That was probably the oddest yet most honest conversation you two have ever had.

And it had only taken thirty years.

Staring down at the envelope, she slowly twisted the metal prongs and the flap sprang up. She wasn't sure what she would find. Had her father dug into Gabe's past and found something? Was it all the dirt he had collected on Kyle?

Dumping the envelope upside down, she let the contents fall next to her on the couch.

And was dumbstruck.

There were pictures, dozens of them, of *her* over the last twelve years. Pictures of her leaving the strip club. Sleeping in her car. Even when she'd been arrested. As she sifted through the scattered photos, she realized that angry, loud sobs had begun wracking her body.

He'd had her followed, had known everything all along.

And for what? What did this prove? That he'd been making sure she was still alive? Had he enjoyed watching her struggle and tread water?

Beneath the pile was a scrap of yellow paper, and with shaking hands, she picked it up, unfolding it to read the words.

Caroline,

Despite the fact that I kept my distance, I needed to know you were all right. I thought if I just gave you time, you would come home, but you never gave up. Your mother was that way—determined. It was why I married her; she never gave up on me, even when I was at my worst.

You may think that you have seen the worst of me in many ways, but I need to confess: Carl Jackson didn't find you by chance. Carl and I knew each other, once upon a time, and I called in a favor. Initially, I just wanted you to get out of that hell hole you were working in; I never expected you to find your passion. Sometimes, it's hard for me to accept that even I might be wrong every once in a while.

> *I know it doesn't mean much to you, but I am* proud *of what you've done.*
> *Your father,*
> *Edward Willis*

Caroline gripped the letter tightly as tears dripped onto the blue ink. She didn't know how to take her father's big reveal. Was she angry? Perhaps a little—just because in all the years she'd known Carl, he'd never said a word.

The path to her success had started with her father's calling in a favor.

Let it go, she thought. *This is his way of making amends. Of showing you he cares in his own, twisted way.*

It was a step in the right direction.

THE NEXT MORNING, Caroline lay in Gabe's arms, listening to the sound of his breathing. It was four o'clock, but she couldn't sleep. Gabe was supposed to take her to the airport at ten, but she wasn't so sure she wanted to be stuck in a car with him for two hours, with so many doubts rolling around in her head.

Last night, after they'd settled in for bed, Gabe had asked her to meet his sister.

Caroline knew how much Honey meant to him and that this was a big gesture on his part. It said he was serious about them and looking toward the future. Yesterday, she'd been so sure, so positive that all her preconceived notions about him were wrong, that this was the guy for her, and he wasn't just like every other guy that she'd fallen for: a big disappointment waiting to happen.

But between the exclusivity talk with Gabe, her father's drop-in bombshell, and all of the emotional upheaval between her sisters and her, she was in intimacy overload. She wasn't used to "sharing her feelings" so much and taking the next step toward something seemingly better.

And suddenly, it was seriously wigging her out.

Just then, she heard Possum scratching in the litter box, and she crawled out of bed to check on him. When he saw her peek around the corner, he started whining.

"Hey, buddy, you miss brother?" she said, sitting down on the floor so he could rub on her. "Me too."

Stroking the kitten, Caroline realized that she needed to take a couple days and clear her head. She was just confused, and with a little distance and perspective, she'd be able to decide if she could ever fully trust anyone.

If she couldn't do that, what kind of future would she have?

SLEEPILY, GABE REACHED for Caroline, expecting a groan of irritation for trying to wake her, but his hand hit cold sheets.

Opening his eyes, he searched the room for any sign of her but saw nothing. He got up from the bed and headed down the hall, stopping off at the bathroom to take a piss.

In the living room, something was different. At first, he couldn't put his finger on it.

Then he realized her luggage was gone.

He went back into his room to grab some clothes and saw that his clock read 10:45. They were supposed to have left at ten to get to the airport by noon. Gabe dressed quickly and went downstairs, just to be sure.

Her car was gone.

It didn't make any sense. Why would she just leave without telling him?

When he walked back into the house, he went to grab his phone from the charger and saw a sheet of paper on the counter.

Gabe,

I just need some time to think. I'll be back on Monday. Please feed Possum.

C.

Gabe stared at the note and started to laugh. He laughed until he couldn't breathe as he reread the letter again and again. For the first time in his life, he'd opened up to a woman and tried to share pieces of himself.

And she had bailed. Taken off without even saying good-bye to his face.

It says she just needs time. Maybe you're wrong.

But Gabe didn't think so and as he crumpled the note in his palm, pain shook his whole body until he was shouting with it. Before he could stop himself, he was hitting the cupboards and the walls, tearing the place apart until he lay on his back, panting, cupboard doors off their hinges and gaping holes in the walls, reminding him that he'd lost control.

That losing Caroline had made him lose all sense.

Crawling back to his feet, he took a few calming breaths before he called Chase. "Can you give me a ride to Home Depot? I only have the bike, and I need to pick up some stuff."

"Sure, what's up?"

"I had an accident." Gabe grimaced as he looked around the room.

When Chase showed up ten minutes later, he gaped at the damage. "What the fuck did you do? Try to take out a wall?"

Gabe smoothed out Caroline's crumpled note and handed it to Chase. "I'll be down by the car."

Before he even reached the door, Chase said, "I'm sorry, man."

"Yeah," Gabe said, heading out the door.

He'd taken a gamble on Caroline and lost.

Look at that, Mom. You and I aren't that different after all.

Chapter Twenty-Four

> "My advice to all women is to accept the fact that
> insensitivity is a common trait in men."
>
> **—Miss Know It All**

IN NEW YORK, Caroline tried not to think about Gabe or what he might be thinking after she'd snuck out on him. If the lack of returned texts or calls was any indication, he must be furious with her.

After the first day, the guilt had started sinking in. Why had she tried to sabotage something that was going so well? Gabe was everything, the whole package. Caring, loyal, accepting…

And she'd run for the hills the minute he started getting too close.

She'd already left two voicemails and six or so text messages, so any damage control she needed to accomplish would have to wait until she got home.

Which had her so tied up in knots, she'd hardly slept at all and missed her alarm clock this morning. She'd woken up with enough time to throw on clothes before she had to leave for her appointment with Mr. Kline. Luckily, she walked into MacAvoy's Tavern with five minutes to spare and immediately saw that the bar was certainly in need of some help.

It was dirty; the kitchen was inexcusable; and the bar staff was incompetent. However, the original wood carvings on the walls, the bar itself, and solid wood bar stools were exquisite, and she wondered if there might be a way to keep them.

"I'll need a day to come up with a solid renovation plan, but I definitely think I can help you, Mr. Kline," Caroline said to the short, round bar owner a few hours later. The man was in his early fifties and seemed like a solid person, which was part of the reason she had a hard time understanding the bar's disrepair.

"I appreciate it, Ms. Willis, but in actuality, I asked you out here in the hopes that you might be interested in saving my bar…for yourself."

"I beg your pardon?"

"I'm getting older, and to tell you the truth, my memory isn't much these days. I can't leave this place to my sons. I let them manage it for me this last year, and they've almost ruined me. Not a brain between them, as you can see. I'd like to sell the bar while it's still worth something, but I can't bear to see it torn down or turned into something that it isn't."

"But I just settled down in Idaho, and I have…"

How about friends? How about a beautiful man who makes you feel whole for the first time ever?

But what if she had screwed that up beyond repair?

Then you still have your family.

"Just take the night to consider," he said. "I assure you, the price I'm willing to sell it for is quite reasonable."

Thanking Mr. Kline, she left the bar and decided that a walk would clear her mind. The problem with New York was, if you were looking for peace and quiet, it was a pretty long taxi ride to get there.

Still, after hailing the cab, she climbed in and said, "Central Park, please."

"You got it," the cabbie said, turning on the meter.

As the cab pulled into traffic, she took her cell phone out of her pocket and checked the missed calls. Three. One from Valerie, the next from a number she didn't know, and the last from Zoe.

Did you really expect him to call you? He's not going to chase you if you don't give him a reason to.

The three calls haunted her, especially Zoe's. Not ready to face that one, she started off with what would probably be the angriest and dialed her sister.

"Is there a reason why you left for New York and didn't even ask me to drive you to the airport?"

"I just parked my car in the extended-stay lot. It's only for a couple of days."

"Still, it would have been a fun road trip," Val said. "Besides, I've been dying for an excuse to go to Boise and shop. I miss real shopping."

"Sorry," Caroline said, laughing. "The guy I'm consulting for just offered to sell me his bar on the cheap, so if you wanted to go into business together, we could move to New York. Then we could do some real shopping."

Silence took over Val's end of the line for half a second before she asked, "Are you trying to tell me something?"

"No, I was just kidding."

"Did he really offer you the bar?" Val asked.

"Yes, but—"

"Then at least some of that was the truth," Val said.

"Okay, you got me. There *is* nothing better than shopping in New York."

"Except for living close to your family and friends," Val said coldly.

"Yes, and so far, that's been *delightful*," Caroline sneered. "People talking shit behind my back. And Ellie…well, she won't even return my phone calls."

"That's because she's going through one of her phases. But you still have me, and didn't you just tell me you were making friends last week?" Val asked.

"Yeah. Look, Val, I'm not being serious."

"And what about Gabe? I thought things were going great between you two," Val said.

"They were…I mean, are…I don't know. I think I may be in over my head. He wants me to meet his sister, and I said okay, but then I just took off for this trip without saying anything to him."

"Okay, so, you snuck out on him, after he asked you to meet his sister? Why, for God's sake?" Val asked.

"Because…you don't know Gabe, okay? Meeting his sister is a big deal, and I'm just scared that—I don't know; maybe I'm just not ready."

"So, what's your plan, Caroline? To never come back, and then you won't have to deal with your feelings?" Val laughed into the phone, the sound coarse and angry. "God, and I thought you were finally maturing. Getting shit off your chest and moving on, but I was just seeing what—and who—I wanted to see."

"I didn't say I was moving here! I just got offered a bar ten minutes ago, and I haven't accepted it yet."

"'Yet' being the operative term," Val said. "You know what? If you want it, take it. Just go. We got along without you before, so it won't be any different the second time around."

"You're acting like a brat."

"And you're a fucking hypocrite! All that bullshit about changing and putting old feuds to rest was a crock. You act like you've put in so much effort, but you were gone twelve years, Caroline. That is a lot of time to make up for in a month."

"Who says I want to make anything up to anyone? I was happy being on my own."

"If that's what you call happy, then I feel sorry for you, because only a person who's completely broken would think that's a life."

Val hung up before Caroline could respond, but the words rushed through her, shaking her to her core. She took several breaths, trying to calm the flood of emotions.

But isn't that what you always thought happiness was? Freedom? That all the men, all the nights drinking away the past were just a part of life?

The cabbie pulled over, breaking through her confusion. "Central Park."

"Keep the change," she said, handing him the cash.

In the park, Caroline took the path along a little pond, smiling at the ducks as they cruised by.

If that was happiness, then what have the last few weeks with Gabe been? Did all the laughter and feelings of acceptance mean nothing to you?

Sitting down on a bench, she put her head between her legs. Lightheadedness and tears overwhelmed her, and she brushed at her eyes as she choked on the lump in her throat.

"Excuse me, ma'am, I don't mean to intrude, but you look like you could use this."

Caroline looked up at a man standing above her, holding out a worn paisley hankie in his hand, just like the kind her grandpa used to have. The man was dirty from head to toe, wearing overalls and a worn ball cap, with a scraggly beard covering his weathered face. His eyes were crinkled but besides that, they were kind.

And then she noticed his other arm was missing.

Pity overwhelmed her as she took the hankie and gave him a watery smile. "Thank you so much."

He sat down next to her. "So is it your family or your fella?"

The question was so forthright, it caught her off guard. "Both."

"I've been there, darlin', yes I have. Had me a girl years ago, sweetest blue eyes you'd ever seen. She wanted me to stay in our little town and get married, but I wanted to make something of myself. Prove her daddy wrong about the type of man I was." His chuckle was raspy, turning into a harsh, wracking cough. Caroline moved to pat his back, but he waved her off, taking in deep, rattled breaths. "I didn't get to do those things, though. I went into the military and lost my arm. Came home bitter and angry, and when she said it didn't matter, I spat on her love. My own brother stopped talking to me years ago, and though I get work from time to time, my demons seem to find me, no matter where I end up."

Caroline smiled sadly. "Mine do the same damn thing."

"My advice—not that you're askin'—is to forget what you've done, what they've done to you, and face down your demons." He patted her knee kindly. "You don't want to end up old and alone, believe me."

Biting her lip, Caroline thought of what her future might look like if she took over Mr. Kline's bar. She couldn't picture making a home here or anywhere else. When she thought of home, it was a two-bedroom apartment above a quiet little bookstore. And in *that* future, when she came home, she pictured a man with deep obsidian eyes and a wicked grin, greeting her with a kiss that would melt her socks off.

"Thank you," she said softly.

"You're welcome, darlin'" the man said, getting up from the bench and moving along down the sidewalk.

Pulling out her phone, she went to dial Mr. Kline to refuse his offer but saw she had a new text message from the strange number that had called before.

Hey, Caroline, this is Chase, Gabe's friend. I don't know if he's ever mentioned me, but look, he's in trouble.

They arrested him this morning for assault, and I don't even know if you care, but he needs you. He won't say that, because he's a stubborn son of a bitch, but he does.

Caroline's stomach dropped out, and a thousand different situations flashed through her mind—none of them good. Jumping up from the bench, she kicked off her four-inch heels and ran to flag down a taxi.

Chapter Twenty-Five

"Revenge is a dish best served cold...and with plenty of gloating."

—Miss Know It All

AFTER EXPLAINING TO Mr. Kline why she had to leave so suddenly and that she couldn't possibly take his offer, Caroline packed up her suitcase and checked out of her hotel. When she arrived at the airport, she spent the night trying to get on a flight to Boise. Finally, she got a 6:00 A.M. flight and arrived in Idaho a little after noon. Surpassing the 80 mph speed limit, Caroline arrived back in town on a mission: she was going to rescue Gabe and try to make up for bailing on him. She was a strong, independent woman who had made mistakes and turned her life around. She wasn't a princess, though Gabe often called her one, and she didn't need a knight to slay her dragons.

She could do that all on her own.

Her first stop was the police station. When she'd called Chase back, he said they were holding Gabe there until

Monday. Chase didn't know who the alleged victim was, but Caroline could only think of one man in Rock Canyon who Gabe would want to beat the snot out of. And if Kyle had provoked Gabe, intending to get revenge, she was going to use every piece of leverage her father had to destroy him.

Though really, if Kyle was involved in any way, shape, or form, she would make him pay. At this point, he'd threatened everyone she loved at one time or another, and there was no way in hell she was about to let him ruin Gabe's life.

Caroline loved Gabe. She'd known it the moment she'd read Chase's text message, but even before that too. Only she'd been too freaked out to face it. He was hers, and she was his. She needed him. And now, he needed her.

She didn't care that she was speeding, and when a cruiser pulled out behind her and flipped on his sirens, she ignored him long enough to pull up in front of the Rock Canyon Police Department.

As she climbed out of her car, she heard a shout behind her. "Put your hands up!"

She turned toward the police officer, who had his gun trained on her, and squinted. "Grady Jenkins, put that fucking thing away."

"Put your hands up first, Caroline," Grady said. When Caroline was in high school, Grady had been a pervy freshman who'd liked to crawl under lunchroom tables to stare up girls' skirts.

"I don't have time for this, Grady," Caroline said, holding up her hands. "Just get your ass over here, and get my shit."

Grady kept his gun out until he was a few feet away and then put it back in his holster. "I really ought to arrest you, you know."

"My purse is on the front seat; insurance is in the glove compartment," she said, ignoring his shout as she turned and ran for the police station entrance. Barging into the front reception area, she walked up and started banging on the bell. "Hello!"

Officer Sam Weathers came running to the front and yanked the bell away from her. "Geez, Caroline, what in hell's bells has gotten into you?"

"Do you have Gabe Moriarty in lock-up, Sam?" She craned her neck to see down the hallway.

"As a matter of fact," he said, flicking the toothpick in his mouth.

"When do you plan to release him?"

"I don't," he said, and when she opened her mouth to argue, he cut her off. "I got a victim that said, and I quote, 'Gabe Moriarty did this to me.'"

"Whatever he said, it's a lie. Gabe wouldn't—"

"Wasn't a guy. It was your sister Eleanor who filed the complaint."

"*What?*" Caroline hollered, sure she'd heard him wrong.

"Yeah, she was here pitching a fit yesterday morning that she'd turned him down at Buck's, and he'd followed her outside to her car. Beat her so bad, poor thing's eye is nearly shut."

Why would Ellie lie? She had to be lying. Gabe would never hurt a woman. He'd sworn he'd never hurt a woman. "You don't understand. I know him. He did not do this," she insisted, panic edging into her voice.

"Well, your 'knowing' isn't enough to trump an eye-witness," Sam said, obviously irritated.

Caroline obviously wasn't going to get anywhere with Sam; she needed to talk to Gabe.

And then Ellie. Her blood was boiling, trying to fig-ure out why her sister would lie. Was this to get back at Caroline for butting into her business?

No, Ellie wouldn't be that cruel. Couldn't be.

"Can I see him? Please?"

Sam hesitated, and she repeated, "Please, Sam, I'm begging you."

After a moment or two, he grumbled. "Fine. Come on back."

She almost passed Sam in her eagerness to get to Gabe, and when she saw him sitting on one of the cots, even though his eyes were closed and a dark shadow marred his jawline, he was the most beautiful thing she's ever seen.

"Gabe!" she cried, racing to the bars.

His eyes flew open, and he looked furious. "What the hell are you doing here, Caroline?"

"I'm going to get you out of here. I know you didn't do this."

"Yeah, well, you and Chase are about the only ones," he said, bitterness clouding his tone. "I have it covered. Got my court-appointed attorney and everything."

"But you don't have to do this alone. I want to help," she said, reaching out for him. "I don't know why she's doing this, but I'll talk to Ellie. We can figure this out."

Then she realized he hadn't moved toward her or even tried to hold her hand. All she wanted to do was touch him, to make sure he was really okay, but he was holding back from her. "Gabe...please...I'm sorry for the way I left. I just got scared and needed a minute to put everything in perspective. Then, when Chase texted—"

"You what? Thought you'd run back to town and save the day? Maybe pull some strings with your dad or, like you said, convince your sister to drop the charges?" Gabe snarled. "The damage is done, princess. Word's out that I'm an ex-con who likes to beat up on women. It didn't take long for people to start digging once the cuffs came out, so my fresh start? The thing I wanted more than anything? It's over with."

"We'll explain," Caroline said, gripping the bars hard. "We can work this out—"

"No, there's no *we*," Gabe said harshly. "You wanna help? Then go home. Whatever you thought, just get it out of your head, because I don't need you."

"Gabe..." she said, shaking with the pain of his words. He couldn't mean it.

He ignored her as he leaned his head back again and closed his eyes.

"Gabe, please look at me," she said, hanging on to the bars as her knees weakened.

"At least you finally got what you always wanted," he said without looking at her. "The apartment is yours."

"I don't want that! I haven't asked for my own space, and I don't want to lose you, so will you stop acting so defeated? You. Did. Not. Do. This. And I'll prove it," she said vehemently.

"Hey, no worries, princess. We both knew that living arrangement was only temporary. At least we got to have some fun along the way."

Part of her knew he was just saying that because he was hurt and angry, but the other, insecure part asked, "Fun? Is that all it was to you?"

"Well, hell, what else was it supposed to be?"

"I thought maybe you had actually turned into a human being, that you might actually be more than just—"

"Just what? An ex-con? A loser?" He opened his eyes to stare right at her. The blank expression in them broke her heart.

"Stop it! I didn't say any of that. I just meant that I know you try so hard to keep people at bay and for a while there, I felt like you were letting me in."

Gabe shook his head. "Just go, Caroline, okay? I'll be fine. We had a good run, but honestly? I'd be happy if I never saw you or your sisters again."

Caroline thought her chest was going to break open, the pain was so intense. Before she could plead or say anything else, Sam put his hand on her arm. "Come on, Caroline, it's time to go."

She started to follow Sam but stopped and said, "I know you think I gave up on you, but you're wrong. I had a weak moment, but I came home. To you. And I am not going to give up this easily."

She didn't wait for him to respond. As she passed through the front doors of the police station, she saw that Grady had shut all her doors and left a ticket on her windshield.

Caroline pulled it off before climbing inside, then glanced down at the total and laughed at the three-hundred-dollar scrap of paper. Her laughter soon turned to tears, and she laid her arms on her steering wheel, sobbing into them. Even if she saved Gabe's reputation, she might have already lost him. He'd given her exactly what she'd needed, accepted her for who she was, but when he'd opened his heart and invited her inside, she'd bolted.

If it was the last thing she did, she would make it up to Gabe. Even if he never forgave her.

CAROLINE STOPPED BY the veterinary hospital on the way home to check on Googlie. Zoe had been happy to report that he was eating and drinking again and had started gaining weight. Caroline had been surprised to find out that Gabe had dropped Possum off on Friday to be with his brother. Apparently, it had been a turning point in Googlie's improvement and although she was happy he was doing better, she'd asked Zoe to keep the kittens a few more days while Caroline sorted out Gabe's situation. Luckily, Zoe agreed.

She parked in front of the bookstore, figuring that Gabe's bike was in the back. When she reached the stairs, she found Ellie sitting at the top, waiting for her. Even from several feet away, she could see the bruises on her sister's face and knew she'd taken a hell of a beating.

"Holy fuck, who the hell did this to you?"

"It was Kyle," Ellie said quietly.

Caroline grabbed the railing, afraid she was going to hurl over the side. "You were seeing Kyle? *He* did this to you?"

"No, I was never seeing him. I swear," she said, confusing the hell out of Caroline.

"Okay, you weren't seeing Kyle, but he's been beating the shit out of you?"

"I wanted to explain—"

"Why you're pressing charges against Gabe?"

Ellie stood up, her eyes shifting away. "So, you heard?"

Okay, that pissed her off. On one hand, she was prepared to dismember Kyle, slowly and with a very dull knife, for hurting Ellie. But on the other hand, Ellie was acting like it was no big deal that Gabe was sitting in jail for something Kyle did.

What the fuck was going on?

"Oh yeah, I heard. What do you mean, *oh, so you heard*? Like it's some casual piece of gossip in that stupid blog you follow?" Caroline's voice rose until she was screaming, "You accused the man I love of assaulting you! Are you fucking insane? If Kyle did this to you, why the hell did you accuse Gabe?"

"Can we just go inside, please, and I'll explain?" Ellie said, starting to stand but she was moving so slowly that Caroline finally put her arm around her sister to help her.

"I would just like to say that although part of me wants to strangle you, the fact that you wouldn't tell Val or me that he was hurting you is just crazy. Why would you let him do this to you? Does he have something on you?"

"It's a long story."

"Good thing we've got some time, then."

Inside, Caroline stopped when she caught sight of the kitchen, which had putty-filled holes in the walls. Some of the doors to the cabinets were on the floor, and there were tools everywhere.

Geez, talk about a disaster zone. She'd ask Gabe what had happened later, once she had him out of jail.

Lowering Ellie to the couch, Caroline plopped down next to her. "Okay, talk. Now." When Ellie winced, Caroline reached out to take her hand. "Do you need something for the pain?"

"No, I took something earlier, but I can't take painkillers if I'm gonna drive."

"Okay," Caroline said, waiting for Ellie to say more, but she seemed at a loss. "Start at the beginning. How did you get involved with Kyle?"

Ellie took a deep breath before answering. "Last year, I was driving home from a bar in Twin Falls, but I'd only had one drink, so I thought I was fine. That I could make it home. It wasn't very far."

Caroline thought back to Gabe's own DUI and the tragic circumstances surrounding it. "You know better, Ellie."

"I know. The worst part was that I drifted into the other lane and hit another car. The driver lived, but she had a broken leg and some other injuries. I freaked out and drove off," she said, running a hand through her hair. "I was underage and driving under the influence. When I hit her, all I could think of was that my life was over. Then the police started investigating and offering rewards for witnesses. Kyle caught me trying to pop the dent out of my beamer, and when I confessed to him, he took care of it."

"How, for God's sake?" Caroline asked, horror mixing with her fury.

"He offered the woman a large settlement to change her story. Since no one else saw what happened, it was easier than I thought," Ellie said, shaking her head. "But when I offered to pay Kyle out of my trust after I turned twenty-five, he said he didn't want my money. He wanted a favor."

"What did he want?" Caroline asked.

They sat down on the couch, and Ellie continued, "He wanted me to dig up dirt on Dad, which is part of the reason I have that file of all his shady dealings. He said we'd be square if I gathered info and gave it to him, but I couldn't. Dad may be a rotten bastard most of the time, but he's still my dad. But when Dad started digging into Kyle's past, he became obsessed with what Dad might know, and he...he started threatening me."

"Is that when the beatings started?"

"When I told him I wasn't going to spy for him anymore, he punched me," she said, waving her hand over her face. "I think he liked hurting me."

Caroline's blood ran cold. "He didn't...he never..."

Ellie seemed to pick up on what Caroline couldn't say. "No, he never went that far."

Caroline's head was spinning. She had no doubt Kyle was capable of blackmail, but why would he do it? He wouldn't really jeopardize his cushy life or his freedom for a little wounded pride and petty revenge.

Wait—this was Kyle. Of course he would. Because in his mind, he could never be caught.

"So why accuse Gabe?"

"Because Kyle said he wouldn't stop until I agreed to press charges," Ellie said, her voice shaky with tears. "And he just kept kicking me and screaming, and I wanted it to stop—"

Ellie's voice broke as she released a choked sob. Unable to resist her sister's pain, Caroline reached out and pulled her into her arms.

Kyle. Everything toxic in her life and the people she cared about came back to him. That was about to change, though. Kyle couldn't get away with hurting her family. For trying to imprison Gabe and go after her father. Caroline's body shook so hard with rage, she was afraid Ellie would think she was crying. She wasn't crying, though. She wasn't scared or cowed, not anymore. It was time for her to fight back, no matter what kind of shitstorm Kyle tried to rain down on her. This time, he was going to pay.

Pulling away from her sister, she looked into Ellie's red-rimmed eyes. "Okay, Ellie. You and I are going to the police station."

"Caroline, I can't," she said, her voice rising. "He'll kill me."

"No, he won't, Ellie," Caroline said, standing up. "Because we're going to file charges and make sure he never gets out of prison. As it is, we have him on several cases of assault, extortion, rape—"

"But how? How are you going to prove what he did?"

"I'm going to have something for the police," Caroline said, standing up and heading for the door. "You're going to have to admit why Kyle was blackmailing you."

"I don't think I can do that! I could go to prison," Ellie said.

Caroline resisted the urge to walk back and slap her sister. Reminding herself that Ellie was a victim and needed support, she said, "Sometimes, part of growing up is facing your mistakes and coming clean."

"Yeah, I know," Ellie said, starting down the stairs. "At least if it all comes out, I won't live the rest of my life with the what-ifs hanging over my head, you know?"

"I know exactly what you mean."

Chapter Twenty-Six

"Revenge is a dish best served cold…and with a
slice of ha-ha, sucker!"

—Miss Know It All

CAROLINE MADE ELLIE wait in the car as she walked
up to her father's door, but she didn't wait for Teresa to
answer before walking inside.

"Caroline, what on earth…" Teresa started, coming
around a corner.

"Sorry, Teresa, I just need something from my old room."

"But all your things are in storage!" she called after
her as Caroline climbed the stairs.

"It's okay," she said, going through the second door
on the right. Teresa wasn't kidding—all of her stuff was
gone—but she was a little surprised that her father had
left the room bare. What should have been a room of
nostalgia and warmth was nothing more than four white
walls protecting an awful secret.

Going into her closet, she knelt and pulled up the loose floorboard she had found as a child. Hidden beneath was a treasure box of keepsakes she hadn't wanted her sisters rifling through, and…

A plastic bag with a knee-length dress, and her underwear from that long-ago night.

Her father's voice came from behind. "What do you have there, Caroline?"

She looked over her shoulder at him. He was standing in the middle of the room.

Caroline stood up slowly, the keepsake box in one hand and the bag of clothes in the other.

"Just some trinkets," Caroline said.

"And in the bag?" he said, pointing.

"This? This is leverage against Kyle," Caroline said. "Did you know he's been blackmailing Ellie for months? Beating her?"

By the affronted look on his face, she guessed not.

"Well, we're going to the police station. Ellie told the police yesterday that Gabe assaulted her—Kyle wouldn't stop hurting her until she agreed. Then he drove her there to make her statement."

"Why would he go to all the trouble to frame your boyfriend?"

"I don't know, wounded pride?" Caroline said, unsure herself. "Gabe worked Kyle over a bit when he found out Kyle had come by the apartment and threatened me."

Her father looked between her and the bag. "When will *you* be going to the police?"

"Now. Why?" she asked, hating that she was still so suspicious of her own father.

"Because before it's leaked to the media, I want to cut all ties with the man."

Caroline laughed bitterly. "Still looking out for the family name?"

Edward Willis hobbled forward. Leaning heavily on his cane, he placed his other hand on her shoulder. "No. I don't want anyone thinking that I don't believe you."

Relief swept through her, and she said, "I'll be going as soon as I get the rest of the dirt you have on Kyle."

"I'll get it now," her father said, limping out of the room.

For the first time in twelve years, her heart warmed toward her father, but she didn't have time to dwell on that. She had some business to take care of.

"BUT ELLIE, YOU came in here yesterday, crying that Gabe Moriarty was the man who hurt you."

Sam's slow uptake was getting on Caroline's last nerve, and she snapped, "Listen to what she's saying, Sam. Kyle Jenner beat and blackmailed her for months and when she refused to accuse Gabe, he beat her some more. To get him to stop, she accused Gabe, but now, she's recanting."

Sam glared at Caroline and then leaned in to whisper to Ellie, "You can tell me if she's pressuring you into this."

"Oh, for the love of God! Are you stupid or just being a pain in the ass on purpose?" Caroline shouted.

Sam's already ruddy face darkened, and his shoulders straightened. "You better watch the way you talk to me, Caroline, or you'll join your boyfriend."

Caroline opened her mouth to retort, but Ellie stopped her by saying, "It's true, Sam. Gabe didn't hurt me. I hardly know him. Here."

Ellie pulled out her phone, scrolling through. When she found what she was looking for, she handed it to Sam. "Here is a video of Kyle kicking me. You only see him for a second, but you can hear his voice on the recording."

Sam seemed uneasy as she hit play.

"You want to say no to me? I'll teach you what happens to stupid sluts who say no to me."

The sounds of blows against flesh sickened Caroline, and despite her anger with Ellie, she pulled her baby sister into her arms.

"I'm sorry I didn't protect you from him," Caroline whispered.

Ellie's shoulders shook as Caroline rubbed her back.

When the video was over, Sam set the phone down and said, "I'll have a car pick up Kyle Jenner at his home."

Tears burned Caroline's own eyes. "You have to release Gabe."

Sam held up his hand. "Once I have Kyle in custody, I'll release Moriarty."

"Fine," Caroline said, handing him the packet her father had given her.

"What's this?"

"Leverage, in case he's uncooperative."

GABE SAT UP on the cot, waiting. He could have sworn he heard Caroline shouting, but it must have been his imagination. Wishful thinking.

What do you expect, man? You cut her off. You deserve it if she lets you rot.

Maybe he had overreacted to her taking off on him, but he hadn't been wrong about the gravity of her sister's accusations. Whatever her reasons, Ellie had ruined any chance he had for getting his business off the ground here. People wouldn't trust him, even if Caroline got her to admit she lied. And even then, Caroline likely wouldn't take his side over her sister's.

It shouldn't surprise him that the minute he tasted a moment of happiness, it was yanked away.

Karma still must have a hold of his short hairs.

"THIS IS BULLSHIT!" Kyle yelled from the interrogation room. "I want my lawyer."

"Sure thing, boss," Sam said, standing up. Caroline stood on the other side of the mirrored window, watching Kyle twist. It would have been sweeter if Sam had left the cuffs on him, but since he'd been cooperative, Sam hadn't felt the need.

As Sam came out the door, Caroline said, "I want to talk to him."

"He asked for a lawyer, Caroline, so we're just going to let him stew for a minute."

"I'm not a cop, Sam. I can talk to him all I want," Caroline said, trying to walk past him.

"There are procedures and rules," Sam argued.

"I just need some time to get him talking. He's an arrogant son of a bitch, and I know, if I can just get him riled, he'll hang himself," Caroline said, touching his arm. "If he had hurt your sister or wife, what would you tell her?"

Sam blustered for half a second before grumbling, "One minute."

"Thank you."

Before he could change his mind, she stepped into the room, her stomach tied up in knots. Kyle looked up at her, shock written all over his face.

"Kyle," she said before she sat down across from him.

"I don't understand." Kyle tugged at his tie. "What are you doing here?"

"I'm here to make sure you never leave the Idaho prison system."

"Oh yeah?" Kyle said, sitting back in his chair. "And how are you going to do that?"

"Well, it's funny," Caroline said. "Did you know that there's no statute of limitations for rape in the state of Idaho?"

"Of course I do," he said warily.

"So, if at any time, even if it's not for another twenty years, I wanted to walk into a police station and say, 'Kyle Jenner raped me in one of his guest rooms when I was fifteen,' I can do that."

Caroline experienced her first zing of triumph as Kyle sat forward, looking nervously toward the door. "I don't know what you're trying to do, Caroline, but even *if* something had happened, it would have been consensual."

"Consensual? Doesn't a girl usually have to say yes for it to be consensual?"

"Oh, you said yes," he said mockingly. "Several times."

Keep your calm. By the time you're done with him, he'll be picking up soap in the shower, with ten other men calling him "sweet cheeks."

"Did I? Funny how I can't remember that," she said, hating the way her voice shook with every word. "What I remember is feeling woozy before you carried me upstairs. I remember you taking advantage of me. You hurt me. And then, you threatened my sisters."

"Whatever story you want to spin to make yourself feel better, that's on you, but I don't have to force myself on women to get laid," Kyle said smugly.

Taking a deep breath, Caroline tried to remain in control. She could hold out long enough to make him hand himself in. Standing up, she continued, "Until recently, I hadn't told anyone what you did, and it was like living in a hell I couldn't escape. And the worst part was, I *let* you put me there. I took what you did and blamed myself for it. But it was never my fault. You're the damaged one."

Kyle's face flushed nearly purple. "Damaged? I work for a prestigious law firm and have my pick of women. You were the one who got drunk and was all over me. I just took what was offered."

"You can try to play it off however you want, but I finally understand that you are just a weak, disgusting waste of a human being," she said, her tone mocking as she added, "I mean, it must take a real big man to force himself on a girl half his size."

"Shut up, bitch," Kyle snarled.

"What's the matter, Kyle? Am I not your type anymore? Because I'm not scared of you?" She forced a laugh.

"Maybe I just realized that underneath all that smarm you're just…pathetic."

He jumped to his feet and grabbed her shoulders, squeezing them painfully as he pushed her back onto the table. Caroline smiled like the cat that got the cream. She'd wanted to make him angry, wanted to throw him off.

"You're the pathetic one. Poor little Caroline; nobody loves her. You were so desperate for my attention," he said, holding fast when she struggled. He leaned forward until he was nose to nose with her. His nearness made her skin crawl. "It was *so* easy. I just added a little nip of whatever I could get my hands on and a few of my mother's sleeping pills. You just kept guzzling that disgusting punch until you were barely conscious."

She'd known he must have drugged her, but hearing the words come out of his mouth made bile rise up her throat, choking her. Caroline heard the sound of the room's doorknob turning, but she had locked it. She had wanted to be alone with him, to make him sweat.

God, she was such an idiot.

"I think my favorite part was when you woke up during and started to struggle, pleading with me to stop," he taunted her.

Bringing her legs up, she planted them into Kyle's stomach and pushed him back. As he released her, stumbling back, she got her bearings and jumped back onto her feet. Just as he started to stand straight, she slapped him, backing away before he could reach for her. She couldn't hold it in anymore, not when he was mocking her with that night.

She wasn't fifteen years old, drugged and helpless. Or walking down a dark alley.

She was ready for him.

"And Gabe? Why did you blackmail my sister into accusing him?"

He rubbed his cheek and tsked at her. "Caroline, I have no idea what you're talking about."

"Forget lying, idiot, my sister has you recorded on her cell phone, beating her. Time stamped and everything."

Kyle paled, and Caroline wanted to laugh that she had finally cracked his cool shell.

"That bastard got right where he belongs, all on his own."

"Well, congratulations, Kyle, because we're gonna be saying the same thing about you in a few hours."

Kyle scoffed, but his eyes weren't so sure. "Your sister is hardly a credible witness, no matter what she might have on her phone."

"Oh, you'll definitely pay for what you did to Ellie, but that's not what's going to put you away for half your life, if not more," Caroline said, crossing her arms. "You know, I was sick every time I thought about what you'd done to me, but I had no idea how many others there were."

"What are you talking about, others?"

"The other women you raped and paid off to keep quiet." For the first time in years, Caroline felt in control. That she had some of her power back.

Sweat was starting to trail down the sides of Kyle's face, and Caroline was enjoying every single second.

"It's funny; once my father contacted them and told them you were being brought up on assault charges, six of them decided to make the trip to town to make statements," Caroline said, grinning. "Three of them are here already. I wonder what they're telling the nice officers about your very"—she looked down at his crotch—"*unimpressive* equipment."

Kyle lunged at her with a roar.

Throwing her right shoulder forward, she twisted under his arm and kicked him as hard as she could in the groin. As he grabbed himself and groaned, she swung her right fist and hit him across his cheekbone, sending him crashing to the floor.

Suddenly, the door burst open, and the room filled with police officers and her father.

"Are you all right, Caroline?"

Shaking her hand out, she said, "Just working out my demons, Daddy."

Sam came in, scowling at Kyle. "We got it."

"Everything?" Caroline said, relief rushing through her.

"Yeah, you were right," Sam said, shaking his head. "I can't believe you got him to hang himself."

"Oh, believe me, I can irritate anyone if I put my mind to it." Leaning over Kyle, she pointed at the camera in the ceiling corner with the red blinking light. "Wave to the camera, Kyle."

Kyle turned his head, and when he saw the camera, he struggled against the cuffs. "Oh, you bitch…you fucking bitch," Kyle groaned from the floor. Two of the officers reached down and hauled him to his feet.

"Caroline?" her father said, his mouth twitching like he was fighting a smile.

"Yes, Daddy?"

"Have you ever considered a career in law enforcement? I have some connections…" he said, his lips still twitching with humor.

Surprised by his attempt to be funny, she laughed.

"Thanks, but I actually love the way my life's turning out." Turning to the chief of police, she said, "Sir, I believe you have something of mine, and I'd like it back."

Chapter Twenty-Seven

"The three hardest words in the English language
are not 'I love you' but 'I forgive you.'"

—Miss Know It All

"Gabriel Moriarty," one of the officers called out as he opened the cell. It seemed a little silly to Gabe, considering he was the only one in the cage.

"Yeah," he said, sitting up.

"You've been cleared, son." The officer opened the door and stepped back. "You're free to go."

"How was I cleared?"

The officer shook his head. "Chief just said you had an angel on your side."

Gabe walked out of the cell and knew exactly who the angel was.

After he finished his paperwork, another uniform drove him down the road to the apartment. He got out of the car and took the stairs two at a time, only to find the front door unlocked.

Caroline looked up from the kitchen table, a pen and paper in her hand.

"You're home," she said breathlessly.

Gabe nodded. "Seems the charges were dropped. I'm guessing that was you."

"Yeah, Ellie had a video of Kyle beating her," Caroline said, standing up. "And I provoked him into admitting what he did to me, and my dad had found some of Kyle's other victims. It's finally over."

All he wanted to do was take her into his arms, but he wasn't sure what was allowed. Or if he should start something up again. Maybe he had put too much pressure on her—and what was between them—the first time around.

"What were you writing?"

She looked away. "I was actually writing you another apology letter. I didn't get very far, though." Caroline picked up the paper and handed it to him.

> *Gabe,*
>
> *By now they've released you. I need to tell you again how sorry I am, over and over if I must. I left in a moment of sheer panic, but I knew it was a mistake the minute the plane took off.*

He could understand what she meant about a moment of sheer panic. Hadn't he been fighting his feelings for her over the last month? Telling himself he didn't deserve her? And when she'd bailed, he'd told himself he deserved it.

"Look, maybe we just jumped into this too fast. Maybe we just need to step back and take things slowly," he said, the words eating him up, even as he spoke them. "I can stay at the shop."

"It's okay," she said, her voice sounding strained. "My sister said I could stay with her. I'll take Possum and Googlie with me, so you don't have to bother with them."

"They aren't a bother," Gabe said.

"I know," she said, walking toward him. She lifted her hand to stroke his cheek before walking past him.

Gabe almost reached out and hauled her into his arms—that's what his impulsive side would've done. But time apart would be good for them, would help them decide if they were really right for each other. Or whether intense pasts and close quarters had brought two people closer who really didn't belong together.

As the front door closed behind Caroline, he sank into the couch, resting his head in his hands. His cell phone rang in his pocket. When he answered it, an unfamiliar voice said, "Mr. Moriarty?"

"Yes?" he said.

"Rick Jameson for the *Rock Canyon Press.* I would like to interview you for the paper tomorrow."

"Interview me? Why?"

"Why? An innocent man set up by an alleged serial rapist for protecting his girlfriend? You, sir, are big news," Rick said. "Now, is your last name spelled M-O-R-I-A-R-T-Y?"

"Yes, but I have to ask you, who leaked the story?"

"I'm sorry, Mr. Moriarty, I cannot reveal my sources."

"That's okay. I have an idea."

Maybe it was too easy, but it was hard not to forgive a girl who fought to prove his innocence *and* save his reputation.

CAROLINE WAS MISERABLE, and she'd only been back on her sister's couch for four days. At least no one had been keeping her up late.

Since Ellie had cut a deal with the DA in return for testifying against Kyle, she'd been on house arrest, except for her court-ordered community service. All in all, she'd gotten lucky, although she certainly didn't seem to act like it.

Then again, Caroline hadn't felt like the world was all sunshine and rainbows either.

"Can I ask you again why you and your devil cats aren't sleeping at your own place?"

Caroline was lying on Val's couch with Googs and Possum sleeping on her chest while she watched *Reality Bites*. Googlie lifted his head long enough to hiss at Val. Much to Caroline's amusement, her kittens had despised Val and her dog on sight.

"I told you; it's being fumigated."

"Right," Val said, whacking her with a pillow and startling the cats. "Letting off a bomb in your apartment takes one day, so explain why you've been a bump on my couch for four?"

"What can I say? We have big bugs," Caroline said, reaching for her Coke and rubbing the wounds the cats' nails had left as they'd escaped. "Now get out of my way. This is the good part."

"No. No more romantic dramas. All this life imitating a movie imitating life is bullshit. I watch movies to be entertained. Not sob into my sister's throw pillows and wipe my snot all over them."

"You know, it wasn't too long ago you were begging me to stay," Caroline said.

"That was when you were Fun Caroline. Now you're Obnoxiously Sad Caroline."

"Ellie and I dealt with you when you were sad."

"I don't get weepy. I get hungry. I eat. You blubber and moan…"

"All right, fine. I'll go home."

"And take those cats with you," Val called over her shoulder as she walked away.

"You're a brat!"

"Freeloader!"

"Anal retentive!"

Caroline flopped back on the couch, depressed. She hadn't told Val she'd given up the apartment because she hadn't wanted to listen to Val tear Gabe apart. Gabe had said he wanted to talk and see where things went, but he still hadn't called. She couldn't blame him, though. Gabe had every right not to forgive her, and she just had to accept that.

GABE FINISHED UP another call and hung up the phone with a wide grin.

"How many orders is that?" Chase asked, his pencil poised above the sketch pad.

"That's twenty-six since Tuesday."

"And I'm sure your recent boom of success has nothing to do with that article the *Rock Canyon Press* printed about you."

"Hey, who am I to look a gift horse in the mouth?" Gabe said. The truth was, the orders had been a good distraction from thinking about Caroline. He kept meaning to call, but every time he did, he lost his nerve. Besides, everything he came up with to say just didn't seem right.

I miss you? I'm sorry I was so quick to judge?

None of it seemed good enough. Especially when he'd been tossing and turning every night, catching himself burying his head in her pillow.

"Yeah, especially when another handful of customers were recommended to you by Caroline," Chase said, setting his pencil down. "Have you even called her, man?"

"I don't know what to say."

"How about, 'I forgive you. I'm sorry it took so long, but please believe I love you'?"

"I don't know, man. What if I took too long?"

"Well, if you wait any longer, you're going to miss your chance. I mean, what are you waiting for? You love her, she loves you, and you're perfect for each other. Stubborn, opinionated—"

"I never said she was anything like me," Gabe said.

But she was. She was his reason to smile in the morning, and he missed the soft touch of her hands on his skin. He could hear her laugh echoing through their empty apartment, and he wanted her to come home.

Home. Their home.

Maybe Chase was right. Their similarities were working against them.

"I read between the lines. Since you complained that you two fought all the time, I decided it was because you were so similar."

Gabe had gone over every scenario for days, but each one left him with the door slammed in his face. Chase was right. She'd saved him, and instead of falling to his knees and telling her he loved her, he'd let her walk out the door.

He kept blaming karma and punishing himself for his mistakes, but this one was on his own stubbornness. And his own fear. If he opened up to her about his feelings, would she cut and run again?

"What if she doesn't accept my apology?"

"Then you'll know where you stand," Chase said, standing up with a grin. "But if I were you, I'd find out sooner rather than later."

CAROLINE HAD BEEN experimenting with the effects chocolate had on spoonfuls of peanut butter when someone knocked on the front door. Sticking the spoon in her mouth, she walked over and opened the door, expecting the UPS man, but instead, Gabe looked in at her nervously with a bouquet of roses in his hands.

"I know I should have called, but I was afraid you wouldn't see me, and I needed to say this."

She waited quietly, somewhere between shock and awe. Plus, the peanut butter was stuck to the roof of her mouth, and she was afraid to try to speak.

"I have tried to be a good guy for years, to prove to my sister, to my mother, even to Chase that I wasn't just the dumb asshole who ruined everyone's lives. I figured when we started hooking up that it was going to be short-lived fun, but I found myself wanting to prove that to you too. And it scared the hell out of me, especially when you left for New York and I wasn't sure if you were coming back. I should have just accepted your apology and moved on, but I sabotage things because I have a hard time thinking anything good can happen to me.

"But you're the best thing that's ever happened to me. Not just because of the way you make me feel—feelings that I've never felt before—but because you don't judge. You've always accepted me, even when I was an asshole. You're amazing, Caroline, and I'd like to spend the rest of my life showing you just how much I love everything about you, starting tomorrow."

Pulling the spoon out of her mouth, she worked the peanut butter until she could swallow it. "What's tomorrow?" she asked breathlessly.

"Our first date, hopefully," he said with a nervous grin. "I'd ask you to come home now, but I want it to feel like the real thing. Like I come to your door and ask your sister's permission. As if we hadn't started things off ass-backward."

Her heart swelled at the sweet, romantic gesture, and she teased, "I don't know. My sisters can be major hard-asses. Not sure they'll let me out the door." Leaning closer, she added, "You look like one of those guys who could get a girl in trouble."

"I used to be that guy," he said, handing her the armful of roses he'd been holding. No sooner had she taken them than he was cupping her face in his hands. "But that was before I fell in love with you."

Holy hell, what do you say to that?

Choking back a sob, she said, "That's pretty convenient, considering I love you too."

He dipped his head, and she met his kiss, dropping the roses to the floor of the entryway so she could wrap her arms around his shoulders.

Finally, he pulled back and whispered, "I'll pick you up at noon?"

"Sure," she whispered, "but first…"

"What?"

She jerked him inside and shut the door behind him.

"What are you doing?" he asked, a smile spreading across his face, lighting up those obsidian eyes.

"People in love have make-up sex, don't they?"

"So I've heard," he said.

She jumped him, wrapping her arms and legs around him, trusting him to catch her. He did, of course.

"Well, come on. Let's get on with it."

"Where am I going?" Gabe asked.

An evil plan formed in Caroline's head. "Val's room is on the left."

"Won't she be pissed?" Gabe said, pushing the door open.

"Too damn bad! Now she'll know what it was like to listen to her loud monkey sex for two weeks," Caroline said, giggling. "Payback is a bitch."

Chapter Twenty-Eight

"Love is about sharing yourself with someone
else. Even the ugly, scary, bumpy parts."

—Miss Know It All

THE NEXT DAY, Caroline stood at the front window of
Val's house, waiting for Gabe. It was five minutes 'til
noon, and although she'd tried not to be a window-
clinger, she was too excited to care.

Suddenly, the back door opened, and Val came inside.
Gus pushed past her to run to Caroline, which sent
Googlie and Possum scurrying for cover. The dog skidded to a stop at her feet, huffing and puffing so hard she
could feel his hot breath through her jeans.

Caroline glanced down at the dog, whose massive jaws
were spread widely into an evil grin, just as he started to
put his dirt-covered paw on her leg.

"Don't even think about it, mutt," Caroline growled,
pointing her finger at him.

The dog actually paused and put his paw down, still grinning at her.

"I told him to do it," Val said as she came into the kitchen. "It's revenge for defiling my bedroom and locking me out of it."

Caroline didn't even bother to look ashamed. Gabe and she had been enjoying a little post-make-up-sex cuddle when her sister had come home to get changed. When she'd tried the door and found it locked, she'd pounded on the door. After a few minutes, Caroline had opened the door, dressed in a sheet and holding an overnight bag stuffed with some of Val's clothes.

"Tell Justin I said hi," Caroline said before closing the door again.

"You better wash those sheets!" Val had ordered, before slamming out of the house.

Caroline started humming as she tapped a finger on the counter, and Val came up alongside her, one of those meal shakes in her hand. "Seriously, why couldn't you have gone to your own apartment to do the deed instead of locking me out of my own room?"

Just then, Caroline saw Gabe pull up on his bike, and she picked her jacket off the counter. As she shrugged into, she said, "Because revenge is a dish best served cold…or sweaty, in your case."

"Aw, gross," Val said, sticking her tongue out. "And what did I do besides give you a place to stay? I sheltered you, fed you, supplied you with plenty of nineties romantic dramas…"

"Made me sleep on your lumpy couch and listen to your barn-animal sex noises," Caroline said, patting her sister's shoulder. "Let this be something you can learn from."

"And what lesson am I supposed to learn, Yoda?"

"That your couch sucks. Get a new one," Caroline said, opening the door and stepping out.

Gabe, about to knock on the door, moved to let her step down next to him. Before Caroline could shut the door, Val caught it and stood there, glaring at Gabe.

"Hey, Val," Gabe said.

Val glared at both of them, before telling him, "You're dead to me."

Gabe turned to Caroline, who just waved. "It's fine."

Val had the door almost shut when she said, "No, it's not!"

The door closed with a click, and Caroline stepped into him, sliding her arms up and behind his neck. "I missed you," she whispered as she tugged on him to come down. He chuckled but obliged her, his lips moving over hers in a lingering kiss that ended too soon for Caroline.

Gabe pulled away, his large hands squeezing her butt. "As much as I want to continue this, we have a lot of driving to do."

Caroline released him with a pout. "Where are we—oh."

Gabe unwound his arms and took her hand, bringing it to his mouth. "If you want to wait—"

"No," Caroline said, holding his hand tight. "I want to meet her."

The smile that lit Gabe's face was worth the butterflies nervously fluttering inside Caroline's belly. His eyes actually sparkled with joy, and she decided then and there, even if she had to walk though hot coals and pokers, that she'd do just about anything to see that smile again.

GABE AND CAROLINE walked into Honey's care facility two hours later. While Gabe signed them in, he never let go of her hand, afraid she'd bolt at any moment.

"Come on; she's up here," Gabe said, heading for the stairs.

"What if...?"

He paused and looked back at her. She was nervous as hell, he could tell, but he wanted her to be good with this. "My sister is the sweetest person and even if she's having a bad day"—he paused to give her a soft, reassuring kiss—"she's going to love you."

Caroline nodded, and he started walking again. When they stood outside Honey's room, he knocked softly, taking his own deep breath. It was the first time he'd ever introduced a woman to his sister, and he wanted it to go well. Despite his brave front, he was probably worse off than Caroline.

Sharla answered the door and, seeing them, gave them a wide, toothy smile. "You must be Caroline," Sharla said, holding her hand out. "I'm Sharla."

"Yes, it's so nice to meet you," Caroline said, shaking her hand.

"Well, come in, you two," Sharla said, stepping back to let them in. "I told Honey that Gabe was bringing a friend, and she's been asking for you."

Gabe gave Sharla a one-armed hug as he passed, and she whispered, "She's very pretty."

Yes, she is.

Caroline was gripping his hand for dear life as Sharla led them into the room.

Honey was sitting at her table, sketching on a thick drawing pad with chalk. As they approached the table, Sharla went around and touched Honey's shoulder.

"Sweetheart, your brother's here with his friend," Sharla said.

Honey looked up, her whole face becoming animated. "Gabe!"

She came around the table at full speed and launched herself into his arms. Gabe let go of Caroline's hand to catch his sister and hugged her hard.

"Hey, baby girl," Gabe said, turning her around to face Caroline. "This is my friend Caroline. This is my sister, Honey."

Caroline held her hand out to Honey and said, "I'm so happy to meet you. Gabe's told me a lot about you. The painting you made him is beautiful."

Gabe held his breath, waiting for his sister to react. Sometimes new people made her nervous. But when she pulled away from him now, he let her go. Honey took Caroline's hand and said, "I want to show you my drawings."

As the two women he loved walked over to the table, he watched as Honey pulled Caroline down next to her.

"Do you like to sketch?" Honey asked Caroline.

"I'm not very artistic, I'm afraid," she said, looking at the picture on the page. "Not like you. This is amazing, Honey."

Honey beamed before turning the page. "I want to sketch you."

Caroline looked toward Gabe, who shrugged. His sister had once detained the pizza delivery guy so she could sketch him.

"Okay, sure," Caroline said.

"Sit very still," Honey said, reaching out to tilt Caroline's head. "Don't move."

"I'm not going anywhere," Caroline said, and Gabe believed her.

CAROLINE SAT ON the bed next to Honey, stroking Honey's hair while they watched *Homeward Bound*. It was so reminiscent of something she would have done with her own sisters as kids, she didn't even feel weird about it. Honey's childlike enthusiasm was addictive, especially when she'd convinced Gabe to go get them fries and vanilla milkshakes, which he'd done after a minute or two of mock grumbling.

As the credits rolled, Caroline glanced over at Gabe, who had pulled up a chair near the daybed to watch. Honey had told him he couldn't sit on the bed with them, and he'd taken it with humor.

"What do you mean, I can't sit up there? I always sit up there!"

"Caroline and I are sitting up here. No boys allowed, even brothers."

Caroline had laughed and agreed. "Yeah, girls only."

Now, Gabe stood up and looked down at them, his eyes a little shiny as he cleared his throat. "Honey, Caroline and I have to leave."

"No!" Honey said, wrapping her arms around Caroline's waist.

"But we've got a long drive home, baby girl," Gabe said patiently.

"You can stay here," Honey said, her voice muffled.

Caroline held up her hand, and Gabe closed his mouth.

"Hey, Honey, did Gabe tell you about our kittens?"

Honey sat up quickly and shook her head. "You have kittens?"

"Two of them. Your brother saved them. He did this thing with his hands—"

"Like the puppy!" Honey cried, clapping her hands.

Caroline looked up at Gabe questioningly.

"I tried it on a stillborn puppy our dog had," he said modestly.

"He learned it from *101 Dalmatians*," Honey said.

"I see," Caroline said, pulling out her cell phone. "Here are some pictures of Googlie and Possum when they're eating." She swiped her finger across the screen. "And this is when they really started moving around."

Honey reached out and started swiping her finger over the screen, searching through the pictures, and Caroline said, "How about the next time we come to visit, I bring a bunch of pictures, just for you?"

Honey nodded vigorously, still staring hard at the images. "I love animals."

Caroline stood up, and Sharla stepped forward. "Honey, it's time for you to see Dr. Hamilton."

Sharla touched Honey's shoulder, and she finally acknowledged her. Caroline waited and watched as Honey stopped to give Gabe a hard bear hug. Gabe kissed the side of her head and said, "You take care now, baby girl."

"You too, Gabey," Honey said, moving on to Caroline. When she hugged her, Honey whispered in her ear, "Take care of him." When she pulled away, Honey was smiling at her, sweetly. "Bye."

Caroline let Gabe take her hand and lead her out of the room. Gabe was walking so fast, she could hardly keep up.

"Gabe, slow down. Did I do something wrong?" she asked as they passed through the main reception area.

"No," Gabe said as he dragged her around the side of the building and pressed her back against the wall.

"What—"

Gabe's mouth slammed down on hers, his hands all over her as he kissed her. She turned to mush as his passion washed over her, pressing her into the building as he made love to her mouth. It was different from every other kiss they'd ever had, almost desperate.

When he pulled away, his hand was tangled in her hair, and neither of them could catch their breath.

Her breathing finally started to slow, and she laughed huskily. "Well, that was definitely new."

His shoulders heaved under her hands, and she realized Gabe wasn't just trying to catch his breath.

He was crying.

"Hey, Gabe," she said, ducking her head to look at his face. He pulled away and wiped at his eyes with his T-shirt.

"Fuck," he muttered.

Caroline stood there, unsure of what she was supposed to do, but finally reached out for him. Pulling him back into her arms, she stroked her hands over his back and kissed his chest. She didn't say anything as she held him, waiting for him to collect himself.

After a minute, he lifted his head and cupped her face. "You are amazing."

Caroline's own eyes stung as she covered his hands with hers. "I didn't do anything."

Gabe dropped his forehead to hers. "Yes, you did." He kissed her softly, tenderly. "I want to take you home," he said, releasing her face and reaching into his pocket for his keys.

"Okay."

But instead of a ring with several keys, he pulled out a single key with a wine-bottle charm attached.

"No, I want to take you back to *our* home," he said, tucking her hair behind her ear. "It's not the same there without you."

Sniffling, she took the key from him and laughed wetly. "We'll have to rescue Possum and Googlie."

"Of course, but first," he said, pulling her into his arms, "I want to take you home and show you how much you mean to me."

"Yeah? So…"

"You should probably call your sister and tell her she's cat-sitting for the night."

Epilogue

> "As I am tasked with reporting *all* the gossip, I should like to be the first to inform you that two years from the day of her return to Rock Canyon, Miss Caroline Willis became Mrs. Gabe Moriarty in a small-but-tasteful ceremony."
>
> —**Miss Know It All**

GABE MORIARTY HAD never expected to fall in love, get married, or live out his dream in a small town in Idaho, but here he was, coming home from a ten-hour day to find his wife asleep on the couch.

Although they no longer lived in the little two-bedroom apartment above Chloe's Book Nook, the furniture still looked the same—with the addition of a brown La-Z-Boy chair Caroline had bought him for their one-year anniversary. All of it fit nicely in their three-bedroom house off Oak Avenue, with a quarter-acre lot and a two-car garage. The house was affordable without straining their finances.

Gabe washed his hands at the sink and came back to hover over his wife, who was being guarded by their cats,

Googlie and Possum, each fifteen pounds and both lazy as hell. Gabe pulled out his phone and took a picture of Caroline, mouth hanging open, with the cats curled up on her chest and stomach.

Coming around the front of the couch, he shooed the cats off and lifted her into his arms, careful of her stomach. The baby bump was just starting to show, and Caroline had been obsessed with getting a picture of it every day, just to show how much it had grown. He'd tried to tell her they could do it once a month and the change would be more dramatic, but she ignored him.

Cradling her against his chest, he leaned over to kiss her forehead. One of his favorite things about his wife was how soundly she slept, even when he jostled her.

As he carried her back to their master bedroom, he peeked in on the nursery Caroline had been working on over the last month, despite the fact that they still had five to go. He took in the lemon yellow walls covered with pictures of zoo animals and smiled at the progress she'd been making. "Good job, princess."

She mumbled something softly, and he continued on into their room, where he could lay her down on the bed. Covering her with a blanket, he started to leave, but Caroline grabbed his hand sleepily.

"Stay with me?"

As he climbed in behind her, he placed his mouth beside her ear and whispered, "Always."

Acknowledgments

WRITING A BOOK can sometimes take a village, and my village rocks! Thank you first to my husband, for his support. My family for cheering me on. My editor, Chelsey, as always, for her feedback and suggestions. The newest team member, my agent, Sarah; how did I live without you? The entire staff at Avon for your savvy style and for keeping us informed. All of the authors from Avon for being such a wonderful support system. For my friends Ellie Macdonald, Candis Terry, Nicole Flockton, and Tina Klinesmith; I adore you! To the ladies of my review crew, for squealing along with me. And thank you to the baristas at my favorite coffee shop, Broadway Java, for keeping me caffeinated on Sundays.

The love doesn't end here!

Keep reading for a sneak peek at
Codi Gary's next Rock Canyon romance

BAD FOR ME

Coming April 2015 from Avon Impulse

"AND THAT WAS John Michael Montgomery, with 'I Swear,'" Callie Jacobsen said into the microphone. "For all you Little Big Town lovers, this one's for you."

Turning on the next track, Callie stretched her arms above her head and yawned. As the morning DJ for Kat Country 106.1, she was at work from four in the morning until noon, even eating while on air. The small radio station had three on-air DJs during the week, and two part-time on the weekends. Although it might have been nice to sleep in and take the afternoon shift, Callie enjoyed the early morning callers.

Okay, well, one caller in particular. He went by Rhett, which probably wasn't his real name, but who cared? He had been calling in for over a year now, the same time every day, but what had started out as simple song requests had ended up striking a chord in her every time.

Mostly because every one of the songs he'd chosen had been a favorite of hers.

Okay, he also had an amazing voice. A rough, deep rumble that made her toes curl every time she heard him on the line. It reminded her of Deacon Clayborne's voice from *Nashville*, her favorite show, and maybe that was what made her so infatuated with him.

It was crazy, really, but each time she heard his voice over the line, the butterflies he woke in her stomach fluttered like crazy. And it had been a long time since she'd had butterflies. Not since high school.

Not since Tristan.

Callie rubbed her chest and felt the bumps and ridges of the scars under her plain T-shirt, a constant reminder of how good love could go bad. Really bad.

Which was why she usually stayed clear of romantic entanglements. It was hard enough to trust anyone, let alone someone looking to get into her pants. She'd had a few stress-relief partners over the years, but she'd never gone back to their places.

And they were never truly alone—not when her dog never left her side.

Kicking off her shoes, she rubbed her feet over Ratchet's belly. The 130-pound Anatolian Shepard went everywhere with her but usually found that sleeping under her DJ table was the best place to get belly rubs. She'd jokingly called him "Killer" to a few folks when she'd first moved to town five years ago, and word had spread pretty quickly that there was a crazy new girl in Rock Canyon with a vicious beast of a dog. She had a few close friends who knew how nice Ratchet really was, but to the rest of the world, her dog's size was enough of a deterrent to keep people from messing with her. And Callie liked it that way.

Little Big Town's latest hit came to an end, and Callie leaned forward to speak into the mic. "Coming up next we'll be taking requests for our 'Crack of Dawn' hour, so all you early birds can listen to your favorite hits as you start your daily grind." She smiled then as their station intern, Dalton, held up a cup in the window with the Local Bean Coffee Shop's logo on the side. "And speaking of grind, try waking up at three thirty and still being as entertaining as me. Let me tell you, it takes work and a lot of coffee, so we're going to take a commercial break. Callie Jay will get herself a little java pick-me-up, and you stick around for more of today's hottest country on the Kat."

Turning off the mic, she waved Dalton in. The kid was a big improvement to the little bastard the University of Southern Idaho had sent her last semester. The intern had been into punk rock and had had an attitude about everything, from the music to the people who came into the station. Despite the fact that he knew what kind of station he had signed up for, instead of putting his whole heart into the job, he had blanched at every task. Callie had sent him packing within a week, after making a call to his professor, stating that he needed a work ethic before being placed in another internship.

Dalton was a complete one-eighty, a good ole boy, just turned eighteen and eager to learn. He had only been there a month, but he'd jump into the next job without her even having to ask. She couldn't have asked for better.

Plus, he was pretty to look at, with a tall, rangy frame and sweet smile. Sure, he was just this side of jail-bait, but Callie would have to be dead not to notice that he was a cutie.

As he came in through the door, Ratchet stood up to say hi. Most of the staff still gave him a wide berth, but Dalton had never been nervous around the big dog. He'd told Callie that he'd grown up on a sheep ranch outside of Shoshone around Great Pyrenees dogs, which were similar to Anatolians but hairier.

"Here's your coffee, Callie," Dalton said. He handed her the cup before kneeling down to pet Ratchet. "Hey, big guy, you gotta go handle your business?" Dalton took Ratchet's leash from the desk and asked, "That okay if I take him outside to go to the bathroom?"

"Thanks, Dalton, you're a godsend," Callie said before taking a small sip of the hot liquid. Sweet spices filled her mouth, and she sighed. "Man, that is good."

Dave, her producer, signaled her for the countdown, and she set her coffee on the desk. When he pointed at her, she flicked the mic back on and said, "And we're back with our all-request hour. So get to your phones and call 208-333-3KAT—unless you're driving or eating. No one wants to hear you talk around a mouthful of bagel, and we all want you to make it safely to wherever you're going."

Her tech held up his finger, and she hit the line-one button.

"First caller, what can I do you for?"

"Hi, I'd like to hear 'Teardrops on My Guitar' by Taylor Swift," a young female voice said over the line.

"Sure, honey, what's your name? And is there anyone specific you want this going out to?"

"Um…do I have to say?" the girl asked nervously.

Callie smiled. Poor kid. "No, of course not. I'll get that on the air for you right now."

"Thanks." The line went dead, and Callie flipped on the track, taking the next call. By the time six twenty rolled around, both lines were blinking, and she had half an hour of music to play.

And Rhett had missed his call-in.

He'd been calling every morning at six thirteen for months and hadn't missed a morning yet. The calls had started off like any other, but lately, they had been getting friendlier and friendlier. Even her friends and coworkers had started to tease her about it, but she swore up and down, there was nothing to it. It's not like she'd ever meet him or anything.

He's just a caller. Stop being a freak about it.

Besides, if he'd had romantic notions about her, he would probably have dropped a hint or two about meeting in person, especially after she started taking their calls off air when their conversations went on too long. But no, he'd never asked, and when she started getting angry waves from her producer and she'd have to go, he'd always just say, *"Have a nice day, Callie Jay."*

Unlike some of the other citizens of Rock Canyon, Idaho, he didn't call up to bitch and moan about politics or what was wrong with modern country music. In fact, just yesterday, he'd called and brought up the fact that he loved October because it was when all the fall drinks and colors started showing up. She was more of a spring person, but when Dalton had made a coffee run this morning, the pumpkin-spiced latte she'd ordered had been in Rhett's honor.

Suddenly, her cell started blaring "Wildflower" by the JaneDear Girls, and she silenced it quickly, picking it up with a hiss.

"I am not going, so stop calling."

"Oh, come on, it will be fine!" Caroline Willis said. "You go to Buck's and Hank's, so what's wrong with this?"

Callie shook her head. When Callie had met Caroline back in April, she had been drawn to the other woman because—for lack of a less "romantic" explanation—she'd sensed someone she could relate to. Someone who had her own demons and was fighting her own past, and she'd been right. Yet in all the time since and as the two of them grew closer, Caroline had never questioned Callie or asked about her past. She'd just taken her for who she was now.

Even though Callie loved her for trying to bring her "out of the army tank you've climbed into"—Caroline's words, not hers—Callie had no desire to go to Caroline's sister's bachelorette party.

"I already agreed I would DJ the damn wedding, but I have no desire to go out with a group of obnoxious women and watch some greasy dudes gyrate to 'It's Raining Men,'" Callie said, catching Dave's frown as he waved the phone at her, letting her know she had more requests waiting. "This whole thing can wait until I see you this afternoon, right?"

"Fine, but I'm not through with you! If you think I'm going to this thing with just my sisters and their crazy friends, you are dreaming!"

"Good-bye, Caroline."

Dave held up his finger, and Callie picked up line one. "You're on the Kat. What can I play for ya?"

"I was thinking a little Blake Shelton, actually," a deep voice said. The caller's smile was evident, even over the phone.

Rhett.

Turning off the "record" button, Callie tried to ignore the giddy butterflies fluttering through her stomach. "You're late."

"You noticed."

"Well, you've been almost OCD about the time you call for seven months, so it's a little hard not to." Callie bit her lip to keep from smiling.

"Well, as a matter of fact, I overslept this morning. Can I just say I'm actually flattered? Were you counting down the minutes?"

Callie's face burned, and even though he couldn't see her, she rubbed her cheeks with one hand. "Actually, it's just because you're the only person who calls in with any taste."

"Coming from you, I'll take that as a compliment."

"You should," she said, turning around in her chair so she couldn't see Dave and her tech, Sam, making kissy faces at her. "Now, what Blake song do you want to hear?"

"Uh-oh, did I get you in trouble with the boss?"

"No, I just… There are just a lot of calls coming in, so I can't talk as long."

"I understand," he said, and there was a pause on the line before he cleared his throat. "Maybe we could talk more later? Off air?"

Callie's heart pounded. Was he asking for her number?

Real names and numbers made it real. What if he was dangerous? What if she gave him her number and he tracked her down—

"I'm going to take it from your silence that I freaked you out," he said, breaking into her panicked thoughts. "I'll let you get back to work."

He hung up before she could say anything. Without his trademark farewell.

Way to go, you paranoid freak.

Callie didn't think she was paranoid; she was cautious. Having your fiancé turn into a complete stranger—a violent stranger—six months before your wedding could do that to a person. Thinking of Tristan was painful, and she tried to push him from her mind. Tried to forget their past together. If she didn't, the nightmares might start up again—and the urge to drink herself into a stupor along with it.

Just then, Dalton came walking in with Ratchet. The minute he let him off leash, the large dog lumbered over and lay his head in Callie's lap, as if sensing her dark thoughts. Stroking his soft fur, she murmured softly to him until he sat down and eventually flopped to the floor.

"Callie, you've got callers holding," Dave said over the intercom.

Pressing the button, she took the next call, but her thoughts were still on Rhett. Was she ready to let someone in and trust again?

She really wasn't sure.

About the Author

An obsessive bookworm, **CODI GARY** likes to write sexy small-town contemporary romances with humor, grand gestures, and blush-worthy moments. When she's not writing, she can be found reading her favorite authors, squealing over her must-watch shows, and playing with her children. She lives in Idaho with her family.

Discover great authors, exclusive offers, and more at hc.com.

Give in to your impulses . . .
Read on for a sneak peek at six brand-new
e-book original tales of romance
from Avon Impulse.
Available now wherever e-books are sold.

AN HEIRESS FOR ALL SEASONS
A Debutante Files Christmas Novella
By Sophie Jordan

INTRUSION
An Under the Skin Novel
By Charlotte Stein

CAN'T WAIT
A Christmas Novella
By Jennifer Ryan

THE LAWS OF SEDUCTION
A French Kiss Novel
By Gwen Jones

SINFUL REWARDS 1
A Billionaires and Bikers Novella
By Cynthia Sax

SWEET COWBOY CHRISTMAS
A Sweet, Texas Novella
By Candis Terry

An Excerpt from

AN HEIRESS FOR ALL SEASONS
A Debutante Files Christmas Novella
by Sophie Jordan

Feisty American heiress Violet Howard swears
she'll never wed a crusty British aristocrat. Will,
the Earl of Moreton, is determined to salvage his
family's fortune without succumbing to a marriage
of convenience. But when a snowstorm strands
Violet and Will together, their sudden chemistry
will challenge good intentions. They're seized by a
desire that burns through the night, but will their
passion survive the storm? Will they realize they've
found a love to last them through all seasons?

His eyes flashed, appearing darker in that moment, the blue as deep and stormy as the waters she had crossed to arrive in this country. "Who are you?"

"I'm a guest here." She motioned in the direction of the house. "My name is V—"

"Are you indeed?" His expression altered then, sliding over her with something bordering belligerence. "No one mentioned that you were an American."

Before she could process that statement—or why he should be told of anything—she felt a hot puff of breath on her neck.

The insolent man released a shout and lunged. Hard hands grabbed her shoulders. She resisted, struggling and twisting until they both lost their balance.

Then they were falling. She registered this with a sick sense of dread. He grunted, turning slightly so that he took the brunt of the fall. They landed with her body sprawled over his.

Her nose was practically buried in his chest. *A pleasant smelling chest.* She inhaled leather and horseflesh and the warm saltiness of male skin.

He released a small moan of pain. She lifted her face to observe his grimace and felt a stab of worry. Absolutely misplaced considering this situation was his fault, but there it was nonetheless. "Are you hurt?"

"Crippled. But alive."

Scowling, she tried to clamber off him, but his hands shot up and seized her arms, holding fast.

"Unhand me! Serves you right if you are hurt. Why did you accost me?"

"Devil was about to take a chunk from that lovely neck of yours."

Lovely? He thinks she is lovely? Or rather her neck is lovely? This bold specimen of a man in front of her, who looks as though he has stepped from the pages of a Radcliffe novel, thinks that plain, in-between Violet is lovely.

She shook off the distracting thought. Virile stable hands like him did not look twice at females like her. No. Scholarly bookish types with kind eyes and soft smiles looked at her. Men such as Mr. Weston who saw beyond a woman's face and other physical attributes.

"I am certain you overreacted."

He snorted.

She arched, jerking away from him, but still he did not budge. His hands tightened around her. She glared down at him, feeling utterly discombobulated. There was so *much* of him—all hard male and it was pressed against her in a way that was entirely inappropriate and did strange, fluttery things to her stomach. "Are you planning to let me up any time soon?"

His gaze crawled over her face. "Perhaps I'll stay like this forever. I rather like the feel of you on top of me."

She gasped.

He grinned then and that smile stole her breath and made all her intimate parts heat and loosen to the consistency of pudding. His teeth were blinding white and straight set against features that were young and strong and much too handsome. And there were his eyes. So bright a blue their brilliance was no less powerful in the dimness of the stables.

Was this how girls lost their virtue? She'd heard the stories and always thought them weak and addle-headed creatures. How did a sensible female of good family cast aside all sense and thought to propriety?

His voice rumbled out from his chest, vibrating against her own body, shooting sensation along every nerve, driving home the realization that she wore nothing beyond her cloak and night rail. No corset. No chemise. Her breasts rose on a deep inhale. They felt tight and aching. Her skin felt like it was suddenly stretched too thin over her bones. "You are not precisely what I expected."

His words sank in, penetrating through the fog swirling around her mind. Why would he expect anything from her? He did not know her.

His gaze traveled her face and she felt it like a touch—a caress. "I shall have to pay closer attention to my mother when she says she's found someone for me to wed."

Violet's gaze shot up from the mesmerizing movement of his lips to his eyes. "Your *mother?*"

He nodded. "Indeed. Lady Merlton."

"Are you . . ." she choked on halting words. *He couldn't be.* "You're the—"

"The Earl of Merlton," he finished, that smile back again, wrapping around the words as though he was supremely amused. As though she were the butt of some grand jest. He was the Earl of Merlton, and she was the heiress brought here to tempt him.

A jest indeed. It was laughable. Especially considering the way he looked. Temptation incarnate. She was not the sort of female to tempt a man like him. At least not without a dowry, and that's what her mother was relying upon.

"And you're the heiress I've been avoiding," he finished.

If the earth opened up to swallow her in that moment, she would have gladly surrendered to its depths.

An Excerpt from

INTRUSION
An Under the Skin Novel
by Charlotte Stein

I believed I would never be able to trust any
man again. I thought so with every fiber of my
being—and then I met Noah Gideon Grant.
Everyone says he's dangerous. But the thing is
. . . I think something happened to him too. I
know the chemistry between us isn't just in my
head. I know he feels it, but he's holding back.
He's made a labyrinth of himself. Now all I
need to do is dare to find my way through.

An Avon Red Novel

He said no sexual contact, and a handshake apparently counts. I should respect that—I do respect that, I swear. I can respect it, no matter how much my heart sinks or my eyes sting at a rejection that isn't a rejection at all.

I can do without. I'm sure I can do without, all the way up to the point where he says words that make my heart soar up, up toward the sun that shines right out of him.

"Kissing is perfectly okay with me," he murmurs, and then, oh, God, then he takes my face in his two good hands, roughened by all the patient and careful fixing he does and so tender I could cry, and starts to lean down to me. Slowly at first, and in these hesitant bursts that nearly make my heart explode, before finally, Lord; finally, yes, finally.

He closes that gap between us.

His lips press to mine, so soft I can barely feel them. Yet somehow, I feel them everywhere. That closemouthed bit of pressure tingles outward from that one place, all the way down to the tips of my fingers and the ends of my toes. I think my hair stands on end, and when he pulls away it doesn't go back down again.

No part of me will ever go back down again. I feel dazed in the aftermath, cast adrift on a sensation that shouldn't have happened. For a long moment I can only stand there in stunned silence, sort of afraid to open my eyes in case the spell is broken.

But I needn't have worried—he doesn't break it. His expression is just like mine when I finally dare to look, full of shivering wonder at the idea that something so small could be so powerful. We barely touched and yet everything is suddenly different. My body is alight. I think his body is alight.

How else to explain the hand he suddenly pushes into my hair? Or the way he pulls me to him? He does it like someone lost at sea, finally seeing something he can grab on to. His hand nearly makes a fist in my insane curls, and when he kisses me this time there is absolutely nothing chaste about it. Nothing cautious.

His mouth slants over mine, hot and wet and so incredibly urgent. The pressure this time is almost bruising, and after a second I could swear I feel his tongue. Just a flicker of it, sliding over mine. Barely anything really, but enough to stun me with sensation. I thought my reaction in the movie theater was intense.

Apparently there's another level altogether—one that makes me want to clutch at him. I need to clutch at him. My bones and muscles seem to have abandoned me, and if I don't hold on to something I'm going to end up on the floor. Grabbing him is practically necessary, even though I have no idea where to grab.

He put his hand in my hair. Does that make it all right to put mine in his? I suspect not, but have no clue where that leaves me. Is an elbow any better? What about his upper arm? His upper arm is hardly suggestive at all, yet I can't quite bring myself to do it. If I do he might break this kiss, and I'm just not ready for that.

I probably won't be ready for that tomorrow. His stubble is burning me just a little and the excitement is making me so shaky I could pass for a cement mixer, but I still want it to carry on. Every new thing he does is just such a revelation— like when he turns a little and just sort of catches my lower lip between his, or caresses my jaw with the side of his thumb.

I didn't think he had it in him.

It could be that he doesn't. When he finally comes up for air he has to kind of rest his forehead against mine for a second. His breathing comes in erratic bursts, as though he just ran up a hill that isn't really there. Those hands in my hair are trembling, unable to let go, and his first words to me blunder out in guttural rush.

"I wasn't expecting that to be so intense," he says, and I get it then. He didn't mean for things to go that way. They just got out of control. All of that passion and urgency isn't who he is, and now he wants to go back to being the real him. He even steps back, and straightens, and breathes long and slow until that man returns.

Now he is the person he wants to be: stoic and cool. Or at least, that's what I think until he turns to leave. He tells me good-bye and I accept it; he touches my shoulder and I process this as all I might reasonably expect in the future. And then just as he's almost gone I happen to glance down, and see something that suggests that the idea of a real him may not be so clear-cut:

The outline of his erection, hard and heavy against the material of his jeans.

An Excerpt from

CAN'T WAIT
A Christmas Novella
by Jennifer Ryan

(Previously appeared in the anthology
All I Want for Christmas Is a Cowboy)

*Before The Hunted Series, Caleb and Summer
had a whirlwind romance not to be forgotten . . .*

Caleb Bowden has a lot to thank his best friend,
Jack, for—saving his life in Iraq and giving him
a job helping to run his family's ranch. Jack also
introduced Caleb to the most incredible woman
he's ever met. Too bad he can't ask her out. You
do not date your best friend's sister. Summer
and Caleb share a closeness she's never felt
with anyone, but the stubborn man refuses to
turn the flirtatious friendship into something
meaningful. Frustrated and tired of merely
wishing to be happy, Caleb tells Jack how he feels
about Summer. With his friend's help, he plans a
surprise Christmas proposal she'll never forget—
because he can't wait to make her his wife.

Caleb opened his mouth to yell, *Where the hell do you think you're going?*

He snapped his jaw shut, thinking better of it. He couldn't afford to let Jack see how much Summer meant to him. He'd thought he'd kept his need for her under wraps, but the too-observant woman had his number. Over the last few months, the easy friendship they'd shared from the moment he stepped foot on Stargazer Ranch turned into a fun flirtation he secretly wished could turn into something more. The week leading up to Thanksgiving brought that flirtation danger-ously close to crossing the line when he walked through the barn door and didn't see her coming out due to the changing light. They crashed into each other. Her sweetly soft body slammed full-length into his and everything in him went hot and hard. Their faces remained close when he grabbed her shoulders to steady her. For a moment, they stood plastered to each other, eyes locked. Her breath stopped along with his and he nearly kissed her strawberry-colored lips to see if she tasted as sweet as she smelled.

Instead of giving in to his baser need, he leashed the beast and gently set her away, walking away without even a single word. She'd called after him, but he never turned back.

Thanksgiving nearly undid him. She'd sat alone in the dining room and all he'd wanted to do was be with her. But how could he? You do not date your best friend's sister. Worse, you do not have dangerous thoughts of sleeping with her, let alone dreaming of a life with a woman kinder than anyone he'd ever met. Just being around her made him feel lighter. She brightened the dark world he'd lived in for too long.

He needed to stay firmly planted on this side of the line. Adhere to the best-bro code. This thing went beyond friendship. Jack was his boss and had saved his life. He owed Jack more than he could ever repay.

"Can you believe her?" Jack pulled him out of his thoughts. He dragged his gaze from Summer's retreating sweet backside.

"Who's the guy?" He kept his tone casual.

Jack glared. "Ex-boyfriend from high school," he said, irritated. "He's home from grad school for the holiday."

"Probably looking for a good time."

Caleb tried not to smile when Jack growled, fisted his hands, and stepped off the curb, following after his sister. He'd counted on Jack's protective streak to allow him to chase Summer himself. Caleb didn't want anyone to hurt her. He sure as hell didn't want her rekindling an old flame with some ex-lover.

He and Jack walked into the park square just as everyone counted down, three, two, one, and the multicolored lights blinked on, lighting the fourteen-foot tree in the center of the huge gazebo, and sparking the carolers to sing "O Christmas Tree."

Tiny white lights circled up the posts and nearby trees, casting a glow over everything. The soft light made Summer's golden hair shine. She smiled with her head tipped back, her bright blue eyes glowing as she stared at the tree.

His temper flared when the guy hooked his arm around her neck and pulled her close, nearly spilling his beer down the front of her. She laughed and playfully shoved him away. The guy smiled and put his hand to her back, guiding her toward everyone's favorite bar. Several other people joined their small group.

Caleb tapped Jack's shoulder and pointed to Summer's back. Her long hair was bundled into a loose braid he wanted to unravel and then run his fingers through the silky strands.

"There she goes."

"What the . . . Let's go get her."

Caleb grabbed Jack's shoulder. "If you go in there and demand she leaves, it'll only embarrass her in front of all her friends. Let's scout the situation. Lie low."

"You're right. She'll only fight harder if we demand she come home. Let's get a beer."

Caleb grimaced. Hell yes, he wanted to drag Summer home, but fought the compulsion.

He did not want to watch her with some other guy.

Why did he torture himself like this?

An Excerpt from

THE LAWS OF SEDUCTION
A French Kiss Novel

by Gwen Jones

In the final fun and sexy French Kiss novel,
sparks fly as sassy lawyer Charlotte Andreko
and Rex Renaud, the COO of Mercier
Shipping, race to clear his name after he's
arrested for a crime he didn't commit.

In her fifteen years as an attorney, Charlotte had never let anyone throw her off her game, and she wasn't about to let it happen now.

So why was she shaking in her Louboutins?

"Put your briefcase and purse on the belt, keys in the tray, and step through," the officer said, waving her into the metal detector.

She complied, cold washing through her as the gate behind her clanged shut. She glanced over her shoulder, thinking how much better she liked it when her interpretation of "bar" remained figurative.

"Name . . . ?" asked the other cop at the desk.

"Charlotte Andreko."

He ran down the list, checking her off, then held out his hand, waggling it. "Photo ID and attorney card."

She grabbed her purse from the other side of the metal detector and dug into it, producing both. After the officer examined them, he sat back with a smirk. "So you're here for that Frenchie dude, huh? What's he—some kinda big deal?"

She eyed him coolly, hefting her briefcase from the belt. "They're all just clients to me."

"That so?" He dropped his gaze, fingering her IDs. "How come he don't have to sit in a cell? Why'd he get a private room?"

Why are you scoping my legs, you big douche? "It's *your* jail. Why'd you give him one?"

He cocked a brow. "You're pretty sassy, ain't you?"

"And you're wasting my time," she said, swiping back her IDs. *God, it's times like these I really hate men.* "Are you going to let me through or what?"

He didn't answer. He just leered at her with that simpering grin as he handed her a visitor's badge, reaching back to open the next gate.

"Thank you." She clipped it on, following the other cop to one more door at the other side of the vestibule.

"It's late," the officer said, pressing a code into a keypad, "so we can't give you much time."

"I won't need much." After all, how long could it take to say *no fucking way?*

"Then just ring the buzzer by the door when you're ready to leave." When he opened the door and she stepped in, her breath immediately caught at the sight of the man behind it. She clutched her briefcase so tightly she could feel the blood rushing from her fingers.

"*Bonsoir*, Mademoiselle Andreko," Rex Renaud said.

Even with his large body cramped behind a metal table, the Mercier Shipping COO had never looked more imposing—

and, in spite of his circumstances, never more elegant. The last time they'd met had been in Boston, negotiating the separation terms of his company's lone female captain, Dani Lloyd, who had recently become Marcel Mercier's wife. With his cashmere Kiton bespoke now replaced by Gucci black tie, he struck an odd contrast in that concrete room, yet still exuded a coiled and barely contained strength. He folded his arms across his chest as his black eyes fixed on hers, Charlotte getting the distinct impression he more or less regarded her as cornered prey.

All at once the door behind her slammed shut, and her heart beat so violently she nearly called the officer back. Instead she planted her heels and forced herself to focus, staring the Frenchman down. "All right, I'm here," she said *en français*. "Not that I know why."

If there was anything she remembered about Rex Renaud—and he wasn't easy to forget—it was how lethally he wielded his physicality. How he worked those inky eyes, jet-black hair and Greek-statue handsomeness into a kind of immobilizing presence, leaving her weak in the knees every time his gaze locked on hers. Which meant she needed to work twice as hard to keep her wits sharp enough to match his, as no way would she allow him the upper hand.

An Excerpt from

SINFUL REWARDS 1
A Billionaires and Bikers Novella
by Cynthia Sax

Belinda "Bee" Carter is a good girl; at least, that's
what she tells herself. And a good girl deserves
a nice guy—just like the gorgeous and moody
billionaire Nicolas Rainer. Or so she thinks,
until she takes a look through her telescope
and sees a naked, tattooed man on the balcony
across the courtyard. He has been watching
her, and that makes him all the more enticing.
But when a mysterious and anonymous text
message dares her to do something bad, she
must decide if she is really the good girl she has
always claimed to be, or if she's willing to risk
everything for her secret fantasy of being watched.

An Avon Red Novella

I'd told Cyndi I'd never use it, that it was an instrument purchased by perverts to spy on their neighbors. She'd laughed and called me a prude, not knowing that I was one of those perverts, that I secretly yearned to watch and be watched, to care and be cared for.

If I'm cautious, and I'm always cautious, she'll never realize I used her telescope this morning. I swing the tube toward the bench and adjust the knob, bringing the mysterious object into focus.

It's a phone. Nicolas's phone. I bounce on the balls of my feet. This is a sign, another declaration from fate that we belong together. I'll return Nicolas's much-needed device to him. As a thank you, he'll invite me to dinner. We'll talk. He'll realize how perfect I am for him, fall in love with me, marry me.

Cyndi will find a fiancé also—everyone loves her—and we'll have a double wedding, as sisters of the heart often do. It'll be the first wedding my family has had in generations.

Everyone will watch us as we walk down the aisle. I'll wear a strapless white Vera Wang mermaid gown with organza and lace details, crystal and pearl embroidery accents, the bodice fitted, and the skirt hemmed for my shorter height. My hair will be swept up. My shoes—

Voices murmur outside the condo's door, the sound piercing my delightful daydream. I swing the telescope upward, not wanting to be caught using it. The snippets of conversation drift away.

I don't relax. If the telescope isn't positioned in the same way as it was last night, Cyndi will realize I've been using it. She'll tease me about being a fellow pervert, sharing the story, embellished for dramatic effect, with her stern, serious dad— or, worse, with Angel, that snobby friend of hers.

I'll die. It'll be worse than being the butt of jokes in high school because that ridicule was about my clothes and this will center on the part of my soul I've always kept hidden. It'll also be the truth, and I won't be able to deny it. I am a pervert.

I have to return the telescope to its original position. This is the only acceptable solution. I tap the metal tube.

Last night, my man-crazy roommate was giggling over the new guy in three-eleven north. The previous occupant was a gray-haired, bowtie-wearing tax auditor, his luxurious accommodations supplied by Nicolas. The most exciting thing he ever did was drink his tea on the balcony.

According to Cyndi, the new occupant is a delicious piece of man candy—tattooed, buff, and head-to-toe lickable. He was completing armcurls outside, and she enthusiastically counted his reps, oohing and aahing over his bulging biceps, calling to me to take a look.

I resisted that temptation, focusing on making macaroni and cheese for the two of us, the recipe snagged from the diner my mom works in. After we scarfed down dinner, Cyndi licking her plate clean, she left for the club and hasn't returned.

Three-eleven north is the mirror condo to ours. I

straighten the telescope. That position looks about right, but then, the imitation UGGs I bought in my second year of college looked about right also. The first time I wore the boots in the rain, the sheepskin fell apart, leaving me barefoot in Economics 201.

Unwilling to risk Cyndi's friendship on "about right," I gaze through the eyepiece. The view consists of rippling golden planes, almost like . . .

Tanned skin pulled over defined abs.

I blink. It can't be. I take another look. A perfect pearl of perspiration clings to a puckered scar. The drop elongates more and more, stretching, snapping. It trickles downward, navigating the swells and valleys of a man's honed torso.

No. I straighten. This is wrong. I shouldn't watch our sexy neighbor as he stands on his balcony. If anyone catches me . . .

Parts 1, 2, 3, 4, and 5 available now!

Parts 1, 2, 3, 4, and 5 available now!

An Excerpt from

SWEET COWBOY CHRISTMAS
A Sweet, Texas Novella
by Candis Terry

Years ago, Chase Morgan gave up his Texas life for the fame and fortune of New York City, and he never planned on coming back—especially not for Christmas. But when his life is turned upside down, he finds himself at the door of sexy Faith Walker's Magic Box Guest Ranch. Chase is home for Christmas, and it's never been sweeter.

Chase had come up to stand beside her and hand her more ornaments. While most of the influential men who visited the ranch usually reeked of overpowering aftershave, Chase wore the scent of warm man and clean cotton. Tonight, when he'd shown up in a pair of black slacks and a black T- shirt, she'd had to find a composure that had nothing to do with his rescuing her.

She'd taken a fall all right.

For him.

Broken her own damn rules is what she'd done. Hadn't she learned her lesson? Men with pockets full of change they threw around like penny candy at a parade weren't the kind she could ever be interested in.

At least never again.

Trouble was, Chase Morgan was an extremely sexy man with bedroom eyes and a smile that said he could deliver on anything he'd promise in that direction. Broad shoulders that confirmed he could carry the weight of the world if need be. And big, capable hands that had already proven they could catch her if she fell.

He was trouble.

And she had no doubt she was in trouble.

Best to keep to the subject of the charity work and leave the drooling for some yummy, untouchable movie star like Chris Hemsworth or Mark Wahlberg.

Discreetly, she moved to the other side of the tree and hung a pinecone Santa on a higher branch. "We also hold a winter fund-raiser, which is what I'm preparing for now."

"What kind of fund-raiser?" he asked from right beside her again, with that delicious male scent tickling her nostrils.

"We hold it the week before Christmas. It's a barn dance, bake sale, auction, and craft fair all rolled into one." She escaped to the other side of the tree, but he showed up again, hands full of dangling ornaments. "Last year we raised $25,000. I'd like to top that this year if possible."

"You must have a large committee to handle all that planning."

She laughed.

Dark brows came together over those green eyes that had flashes of gold and copper near their centers. "So I gather you're not just the receptionist-slash–tree decorator."

"I have a few other talents I put to good use around here."

"Now you've really caught my interest."

To get away from the intensity in his gaze, she climbed up the stepstool and placed a beaded-heart ornament on the tree. She could only imagine how he probably used that intensity to cut through the boardroom bullshit.

As a rule, she never liked the clientele to know she was the sole owner of the ranch. Even though society should be living in this more open-minded century, there were those who believed it was still a man's world.

"Oh, it's really nothing that special," she said. "Just some odds and ends here and there."

When she came down the stepstool, his hands went to her waist to provide stability. At least that's what she told herself, even after those big warm palms lingered when she'd turned around to face him.

"Fibber," he said while they were practically nose to nose.

"I beg your pardon?"

"You know what I do for a living, Faith? How I've been so successful? I read people. I come up with an idea, then I read people for how they're going to respond. Going into a pitch, I know whether they're likely to jump on board or whether I need to go straight to plan B."

His grip around her waist tightened, and the fervor with which he studied her face sent a shiver racing down her spine. There was nothing threatening in his eyes or the way his thumbs gently caressed the area just above the waistband of her Wranglers.

Quite the opposite.

"You have the most expressive face I've ever seen," he declared. "And when you're stretching the truth, you can't look someone in the eye. Dead giveaway."

"And you've known me for what? All of five minutes?" she protested.

One corner of his masculine lips slowly curved into a smile. "Guess that's just me being presumptuous again."

Everything female in Faith's body awakened from the death sleep she'd put it in after she'd discovered the man she'd been just weeks away from marrying, hadn't been the man she'd thought him to be at all.

"Looks like we're both a little too trigger-happy in the jumping-the-gun department," she said, while deftly extricating herself from his grasp even as her body begged her to stay put.

"Maybe."

Backing away, she figured she'd tempted herself enough for one night. Best they get dinner over with before she made some grievous error in judgment she'd never allow herself to forget.

She clapped her hands together. "So . . . how about we get to that dinner?"

"Sounds great." His gaze wandered all over her face and body. "I'm getting hungrier by the second."

Whoo boy.

www.ingramcontent.com/pod-product-compliance
Lightning Source LLC
Chambersburg PA
CBHW010133150626
46552CB00023B/3241